The Rest is Silence

Also by Keith McCarthy

A Feast of Carrion
The Silent Sleep of the Dying
The Final Analysis
A World Full of Weeping

The Rest is Silence

Keith McCarthy

Constable • London

Constable & Robinson Ltd
3 The Lanchesters
162 Fulham Palace Road
London W6 9ER
www.constablerobinson.com

First published in the UK by Constable,
an imprint of Constable & Robinson Ltd, 2007

A copy of the British Library Cataloguing in
Publication Data is available from the British Library

ISBN: 978-1-84529-253-9

Printed and bound in the EU

Prologue

The night was warm, too hot, the humidity abnormally high. The usual chill of an English summer evening had not descended, and the atmosphere was a Mediterranean one; it seemed to have brought the wood alive around them.

He leaned against the beech tree with Ben's head on his lap, looking up through the branches, able to see in the clear skies Orion's belt, even the sword; if he closed his eyes he could make out the nebula.

He was happy, happier now than he had ever been before. He knew that it wouldn't – couldn't – last, that the universe would exact its inevitable vengeance, but over the years he had learned to take each second as it came, to live for the moment. *Carpe diem.*

Ben asked, 'What are we going to do?'

He looked down at Ben, stroked his soft, newly washed hair; it was so fine, so beautiful . . .

'What do you mean?'

Ben looked troubled. He had a serious frown on his face, one that he found adorable; Ben had so many adorable qualities, part of the reason he loved him so. 'This can't go on, can it?'

'Winter will come, because come it must.'

'Is that a quote?'

He laughed. 'Only in the broadest sense.'

They were quiet for a while until Ben said, 'But us . . . it can't last.'

He was looking at the sky again, his eye caught by Taurus. 'Why not?'

'Nobody understands . . .'

A bat flew through the clearing, not ten metres away; it was gone before they knew it had been there, not seen but sensed.

He sighed. 'Things change, Ben. Things always change. One of the few certainties is that we don't know how they're going to turn out.'

'Not much of a life then, is it?'

He laughed softly and he really meant it. 'No, Ben. That's the point. Life's only worth living because you don't know what's going to happen next. The worst curse you can put on someone is to tell them the exact day when they're going to die.'

'But what about us?' Ben was distressed.

He looked down at Ben and, as with every time that he looked at him, was reminded how much he loved him. 'It's not written in the stars that it will all go wrong, Ben. We're not star-crossed, you know.'

He saw Ben becoming frustrated at his inability to express his feelings. 'Doesn't it mean anything to you? Aren't I important?'

He saw that he'd taken things too far. He sat up slightly, put the backs of his fingers against Ben's cheek, feeling the lightest of bristles. 'God, Ben! Of course you are! You're the most important thing in the world to me.' Something moved through the undergrowth ahead of them; a fox, perhaps, or maybe a badger. He continued, 'I can't promise you anything, Ben. Nothing at all. All I can tell you is that I'll never let you down.'

He was too honest; someone more mendacious would have left it there. He couldn't resist adding, 'But, yes, you're right. The odds are against us.'

He smiled but it was a thing of pathos, weak and neonatal, and it didn't fool Ben.

2

'No!' He began to cry quietly.

He was trying to comfort Ben when he became aware of a noise in the distance; voices, people moving through the undergrowth.

'Shh!'

They were some distance off but the night was still. Ben reacted only slowly to his entreaties but was eventually silent and listening. By this time the newcomers were quite near.

Talking and laughing.

Ben suddenly found something familiar in one of the voices.

'You're not drunk, are you?'

Whoever he was with was clearly drunk. His voice was slurred, sounded thick with stupidity. Ben couldn't make out what he was saying.

'There's a special surprise for you tonight, Jacob.'

More mumbling. They were very close now. Ben was holding his breath.

'Oh, yes. Really special. You'll love it.'

Ben heard something in the voice that he couldn't name.

The voices were moving away again, tramping through the woods, through the night. The last thing they heard were the words, 'It's going to be a night you'll never forget.'

They didn't move, didn't speak for a long while after silence had enveloped them again. The voices had been indistinct but Ben could not stop thinking that he recognized one of them, although he could not put a name to it. He turned to his companion. 'See? It could go wrong at any moment.'

A sigh. 'I know, I know. But it didn't happen tonight and maybe it won't happen tomorrow. Maybe it won't ever happen.'

'Maybe it will.'

He laughed. 'Ben . . . Ben . . . Just enjoy what you've got when you've got it. Tomorrow is another day.'

There was a pause. 'Is that another quote?'

He couldn't help laughing again. 'Yes! Yes, it is!'

He bent forward and Ben craned upwards and they kissed full on the mouth.

Part One

The smell of chopped garlic frying briskly in olive oil filled the room while in the background Bing Crosby sang about a white Christmas. The corpse was not yet quite dead, still breathing but barely, the eyes not yet clouded but seeing nothing nonetheless. Before the garlic was little more than ochrous a small onion, finely diced, was added, the noise increasing for a short while as the food was stirred with a wooden spoon still pale with youth. While the onion softened and browned gently in the oil, the sharpest of knives was used to cut through the raw flesh, carving the pale grey of the capsule, the softness of the orange interior, into slices only a few millimetres thick. Mixed herbs were added to the onions, allowed to cook for a few seconds, and the slices were put in, each laid carefully in the pan and covered in the onions, herbs and garlic. After less than a minute the slices were turned; a minute more and were taken from the pan, all of them placed upon a heated plate, submerged in the onions.

The hands that used a knife and fork to cut into the slices trembled, were almost hesitant, yet somehow eager.

The sigh that the taste of these sweetmeats brought forth was almost a thing of passion.

Secret, guilty passion.

Outside single drops of rain began to fall whilst inside Bruce Springsteen warned the listener to be good, not to cry and not to pout, because Santa Claus was coming to town.

Part One

Part Two

She climbed quietly back into bed.

'That was good.'

She had thought that he was asleep but he opened his eyes and looked at her as he said this. She leaned across to kiss him on the lips and enjoyed the feel of his hand as it held the side of her chest, the side of her breast.

She then said thoughtfully, 'It wasn't bad, I suppose.'

He paused, pursed his lips and said, 'Well, it had better do. It's the last shag you'll get this year.'

Raised eyebrows, a glance at her watch. 'But it's New Year's Day . . . surely you can manage it more often than that?'

He closed his eyes and turned away. There was a long pause before he murmured into the pillow, 'I don't seem to have any trouble with my other girlfriend.'

'Bastard.'

'Bitch.'

She lay back, smiling, then switched off the light.

Silence for a long while before abruptly he turned over on to his back and said thoughtfully, 'I love you.'

Three words, a cliché, a phrase that ought to have been meaningless, a phrase that might even have been menacing, given the wrong circumstances. As far as Helena was concerned, though, these were very much the right circumstances; they were perfect words uttered in the perfect tone, with perfect timing. And their rarity – until that moment a thing of intense irritation to her – she suddenly saw in a different way, one that cast them into delightful, spotlit prominence; if she heard them three times an hour, every hour, every day, they would not have meant so much to her. This scarcity made her appreciate that they came from the heart.

It might have mattered that Eisenmenger was half asleep, that it was conceivable he was dreaming about a boyhood pet or his first girlfriend, or even some old sports car he had once owned, except that his hand sought hers under the duvet and squeezed it slightly.

She was unsure what to say, fearing to react too eagerly (although it momentarily seemed an extremely good notion), wondering if it would be best to say nothing at all. In the event she was spared the decision for, with a sigh, he turned back over on to his side and apparently fell deeply into sleep, leaving her lying in the bed, freshly washed after their lovemaking, naked and strangely moved, listening to the unending rain as it beat softly against the bedroom window.

The man stood in the open doorway, crates of equipment behind him in the hall.

'What the hell is she doing here?'

The sight of a small, portly old woman walking up the lane towards the farmyard was not, to the independent eye, one that would be considered likely to inflame anyone, yet this question was posed with a startling degree of aggression.

Cherie's eye, though, was far from independent; she had long ago lost all equipoise when it came to consideration of her husband's behaviour. 'It's Mrs Christmas. She works here, dear.'

Judging from the tone alone she might have been speaking to an educationally backward eight year old; it was one that she employed quite often when engaged in dialogue with her better half.

'I know that. She shouldn't be here today, though.'

Cherie Verner-Morrison sighed. 'It's Tuesday, Alec. It's one of her days.'

'Didn't you cancel her?'

She exuded studied patience that broadcast suppressed irritation. 'No.'

He turned to her. 'Why not?'

She was still beautiful despite the advance of the years, the unrelenting chronological ravages of living. Small, blonde and as ever immaculately made up, she still reminded him of his own personal version of Barbara Windsor in her middle years. Their marriage was now a thing of bickering and sniping but none the less affectionate for that.

. . . Or at least that was what he thought when he was in a good mood.

When he was in a bad mood he looked back through the cheque stubs and totted up how much money he'd spent on plastic surgery.

'Because I didn't know we were going to carry on until today. You didn't tell me.'

'I did.'

'No, Alec. You didn't.'

He knew better than to argue. She might have been short but she was also a formidable opponent and he had heard that particular vocal timbre too many times before to ignore it.

'Well, anyway, you'd better get rid of her, and quickly.'

Their visitor had nearly reached the gateway into the courtyard. Already her eyes had spotted the luxurious minibus and the small van parked side by side in the barn opposite the house.

'Nosy old bat,' he muttered as his wife advanced towards her.

'Good morning, Mrs Christmas. I'm afraid you've come unnecessarily.'

Mrs Christmas had a lined, slightly pudgy face in which were set eyes of faded blue; she frowned. 'No,' she disagreed doubtfully. 'I don't think so. It's Tuesday.'

'We should have told you that there's no need to come today. We've got visitors.'

'Have you, dear? Party going on longer than expected?'

There was something of ambiguity in her tone. It might have been an innocent question, it might equally have been laden with cynicism.

'That's right. They decided to stay over.'

'Well, don't mind me. I won't disturb anyone. I'll just get on with — '

'No.' Cherie Verner-Morrison tried unsuccessfully to leaven her abruptness with a smile. 'I told you. Not today.'

'Oh . . .'

'We'll pay you, of course.'

For a second it seemed that Mrs Christmas might continue to argue, might insist that somehow she had the right to do her job whether or not the Verner-Morrisons desired it. Then, with a flicked glance once more at the vehicles in the barn, she nodded and said, 'All right, then.'

She actually sounded sad to Cherie's ears. She said, 'I'm sorry.' Although as she heard her own words, she couldn't think why she should feel guilt or remorse.

Mrs Christmas nodded. 'I'll see you on Thursday, then.' And with this forlorn rejoinder she turned to retrace her steps.

Cherie watched her walk slowly away. When she went back inside her husband remarked, 'I don't trust her. She's too curious.'

'She's OK. She's like all old women – nothing to do but gossip.'

'Well, I don't want anyone gossiping about me and my business.'

'She doesn't know anything.'

'Well, make sure it stays that way.'

Eisenmenger hated second autopsies but the path his career was taking meant that they were becoming a frequent occurrence. Too often he seemed to discover things that his colleagues, either through haste or laziness, had missed, too often he seemed to find an interpretation that the first pathologist had overlooked, that opened up possibilities previously unconsidered.

It was those possibilities that worried him. In truth he felt very uncomfortable in his self-appointed role as 'pathologist for the defence'. Whilst in principle his libertarian instincts found the concept of 'freeing the guilty to prevent imprisoning the innocent' a worthy one, he hated to think that he might be instrumental in releasing a murderer to murder again. He knew that all he had to do was throw dust in the eyes of justice, suggest that what everyone else had been convinced was probable was only possible, and – hey presto! – he had succeeded.

But at what later cost?

He had particularly bad feelings about this new case, that of Martin Bell, on remand for the murder of his wife, Suzanne.

He could not explain why he felt uncomfortable, but uncomfortable he certainly felt as he tied the wrap-around gown at the neck and the side and slid his feet into rubber boots. When he emerged into the huge dissection room (replete with eight – count them, eight – dissection tables, as if this were some form of commercialized, high throughput concern) two pairs of eyes turned towards him and once more the entrance he made felt less like that of the star, more the character actor who plays the villain.

There were no friends in this audience; everyone there, with the exception perhaps of Suzanne Bell (who, he fervently hoped, neither knew nor cared), wanted him to fail or at best to falter. Police Inspector Starry – thin and tall and ascetic – was not about to welcome some Johnny-come-lately cocky pathologist who wanted to upset his case against Suzanne Bell's widower husband. He did not, in consequence, rush forward to embrace him. Nor was it surprising that the pathologist who had been retained by the Crown and who had performed the first autopsy was not best pleased either; that it was Dr Debbie Addison, who had been bested by him before, only added spice.

Cayenne pepper, actually.

No one greeted him, either formally or otherwise. He went to a peg on which were hung disposable plastic aprons, took one and put it on. He was just wondering where to find the plastic gloves when this small and select company was joined by a short but powerfully built man who opened the red mortuary door with such force it swung back and collided loudly with the wall. This was Roy, the mortuary technician. He sported a well-moussed quiff above an extremely angry face.

The atmosphere became even more unwelcoming and Eisenmenger realized that this was not going to be an easy experience. He only discovered the whereabouts of the plastic gloves because this was the first port of call for Roy. Whilst he was putting on the second pair (he always double-gloved) he was invited to start.

'When the fuckin' 'ell are we going to get going? I was going bowling tonight.'

Eisenmenger fought a feeling of irritation, not because he considered this question unreasonable but because he considered it unnecessary. 'Why not now?'

As if it hadn't already been quite obvious he was in the room, he was now granted the privilege of withering scrutiny. 'What do you need?'

'For now, some paper on a clipboard and a pen; later a PM 40 knife and some robust, toothed forceps. You stay close by but you don't need to do anything unless I say so. OK?'

If Eisenmenger had hoped that a clipped, professional attitude would somehow ameliorate the situation . . .

'Everything's over there. Help yourself.'

And so it progressed while he examined the cold, white thing that had once been Suzanne Bell and noted what he saw on a clipboard. On more than one occasion he was aware that

12

Dr Addison and Inspector Starry exchanged amused glances; that he was participating in a floorshow for their entertainment was scant comfort.

He decided not to involve his assistant too much.

Suzanne Bell had been beaten to death but not in a casual manner. This was not in any way a thoughtless assault. Eisenmenger looked at her and saw someone who wanted to sculpt in bruising. Someone had done this with not only deliberation but also dedication; worse, with enjoyment. Her eyes were puffed and deepest purple, her lips bloodied and swollen; when he pressed her right cheekbone, also bruised, he felt the strangely unpleasant crunch of bone fragments grating against each other.

Yet, despite this, her body was almost untouched. Eisenmenger noted abrasions around the wrists and ankles, love bites on the neck and breasts, but little else. Dr Debbie Addison had been thorough and examined all these injuries by careful dissection of the skin and subcutaneous tissues of the limbs and face leaving an extensive network of stitching that Eisenmenger felt it wise to unpick himself.

He found nothing that he had not already known and began, therefore, to unpick the stitching that ran from her throat to her pubis. He made the mistake whilst in the midst of this to glance up at Roy and regretted it at once; the technician's eyes were filled with a light of loathing. It was at this point that Starry said quite loudly to Dr Addison, 'This is obviously going to take a lot longer than I thought.'

Eisenmenger pressed on regardless. When he had finished he said to the mortuary technician, 'Nice stitchwork.'

Roy scowled and Eisenmenger sighed inwardly.

She hadn't been unattractive. He hated to feel anything for the dead on whom he was forced to work, not because he was unemotional but because he felt too much; he had tried to escape forensic work because of this empathy but forensic work had proved too persistent, something of a stalker. This was slightly easier because he did not actually have to cut the flesh but it was not exactly *pleasurable*; how could it be conducive of enjoyment to place one's hands *inside* another human being, to rummage in blood and bile and gut, exactly as the most depraved barbarian might do, to wade through this depravity whilst pretending to be a professional, a scientist, an expert?

She was cold, too. He had performed thousands of these desecrations and during this journey he had somehow come to expect his fingers to feel a certain temperature. Sometimes, when circumstances had forced him, he had had to autopsy a body still warm and he had then had to fight a near-overwhelming sense of revulsion as part of his brain insisted that life still lingered here, that he was participating in butchery. At other times, as now, the body was too cold because the refrigerators were set too low or because it had been frozen and improperly thawed; then the discomfort would come not just from the frigid pain in his fingers but also from the rubbery feel of the flesh, the feeling that all was not quite right.

As was customary all of the organs had been placed inside the body cavity, brain and all. Two stainless steel bowls, one inside another, were banged down on the dissection table as he began to fish out slices of liver, brain and spleen, coils of intestine large and small; he looked up at Roy and said pleasantly, 'Thank you.'

Roy nodded. His face was still an angry mask but Eisenmenger thought that he detected a slight softening in his demeanour.

Both bowls were soon filled with what had once been the clockwork that kept Mrs Suzanne Bell alive but now resembled a consommé that might be served as a first course in a banquet of the elder gods, come to enslave mankind. When Roy helped him carry these across to the bench, he knew that he had won a small battle. He tentatively asked, 'I'm sorry to have to ask you to do this, but would you mind reopening the head?'

For a heart's beat he thought that he would lose all the ground he had won, but then there was yet another nod (clearly Roy was a man possessed of a limited range of gestures), accompanied by a terse, 'OK.'

Dr Debbie Addison came a little bit closer; Starry proved more resistant.

For the next fifteen minutes Eisenmenger rearranged this mish-mash of entrails into some degree of order, washing off the blood from mucosal surfaces, examining each and every part of each and every organ minutely. He was unaware of Starry's expression of disgust directed at his back, wouldn't have been bothered by it anyway. He straightened and felt a twinge of pain in his back, a brief spasm that came and went rapidly but left behind a definite sense of something wrong. If anyone noticed the passing grimace no one acknowledged it and he was forced to rue the signs of ageing alone.

He began to take tissue samples that Roy, by now sufficiently thawed to be, if not whistling a cheery air at least not plotting murder, labelled according to his instructions. And still Dr Debbie Addison said nothing.

Leaving the organs displayed as if for some later inspection by teacher, Eisenmenger went next to the empty skull, the scalp folded back to expose this bony box. He crouched down in front of it, examining its interior, the sharp ridges and soft curves, the tiny foramina, the blue-grey of the bone. He grasped the top and bottom of the crescentic opening that had been cut in the vault of the skull and pushed and pulled to see if he could expose a hidden fracture, then he inspected the inside of the scalp looking for bruising, finding none.

After a further brief perusal of the main body cavity in which he wiped out the excess blood better to see its finer points and tested each and every rib, each and every vertebra, the pelvis in on both sides, he went once more to the organs on the bench.

Starry's sigh might have been an attempt to imitate a high-speed lift descending from the hundredth floor; certainly his irritation had reached colossal proportions. He asked irritably, 'How much longer is this going to take?' Since he addressed this enquiry to the ceiling Eisenmenger didn't feel obliged to furnish a reply.

In the event he was only a further five minutes. His last action was to examine Suzanne Bell's external genitalia with a gynaecologist's zeal, a scene in the performance that he sensed caused some degree of curious consternation amongst the onlookers. Then he straightened up (gingerly) before turning to Roy. 'Thanks. I think I've finished.'

He turned to Debbie Addison and smiled. 'All right?'

She was pretty but precious and precocious, her lack of confidence translating to defensive obstreperousness, deforming her mouth into a pout and furrowing a frown on to her forehead. Eisenmenger tried to like most people and with Debbie Addison he had tried, but then failed. 'Well?' she demanded, as if he were under some obligation – perhaps a blood-oath or tightly binding contract.

'Well what?'

Roy was emptying the bowls back into the body and, like Starry, was listening to this exchange with some interest.

'What did you find?'

From the look on his face she might have addressed Eisenmenger in Venusian so perfect was his expression of puzzlement. 'Don't you know?' he asked her. Before she had even finished drawing breath for her exasperated reply he waved his hand in the direction of the cadaver that had once been Mrs Bell. 'I should imagine exactly what you found – no sign of natural disease of significance, the fractures, the bruising . . . '

He went to the washbasin, rinsed his gloves then pulled off the outer pair.

'But what's your interpretation?'

Since he was under no obligation to tell her anything, he was unable to resist goading her. With admirable attention to mortuary hygiene he rinsed the second pair of gloves then pulled these off before stripping off the gown. He now proceeded to scrub his bare hands with soap. When he spoke again it was actually in Starry's direction. 'I haven't got one . . . '

Only as he completed the sentence did he turn to his colleague. ' . . . yet.'

Before he left the mortuary he made sure that he placed three ten-pound notes in Roy's open palm, thus ensuring that at least one of the three of whom he took his leave had a smile for him.

Ben Verner-Morrison was an intelligent, tall and athletic boy of fourteen, good at cricket and rugby, an excellent squash player and leaning academically towards the languages. His aims, as yet little more than half-formed, were to read humanities at university; probably not Oxford or Cambridge, more likely Durham or London. He attended a good day school, paid for by his father, and enjoyed a reasonable social life with his school friends, all of whom were male because it was a single-sex institution. Unfortunately, he neither enjoyed nor had a feel for mathematics or science; he had consistently performed poorly in these subjects, something which didn't bother him but which bothered his parents a good deal, and when his father was bothered he let it show.

Alec Verner-Morrison had achieved a good deal by force of will; he had made a fortune, acquired a comfortable, not to say luxurious lifestyle (as well as irritable bowel syndrome, duodenal ulcers and a slightly dysfunctional liver) and ample pension provision. He could not, however, work similar magic upon the mathematical and scientific ability of his son; Ben was, as his father pointed out at monotonously regular intervals, crap at these subjects, regularly achieving percentages in the low twenties. To Ben this was of little consequence, but his parents were mindful of the importance of a pass in mathematics at least at GCSE. Ben's father, having failed to work the miracle by remonstration, anger, threats and (the last resort) bribery, was forced to seek extra tuition. Ben, however, refused absolutely to work with the maths teachers at his school, claiming that he did not like any of them and that most of them disliked him.

Thus Cherie had been absolutely delighted to discover that they had a suitable tutor living not three kilometres away.

It was the third time that Helena had been to see Martin Bell and familiarity was working its customary magic, only it wasn't just contempt she was starting to feel for her client – there was a good deal of anger, disdain and, on occasion, fear. When he was shown into the interview room he looked relaxed and confident, almost aggravatingly so. He was humming something, a simple tune that she knew but couldn't recognize. A nursery rhyme or something.

He flopped down into the chair as if he'd just come in from work and before she could open her mouth he said, 'I didn't do it. I'm not bargaining, or anything. They can stick their "manslaughter".'

As no one had actually mentioned a bargain, she thought this a tad presumptuous.

'Very well, Mr Bell. However, I feel compelled to point out a few peripheral facts that might prove tricky for you.'

'Such as?'

'You used to hit your wife, didn't you, Mr Bell?'

He didn't look ashamed, didn't even look particularly shocked that he should have been accused, didn't even bother to keep a straight face. 'Only when she deserved it.'

Helena was finding it hard to like Martin Bell. She readily admitted she had a problem liking a good many of her clients, but she accepted that as an occupational hazard of defence work – Martin Bell, though, didn't even try. He was of a breed who took the grand old British legal system at its word, opting for the strategy that he was entitled to a defence, that someone

– in this case, Helena – was going to provide a defence, and therefore he didn't need to come across as in any way likeable, agreeable, well behaved or even human. Or humane.

'She was a bitch.'

So what? So you had the right to slap her about a bit? What's the phrase – teach her the rules?

It didn't help that most of her interviews these days seemed to take place in prisons. What was the worst? Was it the odours? – no matter what was cooked, she could always detect cabbage mixed with the stalest of sweat, and foot odour, and damp and . . . generally too many human beings in too small a space. Was it the drabness? – even the modern penal institutions were *institutional*, places established for a purpose, a purpose not in any way congenial. Was it the sounds that she heard as she sat there and waited, was therefore forced to sit there and listen to? – the shouting, occasionally the moaning or the weeping, always the doors slamming.

She said tiredly, 'Unfortunately, Mr Bell, whatever your perception of the provocation, the fact is that you used to hit her and she was battered to death.'

'But I didn't do it.' If insistence won cases, Martin Bell was flying free.

'So, help me. Tell me who might have done.'

But he couldn't. Faced with this impotence he began violently to shake his head and to protest, 'I don't know! I don't know!'

She believed him, too; she disliked him intensely, but she believed him. In an effort to calm him she said, 'OK, I know that. I'm on your side, remember?'

He did remember, but only after some seconds and then, when he was calmer she looked down at her file and said, 'Suzanne was found in your house, in your bed.'

A nod, curt as if unwilling to participate in this game but forced to do so anyway.

'There was no sign of forced entry.'

The shake of his head was no happier, no more freely given, than the assent.

'The body was found by her mother, letting herself into the house using a key that she had been given . . . ' She glanced up at Bell. He was staring at her, nervous at what she was reading out to him. ' . . . because she feared for her daughter's well-being.'

She couldn't help herself, her voice falling into embarrassment.

'Her mother never liked me.'

Who can blame her? Helena watched the thought blossom and turned away from it.

He went on sourly, 'She insisted that Suzanne should give her a key.' He shook his head. 'Just in case.'

He was small but powerfully built; dark to the point of swarthy. He hadn't shaved and, although she couldn't really blame him for that given the circumstances, it didn't help. She tried not to sound too negative as she went through the next part of the case. 'You were in the pub, not a hundred metres from the house.'

'We'd rowed.'

She looked up at him across a battered wooden table. He wasn't stupid, but he was clearly not going to give Einstein a run for his money. She pointed out, 'That's very honest of you, Mr Bell, but not likely to improve your case.'

It took him a moment to follow then he dropped his head. The chairs were hard – she assumed deliberately so – and perhaps that was why he kept shifting his position.

She continued, 'You were drunk when the police found you.'

'You'll find a lot of people tend to be in a pub.'

'You claimed to have been there since noon, which is good because Suzanne was seen by the postman, still alive, at twelve fifteen . . . '

'So what's the problem?'

'You were sat in a corner and no one is able to say with absolute certainty that you were there continuously.' She looked up. 'That's the problem.'

He reverted to his mantra. 'I didn't kill her.'

Clients were like children. It was the first thing you learned after you graduated.

'You last saw her when?'

'Ten, maybe ten past.'

'And did you have a row at ten past ten?'

'Not really.'

She returned to the documents that were piled in front of her. This time she didn't bother hide her exasperation. 'You live in the middle of a terrace and you have neighbours, Mr Bell. Both sides report shouting and some fairly foul language at about ten o'clock in the morning that day.'

'Oh, for God's sake. Yes, we argued, OK? That doesn't mean I fucking killed her! We rowed a lot. That was the way we worked.' He stopped, shaking his head. She let him stew for a while and eventually he looked up at her. 'I didn't kill her, all right?'

The lights weren't bright but they sparkled in his eyes.

'Was she naked when you left her?'

'No.'

'She was naked when she was found.'

Just for a second it was as though she had struck him; his face collapsed into shock, then vacancy.

Just for a second.

'Yeah. I know.'

His tone was unreadable.

When she was out of the prison and in the relative safety of the taxi, she realized that she was herself humming the same tune as Martin Bell. It took her most of the journey to work out the title.

Green grow the rushes-oh.

It had been years since she heard that song and she wondered what significance it could have for Martin Bell.

'No flashes of inspiration?'

Eisenmenger shook his head. 'Not this time.'

Helena knew that she shouldn't feel disappointed but, as so often, knowledge and emotion were mutually repellent. She tried for a positive approach. 'But nothing directly detrimental to his case?'

'I didn't find an impression of his signet ring in the middle of the mark from the fatal blow, no.' He sounded cynical.

They were eating sandwiches in her office, the wind gusting outside while an ancient gas fire sputtered before them. It was cosy and warm, detached from anything as unsavoury as beating the wife to death; they were having an academic discussion that could have been about five down in that morning's *Times* crossword or perhaps the likelihood of a rise in interest rates but just happened to be about Suzanne Bell who now lay in refrigerated darkness on a shiny metal tray in the mortuary.

She asked, 'There's no doubt that that's how she died? Beaten to death?'

'None at all. She had no natural disease of significance and all her injuries are consistent with repeated blows with the bare hands to head and face and neck.'

Helena shook her head in disbelief, her eyes closed . 'That's savage,' she said softly.

'The blow that almost certainly ended her life was one to the throat that fractured her larynx; she died of asphyxia.'

'She was tied down – is that right?'

'She was naked and tied to the bed. Common or garden twine – the kind a gardener might use.'

Helena was reading through the file while eating an apple. 'There was evidence of sexual intercourse?'

He nodded. 'But not rape. She consented.'

'And two types of semen; one from her husband, one not.' She looked up. 'Was this some kind of group sex thing?'

He chewed through a mouthful of bacon, lettuce and tomato then swallowed it. 'I'd say not. Mr Bell's semen traces were considerably older and more degenerate than the other type.'

'Well, that's good. It fits with his story. It also suggests that there's someone else involved.'

'It also gives him a grade A, copper-plated and pretty suggestive motive, doesn't it? I assume that he wouldn't have taken too kindly to someone playing hide the saveloy with his trouble and strife.'

She was forced to agree, but then added, 'But he says he knew nothing about a lover.'

'He would, wouldn't he?'

'You're not being very positive.'

'Only as positive as the courts are likely to be.'

She sighed.

'Do you think he did it?' he asked.

She frowned, didn't answer immediately. 'I don't like him,' she said at last and cautiously.

'Why not?'

'Because he was a bastard to her. He's admitted that he used to hit her – says that she "deserved it".'

'So you think he's guilty?'

Once more she hesitated. 'I think I *want* him to be guilty, probably think it would serve him right, but . . . '

He sipped from a mug of black coffee; he had recently stopped taking milk or cream in an effort to prolong the life of his wardrobe and was finding the going hard. He didn't say anything, just waited. She sighed. 'He says he didn't kill her and I believe him.'

She sounded as if she really wished that she didn't.

This he considered, eating the last of his sandwich and watching her. He saw, as he always saw, someone passionate and angry, hard as glass and just as easily shattered, someone

23

who had a hatred of what she perceived as injustice. He asked tentatively, 'So . . . ?'

She snorted. 'So we have a job to do.'

She was refreshing the feeding trough in the chicken run when she heard the tractor driving into the yard. At once she stood up, the hens swarming unnoticed around her feet, the cockerel strutting self-importantly at the periphery of the crowd. She lifted the half-empty bag of mixed grain with easy strength, then strode through the birds on the ground, forcing a path. The cockerel, who was a coward, made his way through his concubines to the feeding trough only when she was out of the run, the door safely secured.

He was out of the tractor, peering behind the wheel. A wind had sprung up, one that foretold rain.

'Trouble?' she asked, coming up behind him.

'I think a bearing's going.'

'Can you fix it yourself?'

He pulled back from the interior of the tractor, looking around at her. 'I wish.'

Another bill, then.

'The bank's written again.'

He knew that it would not be a round robin, a chatty epistle on how well the children were doing at school and how they had bought a time share in the Algarve.

She said, 'They want to see us.'

They both knew what the subject would be.

She asked, 'What are we going to do, Richard?'

His expression was blank. 'Find some money.'

The last thing she needed was facetiousness. 'Oh, don't be stupid, Richard. Where from? The well's run dry, remember?'

'I've been thinking . . .'

'What?'

He was frowning, working something out. 'Maybe we should think about digging a new well.'

'What does that mean?'

Quite suddenly and apparently inappropriately he grinned. 'Friends Reunited.'

She didn't understand what he meant.

She never would.

'Marty was a good bloke.'

Eisenmenger's nod and its friend, the smile, were minimal, there to encourage further discourse rather than to signal genuine agreement. His informant, a thin and weaselly man called, according to his name badge, Gavin, was clearly outraged that anyone should consider Martin Bell guilty; presumably 'good blokes' didn't beat their wives to death.

'He'd do anything for you.'

Anything? Eisenmenger wondered quite what that meant. He asked, 'As far as you know, he was happily married?'

'Oh, yes. He never had a bad word for her. Whenever I saw her, she seemed OK.'

'Very much in love?'

They were standing just inside the garage, watching the water drip from the edge of the canopy and the rain sweep across the forecourt beyond. Behind them the entire rear wall was covered in rows of tyres while to their right were racks of exhausts. There was only a single car inside, this raised on a hydraulic ramp.

Gavin found the question odd. 'I wouldn't say that. I mean, they weren't newly-weds.'

'But you never sensed that there was a problem?'

Gavin shook his head. His badge not only boasted his name but it also proclaimed that he was the deputy manager. Presumably in recognition of this elevated position he wore a short-sleeved white shirt and bright red tie; both were smeared with grease and the latter was slung so loosely around his neck that Eisenmenger could see his second shirt button above the knot.

'Nah. If anything he was quite proud of her, I thought. Used to like to show her off.'

'And is he a violent man?'

'Of course not!' Gavin was shocked at the suggestion.

All the while Eisenmenger was nodding at Gavin's answers, ostensibly fully understanding of what he was saying, completely approving of all the sentiments. He said slowly, 'But he didn't take things lying down. He wasn't afraid to stand up for himself.'

'Christ, no. Marty didn't take no shit from anybody. Why a little while ago . . . ' He stopped, eyeing Eisenmenger. 'Well, anyway . . . '

'No, tell me. I'm on his side, you know. I'm trying to clear him.'

He began again slowly. 'He had to smack a bloke about a bit because he was rude about Suzanne.'

This sounded to Eisenmenger to be exceedingly euphemistic. 'How badly did he "smack him about a bit"?'

Gavin was suddenly reluctant. He shrugged. 'The bloke knew he'd been in a fight.'

'When was this?'

'About two, three months ago.'

A car, sounding like a hundred Hell's Angels throbbing in unison, pulled on to the forecourt and an elderly man dressed in a homburg and a bright red ski jacket got out, looking around him. Gavin didn't seem in much of a hurry to attend so Eisenmenger asked, 'He was very protective of Suzanne, then.'

'Absolutely. That's why it's obviously crap that he killed her.'

Eisenmenger hadn't expected much from this interview, so he wasn't particularly disappointed. The man with the homburg at last located the door to reception and headed for it. Gavin still wasn't showing obvious signs of a desire to serve him.

'I mean, when that dickhead started laughing at Marty, saying that it was well known that Suzanne was being poked by someone else, Martin went berserk . . . ' He was suddenly aware that Eisenmenger was staring at him. 'When I say "berserk" I don't mean nothing untoward. Marty was very cool, very measured. He just roughed him up a bit. Nutted him; kicked him in the balls, too, I think.'

Through the back window of reception they could just see the homburg hovering above the backs of posters informing punters of the desirability of renewing shock absorbers and tyres. It was wandering backwards and forwards, presumably because its wearer, invisible to them, was pacing the floor.

Eisenmenger asked, 'You don't happen to know who this chap was, do you?'

Gavin shrugged. 'No idea.'

'But presumably Marty knew him?'

'I suppose. He certainly seemed to know Marty.'

Eisenmenger left Gavin then, a feeling of dislocation suddenly settling on him. He knew that here was something important, a nugget of gold panned from the river's mud but it was a feeling aloft, without anchors. Gavin watched him as he climbed into his car. Even as Eisenmenger drove away he wasn't rushing to help the homburg which was now stationed in front of the reception desk and bobbing up and down impatiently on the spot.

Sauerwine had been off for three days with a stomach bug and was still suffering the after-effects; he had eaten nothing for four days and had spent so long doubled up on the toilet that he was fairly sure he had an indelible red mark framing his backside. He felt as if he had been desiccated to the point of mummification and he had a headache that filled his skull and seeped down into his face and neck like warm acid.

And now this.

He could have done with a few days in the nice, warm station; it was scant comfort as he got out of the car and was at once assaulted by the eternal rain that he was presently assigned to a station that was neither warm nor nice.

Of Beckwith he asked irritably, 'Just how long has it been pissing down? It feels like years.'

Beckwith was becoming no less wet but was considerably less bad-tempered. A cheerful soul with blond hair and an air of bumbling that no amount of efficiency was going to counteract, he said, 'Since Christmas Day. That'd be more or less three weeks now.'

Sauerwine sighed. 'A happy bloody New Year.'

'I reckon it's global warming.'

'I reckon my right foot's getting wet.' He looked at Beckwith suspiciously. 'Did you know that these boots had a hole in?'

The boots were station issue and Beckwith had chosen them as they had set out. Sergeant David Beckwith shook his head strenuously; had they not been so wet his golden locks would have swished about his head so vigorous was his denial. Sauerwine gave him a stony glare but said nothing.

They began to trudge up a slight incline across open countryside, through a relentless drizzle that lent a dankness to the darkness even an eternal optimist such as Beckwith found troubling. It wasn't particularly cold, but that only made it worse. On a frost-crisp day at noon it would have been a wonderful, invigorating walk over farmland, views of low, rolling hills to distract; on a damp, almost humid afternoon when there was little more than gloom and mud to look at it, the overall effect was one of despair.

There wasn't much more silence before Sauerwine observed, 'How far from the station are we? Fifteen kilometres?'

'Nearer twenty.'

He shook his head. 'I never realized that the backside of the world was so close.'

Beckwith seemed to find this assessment unfair. 'This is a site of special scientific interest. It's one of the largest in the country.'

Sauerwine snorted. 'It's muddy, damp and a long way from anywhere.'

Beckwith thought about pointing out that given the amount of rain that had fallen, most of the country was almost under water, then decided not to pursue the subject.

They breasted a small rise and the familiar sight of a temporary white marquee was there before them. It perched, the fabric rippled by the wind, on a flat piece of grassland; behind it was the broad expanse of the River Ross while around it were scattered gorse bushes and small copses. Two houses were visible; about a kilometre distant on the opposite bank was a farmhouse and to the right, at about the same distance, was a small cottage. Fluttering before them two long ribbons supported by strategically planted metal rods formed a tortuous pathway to the marquee.

Sauerwine asked, 'Am I missing something? Is it a minefield?'

'A bog.'

Sauerwine could never tell with Beckwith. He had been working with him for four months now and still he wasn't sure if Beckwith were an idiot or a genius, if he despised his superior or merely didn't yet always understand what he was saying.

He wasn't entirely sure if he wanted to discover the answers to these imponderables.

They began to walk down the slope, guided by the ribbons. Outside the marquee stood two uniformed constables; six more had found their way to the riverbank beyond where they had fanned out and were wandering slowly around, staring at the ground. They wore thigh-length waders and walked with obvious difficulty; even from some distance Sauerwine could see that their feet were sinking into the ground. Sauerwine eyed the grass either side of him. 'Just how boggy is it?'

Beckwith considered this. 'Well, we haven't lost anyone yet.'

What does that mean?

Sauerwine's next question came merely because there was nowhere else he felt comfortable going. 'Who discovered the body?'

Beckwith gestured with his head towards the other side of the river. 'Mrs Gillespie. The Gillespies live over there. This is their land.'

When Sauerwine didn't respond, Beckwith continued, 'The river burst its banks last night because of all the recent rain. When it receded, it left behind a body.'

There was a sudden faint flash from inside the marquee, almost gone before it was born, so brief and so slight it might never have happened.

'Has it been in the water long?'

Beckwith said cheerfully, 'Oh, yes.'

There was something perturbing in his tone and all Sauerwine could do was make a noise from the back of his throat, then recommence his march towards the marquee. His right foot was now soaked in water and so cold he was sure that he was starting to get trench foot. A gust of wind rippled the grass around them; some sort of waterfowl landed on the river's edge. Before he ducked under the tent's flap Sauerwine looked around. From here he could see a few more buildings on the opposite side of the river – barns and low huts – that presumably formed part of the Gillespies' farm.

As soon as he entered the marquee any thoughts of wedding receptions or parties on the lawn died and crawled away.

The stench was so strong he coughed and his eyes began to water. He could not only smell it, he could taste it; it settled at the back of his throat and camped there, making phlegm on which he found himself choking. He wanted to take a deep breath but didn't dare.

As well as one dead person there were two living people in the marquee. The living were dressed in white forensic suits that blunted their humanity so that they were little more than figures in a playlet; the dead member of this triptych was very, very dead and partly hidden from view because white suit number one was crouched down by it and pointing at the scarf while white suit number two took a photograph, the

30

flashlight blindingly bright for a brief moment. Then the crouching figure stood and turned and Sauerwine recognized Charles Sydenham, Forensic Pathologist.

'Inspector. Come and join the party.' This was a drawl, uttered from a position of overwhelming certainty of superiority.

Sydenham. Oh, great.

He had already been feeling bad, yet the discovery that this relic of an unlamented era was to inspect the scene and dissect the corpse plunged him into deep gloom. His facial muscles assumed a representation of a smile for about a second, his throat doing similar things to feign some sort of vocal acknowledgement. He quickly looked down at the corpse . . . and immediately regretted this choice.

It was overwhelmingly wet and this wetness had partially distorted it, as if he were looking at it through slightly frosted glass. It was naked save for a black silken scarf around the neck, but that was the least of it because it was puffy and wrinkled, pale to the point of fish flesh. The eyes were ragged tears of grey mucus, the tattered skin covered in silt and weed. It might have been born from slime. Sauerwine opened his mouth to speak, sucked in miasma and shut it quickly again. He gestured quickly with his head that Sydenham should join him outside, then retreated. Sydenham instructed the photographer – SOCO man George 'Woodie' Guthrie – to continue with general positional shots, emerged into the open air, where the air was filled with drizzle but at least breathable.

'Lovely day,' remarked Sydenham. He sounded supremely contented, as if there were no other place to be, as if he drew joy from the situation. Sauerwine spotted that Beckwith was about to reply and before his subordinate could join in the persiflage said sharply, 'What have you got for me?'

Sydenham was about fifty-five and rotund with boyish features and grey-blond hair. In common with his breed he enjoyed seeing the discomfort engendered by rotting, stinking

31

corpses within senior policemen. He said, 'Well, he's fairly ripe . . . but then you spotted that.'

'Tell me something I don't know.'

Sydenham considered. 'It's very early days . . . '

Impatiently Sauerwine said, 'OK, OK. I know. I won't quote you and I won't hold it against you if you subsequently change your mind. Just give me first impressions. For a start off, is it murder?'

'My dear Inspector, isn't that for you to decide? I can tell you only whether it was natural or unnatural, and whether there was another party involved.'

'And was there?'

Sydenham, however, ignored this question. 'Male, young – possibly very young. A fair amount of predation by our friends in the piscine world; I'd hazard a guess that he's been in the water about three, maybe four weeks.'

'How did he die?'

Sydenham shrugged, a gesture that was muted by his shape and the body suit. 'If I knew that now I wouldn't need to do a post-mortem.'

'But he's naked. I mean, that must mean there's a second party involved.'

Sydenham, head on one side, considered this. 'Maybe he went for a skinny-dip on Christmas Day.'

Sauerwine said through clamped teeth, 'Did he drown?'

Sydenham hesitated before replying. 'Can't say yet.' Then, 'The scarf's interesting, though . . . '

'Why?'

'I'm no expert, you understand, but I'd say that it's a woman's scarf. Also, it's tied pretty tightly around the neck.'

'Strangulation?'

'Possibly.'

Sauerwine frowned. 'You're not suggesting a woman did it?'

Sydenham laughed. 'I'm not even suggesting that it caused his death, Inspector. I'm merely reporting my observations. It may not be significant and, even if it is, I don't think you should forget about auto-asphyxiation. I hear the feel of silk around the neck while dipping in and out of consciousness can be quite a thrill, if you're that way inclined.'

Sauerwine stared at him and then was surprised to see Beckwith nodding sagely at this: was this professional or personal experience? He asked Sydenham, 'When will you be doing the post-mortem?'

'This evening.'

Sauerwine turned without saying any more. He had taken two steps away when Sydenham called, 'Inspector?'

'What is it?'

'There's one other thing.'

Sauerwine turned and waited.

'Not only was he naked, not only was there a woman's scarf tied around his neck, and not only was he quite well endowed – did you spot that? – but there was something tied around his feet.'

'What?'

Sydenham smiled. 'Fishing line.'

Sauerwine heard this, frowned, opened his mouth, but before he could speak Sydenham drawled, 'Perhaps he was a fisherman.'

'Is everyone a bloody joker?'

Beckwith opened his mouth and Sauerwine, fearful that he would receive a considered and well-balanced dissertation on this proffered subject, said quickly, 'I want the riverbed searched.'

'There's a diving team on their way.'

'Good.'

'Where do you want them to search? If he's been in the water for four weeks, he could have been thrown in a long way from here.'

'They can start here and then begin to work their way upstream. Meanwhile, you're going to take a team and begin house-to-house along both banks, again going upstream; someone might have seen something suspicious.'

'Rightio.'

Of all Beckwith's many irritating habits, his use of this word was close to being the most aggravating. Especially when, as he did now, he followed it up with questions, questions.

'What about Mrs Gillespie?'

'I'll see her.'

'What about the post-mortem?'

Clamping down on the impulse to enquire, 'What about it?' he said tersely, 'I'll attend. You just start the house-to-house, OK?'

'Sure thing.'

Another irritating phrase.

Maeve Gillespie was quite strikingly attractive. She had bobbed, light-brown hair, large, slightly inclined eyes and lips that looked comfortable enough to go to sleep on. She wore an open-necked, pale-blue shirt and dark-blue jeans; it was almost a Country and Western look but her accent was distinctly, almost falsely English. When she opened the door to the farmhouse, Sauerwine saw anxiety and tiredness. Behind her he saw a large, cavernous hallway with high ceilings and original plaster mouldings.

After the introductions he asked, 'Can I ask you some questions?'

She frowned slightly as she said, 'Questions?'

He smiled. The shirt revealed a pleasantly soft, pleasantly deep bust and he found himself envious of Mr Gillespie. 'I understand you found the body.'

'Oh, no. I wouldn't say I found it. I spotted it. I didn't go anywhere near it.'

'Whatever,' he said gently. 'I still need to ask you a few questions.'

He raised his eyebrows and gestured slightly with his head, indicating that, although because he was under her porch he was out of the rain, he would still quite like to escape the cold and the wind.

The kitchen was larger than his living room. It boasted a cast-iron range cooker, a central breakfast bar, a huge double-doored fridge-freezer and two butler sinks. They sat at the breakfast bar and drank coffee from a percolator. There was a smell of dog in the air – not unpleasant, just there. High up in the corner was a large, flat-screen television that showed silent images of meaninglessness.

'What were you doing when you found the body?'

'*Spotted* it.'

He bowed his head in apology. 'Spotted it.'

'I was walking Bessie.' Sauerwine, who was no mean detective, decided that Bessie was her dog. 'She's a Labrador,' she continued, confirming his deduction.

'Where were you?'

'In the bottom field. I usually go along by the river's edge, but I couldn't because the river's broken its banks.'

'When did that happen?'

'Only last night.'

He nodded and smiled. 'So you were walking the dog? What time was that?'

'About ten, I think.'

She had a low voice and the habit of wetting her lips with her tongue; somehow he discovered that he was dreaming of doing the job himself. It took a distinct effort to point out, 'That's rather late to walk the dog.'

She asked, 'Is it?' She shrugged. 'It's the time I always walk her.'

'So what did you notice?'

She considered. 'The birds, I suppose. The crows. They always make a dreadful racket, but this morning it was worse than usual. I saw a lot of them had settled on the opposite bank. At first I didn't take any notice, but then as I walked along, I suddenly saw what it was they were clustered around.'

'A body.'

She suddenly shivered. Sauerwine would dearly have liked to take her in his arms and comfort her but official protocol steeled him. 'I thought at first that it was a sheep, or something. They fall in the river every so often – stupid beasts – and then get washed away, but when I looked closer, I saw that it was . . . pink.'

She uttered the last word with revulsion.

'"Closer"?' he asked.

'I'm sorry?'

'You said, "closer". Does that mean you actually approached the body?'

'Oh, God, no! How could I? The river's normally ten metres wide, and now it's swollen to twice that.'

'So . . . ?'

'I stopped and I looked properly. It was only when all the birds flew up that I saw what it really was.'

He thought about this. It was in a contemplative tone that he enquired, 'Why did they fly up?'

This provoked apparently genuine consternation and Sauerwine watched it with curious pleasure. 'You know, I don't know. Perhaps it was a shot. A lot of shooting goes on around here.'

He didn't doubt it. He wanted to ask her if she could hazard a guess as to who the corpse might be but didn't know how to construct the question. Whilst he was pondering this she pre-empted him. 'Who is it?'

'We don't know yet.'

With some hesitation. 'It looked like he was . . . naked.'

She was assuming the sex of the body and he wondered if that were significant.

'Not quite,' he remarked non-committally.

She nodded acceptance, apparently not daring to delve more deeply. He asked then, 'Have there been any strangers in the neighbourhood recently?'

A pause. ' . . . No.' Then with more thought and more confidence, 'No.'

'Could I have your husband's name?'

'Richard.'

'Where is he now?'

She was disconcerted by the sudden change in direction and seemed to have to bring the answer forth from regions previously unexplored. 'He's repairing some fencing. Up in the Longacre Field.'

'He's been there all day?'

'Pretty much.'

'Anyone with him?'

She suddenly found resistant indignation. 'Is this relevant? He wasn't anywhere around here when it happened . . . '

Sauerwine, who didn't necessarily ask questions that were in any way relevant, repeated his enquiry as if she hadn't spoken.

'No, he's alone.'

'Were you at home for Christmas?'

She didn't understand, of course, but that was no surprise. 'Yes. Why?'

'Both of you?'

And he saw hesitation as she said, 'Yes.'

'Did you have guests to stay?'

Her answer came replete with a certain temerity that he didn't miss and couldn't explain. 'Why does this matter?'

But Sauerwine had a bad case of selective deafness. 'Did you?' he asked again.

'No.'

'And you were at home all the time?'

Now the hesitation spawned irritation. 'This is a working farm, Inspector. It doesn't stop for anything, not even the birth of Jesus.'

'So there were times when your husband wasn't in the house.'

A pause supervened, only adding to Sauerwine's curiosity. He looked at her, she looked at him; his expression was of polite and expectant interest, hers one of near anguish and one, moreover, that he quite adored.

Then she sighed abruptly and admitted, 'Look, there's something you should know . . . '

He'd guessed as much but asked only, 'And what would that be?'

'My husband and I are effectively separated. We lead independent lives; this is my house, his is over towards Rendcomb.'

Rendcomb was a small village, barely more than a hamlet.

Sauerwine said, 'Ah.' His face remained one of professional aloofness whilst inside he was doing a lively and energetic jig and shouting loud hurrahs to heaven. He added for completeness, 'So you couldn't really speak for him.'

'No.'

He looked about the room. 'What about running the farm?'

'We have a business partnership, nothing more.'

He was about to enquire further but she added, 'Is there anything more you want to know?'

It took him a moment to come back to the reason for his visit. 'Did you notice any strangers about around Christmas?'

'What's that got to do with . . . that thing?' She waved her nicely manicured hand towards the river.

His coffee was cold and he hated cold coffee. As he drained the mug he wondered if she had children. 'You might have discovered the body today, Mrs Gillespie, but that doesn't mean the death was a recent one.'

'But it must be . . . I'd have noticed it before. When I walk Bessie . . . '

She stopped, and it took her a moment to realize. Her face screwed itself into disgust. 'Oh, God! You mean he's been dead since Christmas?'

'Possibly.'

She digested this, found it gave her heartburn. 'But if the body came out of the river, then he probably died miles away from here.'

He couldn't blame her for being keen to place the death as far away as she could. 'Quite likely, Mrs Gillespie, but not certainly. I still have to ask the questions.'

She proffered more coffee but he declined. While she poured more for herself he asked, 'So do I take it that you were completely alone over Christmas?'

'That's right.'

No boyfriend then.

'Has anyone around here gone missing recently?'

She had sat back down. Her perfume was strong. 'No one, I'm sure.'

'Who are your neighbours?'

She seemed to think the question odd and her tone as she replied betrayed this. 'Well, there's Miss Flood – she lives behind us, in the cottage on the hill – and then there's the Verner-Morrisons.'

'Where do they live?'

She waved a hand past his face towards the place that the body now lay. 'Over there.'

'Do they own the land on the opposite bank?'

She nodded.

'Where's their house?'

This time her hand was waved even more closely to his face. 'It's about four or five kilometres away, I'd say. Towards Rendcomb.'

She said this as if she weren't rolling in money herself. He smiled at her and asked, 'What do you farm here?'

'Arable, mostly. A few beef cattle, some pigs.'

It was immediately obvious to him from her tone that he had asked a stupid question and he only asked how many acres to hide his embarrassment.

'Getting on for two thousand.'

39

Dragging up ancient episodes of *The Archers*, he said tentatively, 'I suppose it's busy, even at this time of year?'

'Oh, yes. It never stops.'

He looked around and thought that she made being busy look amazingly relaxed.

He suggested timidly, 'Do you have anyone to help you on the farm?'

'We get occasional students, but they're more trouble than they're worth.'

'Does anyone else live around here?'

'Not really.'

He observed, 'It must be lonely.'

There was something beautiful about her smile as she said, 'Sometimes.'

Beckwith would have liked to attend the autopsy. He had enjoyed biology at school and considered that he had done his rat dissection quite well (all except the brain, which had been damaged by his extraction technique and had resembled at the end a small serving of grey blancmange dropped on the floor). He had thus far been present at only three post-mortem examinations and had seen little at any of them, not only being relegated to the back but also being required to run a constant stream of errands for his superiors. He had hoped that this time he would get to see a little more of the *nitty-gritty* of the procedure, the details of the anatomy.

Oh, well . . .

He called for an Ordnance Survey map, not having the faintest idea where most of the properties in the neighbourhood were, but even when it was produced he was still completely lost about where to start. Rescue came in the form of Constable Meckel who spotted Beckwith examining it as it became damper and damper in the increasing rain and noted that his whole demeanour clearly signalled a man who didn't have the foggiest what to do next.

'Sergeant?'

Beckwith took a moment to look up. He saw a uniformed constable he didn't know from Adam. Sherlock Holmes might have noticed that he was perhaps forty-five, tall and slightly stooped, that he had a scar down the right-hand side of his nose and that in his eyes was a comforting sense of calm and stoicism. The Baker Street sleuth might then have deduced a plethora of facts – that the constable had three teenage children, that he had served in the army for a short while before joining the force, that he had recently run a marathon for charity, even that he was currently reading *Pride and Prejudice*.

Beckwith wasn't Sherlock Holmes, wasn't even Dr Watson, and he neither noticed nor deduced anything. He even failed to spot the scar, although in his defence the light was exceedingly poor.

'Yes?'

'If you want a hand with working out the lie of the land, I think I can help you. I'm stationed at Bishop's Shrieve. I know the area pretty well.'

Beckwith opened his mouth, ready to accept with alacrity, but then he remembered protocol. Clamping lips back together he assumed the obligatory air of disdainful superiority and said slowly and doubtfully, 'Do you?'

'Been here seven years come February.'

'And you know these people?'

He shrugged. 'Some of them. It's not a high-crime area, but I've got to know the lie of the land.'

Beckwith considered this carefully then, as if he were handing out a reprieve from a sentence of death against his better judgement, he said, 'OK.' He thrust the map – now rapidly reverting to wood pulp – at Meckel. 'We've got to work our way up the river, calling on each property. You highlight on the map all the inhabited premises while I organize two parties to work each bank. Then I want you to take charge of one, I'll lead the other.' He walked off without waiting for further comment, appearing to be perfectly in command of the situation, in actuality fearful lest Meckel should find something to criticize in his plan.

It took thirty minutes to find a total of ten men, during which time the light had weakened still further in deference to the strengthening rain. Like ants attracted to nectar, various shades of police and subsidiary personnel had come scurrying to the area, bringing with them a motley mix of chaos and organization. A temporary pathway across the drier parts of the flooded meadow had been unrolled down the hill to the marquee by the river's edge; floodlighting had been erected, bringing stark grey-white light to the grass and rippling, flowing water. There were now about a dozen officers in thigh-length waders moving slowly in a line between the marquee and the shallower part of the river, the man nearest the water having difficulty pulling his feet from the mud and slime and therefore walking like a poorly designed robot. A group of four men – two young, two old – in black suits and incongruous green rubber boots stood with folded arms outside the marquee; they looked mostly at the ground and were clearly cold.

They were, with equal clarity, undertakers.

By now, Beckwith was in that part of cold, miserable wet-ness that allowed him some peculiar pleasure in his condition. When Meckel came back to him he was feeling strangely noble, oddly contented. He looked over the markings that Meckel had made on the map; relevant properties ringed in red with the names of the owners scribbled in a near-legible hand alongside.

'Looks OK,' he pronounced after a protracted pause and with colossal reluctance. Before Meckel had a chance to draw anything approaching a breath he continued, 'I want you to take the opposite bank. We need to know if they've seen anything odd recently – especially odd activity down by the river. Also, if there have been any strangers in the neighbourhood, or if anyone has recently gone missing.' Meckel was nodding and might have been about to speak as Beckwith drove relentlessly on. 'I think we should be able to cover about three kilometres along the river tonight, just calling on those properties that front the river. Then tomorrow we'll cover the same distance but calling on houses a little further back.'

Beckwith paused for breath and thus allowed Meckel to say, 'There's no point.'

His superior frowned. 'Why?'

Meckel's face was completely neutral, his voice similarly colourless as he explained, 'I reckon he was dumped in the river at Rendcomb.'

Beckwith struggled with squabbling emotions of anger and embarrassment; fortunately the bitterness of the wind bleached his skin of a blush. 'And what makes you say that?' he asked slowly.

'The river's shallow and slow-flowing, yet the body's been in the water for a long time. The only place he could have been put in around here is at Rendcomb. There are some very deep pools there; anywhere else the body would have been obvious.'

Beckwith hated Meckel at that moment but was fully occupied hauling himself out of a steep-sided chasm of belittlement. He could hear his voice shot through with half-heartedness as he said belligerently, 'Maybe he was put in a long way upstream and only just got here after a long time.'

But Meckel was a relentless adversary. 'But it's just as shallow higher up, and anyway he'd have been seen before now.'

Beckwith was forced to resort to the somewhat ineffectual combination of a glare and a rather weak, 'Well, let's just wait and see, shall we? It doesn't do to assume too much too early when it comes to crime detection, Meckel.'

And Meckel, to his credit, kept a straight face as he nodded and said seriously, 'I'm sure you're right, Sergeant.'

Maeve Gillespie watched Sauerwine depart, Bessie the dog at her heels. A large black Labrador that she had owned for ten years and nursed through a road traffic accident that had dislocated her hip and still caused her noticeably to limp, Bessie was dearer to her than anyone else in the world.

She returned to the farmhouse, collecting a cup of coffee from the kitchen and going through to the farm office where she worked for an hour on the accounts. As she always did, she concentrated so hard that the dying of the day and the falling rain that was occasionally driven against the window behind her failed to disturb her. Only when her husband came in did she look up. Bessie remained in her basket, head down, eyes following him.

Without a greeting he asked, 'What's going on? Police are crawling all over the valley.'

'A body was washed ashore.'

He was tall and the life had weathered him, given him arms that were sinewy and a face that was sculpted into a mask unwilling to let anything in or anything out. This news brought forth a deepening of his frown but no more. 'A body?'

She barely nodded. 'Bessie found it.'

He glanced at the dog as if she might add to this modicum of information.

His wife continued, 'Pretty bad it was. Must have been in the water a long time.'

He looked back to her and for a moment they were content to stare at each other. It was she who switched her gaze first. She asked of the figures on her computer screen, 'Did you finish the fencing?'

'Ay.' He dropped into a chair in the corner, causing the dog's head to jerk up, ears slightly erect. 'The badgers are back in Chase End.'

Genuine interest was sparked by this. 'Really? Already?'

It was only eighteen months since he had gassed them.

'Ay.'

'What are you going to do?'

'Gas 'em again.'

She nodded slowly. He was breaking the law but it was no business of hers how he did his job. 'Fine.'

He sat and watched Bessie while she lay with her chin on the edge of her basket and returned the compliment through eyes half-closed. His gaze was less than friendly; she was Maeve's dog, not his. After several minutes of silence in which his wife, immersed in her work, ignored him completely and the dog regarded him with a look that suggested she knew exactly who her friends were, he stood up. 'I'll be off, then.'

'OK.' This to the computer screen.

He watched her for a second then said gruffly, 'See you tomorrow.'

As he strode from the room she looked up at his back just as it disappeared out of the room. 'I suppose you will,' she murmured. 'I suppose you will.'

Darkness had descended on – in fact had completely subsumed – the landscape as Beckwith made his third call. Of the first two, one had been on an empty, near-derelict cottage perilously close to the flooded river's edge and another had been on an elderly couple, the Wiedemanns, who were not only deaf but also nearly blind. Their small semi-detached house nestled at the foot of a small hill facing away from the river on the outskirts of Rendcomb. They had been fearful and suspicious of Beckwith, claiming to know nothing and not to care either; they never saw strangers, knew of no one who had recently gone missing and had problems of their own without being burdened with those of others.

Their neighbour was a widow, Mrs Christmas, on whom they relied for much support. She conjured in Beckwith's mind instant images of cream meringues, sticky toffee and black-and-white television. Beckwith was invited in at once and with equal alacrity he was given a seat in an uncomfortable sagging armchair and tea was proffered. Even though he shed his sodden raincoat and boots, his trousers were still so wet that it wasn't long before steam began to rise gently before his eyes as the gas fire hissed in the background. Was it his imagination or could he smell mothballs? He found himself becoming drowsy and half expected a talking faun to make an entrance.

His introductory comments setting the scene – unidentified body washed ashore downstream – had a curious effect on Mrs Christmas, seeming to provide direct stimulation of her prurience glands (already, he guessed, well developed).

'Oh, my goodness! A body, you say?' This in a pitch that threatened the cut glass liberally decorating the bookshelves.

Beckwith nodded. 'We're making house-to –'

'Was he murdered?' The pitch had dropped – plummeted – into a low whisper that the unwary might have interpreted as horrified but that Beckwith suspected was excited.

He played the straightest of bats, a perfect forward defensive so that Mrs Christmas's attempted googly rolled back harmlessly down the pitch. 'I really couldn't say until we have the results of the post-mortem.'

The disappointment was almost painful to behold. He took advantage of this deflation to press on and so, while Mrs Christmas plied him relentlessly with biscuits, he tried to advance the investigation and she introduced irrelevancy in an astonishing display of flight of ideas.

'Have you seen any strangers in the area recently?'

Not that she could think of . . . although when she came to think of it, there had been a couple camping by the river's edge . . . just before Christmas, it was . . . nice couple . . . not very old . . . they had a dog, a spaniel . . . she liked spaniels . . . couldn't abide Jack Russells . . . she'd once been bitten by a Jack Russell and the wound went septic . . . spent three weeks in hospital . . . hadn't liked the sister on the ward . . .

'You don't happen to know their names, do you?'

She wasn't sure . . . she had spoken to them on several occasions, certainly . . . they'd asked to use her phone because their mobile phone had stopped working . . . that's modern technology for you . . . only yesterday her iron had made a loud bang when she plugged it in . . . things didn't last like they used to . . .

'About how old were they?'

Goodness, she didn't know . . . she wasn't very good at guessing people's ages . . . anything like that . . . she'd only once won the 'Guess the Weight of the Cake Competition' at the summer fête . . .

'Any idea at all? Over thirty or under?'

Mrs Christmas laughed. 'Goodness! Well over thirty . . . possibly over fifty . . . '

Beckwith crossed out the notes he had been making with a silent but heartfelt sigh. Mrs Christmas suddenly blurted out a single word: 'Symmers!'

'Pardon?'

'Symmers. That was their name . . . he was a retired solicitor . . . keen birdwatcher . . . we have quite a few of those coming here, you know . . . there have in the past been quite a few sightings of rare species . . . '

And so it went on until feeling peculiarly punch-drunk (full of biscuit and empty of useful information) Beckwith surrendered, acknowledging that he had met a superior opponent and the victory was fair. He made his apologies and departed into the rain.

Back in the car he contacted the other members of the house-to-house team to request updates. In all, they had visited twenty-two households and no one had seen anything of relevance in the past few weeks. Beckwith moved on to his next call.

***

Even in the darkness Meckel could see that the house was well cared for. The front garden was narrow and long, the path along which he moved free of weeds. It all contrasted sharply with the cottage as he remembered it; for years it had been rundown and untidy, undecorated and widely regarded as an eyesore. The then owner – a reclusive old man with a history of mental problems – had used it as a place in which to shelter, nothing more, and on his death some six years ago it had remained empty for some months before a local property developer had bought it, almost gutted it completely, then rented it out to its present incumbent, Kenneth Girdlestone. Meckel didn't know Girdlestone, hadn't even heard anything about him, which, in Meckel's book, was good. Policemen rarely noticed people who were nice and harmless.

He rang the doorbell and waited only a short while under the light of the small porch before the door opened and the face of a tall, distinguished-looking man peered out at him. He had on a thick woollen dressing gown over paisley pyjamas; round glasses, thin-framed and delicate, perched on his nose.

Meckel knew that something was wrong at once. The face didn't change when Girdlestone saw his uniform, but that didn't mean this man wasn't alarmed at the sight.

'What is it?' Not querulous, but too sharp, as if anxiety drove the voice.

'Mr Girdlestone?'

'What's wrong?'

'Are you Mr Kenneth Girdlestone?'

'Yes.' Meckel heard the hesitation of foreboding and saw a tinge of fear behind the lenses. He was used to apprehension when he called at people's houses, but this was something more.

'I was wondering if you would be able to help us. We're talking to everyone in the neighbourhood.'

'What about?'

'May I come in?'

He didn't want him to, that much was obvious. It struck Meckel that it was very early to be dressed for bed. Girdlestone seemed to debate the wisdom of a refusal while Meckel waited, never taking his eyes off his face. Eventually, 'OK.'

He stepped aside allowing Meckel to enter. While Girdlestone stood and watched, Meckel took off his boots and shed his soaked raincoat, hanging it up by the telephone. Then Girdlestone led him into the living room where Meckel was able to conclude that the developer had done a good job; it was small but warm, a coal fire burning in the grate, wall lights turned down low, the upholstery too chintzy for Meckel's taste but comfortable nonetheless.

Girdlestone sat down on the edge of his seat, an embodiment of nerves. 'What's wrong?' he demanded.

'A body's been washed ashore a few kilometres downstream. We're making house-to-house enquiries to determine whether anyone can shed light on who it might be.'

And Girdlestone relaxed, only slightly but quite noticeably, sitting back further into the chair, breathing a little more deeply. 'A body? Who?'

'We don't know yet. That's one of the things we're hoping to discover. Have you seen any strangers around the place recently?'

'No. No, I haven't.'

'And as far as you're aware, no one who lives around here has gone missing?'

'No.'

'We think the deceased was quite a young man . . . does that ring any bells?'

Girdlestone had developed a smile that was nothing more than a slit in his face, one that quivered at high frequency. With a shaking head he said, 'Not at all.'

Meckel could smell fear, a scent as potent as ammonia once the nose became attuned, but he was canny enough to act as if the only odours in the room were from furniture polish and the freshly cut flowers in the vase in the corner. 'The river runs along the bottom of your garden, I believe?'

'That's right.'

'I don't suppose you've seen anything odd in the last few weeks?'

'Oh, no.' Girdlestone was positive, like a cathode.

Meckel smiled, nodded and made a note because policemen always make notes. Having done this he looked up. 'Do you live here alone?'

'I do.'

'Not married, then?'

'No.'

And why not? A man who appeared to be in his fifties had every right not to be married; it was unfair to suggest there was anything untoward in this.

'How long have you lived here, Mr Girdlestone?'

'Four, maybe five years.'

'And before that?'

Somehow the smile remained while he frowned. 'Why?' The quivering didn't stop either.

Meckel could have modelled for the goddess of innocence. With a shrug that barely disturbed his jacket he said cheerfully, 'I haven't seen you around, that's all. I'm the local copper around here.'

There was a degree of guardedness about the way that Girdlestone said, 'I moved here from London.'

'A long move, then.'

'Yes.'

Meckel nodded companionably. 'Forgive me for being nosy, Mr Girdlestone, but what do you do for a living?'

'I'm a teacher.'

'Really? Which school?'

'I give private tuition.'

'What in?'

'Mathematics.'

Meckel smiled and nodded and let silence settle while he did nothing more than look at Girdlestone; it wasn't a hostile expression but the fact of its existence was itself unsettling. Eventually Girdlestone, his face still bearing a mask-like smile, asked, 'Is there anything more I can do for you?'

Meckel could think of no further reason to prolong his call. He closed the notebook and said, 'No, I don't think so at present, Mr Girdlestone, but if you should think of anything else, you'll be sure to let us know?'

'Oh, yes.' He was standing already, a sudden fit of enthusiasm, practically herding Meckel out of the room, the house, his presence. Meckel, though, felt slightly Newtonian and decided to resist with a force that was equal and opposite. He paused and said in a conversational tone, 'But you used to teach in a school, I take it.'

'Yes.' This was said much as he might have approached an angry bear.

'Where? In London?'

Meckel found himself trying to work out why this paradigm of innocuous small talk, this snippet of conversational inconsequence, produced a relapse in Girdlestone so that he became once more distinctly agitated. The frown and the smile – inseparable partners, it seemed – returned.

A head was shaken. 'Manchester, actually,' he admitted, but it was not to Meckel a convincing display and he thus came across an irresistible impulse to probe a little further.

'Really? I used to be stationed there,' he lied. 'Which school?'

There passed briefly into Girdlestone's face a look of panic. 'Manchester Grammar.'

Meckel nodded. 'A good school.'

'Yes. Very.'

Girdlestone was shifting his weight from foot to foot, edging forward to reach past Meckel and open the door.

'When were you there?'

He had opened the door so that the cold and the sound of falling rain enveloped them. 'Ten, eleven years ago.'

Meckel nodded. 'Retire, did you?'

Girdlestone agreed at once. 'That's right.'

Meckel sighed. 'I wish I could afford to retire early.'

It seemed to Meckel that had he had the courage Girdlestone would have pushed him out into the night; he seemed about ready to explode, or faint, or possibly both. 'Ah, well . . . ' he said weakly, a tremor lurking beneath these words.

Meckel smiled. 'Well, anyway. I'd better be off.'

The residents of Mafeking would not have looked more relieved at the departure of the Boers than Girdlestone did as Meckel walked out into the rain.

Sydenham shouldn't have been a pathologist, Sauerwine had decided. He was more a lawyer, perhaps; maybe a company director. Sauerwine could imagine Sydenham behind a desk or around the polished mahogany of a boardroom table, but not wearing silly clothes and a mask with his hands deep inside someone's offal.

Not that you would have known it from the constant river of sometimes inane, sometimes relevant words that issued in cultured tones from his mouth. Sauerwine had heard things about Sydenham – how he wasn't as good as he liked to think he was, how he had, on one or two occasions, fouled up completely – and the impression created over this present body was doing nothing to reassure him.

'Of course,' remarked Sydenham cheerfully, his head down over the pelvis as he encountered a particularly interesting blemish on the corpse's backside, 'one must be grateful that the olfactory nerves swiftly tire.'

Sauerwine's olfactory nerves weren't swiftly tiring; indeed they were hanging on in there, proving to have the staying power of Olympic marathon runners. The stench had been bad when he had walked into the mortuary, had worsened with each manipulation of the corpse, and had since stayed at the same intensity. Then there was the sight of the bubbled flesh, in a shade of green that was peculiarly obnoxious; the fact that the slimy skin peeled every time it was touched added a piquancy that only a truly sadistic Supreme Being would have conceived. Sauerwine said nothing, choosing instead to look around him and observe the decor.

Not that it was particularly pleasing on the eye. Sauerwine had spent many hours in a lot of mortuaries and felt that he had experience enough to judge. None was what he might have considered 'homely' but there were some that were at least modern and reasonably intact; this one was decrepit, with intricate and wide cracks in the ceiling plaster, a large patch of damp in the corner by the sluice, dark-brown wood everywhere and dim globe lights suspended from the ceiling by dark metal rods. It was also cavernous and echoing; the dissection tables stretched away into the far distance.

Sydenham looked up at him, a look of triumph on his long face. 'He's been buggered, Inspector.'

It was the prince, the king, the emperor of non-sequiturs. Thankfully Sauerwine was saved from inadequate response by the pathologist, who added, 'More than once, I think. He's got a "funnel anus".'

Oh, good. He didn't dare ask what that meant, fearful that he would be given a demonstration at an unhealthily close proximity. Instead he nodded and said, 'A homosexual, then.'

Sydenham lived for superciliousness. 'Not necessarily. He might have been a male prostitute.'

'Aren't they all gay?'

Sydenham couldn't believe that he was witnessing this display of naivety. 'Goodness, no. It's a business to many of them. Men or women, dwarves or giants, missing limbs or extra limbs – it doesn't matter. Animals, almost certainly, if you paid them enough.'

Once more, Sauerwine expressed silently his gratitude to be

given the wisdom of the good Dr Sydenham. 'Shall we say, then, that he indulged in unusual sexual practices?' he suggested. For an instant he feared that Sydenham would enter into a debate on his choice of the word 'unusual', but thankfully the pathologist opted merely to grunt and return to the corpse.

'Any chance of fingerprints?' he asked optimistically.

Sydenham didn't reply, merely proffering a look of tired and amused contempt before turning to the mortuary technician and saying, 'You can turn him over now.'

The mortuary technician was female, something that Sauerwine had noted was an increasing tendency. Quite what the distaff side got out of the job was completely lost on him but since not all of them were complete losers in life's beauty handicap stakes, he counted it a blessing. The case in point, for instance; only thirty or so, he judged, and fairly slim; not bony but certainly not a porker. As his sex life of recent times had been vaporously attenuated, he toyed with the idea of getting to know her a bit better. It was a shame that he was forced by the health and safety procedures to dress in a billowing paper gown coloured a strikingly unattractive shade of green. He felt like one of the three little maids from school. And anyway, how would it look if he were seen in her company? He feared that it would provide fertile ground for gossip and outright bawdiness amongst his colleagues at his expense.

On the other hand he feared that if he didn't indulge in some romance soon certain parts of his anatomy would either explode with frustration or drop off due to underuse . . .

'He's had quite a bit of dental work done, Inspector. Some dental practitioner somewhere has made a bob or two out of him; that should help you to identify him.'

'What about DNA?'

Sydenham snorted. Sauerwine had noticed that the Sydenham snort was an impressive thing, one that stood in for any or all of impatience, amusement, disdain or incredulity, depending on circumstance. It was one of a complete range of sounds that Sydenham could summon depending on circumstance. It was a form of communication somewhere between verbal and non-verbal, and as such perhaps it was a relic of man's earliest attempts at talking.

'What about it? It's no better than teeth, you know, Inspector. It's just a modern fad, one foisted upon us by the technocrats; those same technocrats who are ruining the British way of life . . .'

The female mortuary technician was standing slightly behind Sydenham's right shoulder and grinning broadly as this diatribe ran its course. When she winked at Sauerwine it required a great effort not to giggle. Eventually he was able to say, 'Nevertheless, Doctor, I would like you to take some samples, if it's not too much trouble.'

Sydenham grunted; not as good as his snort, but a close second.

Sauerwine decided to retreat for a cup of coffee and, he hoped, a chocolate digestive biscuit. Having, he felt, done his duty and been there at the start, he would let Sydenham do his stuff in private from now on; he would return for the final summing up.

Meckel saw at once that it was more than just a farmer's house. He knew farms and farmers well, having been stationed in the country for most of his police career. Almost without exception, farmers were practical people with little interest in the appearance of things; they had no regard for superficiality, distrusted those who did. As long as it worked that was good enough for them. The places, therefore, where they lived and worked tended to be as untidy and ramshackle as if abandoned; invariably mud (or muck) adorned everything, rust decorated all exposed surfaces and there was an air of decay everywhere that one looked. Here, however, all was spick and span, neat and tidy, just tickety-boo. There wasn't even a smell around the place, unless it was one of perfection.

As soon as his car drove into the yard several hundred –
possibly more than a thousand – watts of security light flicked
on so that he had the impression that he was standing on a
film set. Still, it gave him plenty of illumination to inspect his
surroundings. He judged that the house had once been
Edwardian, although it had been renovated and extended
almost to destruction. He suspected that it now housed at
least eight bedrooms and over on the left of the house he saw
through large picture windows an indoor swimming pool.
What had once been the farmyard was now paved with pristine
stone, two barns converted into offices and workshops. A
vintage tractor standing in the middle of the farmyard – also
renovated and turned back into perfection – was clearly meant
to be some form of decorative artefact, meant to impress; to
Meckel it seemed merely to serve to underline a blasphemy.

He knew that the property was owned by the Verner-
Morrisons and, against all the evidence, that it was a working
farm; he knew also from gossip that the Verner-Morrisons
were not farmers. They owned a luxury car business, one
which reputedly had made them millionaires; their farming
was done by William Sneddon, the manager and, according to
local gossip, the only one within a mile or two who knew
which end to feed a cow.

Meckel was a fair man, calm and beyond the point where
mankind's grosser iniquities caused him angst, and therefore
little in his working life ignited the fires that burned low
within him. Not even the small, portly and clearly arrogant
man who emerged from the imposing black front door and
began shouting at him, even though Meckel had only just
emerged from the car into the rain.

'Clear off! This is private property! Clear off!'

The rain wasn't now raining, it was deluging and Meckel
felt that he was dressed in clothing composed of sponge. He
decided that he didn't want to clear off.

'Mr Alec Verner-Morrison?'

This produced a brief pause and retrenchment. 'Who's asking?

Meckel trudged through the rain and the coalescing puddles. His single word of reply – 'Police' – was partly obscured by the amount of water running down his face.

Verner-Morrison was fair-haired and pale-eyed. He was dressed in a pallid yellow jumper above which a brilliantly scarlet cravat poked pompously. He had in his hand a large but unlit cigar. 'What do you want?'

The emphasis was on the third syllable.

To get dry. To get warm. To get away from people like you.

'I'd like a brief word with you.'

'What about?'

By now Meckel was standing in front of him, under the broad, deep porch and out of the rain. Meckel's relief was only partial because there was still a fair volume of water shifting downwards about his person as gravity worked its magic. 'We're conducting house-to-house enquiries in the area. Could you spare me a couple of minutes?'

Verner-Morrison frowned. 'What's going on?'

'Could we step inside, sir? I am rather cold.'

So was Verner-Morrison, but he didn't seem keen to comply with the request and Meckel had a sense of déjà vu. After a hesitation he asked, 'Is that necessary? I don't want my wife disturbed.'

Meckel wondered why and decided that, yes, it was necessary. 'I'm sure that there's no need to do that, sir. It won't take more than a few moments . . . '

Verner-Morrison tried to outstare him and lost with an audible and angry exhalation of air through his nose and mouth simultaneously. 'Oh, very well.'

He turned and pushed the door open, striding into the high-ceilinged entrance hall behind him; unbidden, Meckel followed and was at once confronted with a life-sized statue of a woman. The woman was very much naked and very well endowed. Meckel, who liked a woman with generous proportions, found himself having consciously and deliberately to remove his eyes from this sight and on to the slightly less prepossessing sight of his host who was standing, arms folded, in the middle of the room. Behind him to his left a staircase ran up the wall to a first-floor landing while three doors led in a variety of directions further into the house and a chandelier hung down above his head.

'Well?' he demanded.

'The body of young man has been washed out of the river by the recent flooding, sir. Are you aware of anyone in the area going missing recently?'

'No.'

'Have you seen any strangers in the area?'

'No.'

From behind a doorway to Verner-Morrison's rear came a voice. 'Who is it, Alec?'

The small and aggravated householder turned irritably. 'No one.'

Meckel raised an eyebrow at his dismissal from existence. Verner-Morrison was again looking at him as he enquired, 'Is that all?'

Imperturbably Meckel rode over the peremptory, irascible tone and asked, 'No unusual activity on the river?'

'No.' Verner-Morrison uttered this through teeth clamped together.

'No travellers, anyone like that?'

'I told you, no.'

The door opened behind Verner-Morrison and in came a short, blonde woman dressed in a bright-blue silk robe that gave Meckel an immediate dilemma – whether to look at the legs that it didn't cover or the breasts that it did. 'Alec? What's keeping you? Oh . . . '

She stopped and looked alarmed. Verner-Morrison closed his eyes, took a deep and impatient breath, then turned with a close-lipped grimace to his wife. Ever since Meckel had first seen him Verner-Morrison had appeared to be angry – seemed to have been built for it, given his squat stature, thick neck and cropped, almost crew-cut hair – but Meckel now realized that he had been duped into accepting a weak substitute for the real thing. Now he saw just how angry Alex Verner-Morrison could be.

'Get out.' This was uttered not as any form of shout, more as a calm and considered command, almost a growl, very much a threat.

Meckel saw that she was torn between the force of his order and curiosity; she hesitated therefore, but only briefly for her husband pointed out almost immediately, 'I said, "Get out."'

The voice just slightly louder but immensely more intimidating.

She opened her mouth and shut it, then appeared to be unsure whether to smile and laugh it off, or screw up her face into tears. In the end she managed a sort of cocktail of the two. Murmuring, 'I'm sorry,' she nodded at her husband, then turned and retraced her steps. Before the door had closed behind her Verner-Morrison was back with Meckel. 'Anything more? Or can I get back to *The Times*?'

Meckel, though, had decided that he didn't like Mr Verner-Morrison. Showing no sign of departing he asked, 'You're in luxury cars, aren't you?'

'What of it?'

He looked around him. 'A lot of money in it, I see.'

Verner-Morrison didn't shrug, didn't smile in self-deprecation, didn't even look down in embarrassment. 'Shedloads,' he proclaimed deliberately. 'Fucking shedloads.'

'But not much in farming.'

'Look, I've told you what you came to find out. It's time to go.'

Meckel nodded slowly and only after appearing to consider whether this fitted in with his plans, said, 'I suppose it is.'

Verner-Morrison came forward and opened the door to let him out. As he was passing through it Meckel said, 'So why do you do it? Farming, I mean?'

From the hesitation he wondered if he had somehow caught Verner-Morrison off guard. Then, 'Right from when I was a kid I wanted to own a farm. Kind of ambition, I guess.'

'William Sneddon's the farm manager, is he?'

'That's right.'

'He lives . . . where?'

'At the end of the track, on the main road.'

'The one I passed? It looked as if no one was in.'

Verner-Morrison shrugged. 'Then maybe he's out.'

Meckel thanked Alec Verner-Morrison and stepped back out into the cold bitterness of the ever-falling rain. As he got into his car he looked across at the farmhouse and wondered.

Wondered what the Verner-Morrisons were hiding.

Wondered why there should be a life-sized sculpture of a naked Mrs Verner-Morrison in the entrance hall.

Helena saw that the strain of remand was starting to get to Martin Bell. She saw a greyness to the pallid skin, a dampening of his ebullient bravado, and she smelled the scent of imprisonment on him. This was an unpleasant, slightly fetid odour, a combination of sweat and anxiety and bad breath, the perfume of the prison.

'What's going on?' he demanded as soon as they were alone. 'Have you got some news?'

'I just need to talk to you about something.'

He wouldn't sit down, another change, she noted. He strode about the small room, his eyes seeming to find the small high window irresistibly attractive despite the fact that it was a rainy night and only gloom was interested in peering through the thick glass. 'Sit down, Mr Bell,' she advised.

He shook his head, and otherwise might not have heard her

invitation. The room they were in was only two by three metres but he strode about it like a man working himself up to something.

Helena said, 'I've been told that a few months ago you beat a man up.'

That stopped him, but the face he turned towards her wasn't calm.

Far from it.

'You what?'

She repeated the sentence.

He came towards her, leaning across the table where she was making notes in pencil on a pad of lined paper, and rested the knuckles of his clenched hands on the laminate top. It was an overtly aggressive posture, one that was emphasized by his expression, and Helena could feel twinges of fear; small ripples but none the less perturbing. 'Is this some sort of game? You're supposed to be proving me innocent, not raking up crap about me.'

'Sit down, Mr Bell.'

'Why should I?'

She felt very nervous now, the ripples a bow wave of disruption. Everything about him had become immediately ugly – the look on his face, his tone of voice, even his demeanour. She saw cruelty in his eyes and she thought, *He's enjoying threatening me.*

'Sit down, Mr Bell.' She raised her voice just slightly, hoping that he would not hear her fear.

When a smile seeped out through his angry face she knew that she was seeing the true man. *He's a bully. He gets off on frightening women.*

'If you don't sit down now, Mr Bell, I'm getting up and leaving and you'll never see me again.'

He responded then; slowly and quite deliberately so but he backed away and sat down on the chair on the opposite side of the table. The smile deepened, broadened and took over his

61

whole face. He put up his hands, palms towards her. 'I didn't mean anything, you know.'

She would rather have liked to argue but she said nothing.

He went on. 'It gets to you, this place . . . '

'I'm sure.'

'It's frustrating, too. Not being able to get out there and bang heads together, make people tell the truth.'

She reflected that his choice of expression was perhaps more apt than he had intended, saying, 'I'm not interested in what you did to this man, Mr Bell, only in what he said and who he was.'

'He was a toe-rag.'

'Be that as it may, Mr Bell, you had a fight with him.'

Bell snorted. 'Hardly. The sorry little prick didn't land a blow on me. I gave him a good seeing-to.' Things had clearly changed; now it was acceptable to admit to, even boast of, how much damage he could inflict on another human being.

'What was his name?'

'Kernohan.'

'You knew him, then?'

'He works the bar at the snooker hall.'

'And he said what, precisely?'

'Said that he'd seen Suzy with someone. Said that they were lovey-dovey. Said that he'd seen them in the pub, that this cunt was tickling her tonsils whilst she had her hands all over him.'

'And you took exception to that?'

His head jerked up as if he suspected she was laughing at him. 'Wouldn't you? He'd been spreading that crap all over the place, telling anyone who'd listen. I couldn't let him make me look a laughing stock.'

'But when we've talked before, Mr Bell, you said that you had no idea about her having an affair,' she reminded him hesitantly.

He frowned. 'I didn't think she was.'

'I don't understand . . . '

He explained impatiently, 'Kernohan's a toe-rag, I told you. I thought he was making shit for me, nothing more.'

'Why would he do that?'

He was hesitant, a coyness that was as unsuited to him as an Easter bonnet would have been. He shrugged. 'That's what people like him do.'

She had been frightened of him a few moments ago but she forgot that as she said, 'Had you done something to him? Is that it? Was he getting revenge in some way?'

Another shrug.

She pointed out, 'I'm supposed to be proving you innocent, but I can only do that if I have the whole story, Mr Bell. *Somebody* beat your wife to death; if it wasn't you, I need to have everything you can possibly tell me about your life and about your wife's.'

'I don't see that this is relevant.'

'I don't see that it's not.'

For a moment there was a standoff, a contest, and she wondered if his pride would let him lose or if his fear of conviction was strong enough to overcome it. Then, quite loudly as if proclaiming this for all to hear, recklessly bringing truth to the ignorant, pointing out that the king was naked, he said, 'I knocked his wife off.'

The vernacular lost her for a second, then, 'You had an affair with his wife?'

'That's what I said.'

'And he found out . . . and you think he was just making trouble for you.'

A curt nod. No smile but an undoubted sense of pride in what he had done. Bell had *alpha male* written all over his attitude. He explained from this position of machismo, 'He knew he couldn't take me in a straight fight – fuck, I proved it, didn't I? – so he starts making up crap about Suzy and some low-life.'

Helena wrote this down but was thinking hard as she did so. 'Did he mention who this "low-life" was?'

There was a distinct increase in aggressiveness as he asked, 'Why?'

She retained as much ice as she could about her exterior as she looked directly up into his face and said, 'Because maybe it was true. If it was, that gives us another suspect to consider.'

'It wasn't.'

She raised an eyebrow and suggested, 'You . . . questioned . . . your wife about it?'

He leaned back in the chair; it creaked as he did so. 'I did mention it,' he offered carelessly.

You gave her a good hiding, you mean.

'And . . . ?'

He made a face. 'And she denied it.'

She was finding it difficult to keep the contempt and disgust away from her voice. 'Did you believe her?'

He changed posture quite suddenly, leaning forward so that once more he was in her face and it became all too obvious that she had been right and that he wasn't brushing his teeth too well. 'Oh, yes.' And this time he couldn't keep the smile of pride away as he spoke.

Verner-Morrison watched Meckel departing and then turned away. He strode across the hall and through the doorway at the back.

'Cherie!'

Nothing.

'Cherie!'

Still nothing.

'Oh, for fuck's sake.' This he said on an exasperated breath. He looked around the room, appeared to make a decision then went to the phone on the table by a large portrait in oils of a loving couple of Verner-Morrisons. He punched in a number, listened to the ringing tone for maybe a minute, then slammed it down again, swearing.

He waded over the thick pile of the bright-white carpet, flopped down on a bright-yellow leather chair, sucked in a lungful of air and bellowed anew, 'Cherie!'

She appeared two long minutes later, drinking champagne, still in the robe. 'Has he gone?'

'Where have you been?'

'Shaving.'

He grunted but didn't speak. Cherie didn't mind – actually, she admitted to herself, she didn't *care* – they'd been too long married for his moodiness to have much effect on her. She sometimes wondered if he were having an affair. Since coming to Rendcomb he had changed subtly, become more tense, less open. There had been times when she had come in on the end of a telephone conversation hurriedly terminated and his explanation had seemed less than convincing. He made a lot of trips, many abroad – *on business*, he said – and she wondered about those too . . .

But the most frequent thing about which she wondered was, did she care?

She sat on a long, low sofa that matched his chair and sipped champagne demurely, a picture of expensive elegance, unaffected by a world gone bad. When she drained the glass she rose and went to the bar that was located in the corner of the room and brought out from the refrigerator an opened bottle. 'Drink?' she asked. Had her tone not been knowing, this might have been taken as solicitude; that he merely scowled in response and that she smiled sweetly suggested otherwise.

'Oh, no, I forgot. You're off the booze.'

'It might do you some good to cut down a bit.'

She sat back down.

'Where's Ben?'

'In his room. Homework.'

More silence between them until he said abruptly, 'They've fished a body out of the river.'

For the first time interest was sparked. 'Really? Where?'

'South of the village.'

'Who was it?'

'No one knows. That's what the copper was trying to find out. Asking about strangers.'

'Oh, my God!' She was now energized. 'Was he murdered?'

'Of course he bloody wasn't.' He pronounced this tiredly. 'Why do you always think the worst?'

She smiled sweetly. 'Because it usually happens, dear.'

He scowled. After a moment's silence she decided, 'Well, that's put the tin lid on business for a while.'

'Why?'

For a second she was nonplussed by his insouciance. 'Because we're likely to have police everywhere, at least until they've found out who it was and how he ended up in the river.'

He shrugged. 'So?'

She was scathing. 'So we don't want the police around here, do we? Especially not this week.'

'They won't see anything,' he reassured her.

She didn't argue but clearly didn't agree, pointing out instead, 'Don't forget that they're interested in strangers. If they find out that we quite regularly have outsiders coming and staying with us, they might take an interest then.'

For the first time he looked directly at her. 'Ah.'

'Exactly. We've been careful, but that doesn't mean someone hasn't seen something. If that's the case, they may ask some awkward questions . . . *and* they might decide to look in a few of the outbuildings.'

He considered this and while he was doing so she added, 'What about William?'

'I've thought of that. He's not answering his phone and the copper seemed to think that the house empty.' He was silent for a moment but it was not a contented interlude. He decided eventually, 'Anyway, we can trust him not to say anything stupid.'

He was confident about that. William Sneddon had as much to lose as his employers.

Sydenham spoke as if he were addressing a particularly retarded child as he presented his findings to Sauerwine. The age difference between them was approximately twenty-five years and so perhaps it was reasonable that Sydenham might look on him as a child, although Sauerwine did not consider himself to be particularly retarded. His only consolation as he listened to Sydenham pontificate and expostulate, explaining details that were either irrelevant or too technical to understand – or both – was to make occasional eye contact with the mortuary technician whose name, he had discovered, was Tricia. She seemed to like him and although the competition in the room was not stiff, she was certainly the most attractive person there. Even the stench didn't seem so bad, he had decided.

'Obviously we'll have to wait for the tox jocks to do their tests' – Sydenham spoke as if they were mere children playing with test tubes – 'but I doubt if they'll add significantly to my findings.'

The implication was that he was speaking from a position of omniscience, stooping merely to please others; what could a mere toxicologist add to the perfectly formed picture he was painting?

'Of course,' murmured Sauerwine. Tricia had very short, very black hair and a slightly upturned nose, giving her an elfin appearance that was enhanced by ears that were ever so slightly pointed. She was quite small but gave the impression of being compact and strong; another impression she gave was that fools were not only not suffered gladly, they were not suffered at all.

Sydenham continued his oratorical exhibition oblivious of the non-verbal communication that was commencing around him. 'The degree of putrefaction makes assessment difficult, of course; immersion always accelerates tissue decay and then there is the degree of predation by wildlife – fish are voracious and rather unpleasant things, I feel; water shrimps are even worse.'

Struggling to catch the odd relevant observation or finding amidst the tiresome and seemingly inexhaustible stream of self-opinionated logorrhoea, Sauerwine asked, 'Can you tell me how long he'd been in the water?'

'Ha!' Sydenham smiled, superciliousness congealing out of his pores. 'I'm bloody good, my dear chap, but I'm not that good. Only the Lord God Himself and the murderer know that for certain.'

'Can you estimate it, then?'

'That's easy. More than two weeks, no more than five.'

'Is that it?'

Sydenham seemed surprised that this gift of knowledge was so ungratefully received. 'What more do you want?' he enquired.

'Something not quite as broad as a three-week time span.'

Sydenham tutted; no one tutted like Sydenham. He accompanied a perfectly executed sound by a slight toss of the head, a lift of the eyebrows and a slow exhalation. It was a tut that would not have disgraced a theatrical knight, even a theatrical lord.

'Would you like the date? Perhaps the time of day? Perhaps even the weather as he was delivered to the water?' He stared inquisitorially at Sauerwine, then asked, 'Mmm?'

'I'd like something a little less ill-defined.'

Sydenham then guffawed. His guffaws were better than his tuts but not as striking as his snorts and grunts. 'Look at him, Inspector! Be grateful that I'm giving you anything useful at all and don't expect miracles.'

Sauerwine gave up. He sometimes felt that it would have been easier herding a reluctant bull than dealing with a pathologist. He looked across at Tricia and saw her smiling at him, accompanied by a slow, knowing wink.

'He was, as I suspected, engaging in some sort of asphyxial stimulatory act. There is a lot of superficial trauma to the neck structures and, in fact, this goes quite deep so that there is some haemorrhage around the subserosal tissues of the trachea. He was suspended somewhere with his feet just off the ground. The method of suspension was almost certainly this scarf.' A pause then he looked at Sauerwine with a slightly unsavoury grin. 'A tantalizing position to be in. The hypoxia and the pain induce sexual stimulation that is, I believe, quite exquisite.'

'Could this be in any way self-inflicted?'

Sydenham was able to stamp on that one and did so with pleasure. 'Oh, no. Not at all. Out of the question.'

'But people do this kind of thing themselves . . . '

'Tell me, Inspector, in your experience, do they bugger themselves as well? If they do, you really must tell me how – I'd be fascinated.'

It was no coincidence that at that moment Sauerwine found that he had his own thoughts of buggery. Trying to stop his temper from throttling Dr Charles Sydenham, he responded, 'Point taken.'

'The last time he was buggered, though, it was rather . . . violent.' There was something about his tone that was distressingly unpleasant. 'Are you sure you wouldn't like to see?'

Sauerwine had visions of hell when Sydenham said this. Suppressing a shudder he shook his head. Sydenham expressed disappointment, his whole demeanour signalling bewilderment at such ingratitude. Sauerwine found Tricia laughing again; he found also that he didn't mind. Sydenham, meanwhile, had picked up another piece of armature with which to continue his assault on Sauerwine.

'Plus, of course, his hands were bound.'

He indicated the green, slimy and quite noticeably nibbled wrists where there were prominent markings, dark and irregular; the fishing twine had been removed. 'I've put the ligatures in a forensic bag.'

Sauerwine thought that he was getting a clear picture of what might have happened but he knew from experience that some cases were illusional, as deceptive as oases; what he thought was truth now might prove in an hour's time to be nothing more than a wisp.

'So he was sexually abused, killed by asphyxiation and then dumped in the river?'

Sydenham was delighted. 'Good grief, no! Whatever gave you that idea?'

Sauerwine couldn't recall. He closed his eyes briefly, then smiled a smile so tight it hurt his lips. 'What did happen, then?' He couldn't keep exasperation from his voice, at which Sydenham raised a patrician eyebrow and Tricia, at that moment mopping the floor (Sydenham was nothing if not messy), looked up and caught his eye. The smile that followed was at once playful, commiserating and enticing.

'If you'd pay attention, my dear chap, I'd tell you.'

Sydenham's sarcasm might have been described as withering or petulant, depending on the perspective; the musculature of Sauerwine's face became so tetanic he had almost lost the ability to speak. 'Tell me,' he suggested.

Sydenham turned back to the body, speaking out as if declaiming great truths, a prophet whose time had come. 'The poor gentleman before us, having been suspended to the point of near asphyxia and the victim – perhaps the willing victim – of anal intercourse and conceivably other sexual practices, was, I am afraid, given up to the Deeps whilst still alive.'

It was like listening to a nineteenth-century actor-manager reciting some turgid gothic melodrama.

Before Sauerwine could ask, Sydenham supplied an answer.

'He was drowned.' He said this brightly . . . *It's going to be a sunny day!*

Momentarily Sauerwine found that he was there, horribly immersed in what it might have been like.

'Whoever did this,' decided the pathologist sagely, 'must have been quite, quite calculating.'

Which wasn't the word that Sauerwine would have used. Warily he enquired, 'Is there anything else I should know?'

But Sydenham had run out of tricks with which to amaze the audience. 'Isn't that enough?' This was asked disdainfully.

Thus dismissed, Sauerwine returned to the mortuary office, having thankfully divested himself of his unbecoming outer garments. He sat down – actually it was more of a slump down – thoroughly depressed. It was still raining, still winter, still night; he had a seriously decomposed body that had been seriously sexually abused and seriously murdered. He had no idea who it was or where the murder had been done or, in a practical sense, when.

And he had a headache.

Tricia came into the office and from something and somewhere he mustered a welcoming smile. She said, 'He's something else, isn't he?'

With a laugh he asked, 'Is it me, or is he a prick with a medical degree?'

'Oh, don't worry. It isn't you. He's a twelve-incher.'

More laughter. She said, 'Coffee?'

Which seemed like a good idea. 'White, please. No sugar.'

When the kettle was boiling and she had put instant coffee in the mugs he asked, 'What's he doing?'

'Dictating his report. Shakespeare should pay attention – might learn a thing or two.'

She poured the water, stirred in milk and handed him a mug. For a while they enjoyed their shared antagonism of Dr Charles Sydenham, FRCPath. When he had finished, Sauerwine did the diplomatic thing and went to the sink, there to wash

71

his mug. Whilst he was doing this he heard her say tentatively, 'I don't suppose you'd like to go out for a drink sometime?'

Beckwith called upon Richard Gillespie's house but found it was empty. He looked through the windows but saw only darkness and he was by now so wet and miserable that he wasn't going to hang about for long. He turned and walked back to the car just as a battered blue Land Rover drove along the lane; Beckwith halted, assuming that it was going to stop, but it kept on going, only slowing about a hundred metres further on as it turned right off the road.

'Oh, well,' sighed Beckwith. He continued back to the car and had opened the door to get in when a second car approached the house, this time slowing and turning in to park beside him.

The man who got out looked at him suspiciously, the rain dripping off the hood of his wax jacket. Beckwith asked, 'Mr Gillespie?'

'Yes?'

'I'm from the police. Sergeant Beckwith.'

'Oh, yes?'

Beckwith thought that he detected a certain degree of hostility. It was difficult to make out the man's face but he couldn't imagine a smile in amongst the shadows.

'It's about the body that your wife discovered. Inspector Sauerwine asked me to have a word with you.'

'Did he, now?' He paused then turned abruptly, walking towards the house as he threw over his shoulder, 'You'd better come in, then.'

They entered by the kitchen door at the rear of the house. Beckwith said nothing about the fact that it was unlocked.

'I won't keep you long, sir.'

Once divested of his outer garments and standing in light, Gillespie could be seen to be tall and muscular, the kind of sinewy tautness that farming seemed to imbue in people. He

72

went at once to the fridge and produced two bottles of beer, one of which he proffered to Beckwith.

Sorely tempted, Beckwith shook his head with a melancholy smile. 'No, thanks, sir.'

Gillespie shrugged, then sat down at the table to open his bottle. 'Sit down.'

After complying, Beckwith asked, 'We're trying to find out if anyone in the neighbourhood has noticed anything odd.'

Gillespie shrugged. 'In what way?'

'Well, have you seen any strangers about in the last few weeks?'

'We had travellers about three month back. Bastards set up camp just outside the village.'

'Are they still there?'

'Naw. Only stayed a week. Good riddance.'

'Nothing since then?'

Gillespie tipped the beer bottle back and took a long drink before replying. 'Can't think of anything.'

'No one gone missing?'

'Nope.'

'So you'd have no idea who the dead man might be?'

'Nope.'

The bottle was empty. Gillespie put it down and picked up the other one. 'You sure?' he asked.

Beckwith stood. 'Quite sure,' he said.

'That's about all for now, Mr Gillespie, but if you should think of anything else. . .?'

Gillespie was opening the second bottle. He said carelessly, 'I'll let you know.'

Feeling as if the interview had not gone well but feeling also that it had gone as well as it was going to, Beckwith went to the door. Gillespie didn't stand up.

'Thanks for your time.'

Gillespie's only reply was a bottle raised and a single nod.

By the time Sauerwine had returned to the station, Beckwith

was there with Meckel. They both looked as though they had fallen in the river not once but on many occasions. They were clearly extremely tired and extremely irritable; neither of them was happy as they sat in the staff rest room drinking an orange-brown liquid that pretended, badly, to be tea.

Sauerwine had his own office and he called to them to follow him as he walked past. As was his habit, the room was superbly tidy; Meckel, who didn't know Sauerwine, was somewhat surprised and not a little disorientated by this parallel world where everything was where it should be, where there were no old coffee cups and overburdened ash-trays and where all the pens and pencils had been mustered, all present and correct, in a plastic pot on the desk.

'Sit down.'

Sauerwine was knackered and even the prospect of socializing with Tricia could not raise his spirits. It was still raining and the night was blacker and gloomier than ever.

'First of all,' he said, 'the poor sod drowned.'

'Drowned?' Beckwith was not unnaturally surprised. 'You mean it wasn't murder?'

Sauerwine laughed sourly. 'Oh, it was murder all right. Sydenham reckons he was suspended by the neck until he was almost dead, buggered, and then thrown into the river tied to some sort of weight. He says sometime between two and five weeks ago.'

Beckwith's eyes widened slightly as he nodded and then said, 'Ah.'

Sauerwine brooded for a second on the task before them; whilst doing so he noticed that around both of his guests there was a spreading patch of damp as they discharged rainwater back into the environment. He rather wished that it was not *his* environment. He said, 'It's late and I'm ready for bed, but before we go I want to establish the strategy.'

They both nodded but said nothing.

'Well?'

74

Beckwith felt that as the more senior of the two he should be the one to begin but Meckel seemed to be unaware of the political niceties involved and said at once, 'Identification, sir.'

Sauerwine nodded, clearly pleased with this. 'Good.'

Beckwith, mouth open, shot a venomous glance at Meckel. *Bloody woodentop.* He said somewhat too loudly, 'We'll need to start by getting possible matches with missing persons.'

Sauerwine sighed. 'You'll have to go back at least six weeks, probably eight.'

Somewhat to his surprise Beckwith, it seemed, had volunteered. He thought about protesting, decided that it would not do to look recalcitrant. 'OK.' Then, 'What have we got if I identify a possible? DNA?'

'DNA and teeth.'

Pleased that he had at last established some sort of stake in the discussion, he was just about to appear to be intelligent on the house-to-house enquiries when once more Meckel upstaged him.

'If he was drowned, I'd say it was almost certain that he went in the river at Rendcomb.'

It wasn't just *the fact* of his doing it, Beckwith reflected acidly, it was *the way* he was doing it; goody-goody to an extreme, it was highly likely that he would next produce an apple from his pocket for teacher.

Sauerwine, moreover, was actually taking him seriously. 'Why do you say that?'

Beckwith was forced to sit and listen again, and express apparent interest in Meckel's theory regarding the deep pools at Rendcomb. When Meckel had finished, he said quickly, 'Obviously that's a possibility, sir, but if the body's been in the water that length of time, isn't it possible – even likely – that it was dumped in the river a lot further upstream? It might be kilometres away; out of the county, even.'

Meckel, the sod, had an answer, though. 'The river's pretty slow flowing, sir. If the body's been in the water five weeks and it broke free immediately, I suppose it's possible that it came from further upstream, but it's so shallow for miles, it would have to have been a long way away, say Dixton; if, however, it stayed tethered for any length of time, it wouldn't have had the time to get this far.'

Smartarse.

Inexplicably, Sauerwine couldn't see this though. He asked thoughtfully, 'How far upriver is Dixton?'

'Another thirty kilometres.'

He considered this, then made a decision. 'Well, obviously, we have to concentrate on Rendcomb first.'

Obviously. Beckwith felt like Napoleon on the field at Waterloo being told that the bloody Prussians had just turned up for a bit of argy-bargy.

'I want a diving team searching the river at Rendcomb first thing tomorrow.' Beckwith, it seemed, was to be entrusted with arranging this. Sauerwine asked of Meckel, 'How deep is it at Rendcomb?'

'There are pools there at least ten metres deep.'

'Why?' Beckwith heard himself sounding petulant, sounding as if these pools were Meckel's doing.

'Subsidence. There used to be a lot of open-cast mining in the area.'

Much as he wanted to have a ready response to this information, Beckwith could think of nothing to say and nothing to do except grunt. Meckel projected meek satisfaction at being so helpful; perversely Beckwith would have preferred an air of smug superiority. Sauerwine had moved on. 'Has the house-to-house turned up anything?'

Thus far they had visited thirty-two households in total. No one had seen anything unusual, no one knew of anyone who had gone missing, no strangers likely to have been the victim had been seen in the neighbourhood. Sauerwine sighed.

He had expected no more but hope sprang eternal . . .

'There is one thing, sir.'

Sauerwine looked up at Meckel. So did Beckwith but his expression was less benign as, indeed, were his thoughts.

'What is it?'

'One of the people I spoke to tonight . . . '

'Yes?'

Meckel was hesitant. 'There was something odd about him . . . something I didn't like.'

'Who was he?'

'Name of Girdlestone. Lives in a house in Rendcomb, by the river.'

'Close to these pools of yours?'

'Very.'

'So what didn't you like about him?'

Meckel didn't know what to say, evinced embarrassment that he had said anything. 'I can't say really. He was uncomfortable that I was there. He wanted me out of the way as soon as possible, I think.' He clearly thought that he wasn't making a good case, for he shrugged then said, 'It's probably nothing.'

Beckwith had opened his mouth and might actually have involuntarily proclaimed aloud his total agreement with this last sentiment had Sauerwine not raced to give encouragement to his junior staff. 'Not at all, not at all. You're an experienced copper. If you've got an instinct about someone, then we're interested.' Unexpectedly he turned to Beckwith. 'Aren't we?'

Beckwith wanted to point out that he was far from interested, that he thought Meckel was a bit of a twat, and he certainly didn't want to encourage him. However he said only, 'Absolutely.'

Having garnered this support, Sauerwine turned back to Meckel, who was now apparently seen as some sort of elderly protégé. 'What do you know about this Girdlestone?'

'Says he's a maths tutor. Retired from teaching. He's lived there some years.'

Beckwith saw Sauerwine considering what Meckel had told him. He said quickly, 'I think Meckel should look a little further at this Girdlestone chap.'

It hurt him but he felt desperately that he had to do something to regain some sort of respect and, more importantly, self-respect.

And Sauerwine agreed, even seemed to think that Beckwith (at last) had made a useful contribution. 'Yes, good idea.'

Meckel appeared to be relieved that he wasn't being dismissed as a thick woodentop.

Sauerwine stood up with a groan. 'OK, that's settled, then. Time to go home, I think. We all know what we're doing tomorrow.'

Which was odd, because he hadn't actually told them what his own plans for the day were.

Having parked the car in the garage at the bottom of the garden, Beckwith let himself into the dark house. He had just kicked a bicycle that had been carelessly discarded in the darkness of the covered back patio, stifling a brief burst of blasphemy. He had bent down to rub his painful shin, then hit his head on a hanging basket as he stood back up.

For God's sake! What is this – an SAS training ground?

Janet loved her garden, spent hours in it in the summer, pined for its relaxations in the winter, and Beckwith admitted that he was grateful for this occupation. She didn't say anything but he knew that she found the life of a policeman far more difficult than she had expected. If the long working hours were not bad enough, the added encumbrance of their unpredictability made them worse; add in a seven-year-old who was too bright for his own good and who suffered from eczema and sometimes disabling asthma, and here was a recipe for depression.

The rain had not in any way relented and he was soaked through. Having taken off his shoes in the kitchen, he tried, as he always did, to make his way through the small house to their bedroom as silently as possible and, as he always did, he failed completely. Doors opened and closed with whinging hinges and clanking catches, floorboards squeaked for attention, a tin of toy building bricks crept out on the landing to be kicked and scattered, spearing his toe with another burst of agony. By the time he reached his destination, he felt that he might just as well have moved through the house ringing a bell and calling the hours. Janet had already switched on her bedside lamp and was lying there sleepily looking and yet not looking at the alarm clock.

'Sorry,' he said in a loud whisper.

'It's late,' she said. Her tone was matter-of-fact, not at all upset or accusatory, and all the more painful to hear.

'Sorry,' he repeated. He sometimes thought that half his conversation with her was constructed of this single word.

'You're wet through.'

'I've been out at Rendcomb for most of the day.'

'What is it?'

He took off his jacket and flung it on a chair by the wardrobe, then sat on the end of the bed to remove his socks. 'A dead body in the river.'

'Nothing nasty?' she asked as if she cared which he suspected that she did; Janet had an infinite capacity for caring.

He removed his tie, flung that, too, on the chair. ''Fraid so.'

He cared as well, but only because it would mean more late nights and early mornings to come. Once he had been like her.

She didn't reply and he divested himself of the rest of his clothes, put on pyjama bottoms and then went out to the bathroom. On his return she was nearly asleep again but he brought her to when he climbed into bed beside her. Before he turned out the light, he asked, 'How's Freddy?'

'Oh, not too bad. He was wheezing a bit this morning.'

'And his eczema?' Whereas his parents were most concerned by his respiratory problems, Freddy was worried only by his itching skin.

'He won't stop scratching. It took him a long time to go to sleep tonight. I had to read to him for ages.'

Which once again invoked the only response he seemed capable of. 'I'm sorry.'

'Don't be silly. You've got to do your work.'

He grunted softly, feeling that such sentiments were all very nice but valueless when weighed against guilt; trinkets that shattered easily and were cloudy in the bright sunshine. He leaned across to kiss her. 'Goodnight.'

'Goodnight.'

He switched out the light and lay there in darkness while he listened to Janet's breathing rapidly become heavy and regular.

And thought, as he often did, of Cindy.

Thought, as he always did, two words.

What if?

Sauerwine returned to his flat and switched on the light in the hallway. It was cold and there was, as ever, a slight odour of damp that he couldn't locate and the landlord, inexplicably, couldn't smell. He took off his raincoat and hung it on the coat rack by the front door, pulled off his shoes without undoing the laces, then went into the kitchen to liberate a bottle of beer from the fridge. As he drank it he sat and looked at the pile of unwashed crockery and cutlery that had accumulated during his recent illness; he looked at it and it looked at him, but there was no love in these stolen glances.

No love anywhere in the flat. No love anywhere in his life, now he came to consider the matter. He thought then of Sally Felty, how he had not realized quite how special she was to him until he had lost her. Perhaps, though, enough time had passed to allow her hurt to heal; perhaps if he called her – he had kept track of her and knew where she was working – she would allow herself to feel forgiveness.

He finished the beer and, leaving the bottle on the table – now forlorn and bereft of its reason for existence – fetched another to meet the same fate. As he sat down again the futility of this hope enveloped him. Sally would never forgive him. His betrayal had been too deep, too blatant; he had become infatuated with another woman and had slept with her; he had compounded the sin by doing so when he had sent Sally away. It was difficult to argue that it had been a spontaneous act of treachery.

Inevitably this line of thought led to the cause of his misery. Beverley Wharton.

Yet whilst he blamed her, he also wanted her. Still he wanted her. She had come into his life and capsized him, and things would never be the same again, yet still he wanted her.

He knew, though, that she would not want him. Nothing had been said but he knew – as he knew that he couldn't breathe under water and that there were bears in the woods – that should he take the trouble to locate her and call her, her voice would be as dismissive as if she were talking to a junior reporter from the *Boghampton Express and Courier.*

Amazingly the second bottle of beer succumbed as easily as the first. No problem there, though; always plenty of recruits ready for combat. Back at the kitchen table and by now feeling slightly light-headed and also increasingly chilly, he began to tackle this new entrant into the ring as his thoughts turned to Maeve Gillespie.

Was he really attracted to her, or merely desperate for a shag? This quandary held him, sprawling on a pin, pinned and wriggling, while he wondered at his motives, his needs, his emotions. Would he have looked twice at her – would he have even seen her? – if he had been in a stable, loving relationship, if he hadn't been tired and cold and wet and living alone in a flat that smelled slightly but not insignificantly of damp?

It was a question that would never admit of an answer, but no less demanding of one for that.

And then there was Tricia.

Bloody typical. Weeks of shaglessness and then two attractive women turn up at once, one of them practically throwing herself at him. Which to pursue, then? Tricia seemed the safer bet but if he were known to be dating a mortuary attendant he would be the butt of endless ribaldry at the hands of his colleagues. Was he really ready for that?

Maeve, though, might not be as interested in him as he was in her; he might fall flat on his face, might make an idiot of himself. It wouldn't be the first time, nor (almost certainly) would it be the last.

If, though, she were as desperate for affection as he guessed, then perhaps . . .

She had undoubtedly been attractive.

The other danger was if she were in some way involved with this body in the river, a possibility as remote as his next promotion being to Chief Constable but potentially as momentous. There were rules about getting involved with witnesses which would be potentially troublesome but only if things became public; of course there was a faint possibility that she was a suspect – in which case he was effectively slicing his own throat – but he felt that this prospect had the luminescence of a brown dwarf.

And she was quite strikingly attractive . . .

And apparently unattached . . .

He felt in his pocket for the slip of paper that Tricia had given him and then sat there and looked at the number she had written on it.

Tricia or Maeve?

He sighed, folded the paper neatly in half and then tucked it under the bread bin with its contents that had progressed beyond stale into mouldiness. He would ring Maeve tomorrow; invite her for a drink.

He went to bed clear in his head as to what he would do, for the first time in a long time feeling quite excited by the future.

The next morning Mrs Christmas stood waiting outside the front door and admired the garden. It had stopped raining but the sky suggested that this was merely a respite. It was damp, too. She hated the damp; it made bones ache. Had it not been so cold, the fact that the air was seemingly filled with steam would have suggested tropical climes.

The door opened and whilst it would not have been accurate to suggest that Mrs Christmas swung round, she certainly rotated slowly to bring her attention to bear upon the householder before her.

She smiled.

'Hello, Mr Girdlestone.'

He looked ill, she noticed. Being naturally solicitous she enquired as she entered his house, 'Are you all right, Mr Girdlestone?'

He tried to smile but it looked as if he were breaking something. 'Didn't sleep too well, Mrs Christmas.'

She smiled once more because she had long ago decided that the best way through anything was always a smile. 'Never mind, Mr Girdlestone. Shall I make you a cup of tea?'

He shook his head. 'Not at the moment.'

She hung up her coat. 'Where would you like me to start?'

He did not appear to care. 'Wherever you like.'

She went to the utility room to fetch the vacuum cleaner and polish.

William Sneddon saw Alec Verner-Morrison approaching when he was still several hundred metres off.

'What does he want now?' he asked of the engine block, which unhelpfully held its views on the matter close to its pistons. Sneddon made no external sign that he knew his employer was heading for him, that said employer was shouting to attract his attention or that same was also angry and impatient. Verner-Morrison was always angry and impatient and, consequently, William Sneddon was always oblivious of it.

'William! William!'

When he did pull his head out of the engine compartment

of the blue Range Rover and turn, Sneddon was showing a smiling face, as if he were deaf to Verner-Morrison's peremptory tone, blind to the angry frown and intimidating body language. He said nothing.

'Didn't you hear me?'

'Sorry, no. Had my head inside this monster.'

Verner-Morrison relented slightly and Sneddon left his smile to speak for him.

'What's up?' That Verner-Morrison was talking about the Range Rover he indicated with a gesture of his head.

'Reckon the fuel line's blocked.'

It was particularly cold that morning and there was half-formed ice on the mud puddles in the field to their right. Verner-Morrison was shivering but then he was only wearing a thin woollen jersey over an open-necked shirt; Sneddon, dressed in thick grey roll-neck and heavy wax jacket, found peculiar pleasure in Verner-Morrison's discomfort. He had a dark, full beard below a thin face in which were piercing blue eyes. It had often occurred to Cherie Verner-Morrison that without the beard he would have been quite handsome.

'Well, fix it then.'

'If I can.'

'That's why I pay you, Will, remember? It's your job to keep this place running.'

'I'm a farm manager, not a car mechanic.' He pointed this out in a tone that sounded quite light and perhaps even jocular, that betrayed none of his irritation.

'A blocked fuel line is a simple job; I'm not giving money away to some crook in a garage. I'm in the business, remember? I know what the mark-up is.'

Sneddon nodded thoughtfully as if considering this nugget and maybe even mentally polishing it. He said nothing, however, perhaps waiting for Verner-Morrison to give him a quick tutorial on unblocking a fuel line in a V8 Range Rover;. Strangely, his boss did not oblige.

Instead, 'I wanted to talk to you. Have the police been to see you?'

Sneddon frowned. 'No. Why should they?'

'Some poor tosser's been fished out of the river. They're trying to find out who it is.'

Sneddon considered this. 'What's that got to do with us?'

'Absolutely bloody nothing, but that didn't stop some flatfoot poking his nose around here last night. Seems they're talking to everyone in the neighbourhood; trying to find out who it was.'

'What about your next party?'

'What about it?'

'You still want to go ahead?'

'Of course. Not got cold feet, have you?'

Sneddon shook his head at once. 'Absolutely not.'

'Good. I don't see any problems. They'll probably find out who it is today. End of story. I expect he was on the piss then fell in.'

'Probably.'

Satisfied, Verner-Morrison said, 'Well, anyway, just to let you know. A bit of advance warning.'

'Thanks.'

Verner-Morrison turned away and had gone two strides before turning back. 'How are things? With the farm, I mean.'

Sneddon just managed to present a neutral face. He said, 'Milk yields are down.'

'Badly?'

Sneddon shrugged. 'I'll sort it out.'

Verner-Morrison nodded curtly. 'Good.'

He walked away back to the house, by now thoroughly chilled. Sneddon watched him until the door had closed behind him.

Beckwith had arrived early but discovered to his incredulous excruciation that Meckel, dressed in civilian clothes, was sitting at his desk. He swallowed feelings of paranoia and doom-laden fears of usurpation, finding them as digestible as lumps of regurgitated gristle, while Meckel smiled welcomingly and said, 'Morning, Sergeant. I hope you don't mind but I didn't have anywhere else to work.'

'What are you doing? Shouldn't you be out on the beat or something?'

'I'm not due on until one. I thought I'd start work on checking out Girdlestone. I've only just got here.'

Beckwith had not previously been bothered by the fact that he had never, ever been at work over four hours before he was due on shift; now he suddenly felt inferior. Meckel at least had the grace to stand up and let him flop down in the chair; it was warm but, despite the cold of the morning, he found it an unpleasant warmth, one that was peculiarly biological and suggestive of an intimacy he did not want to feel.

'Where can I work?'

Beckwith thought about suggesting the men's room, decided that dignified silence was the better option. Eventually Meckel wandered off, leaving Beckwith to try to analyse why his perfectly proper exercise of superior rank had left him so miserably deflated.

Meckel eventually located a spare desk in an adjacent office that he was told by the duty sergeant was temporarily unoccupied. He had already worked out his plan of campaign and since it was now well past nine o'clock he thought it time to commence. He lifted the phone to call Manchester Grammar School having found the number from the Internet. For the next fifteen minutes he struggled to get to speak to the right person. Eventually he found himself in conversation with a very suspicious bursar.

'Our personnel records are confidential.'

'I'm sure they are, Dr Masson, but this is a police investigation. It's not as if I'm asking you for information that is in any way sensitive. All I wish to know is if you had a Mr

Girdlestone working there as a mathematics teacher about ten or eleven years ago.'

Dr Masson breathed out through his nose loudly and unhappily. 'How do I know this isn't some sort of hoax? You might be anybody . . . '

'If I give you the number you can call me back. You'll be put through to the police switchboard who will verify my identity. If you like you can check the number I give you with your local station to ensure I am giving you an authentic number.'

But Dr Masson decided that he was not as suspicious as all that.

'Girdlestone, you say?'

'That's right. Kenneth Girdlestone. Teaches mathematics.'

'Well, the name doesn't sound familiar . . . Hang on a minute.'

He put the receiver down, came back in about five minutes. 'Nothing. Never had a teacher of that name in any depart-ment. I've looked on the computer right back to 1990.'

Which might have been that, except that Meckel was by nature obdurate. 'Could you go back a little further? Say another five years?'

Dr Masson didn't want to but he did, albeit with obvious exasperation. When he returned to the phone he sounded triumphant, as if he had won a bet with Meckel. 'Nothing.'

'Oh.'

'I was fairly sure that there wasn't anyone around of that name at that time, and I was proved right.'

He had all but put down the phone as Meckel asked, 'Why?'

'Pardon?'

'Why were you sure?'

'Because of the fuss.'

'What fuss?'

'Oh, well, I don't see that it's relevant . . . '

'I'm intrigued, though, Dr Masson. Could you elaborate?'

The bursar, though, didn't want to. 'It was nothing . . . an internal matter.'

Meckel sensed something important; it was hardly anything, just a faint spectre that beckoned from his peripheral vision. He persisted. 'Did one of your teachers leave under a cloud?'

'Well . . . it was very awkward . . . '

To judge from his voice, the bursar still found it awkward. Meckel asked, 'What was the teacher's name?'

'I don't see . . . '

'His name, please, Dr Masson.'

'Well . . . it was Gerard. Kenneth Gerard.'

At which Meckel *knew*.

'And the fuss was what?'

The bursar found that he had stepped on to a moving psychological walkway that carried him inevitably, no matter how reluctantly, into further revelations. 'Nothing was proved, you understand . . . '

Meckel's question was perfectly reasonable. 'About what?'

'And the boy was slightly . . . odd . . . '

The bursar, it seemed, had lost the ability to utter more than half a dozen words without relapsing into ellipses.

' . . . He'd made accusations about other teachers . . . '

'Accusations about what?'

There was a long pause but no matter how strenuously the bursar tried to resist he was carried relentlessly onward until it came out with a sort of dying sigh, as if Dr Masson relented through overwhelming exhaustion, a spent force.

'He said that Gerard tried to assault him. Touched him inappropriately.'

Meckel's spectre moved ever so slightly further into his line of vision.

'Perhaps you'd better give me a description and full particulars of Mr Gerard.'

Beckwith had arranged for the divers to start at nine o'clock and had delegated the house-to-house enquiries to Detective

Constable Crick, a man who was large and jolly and reliable if not inspiring; he was close to retirement and prone to somnolence but Beckwith knew that he could rely on him to organize the teams with reasonable efficiency. Sauerwine left his sergeant beginning the trawl through the missing persons and went down to the river at Rendcomb.

He had a headache and his stomach was threatening to relapse; also it was again raining. For some reason the only thing that gave him cheer was the prospect of ringing Maeve and asking her out for a drink.

At least Rendcomb was linked to civilization by road.

It would have been picturesque had the weather had any clemency at all. Along a winding and exceedingly narrow road that ran through the middle of it, quaint and thatched cottages seemed to overhang the tarmac, a church and church hall were set slightly back and two pubs, both hiding from the modern trend of designer themes and live music on Friday nights, lived quiet and productive lives. Television murders took place here, ones that were sanitized and replete with red herrings, odourless and sightly corpses, dim policemen and an expected surprise before every commercial break.

The river was reached by a wide lane between meadows in which sheep grazed; perhaps it was the rain but they looked as if they had just been laundered, then placed with a designer's eye, on brightly painted and stretched felt fabric. Sauerwine found himself in an unpathed parking area at one side of which there was a sign that forbade bathing (rather unnecessarily, Sauerwine thought). He saw a silhouette through a thin line of trees ahead and headed towards it. As he approached this image resolved into a man dressed in blue rubber; he was standing on a short wooden jetty that projected into the river.

The river at this point was perhaps fifteen metres wide. To the right of the jetty, about twenty metres away, was an old stone bridge, traversing the river in a double span. A small line of hardy spectators was spread along the bridge observing the police activities with interest. Sauerwine wondered what drove the public to endure such hostile conditions; he could imagine no amount of prurience would ever be sufficient to cause him to forsake warmth and shelter for this particular spectacle.

'It shouldn't take long.' The leader of the diving team was inexplicably cheerful, as if he had been made for just such an occasion, as if he were fulfilling his destiny. Sauerwine, on the contrary, felt chilled to the marrow just watching the diving team move slowly around the dark grey waters. For much of the time it was so shallow the water barely came up to their thighs but there were clearly areas where the river bed dropped precipitously away.

'How deep are those?'

The team leader, seemingly impervious to the wind, wet and Antarctic chill in his striking attire, replied happily, 'Some of them are nearly twelve metres deep.'

'And how many are there?'

'Nobody seems to know. We've found six so far.'

Sauerwine could see houses of various sizes and types in the woods on the far bank. Smoke rose from the chimney of the nearest. The rain that had until then shown unaccustomed mercy was now gradually but remorselessly increasing in strength, fine drizzle that was almost a heavy dripping mist.

There was a commotion from the river. Amid a swirl of blackness and bubbles a rubber-suited figure suddenly emerged in a spot surprisingly close to the far bank. He began to wave his arms.

'He's found something.' Sauerwine heard disappointment in his companion's voice, presumably because there was now a possibility that his time frolicking in the frigid waters might be coming to an end.

He had started off with nearly a thousand names listed as

officially missing on the Police National Computer but by the time he had eliminated those who were female, those who weren't Caucasian, those who were over forty and under fifteen, those with missing limbs and those who were bald, Beckwith had reduced this terrifyingly large collection to an only slightly less terrifying one hundred and forty-nine. His problem then was to prioritize this list and, after much furrowing of his brows and several cups of coffee, he rang Charles Sydenham.

'Sorry to bother you, Doctor.'

'What is it, Sergeant? Please be brief – I have sixteen Coroner's cases awaiting me downstairs and only three hours to do them in because after that I am due at court.'

Beckwith drew some comfort from the fact that he would not be required to witness the carnage that Sydenham was about to wreak. 'I was wondering if you could give me a rough age for the victim. It would help narrow down the search.'

'Between fifteen and forty. I told you.'

Beckwith had hoped that Sydenham might by now have found evidence to reduce his estimate from a third of a lifetime to something a little less vague. 'Can you narrow it down any further?'

'You did see the body, didn't you, Sergeant?'

'Yes, sir, briefly . . . '

'Well, I saw it at great length . . . and depth. I saw it at close quarters and from a distance.'

'Yes, I know . . . '

'It was practically compost, Sergeant. I've seen bags of John Innes No. 1 with more resemblance to a human being. They dig up warriors from frozen peat bogs who look healthier.'

Sydenham didn't so much make his points as construct them from the finest materials, gild them and put them on public display.

It would be untrue to say that Beckwith was totally undaunted, but he was a brave man who was not yet completely daunted. 'If you were to hazard a guess, sir, would you put him towards the younger end or the older end of the spectrum?'

'I don't guess, Sergeant.'

'Estimate, then.'

A sigh came at him from the telephone receiver; it was a bit like a spring zephyr. 'I suppose if I had to *estimate*, I would say closer to fifteen than forty.'

'Thank you, Doctor. Thank you very much.'

'Not all, Sergeant, not at all.' Sydenham was so patronizing he might have been accepting thanks for donating a few million to the Police Benevolent Fund.

Beckwith put the phone down and would have begun work on prioritizing the list had Sauerwine not returned, exuding triumph.

'My office, Sergeant.'

He followed obediently and quite happily until Sauerwine stopped in the corridor and asked, 'Where's Meckel?'

Beckwith frowned both within and without. 'Don't know.'

'Well, find him and bring him with you.'

Bloody marvellous. What do we need Supercop for?

He rather hoped that he might be unsuccessful but eventually he bumped into Meckel emerging from his temporary hiding place, upon his face a suppressed smile of excitement. 'I've got some news . . . '

'Come on. The Inspector wants us.'

He turned at once and thereby made it abundantly clear he wasn't in the least interested in any news Meckel might have. PC Bumpkin's theories might play well in Toyland but not, he was sure, in the real world.

Yet when the door to Sauerwine's office was closed, Beckwith's construct proved dangerously frail.

'It looks as though you were right,' Sauerwine announced, looking at Meckel. 'The diving team found an anvil in one of the Rendcomb pools, and there was fishing twine around it.'

Beckwith found that the appreciative smile on Meckel's face was painful to behold. He said, 'Is that necessarily significant, sir? Might it not be completely unconnected?'

Sauerwine stared at him, a completely unreadable expression presented. He said after a pause that became uncomfortable very quickly, 'Someone fishing, perhaps, who lost their sinker? Angling for sperm whale presumably.'

'No. I just meant . . . '

'Why else would there be an anvil with fishing twine tied around it?'

And Beckwith, feeling that he ought to be able to come up with a million explanations for this superficially simple situation, found only a frustrated wordlessness.

Thus dismissing him, Sauerwine continued, 'Forensics are going over it now but it's quite heavy enough to have weighted a man down.'

Meckel asked, 'How deep was the pool?'

'Over eight metres.'

Meckel nodded and Beckwith had a sense that there was a rapport between his superior and his inferior that was beginning to exclude him. Sauerwine hadn't finished basting Meckel with praise, though. 'That was smart thinking, Meckel. It saved us a lot of time. It certainly means that we should concentrate our investigation in and around Rendcomb.'

Meckel had clearly been keen to pronounce his news for some time and now he had his chance. 'I've uncovered something very interesting, sir. About Girdlestone.'

'What?'

'His story was a pack of lies. I think his real name is Gerard and he's a convicted paedophile.'

This was as effective as exploding a skunk in the middle of the room. Sauerwine looked startled, his mouth falling open, his gaze becoming adherent to Meckel. Beckwith felt himself twitch, the action coming just before he thought, *Oh, for fuck's sake!*

Meckel had handed Sauerwine his notes and supporting documentation. Beckwith watched as these were read through. Meckel said, 'Manchester Grammar had never heard of Kenneth Girdlestone but Kenneth Gerard was a maths teacher who left in the middle of some sort of scandal concerning a pupil who said he'd been molested – that might have been something and nothing but I think it's interesting he chose to leave rather than fight it out.'

Beckwith couldn't resist asking, 'Is that it?'

Unperturbed, Meckel strode onwards, his eyes on Sauerwine who was reading intently. 'Three years later, Kenneth Girdlestone was arrested for a sexual relationship he was having with a fifteen-year-old boy. Girdlestone was a pseudonym that was being used by Gerard. He was inside for four years.'

Sauerwine looked up briefly. 'Anything nasty?'

'No. It was consensual.'

As Sauerwine returned to the documents, Meckel added helpfully, 'There's a faxed photo of Gerard at the back. It's definitely our man. And, of course, it was before the Sex Offenders Register. He just came out of prison and disappeared.'

Beckwith said, 'I don't really see what this has got to do with our corpse.'

Sauerwine looked at him, surprised. 'Don't you?'

'Just because this bloke Gerard fancies adolescent boys doesn't mean he's going to hang them from the rafters, have his way with them and then throw them into the river attached to heavy weights.'

As Sauerwine was considering this Meckel said, 'I appreciate that, but I think we should check this chap out.'

Beckwith might have committed himself further had Sauerwine not said, 'Actually, we don't know that this was a deliberate act of murder. It's conceivable that it was a sexual game that went wrong. Perhaps he really thought the victim had been accidentally asphyxiated, then panicked. He thought to get rid of what he assumed was a corpse, not knowing that he was drowning someone in the river.'

Beckwith thought that this was crap but he didn't feel like sticking his head between the lion's jaws on that particular issue. Sauerwine looked up at Meckel. 'Where is Girdlestone's house in relation to the place where we found the anvil?'

Beckwith could not think of anything he wanted to hear less than the words Meckel then uttered. 'It's right by there. In fact, it's probably the nearest house.'

'Right.'

Sauerwine sounded energized. To Meckel he said, 'Get a car. We'll drive over there now. Have a chat with Mr Girdlestone and see what he's got to say for himself.'

Meckel looked pained, almost upset. 'I'm sorry, sir. I'm due on duty . . .'

To Beckwith's anguish Sauerwine's face collapsed. 'Oh . . .'

Meckel was apologetic, as if he were the star declining to give yet another encore. 'I'm sorry . . . I've got to meet a Neighbourhood Watch group in Dixton.'

Beckwith heard a sigh – he didn't believe it but he heard it – before Sauerwine said, 'Very well . . .'

Meckel left.

Sauerwine might have just lost a relative. He said in a doleful tone, 'You'd better arrange the car.'

But Beckwith hung back. 'Sir, there are over three hundred people living in Rendcomb.'

'I know that, Beckwith.'

'Well . . .' He paused, uncertain how to proceed. 'Don't you think we might be jumping to conclusions?'

Sauerwine frowned. 'I don't think so.'

Beckwith was perceptive enough to decide upon retreat at this point and would not have said anything more had he not been outflanked, and his line of retreat cut off, by Sauerwine asking in a tone that was both dangerously innocent and dangerously curious, 'Do you?'

'I just think that we shouldn't make assumptions too early.'

'Is that what you think I'm doing?'

This was one of those questions that was as dangerous as an elephant trap, and just as well camouflaged.

Beckwith hopped nimbly to the side. 'I wouldn't have said that . . .'

Sauerwine shook his head sadly. 'It would be nice if you had a little more confidence in me, Beckwith. Of course I realize that we can't just assume it's this chap Girdlestone, but are you seriously suggesting that we should ignore him?'

'No . . .'

'I think you're being very negative, Beckwith, you know that? I'm slightly surprised. To pick up a lead so early in the investigation is quite a stroke of luck.'

'Yes, sir.'

'Mind you, we have to thank Meckel for that. He's a good man, I think. Wasted in uniform.'

Beckwith struggled to make his voice sound fully in agreement as he said again, 'Yes, sir.'

Sauerwine glanced at him keenly. 'Do you like Constable Meckel, Beckwith?'

Beckwith hurried to play the team game. 'He's clearly a very competent man.'

'But do you like him?'

'I hardly know him.'

Sauerwine nodded slowly. 'And anyway, it's not necessary to like someone to work effectively with them.'

'Exactly.' As soon as Beckwith said this he knew that he had been caught, that he had avoided one trap to be snared by another. He added, 'Not that I — '

Sauerwine interrupted, 'I've got no time for sniping, Beckwith; no time for prima donnas, OK? Put up and shut up, or get out.'

Beckwith knew better than to say anything other than, 'Yes, sir.' He bowed his head in contrition and Sauerwine asked, 'How are you getting on with the list of missing persons?'

'It's narrowed down to just under a hundred and fifty, but beyond that it's going to be difficult. I thought to rank them in age order, the youngest first.'

This found favour. 'Good. And the house-to-house?'

'Crick was going to move further up the river, according to previous instructions, but I guess they'd better fan out and cover just Rendcomb.'

'How many households have we contacted so far?'

'Last I heard about sixty.'

'Anything of interest?'

'Not so far.'

Sauerwine said nothing for a moment then stood up. 'I think I'll try and get Meckel seconded to us for a while. I'm sure Burr will agree.'

He left without looking towards Beckwith, thus he didn't see the slightly strained expression on his sergeant's face.

Superintendent Burr occupied an office on the top floor of the station overlooking the entrance and commanding a view of a small park. He was an extremely corpulent man, heavy of breathing and heavy, too, of sarcasm; he seemed suited to his name to a degree that was beyond coincidence, as if he must have grown to fit it, much as a fish grows to a size suitable to the tank in which it swims.

When Sauerwine knocked on the door, of course he was in. Burr's occupation of this office space was more than mere presence; he had never been seen outside it, seemed to live there. More than that, Sauerwine had only rarely seen him out of the chair behind the desk. This near-permanence behind the office furniture might have proffered the impression that Burr was the nerve centre of the station, issuing commands, receiving reports and assessing situations in perfect serenity while all about him whirled with activity, that he was the focal point of a network of afferent and efferent mechanisms.

Might have, except that he had only a single phone on the desk.

What did the man do?

'What is it, Inspector? I'm rather busy.'

Sauerwine reflected that he was glad Burr had told him this, for there was not a wisp of evidence to support the contention. He said, 'I thought I'd better update you on the body in the river, sir.'

'Ah, yes. Progress?'

'I think so, sir. Meckel's been helping us and he's come up with an interesting lead.'

He told Burr of Girdlestone. 'He might not be a perfect fit, but if it is the same chap, we've got to talk to him, especially given the proximity of the body to his house.'

'A bit too close, perhaps?'

Burr might have been sedentary to the point of paralysis but he hadn't risen to his elevated rank purely by brown-nosing and Masonry, Sauerwine reflected. He said, 'Judging by the weight of the anvil, it would have been difficult for him to get it much further away. It must have been bloody awkward as it was – he'd have to have dumped the body in the dark and over the side of a boat.'

'How did he know just where to dump it? If he'd hit the wrong spot the body would have been plainly visible.'

'Possibly a plumbline, sir.'

He couldn't tell whether Burr was convinced or not. He decided on a small tactical withdrawal. 'I'm not ruling anything else out, sir. I'm not completely sold on him as the murderer.'

But Burr, through cussedness that was possibly deliberate, possibly accidental, replied, 'I don't want him forgotten, Sauerwine, whether he did it or not. If he's a paedophile, I want him off my patch. If he did it, I want him to swing. If he didn't, I want him to be advised on a good firm of removal men.'

This sentiment perhaps overstated the case as far as Sauerwine was concerned but he swallowed his irritation and said, 'I'll go and see him. Ask him if he'd like to co-operate with the police.'

'And perhaps remind him that if he doesn't, someone might accidentally tell the local paper who they've got living in their rural paradise.'

With something less than enthusiasm Sauerwine said, 'Let's hope it doesn't come to that, sir.'

Burr grunted, implying that he would be rather pleased if it did. Sauerwine hastened to change the subject. 'I don't suppose we could borrow Meckel for a few days? His local knowledge would be useful and he's already proved himself worth having.'

Burr hesitated, then said cautiously, 'Possibly. I'll see what I can arrange.'

Sauerwine left, wondering if this reluctance were born of the thought of actually having to do something.

Mrs Christmas just happened to be walking down the lane that took her past Kenneth Girdlestone's house, over the bridge and back into the main part of Rendcomb when Sauerwine and Beckwith arrived. She carried on walking in her slow, ambling pace, but her whole attention was on the dark-green Volvo that had just pulled up outside Mr Girdlestone's neatly painted garden gate. When Beckwith returned her stare she called politely, her breath showing as streaming mist in the drizzle, 'Good afternoon.'

Beckwith smiled tightly and nodded. Sauerwine, more graciously, called, 'Good afternoon.'

She moved on and Sauerwine asked, 'Do you know who she is?'

'Mrs Christmas. Lives in the village.'

Sauerwine caught a tone in his voice. 'Don't you like her?'

'Archetypal old woman. Rambling, irrelevant and irritating.'

Having just insulted and dismissed the commonest social subgroup in the country, Beckwith opened the gate for Sauerwine. They walked up the path, through a garden that was surprisingly colourful despite the time of year. It was Sauerwine who knocked on the door, ignoring the bell.

It took a long time for the door to open.

'Yes?'

'Mr Girdlestone?'

'Yes.' His eyes flicked to Beckwith.

'Mr Kenneth Girdlestone?'

This time an added frown. 'Yes.'

Sauerwine showed his identity card. 'I believe you were christened Gerard.'

He was smiling but that was purely a mask, as insincere as a hooker's moan of ecstasy. Girdlestone didn't even look at the white laminated card. He opened the door wide and said tiredly, 'Come in.'

In the lane outside Mrs Christmas continued to stare curiously as the front door closed. Then she sighed and shook her head.

'You don't seem suprised to see us, Mr Gerard.' Like Meckel the day before Sauerwine admired the interior furnishings; also like Meckel he saw stress in the man before him, the man who was trembling noticeably. Attempting to smile but even the lips were quivering and when he spoke there was an undoubted tremor to his words.

'I'm not.' He smiled as if not to do so would kill him.

'Why would that be, sir?'

And suddenly Gerard stopped trembling, an abrupt cessation, a rush into serenity. His smile was unchanged but now different, because it was genuine, no longer forced. There was even humour in it now. With a deep sigh he leaned back in his chair, the master of the situation. 'Shall we stop playing games, Inspector? I know exactly why you're here.'

Sauerwine wasn't about to make it easy. 'Really? Perhaps you'd like to let me in on the secret.'

For a second Gerard looked uncertain, then he laughed, an explosive and short sound of exultation. 'Ha! Very good, Inspector!'

Sauerwine said nothing. He saw Beckwith looking at him curiously.

Gerard went on in a steady tone, innocent of any emotion at all, 'You've discovered the truth about me. That I have served time for what is colloquially known as "paedophilia".'

'And what is it known as to you?'

'He was fifteen, Inspector. A consenting adult in everything but age. I didn't pluck him from the baby-seat of a car, or entice him away from kindergarten.'

'You broke the law.'

'I broke *your* law. I happen to believe that it is a stupid law.'

Sauerwine turned to his sergeant. 'That's always the line with paedophiles, Beckwith. They refuse to see that what they do is wrong. Worse, it's disgusting in most people's eyes, whereas they enjoy what they do.'

Now that he was shorn of his fear of discovery Gerard seemed to be growing in self-righteousness. 'One man's sexual enjoyment is frequently disgusting to others. I'm sure the thought of your parents indulging in perfectly reasonably sexual congress fills you with something approaching nausea.'

Sauerwine was shaking his head. 'It doesn't work, Gerard. You're deliberately muddying the picture. What you did – what you do – is illegal, it's morally wrong, legally wrong and has to be stopped. What if your fifteen-year-old had been twelve and looked a lot older?'

But Gerard dodged that one easily. 'Jailbait? A problem whatever your sexual orientation, I think.'

Perhaps because he thought that Sauerwine was losing debating points Beckwith weighed in with, 'You're still calling yourself a tutor, aren't you? Still in close contact with young men.'

'It's what I do. I'm hardly built for ploughing the fields or hod carrying. All I have ever done is teach. I do this or I starve.'

Sauerwine found himself becoming more and more irritated by this sangfroid. The script was being rewritten by Gerard's

101

liberation from his anonymity. 'That's crap, Gerard. You disappeared as soon as you could, didn't you? And what did you do? You came somewhere where nobody knew you, but it wasn't to lead a life of good works and Samaritanism, was it? No, it was to set up shop as a "maths tutor". The first thing I want from you is a list of everyone you're teaching.'

'Of course.'

He rose and went to a small table beside the television. He brought back a neatly printed list of names and addresses which he handed to Sauerwine, who then passed it on to Beckwith. Sauerwine said, 'Anyone would think you were guilty.'

He shrugged. 'My time here is ended, anyway.'

Which insouciance only infuriated Sauerwine further. 'You do know why we're here, don't you?'

Gerard nodded. 'The body in the river.'

'The young man in the river who was finally drowned, having been suspended from the neck and then repeatedly sodomized.'

Beckwith was watching Gerard as Sauerwine said this and he saw someone who was listening to a voice first, only hearing the words second. He saw confidence appear to dissipate, suddenly as insubstantial as the integrity of a politician.

'I don't understand.'

'He was murdered, Gerard. Didn't you know? Come as a shock, has it?' He asked these last two questions in mock concern.

That was something of an understatement; Gerard looked as if he had just been told he was scheduled for execution tomorrow at dawn. Beckwith saw this and thought it was genuine, thought therefore that they were dealing with innocence; Sauerwine saw it and was contemptuous. 'Don't overdo the surprise, Gerard.'

'But I assumed . . . '

'What did you assume? That he wouldn't float up so quickly?'

'No . . . '

'That we wouldn't recognize what you did to him? In that case you underestimated what we can tell from a corpse.'

Gerard closed his eyes; the tremor was back, this time accompanied by a look of grey sickness. Beckwith, who had seen his grandfather die, thought that he was possibly having a heart attack; in contrast Sauerwine thought he was getting somewhere. 'Who was he, Gerard?'

Eyes still shut, voice now weak as if he were very far away in a land that was lost, he said, 'I don't know.'

'One of your pupils, perhaps?'

He shook his head but his eyes wouldn't open, as if sewn together. 'No. I've given you their names.'

'How do I know it's complete?'

Gerard apparently couldn't supply a reassurance on that. He had by now dropped his head and seemed to have sunk into the upholstery of the chair, bones dissolved by shock. Sauerwine said to Beckwith, 'Search the house and garden.'

If Gerard protested at this infringement of his rights it was without external sign. Beckwith knew better than to start a discussion group on the precise legal and moral implications of this command; he went out without a word, leaving Sauerwine sitting and staring at Gerard while in turn Gerard sat with head bowed low and shaking slowly.

'It certainly changes things.'

They were queuing for the delicatessen behind a woman who couldn't decide how much Brie she wanted and an elderly man who wore two hearing aids. It was very cold inside the shop and Eisenmenger's feet were cold.

Helena said, 'I don't know if I can go on representing him.'

'He can't be the first obnoxious pig you've met professionally.'

'Far from it – and that goes for personally, too – but he is the worst. By a long way.'

'Doesn't mean he's a killer.'

The man with the hearing aids had previously exhibited signs of impatience with the Brie woman (who had now moved into indecision about which variety of olives to acquire and was sampling every single one), but this remark had the effect of distracting him. His head twitched slightly at the sound of the 'k' word; not much but enough for them to understand that they were now officially in the presence of an eavesdropper.

Helena said with her eyes on the hearing aid closest to her, 'It gives him an even better motive, though. We've only got his word for it that she denied the affair; anyway, if she *was* committing adultery with this "low-life", Martin Bell is not the kind of man to agree to counselling, take a deep breath and then move on. He'd have killed her, John. As simple as that.'

'You can't be certain.'

At last the olives were chosen and the money proffered. The eavesdropper, to his patent frustration, was forced to abandon his hobby and pay attention to the shop assistant, asking in a loud, stentorian voice for some Mountain Gorgonzola. Eisenmenger wondered what thoughts were arising between the tearing aids as Helena insisted, 'I can, John. You weren't there. He's violent – controlled but not eternally confined. He made it plain that he didn't like the thought of his wife having an affair, his pride wasn't going to allow it. It was like being in the room with a hybrid of an African lion and a Mongol emperor.'

Eisenmenger didn't reply and they were served and outside the shop, back in something that was cold damp rather than outright rain, before he said, 'He didn't do it, you know.'

It was one of his most endearing and yet most aggravating traits to do this, to conjure certainty from nebulousness.

It was one of Helena's to explode. 'What the hell gives you the right to say that? You haven't met him, and you should give thanks to the Lord God Almighty that you haven't.'

They were hurrying to his car, parked about three streets away in a Pay-and-Display. He didn't want a row and said humbly, 'Sorry.'

She glanced at him sharply but said nothing more until they were in the car. 'Why did you say that?'

He started the car and was pulling into the traffic before he said, 'I shouldn't have spoken. You're right, I don't really know enough to judge.'

Which apology paradoxically enraged her even further. 'What did you mean?'

Just a few spots of rain fell on the windscreen. 'You're absolutely right – I *haven't* met him and he does sound quite capable of beating his wife to death,' he began.

'But?' she prompted when he said nothing more.

With a suppressed explosion of exhalation he said eventually, 'He claims that he didn't know that she was having an affair, although there is evidence to suggest that he had been told otherwise by this man, Kernohan.'

'So?'

'So he goes home, gives his wife some third degree and she denies it. She would, wouldn't she? If what you say is right, he almost certainly would have killed her if she had admitted it.'

'I suppose.'

'I've met men like Bell before, Helena. You say he's like an African lion, well I bet his self-esteem wouldn't allow him to believe that he was being cuckolded. It's necessary for his ego to deny that fact at all costs; to himself just as much as to others.'

She saw what he was getting at. 'He believes Suzanne because he has to, which means he finds Kernohan and, content that Kernohan is deliberately lying about the affair, takes it out on him.'

'It's consistent, both with that type of personality and with what we know.'

She pondered this and while she did so he added, 'Also, the manner of the beating has been bothering me.'

'In what way?'

He turned off the main road, heading for the street in which they lived. 'It wasn't frenzied, it was measured.'

'I think Bell could be quite measured if he wanted to be,' she said with memories of his menace still fresh.

'Maybe.'

There was no further discussion until they were in the lift ascending to their flat, bags of shopping retrieved from the boot of the car. Helena said thoughtfully, 'We shouldn't forget Kernohan. He had a perfect motive for framing Bell.'

He hadn't thought of that.

'One thing's for sure,' he said. 'We need to talk to Kernohan.'

Although seen from the outside the house did not look particularly large, it had been cleverly designed and Beckwith discovered four reasonably spacious bedrooms, a good-sized kitchen-diner at the back and a utility room. Gerard had converted the second bedroom into a study and Beckwith was interested to note that it had a good view of the bridge and the river. He wondered if the tutor had watched as the anvil had been pulled from the water, and he wondered too what his feelings might have been had he done so. There was quite an elaborate computer system that made Beckwith somewhat envious; the casing was black plastic, the screen a large flat panel, and there was a colour laser printer nearby. He made a note of all this, knowing that it would be confiscated and a computer forensics team called in to go through Gerard's life in virtual reality. Around the walls were bookcases, one of which was given over to mathematical texts, the others containing mainly fiction; many of the books were old, only a few were paperbacks. Beckwith flicked briefly through a few, just to see if child pornography would flutter out of any, but none did. He switched the stereo system on and some discordant cacophony came through while the display told him he was listening to Radio Three; he had never listened to Radio Three before and now he knew why.

Two of the rooms were clearly unused, empty and cold, the furniture unwelcoming. The fourth bedroom, the largest, was where Gerard slept. It was neat and tidy – Beckwith thought unnaturally so for a man – but his perusal brought forth no items of bondageware, no sex toys, no items of women's clothing, no pornographic material either legal or illegal. He went back downstairs and into the kitchen. No washing up, no stains, no half-empty milk bottles left by the kettle; the scene that met Beckwith's eyes was so tidy and clean that he was illogically suspicious. Surely no one normal lived like this? His own experience suggested that such pristine virginity only occurred in the kitchen showroom, and he wondered what this portended. He began to wonder if, inexplicably and extremely irritatingly, Meckel might be on the right track. Had Gerard scrubbed the place down following some act of barbarity?

His search, though diligent, found no evidence to support his hypothesis, however, and he moved out into the back garden.

More neatness. Sauerwine was neat but this degree of tidiness suggested to Beckwith psychopathy. It had to hide something, he decided and, using some sort of intuitive and unspoken formula in his mind that directly correlated neatness and madness he reckoned that whatever it was that Gerard had done was truly hideous.

There seemed little point in poking amongst the hydrangea bushes and gaunt, dormant roses so he walked past these down the path to the bottom of the garden where he discovered an old well, a greenhouse and the garden shed.

The well was small – perhaps a metre in diameter with a crumbling stone wall about a metre and a half high – and clearly unused. The remains of a rotten wooden frame that had presumably once supported a bucket could still be seen lying at an angle beside it. A heavy metal lid had been placed over the top of the well and on top of this about ten heavy breeze blocks had been placed. Beckwith thought about trying to shift these to look inside the well but decided quickly that it would take too much effort and that his life was already too short and too full of woe to bother. It would be done later.

The greenhouse was small and, he was not surprised to note, neat. It contained numerous flowerpots, a range of implements, a free-standing set of shelves on which were various herbicides, fungicides, insecticides and even rodenticide. There were bags of compost and bags of fertilizer, bundles of sticks and a box full of labels.

And a roll of plastic fishing line.

Beckwith actually jumped slightly when he recognized what he had discovered. He hadn't yet seen the twine that was wrapped around the feet of their unidentified victim but this was suggestive enough to convince him it was significant. He pulled a resealable evidence bag from his pocket, opened it and put it over the twine, careful not to touch it. He sealed the bag, wrote the time, date and location on the label, which he then signed.

Having found nothing else of potential interest he left the greenhouse and went across to the garden shed opposite. It was old, rotten around the bottom, with a door that was warped. It was padlocked but when he peered through the wide gap between the door and frame he saw a small petrol-engined lawnmower and, because of the dark, little else. He would have liked to force an entry but decided that it could wait for proper legal authority.

He looked around. He was at the end of the garden, bushes obscuring the views. It was untidy here, as it was at the end of so many gardens; ashes and a largish area of burnt ground suggested that Gerard had had bonfires here. Beckwith eagerly inspected this, aware that a myriad of murderers had used such a place to dispose of the evidence, but was disappointed once again.

With depressing inevitability it began to drop water from the sky.

He poked in the compost heap and found no limbs, no eyeballs. He peered over the chainlink fence into the bushes but no bleached bones were to be seen. He turned around and looked up the long length of the garden. Behind the shed some wood had been carelessly piled. He walked over to it and looked at it. Was he being overly suspicious or did it looked *deliberately* artlessly piled? Was it hiding something?

He bent down and began to pull away damp and rotting planks of wood of all shapes, sizes, ages and provenances. There was a lot of it but he wanted to see what, if anything, was under it.

Nothing.

Except that it was very significant nothing.

He came into the sitting room as casually as he could, his face neutral, his pace measured. They both looked at him, of course, but he only had eyes for Sauerwine. 'I've come across a problem, sir.'

Sauerwine, without understanding, frowned. 'What?'

Beckwith allowed his eyes to flick across to their lone spectator. 'An *evidential* problem.'

Sauerwine stood up. 'You won't leave, will you, Mr Gerard?'

He didn't wait for a reply.

As they walked along the garden path Beckwith produced the bag with the twine in it. 'Is this relevant?'

Sauerwine took it, squashed the plastic against its contents for a better look, then said excitedly, 'That's the twine!'

Beckwith nodded, pleased that his instinctive correlation between tidiness and extreme criminality had been proved. 'And, also, I don't know if this is significant . . . '

He led his superior to the ground he had exposed beneath

the pile of wood. He pointed at a rectangular depression about two centimetres deep in the ground and asked hesitantly, 'Would the anvil have fitted in that?'

Sauerwine bent down, his spirits rising exponentially as he did so. He looked up, Beckwith seeing for the first time in many days a look of joyful appreciation. 'I do believe it would.'

Helena was struck by the change in Sauerwine. He had lost his boyishness and with it, some of the superficial charm; he was far from haggard but he certainly looked tired. He was slightly thinner too, although she had previously thought that he had too much puppy fat. When he greeted her there was no smile, only formality; when he interacted with his subordinates she saw impatience. She was sure that these were new acquisitions and, despite herself, she was sad. The old Andrew Sauerwine had possessed a vital innocence that she had found invigorating.

'Miss Flemming.'

'Inspector.' She smiled but he didn't reciprocate.

He asked her to sit down. She noted that his office was still as tidy and she was curiously reassured.

'Good journey?'

'Fine.' This glowing reference was spoiled by her follow-up remark. 'The train wasn't too late.'

Not that he cared. 'Tea? Coffee? Only Rich Tea biscuits, I'm afraid, but good to dunk.'

'Nothing, thanks.'

'Dr Eisenmenger not with you, then?'

'No. Should he be?'

He didn't know how to react to this but his dilemma was relieved by a knock on the door. Before he could command the interloper to enter the door opened and a fair-haired, blue-eyed man of about thirty came in. He stopped abruptly when he saw Helena.

'What is it, Beckwith?' demanded Sauerwine.

'Sorry, sir. I didn't know . . . '

'What is it, Beckwith?' The repetition came with added asperity.

A file was proffered. 'Preliminary forensics report on the computer. They've got something.'

Sauerwine's irritation at the interruption did not dissuade him from reaching impatiently for Beckwith's gift. As he leafed through it Helena was aware of Beckwith standing awkwardly, casting covert glances at her and, she guessed, wondering who she was. She waited patiently and watched Sauerwine, noting the contented expression that settled on his face.

He looked up at Beckwith as if to ask why he was still there, then dismissed him with a brief, 'That's fine.'

Beckwith appeared dissatisfied with this, but did not vocalize any dissent. As the door closed behind him, Sauerwine said to Helena, 'Sorry about that.'

She couldn't actually tell that he was sorry; if anything he looked rather pleased.

He continued, 'The suspect asked for you by name.'

'I was involved with his defence once. On a charge of gross indecency with a minor.'

'He went to prison.'

She smiled sweetly. 'Let's hope he was guilty, then.'

'You know what the charge is now?'

'Murder.'

Sauerwine nodded. 'He was calling himself Girdlestone again. Still pretending to be a tutor.'

'From what I remember he was quite a good teacher; certainly nobody said otherwise.'

'I'll tell you now, Miss Flemming, because you'll find out soon enough, I've got a bloody strong case against him.'

She bowed her head in acknowledgement, then enquired, 'So . . . what? You think I should pack my bags and steal away?'

111

Sauerwine shrugged. 'I can't see him getting off this one.'

'Not worth defending? Is that it?'

Sauerwine held up his hands as if to say, *Do what you like. Take a toothpick and go kill a dragon, if you want.*

She pointed out, 'Everyone's entitled to a defence.'

His nod deliberately patronized her, as insulting as a raspberry blown in her face. 'I know that, Miss Flemming.'

Not so long ago she would have been enraged by this attitude, this treatment, but time and experience had changed her. Now she used the anger that she might once have expressed as fuel. 'Why am I here, Inspector? It's not normal to entertain the solicitor for the defence.'

And in truth, now that the question was asked, now that it was a thing born and, no longer non-existent, seeming to fill the room so that he could not ignore it, he did not know. Savagely thrusting away the impudent voice within his head that suggested, *She is very attractive, don't you think?* he replied slowly, 'Since we know each other of old, I thought we might be civilized . . .'

She thought, *By which you mean civilized as in expressing sorrow while you insult me.* She stood up. Smiling amiably and in the politest of voices she suggested, 'Well then, now that the civilities are disposed of, perhaps I could see Kenneth Gerard.'

He stood at once, action to conceal his embarrassment. 'Absolutely.'

He ushered her out of the room and led the way to the interview rooms. By the time they had reached them he had recovered sufficiently to add one more goad. 'By the way. I think that you should know now rather than leave it till later. The report that Beckwith just gave me – it doesn't help your client.'

'Oh?'

He shook his head. 'No. I'm afraid a preliminary scan of his computer has shown quite clearly that Kenneth Gerard was accessing child pornography on the Internet.'

***

'Good day, Miss Flemming.'

He actually stood when she came in, something so alien to this situation that was otherwise so typical it was almost comical.

'Hello, Mr Gerard.'

'Please call me Kenneth. You used to, you know.'

She sat down. 'Kenneth, then.' She had put her battered briefcase on her knees and having opened it she produced the same pad of paper on which she had written Martin Bell's evidence. The bag back on the floor by her side, she asked, 'Are they treating you well?'

He shrugged. 'They're treating me as they should. I'm not sure I can stretch that to cover the word "well".'

'But nothing you wish me to complain about?'

'Only that they have arrested an innocent man.'

'Have they explained what the charges are?'

'Murder doesn't require much explanation, does it? Probably one of the simpler laws; certainly one of the earliest. The Mark of Cain, and all that.'

'Tell me, then.'

'Tell you what?'

'First what they say, then what you say.'

His composure weakened, a tremble running through the shell she saw that he had secreted about himself. A small smile crept on to his face, almost a plastic mask or a botox disaster, and she remembered at once that this was a sign of stress; she had seen a lot of it during the course of their earlier acquaintance. 'Inspector Sauerwine believes that I enticed this gentleman to my house, there to indulge in sex with him. He is gracious to admit that I may not have deliberately killed him, but he believes that the result of my actions was that this gentleman was rendered unconscious and that, possibly callously, possibly unaware that he was still alive, I then weighted him down in the river where he remained for some weeks until recently.'

'And on what evidence does he base this?'

He took a deep breath. His words had taken on a despairing note that was almost chilling to hear. 'The body was tied to an anvil taken from my garden and it was done with twine similar to some found in my garden shed.'

She was noting this down and he seemed to have stopped so that she was preparing to speak again when he unexpectedly went on, 'Perhaps I should also mention that the body had been dumped in the river less than fifty metres from my house.'

The smile was wider but tauter and threatening to snap.

She asked, 'Is that all?'

'Thus far.'

'First, Kenneth, I have to ask a single, simple question.'

He nodded and said at once, 'No, I did not do it.'

She didn't want to but she had to tell him. 'They've been looking at the hard disk on your computer.'

He knew at once. 'Oh.'

'You know what they found?'

He took a while but it came eventually. 'I can guess.' She thought that he sounded genuinely ashamed. He took inside himself a deep, shuddering breath. 'Oh, God.'

She waited a while before asking again, 'Did you do it?'

He had sunk down, arms folded on the table, head down on them. When he looked up she saw the tears that he had been crying. He began to shake his head only after staring at her as if seeing not her but the lights of the train heading down the tunnel towards him.

'No.'

This was only a whisper.

Later that day, as he had done with the report on the computer, Beckwith brought in to Sauerwine the reports on the twine found in the shed and the soil traces taken from the rectangular depression in the garden. They were conclusive;

the twine was the same – there was even a match in the cut ends – and the metallic oxides in the soil had come from the anvil.

Beckwith, who had glanced through the reports before bringing them in, said, 'It looks pretty conclusive.' He mustered some artificial enthusiasm for this sentence, trying to be philosophical and accept the inevitable; Meckel had been right.

Right, but lucky.

Sauerwine tried on modesty as he replied, 'Yes, it does, doesn't it?'

It didn't fit him, though.

Which was when the phone rang. He picked it up and listened. Beckwith watched his superior's face transmute from slight interest to disbelieving shock, stopping off briefly on the way for something that a medical man might have taken for concussion.

'You're joking.' This in a hushed tone.

But it appeared that this was not a jest.

'I'm coming straight away.'

He slammed the phone down and picked up his jacket from the coat hook without informing Beckwith of this apparently stunning news; he didn't even seem to realize he was there.

'Sir?'

Sauerwine looked towards him; not at him, but towards him. His voice, when it came, came from far distant lands. It had faint tones of wonder and unbelief, yet also something else. 'Yes?'

'What's wrong?'

Sauerwine stared at him, then seemed to come to. He took a deep breath then said, 'Get your coat. We're going back to Gerard's house.'

'Why?'

'The team searching the garden have found something.'

115

Beckwith at last understood what else there was in Sauerwine's voice.

Satisfaction.

Helena sensed that things had changed as soon as the door to the interrogation room opened and Sauerwine, followed by Meckel, entered. He switched on the recorders, gave time, date and place as well as the names of those present, then fell into silence, his eyes seeming to find nowhere else worth resting other than on Kenneth Gerard's terrified face.

The silence expanded, filling every dimension of the room, seeping into the very fabric of the space that they occupied, becoming a presence as real as any of the four people there, growing into the chief player in the drama. Meckel, having begun with eyes looking around as if on a sightseeing tour of the area, became entangled and soon his gaze, too, found its way on to Gerard's grey abjection. Helena wanted to break this beautifully judged interrogation, this perfectly legal pressure, this battering as physical as blows landed on flesh, but she knew also that that was what Sauerwine wanted; Gerard didn't seem to even notice it. He had retracted all contacts with this hell in which he found himself, presenting only a physical representation of an absent spiritual being.

Abruptly Sauerwine said, 'There's a well at the bottom of your garden.'

Gerard didn't respond; Helena only frowned.

'Do you use it?'

These verbal thrusts were taking their time to reach the place that Gerard occupied. Helena looked at her client and only slowly saw him react, as if sedation blanketed his senses.

'Well?' he asked.

'At the bottom of your garden.'

Gerard shook his head, an old man in a dry month, beset by too much of life's experiences to raise vitality within himself. 'It's disused, old. Nothing but slime and mud . . . '

'So you don't use it.'

'No.'

'You just store breeze blocks on top of it.'

Gerard frowned, not following him. Helena asked, 'Is this leading anywhere useful?'

Sauerwine didn't hear her words. 'You put breeze blocks on top of it.'

Gerard's nod was slow. 'Yes, that's right.'

'It made it difficult to get at. Took my men quite a while to lift them off.'

'It was dangerous. The bolts holding the metal cover came loose and it was no longer secure. I didn't want anyone falling down it . . . '

'Very commendable.'

Gerard looked at him at last. 'I was going to get the landlord to fix new bolts but I forgot . . . ' He suddenly awoke. 'There hasn't been an accident, has there? I put the breeze blocks on it in case some silly children played . . . '

'No, don't worry. No accident.'

Gerard seemed reassured. Helena tried again. 'Look, Inspector . . . '

She might just as well have been talking in a soundproofed booth.

'And you covered it up to stop people looking inside it?'

Helena tried once more. 'Haven't we established that?'

She succeeded this time. Sauerwine suddenly shifted his gaze to her. 'I wanted it to be absolutely without possibility of contradiction that Kenneth Gerard deliberately made that well difficult to access.'

At which Helena sensed the trap into which she and her client had just blundered. She asked, because she had to, 'Why?'

But Sauerwine had dropped her and was back playing with his suspect. 'You covered it up to stop people looking inside it?'

Gerard, too, knew that there was more to this question than a matter of interest to the Health and Safety Executive; when he nodded it was with slow, turgid dread. Sauerwine announced to their unseen, future audience, 'The suspect has just nodded.'

Gerard added quickly, 'It would have been dangerous. I'd seen a couple of village children crawl through a gap in the hedge and get into the garden; if they'd moved the cover, they might have . . . '

Sauerwine interrupted, a wicked grin shaping his words. 'Seen what was in it?'

' . . . fallen in.'

Sauerwine raised his eyebrows. 'Suddenly you're worried about children? You? A paedophile?' The sarcasm threatened to melt his fillings as the words flowed over his tongue.

Gerard found some pride from somewhere about his person. 'You refuse to understand, don't you?'

'I think the reason you made it so difficult to get at the well was that you had something to hide down there.'

'That's rubbish. I told you the reason. It was potentially dangerous.'

'The bolts that secured the cover hadn't rusted through, they'd been sheered, the lid had been deliberately loosened.'

Gerard stared at him for a moment. 'No, they were rusted through, or something. Why should anyone saw through them?'

'Not just anyone – you. You sawed through them to get at the well.'

'Why?'

Sauerwine sighed. 'I told you. To hide something in it.'

Gerard was trembling again. His question when it came barely made it past his incisors. 'What?'

Sauerwine leaned forward so that the microphone would pick up what he was saying with optimal clarity.

'Five more bodies.'

***

118

Cindy had been a clerical officer in the station where Beckwith was posted about eight years before and he had fallen in love with her.

He still didn't know how or why, but boy had he fallen for Cindy.

Except that somehow he did know. She had come to entrance him, enchant him, obsess him.

And even though she had been gone from his life for seven years now, she still obsessed him – but quite why he could not say. His thoughts stopped short in regard for her beauty, her person.

She had had flared copper-red hair, full and luxuriant and resting on her shoulders, falling down her back. Pale-blue eyes, high cheekbones, a wicked smile, good figure. Fiercely independent, she had talked quite openly about her single-ness, keeping the more lupine members of the staff at bay with easy grace. The pay was poor and so was she, but she was somehow glamorous nonetheless.

His awareness of her had crept up on him, a shadow that stalked him without any knowledge on his part. At first they had worked together only a little; her job entailed fetching files, typing reports, answering the telephone, but only for senior officers. She had thus been a peripheral player in his life, glimpsed uncommonly and talked to only rarely. Yet as the months had passed, she had moved stealthily from the background to the fore, and their conversations had grown gradually longer and deeper.

More intimate?

Looking back on them, he could only think that they had been; not intimacy in a profound, emotional way, but intimacy gilded by jocularity, so that they touched on personal thoughts and hopes and fears and desires in a less meaningful but none the less truthful manner.

He had learned much about Cindy, been even more intrigued by what he did not discover. She lived in a flat, had lost her father to lung cancer, had a single, older brother. She had, it seemed to him, a stream of lovers, none a serious attachment. This independence of spirit only added to her lustre; she would explain to him over drinks in the pub (just the two of them) that she had to be hard to survive. He now suspected that he had thought perhaps to conquer this resilience, to dismantle that adamantine resolve. It was doomed to be an unrealized dream.

Yet not before long attraction had transformed itself first into passion then into obsession. He had begun to want to see more and more of her, talk to her more and more, first at the office, then when she was at home and he on duty. At first she had not minded, possibly she had even been flattered; she seemed to enjoy their hours together when they talked of their lives and hopes. Like many before him, though, he had taken this easy companionship as something that, he saw now, it had not been.

She liked him – liked him a lot, even – but she did not love him.

This is what still hurt, even after seven years of analysis and dissection, torture and recrimination.

Why? Why was there this gap between affection and love, a gap that was too small to see, too wide to bridge?

He had tried to force the issue. Not in an aggressive way, but hard enough he saw in retrospect through bitter experience to force them apart. Like a man standing in a boat and hitting at the lock gates he found himself drifting away from where he wanted to be; the harder he struck, the further he wandered from his target. His obsession (desire, lust, crush – it could be called any or all of these names) at last broke him down so that in tears he had begged her to recognize that theirs was more than friendship, that he wanted her, and wanted her to want him.

He had scared her, of course. She had told him time and again, both directly and otherwise, that she didn't want commitment; didn't want to be forced to commit and didn't want others to commit to her. Hence the steel perimeter. Hence the self-possession that was unbreakable.

She certainly didn't want an affair with a married man with a pregnant wife.

That had been the beginning of the end. He had pulled himself together (after arguing but only without hope and without success) and thereafter they had met on odd occasions – perhaps enjoyed a meal or even a drink or two – but things were changed and what had passed was past and would never be again.

A kind of death.

Beckwith had returned to his pregnant wife and nothing like it had ever happened to him again.

Sometimes he wished it would; sometimes he blushed with shame to think of how he had behaved. Often, though he looked back and thought that it had been the happiest time of his life.

And, especially in the night when he was hidden by darkness, he would lie and think of Cindy and what might once have been.

Shameful thoughts that he found now were coming ever more frequently.

They were made all the more shameful because three years before Janet had been diagnosed with motor neurone disease.

'Will you continue with the case?'

'Of course.' She implied that she was surprised, appalled even, that he should consider posing the question. Helena Flemming, Superstar Lawyer, never turned away from a client's cry of distress.

'So you think he's innocent?'

If he had deliberately compiled a list of questions to rile her, he could not have done better.

'What the hell does that matter?' She was telling him that he should have known better than to have asked such an imbecilic question and, in retrospect, he had to agree. Helena did not care whether Kenneth Girdlestone, né Gerard, was innocent; he required a defence.

Enough said.

'As a matter of fact, I do,' she conceded in a slightly less caustic tone.

The toaster disgorged two slices of toast with a mechanical twang and Eisenmenger stood up to retrieve them. 'Will you want more?'

She shook her head.

He put the two slices of granary toast in the stainless steel rack then sat back down with it to finish his half of the grapefruit. It was, he noted philosophically, a definition of partnership – sharing the same grapefruit.

'Why?' he asked, referring to her support for Gerard.

'Because I do.'

Perhaps she hadn't slept well. Perhaps, though, it was because it was Helena talking.

He knew that it was not the most auspicious time to raise some practical problems.

Nevertheless . . .

'We've got the Bell inquiry as well.'

She was applying olive oil spread to the toast with a sadistic vigour, as if it deserved everything it was getting, but his observation gave it a respite. 'I know.'

It would have been explicable had he forgotten her birthday but that (he was certain) was ages away. Had he, he wondered, neglected some other anniversary? The first time he had taken her to dinner? Twelve months since he had moved in? Was it possibly, he wondered (and thereby wandered into political incorrectness) a more regular happening known only to the distaff side?

'Can we handle both?'

For a moment it looked as if the toast was in for another pasting and one, moreover, of more than marmalade, then she sighed and put down knife and victim. 'I think so . . . no, I hope so.'

He picked up his own slice of toast and began to smooth spread over it, treating it in a more kindly fashion than Helena had treated her chosen victim. 'But you want to try.'

'Certainly.'

He applied Marmite to his toast. 'Why is he innocent?'

She didn't hesitate. 'Kenneth Gerard might have a "sickness" that society defines as a crime but he was never a killer. He is, if anything, a romantic. He isn't interested in children, only in the love of young men. There was no evidence that he ever harmed anyone.'

'But he admits accessing child pornography via the web. You can't surely defend that?'

'No. Not at all.' She found it difficult to express what she felt. 'What he does is wrong, sick, disgusting to the vast majority . . . but . . . '

She faltered and he prompted, 'But what?'

'But he is not a serial killer.'

He pointed out gently, 'He wouldn't be the first.'

She shook her head vehemently. 'No . . . '

He said nothing and she went on, 'It's not even as if he goes after small children . . . '

'Does that matter? If I had a fourteen-year-old child, I wouldn't be too happy about having him live next door.'

'But he wasn't living next door to anyone. He wasn't trying to impose himself on anyone.'

Eisenmenger knew that a strong liberal streak ran through Helena but he wondered if she were merely being naive. Kenneth Gerard might have thus far limited his interests to young men just below the age of legal consent but he had undoubtedly exhibited the characteristic behaviour patterns of the paedophile – denial, evasion and working in the shadows. What Gerard said and what he believed and acted upon were almost certainly connected only in a very insubstantial and discontinuous manner. His uncertainty was presumably apparent to her as she said, 'Anyway, this is irrelevant. He needs someone to defend him.'

There were times when Eisenmenger wondered if it would have been any easier living with Joan of Arc.

'And the Bell case? We haven't got long before his case is due to be heard.' *Not long* as in four weeks.

She had the answer at once. 'We'll have to work separately.'

He had an inkling that he knew where this was going. 'And who takes the Gerard case?'

She chewed her toast for an inordinate length of time as if considering but he could see with unnatural clarity that she had decided long, long ago. 'It makes more sense for you to go to Rendcomb.'

'Does it?'

'There are the autopsies for a start. I can't do those.'

He nodded and smiled. 'Just what I need. Autopsies on six bodies that have been dead and decomposing for several months.'

'They have to be done.'

In Eisenmenger's experience second post-mortem examination of remains that had putrefied to the point of worm food were rarely informative but he knew that to argue would be seen as dangerously subversive of the cause. He merely made a neutral noise. Content that things had been settled very much to her satisfaction, Helena finished her toast and turned to her coffee. 'And I'll find Mr Kernohan and talk to him. Try to find out just who Suzy Bell's lover was.'

Sauerwine was more nervous than he cared to admit, more nervous than he had ever been before in this situation, and this perplexed him. The circumstances were generic – first date, pub, attractive woman – and he was well versed in them, so why should he be so anxious?

He resolutely refused to contemplate the possibility that it was desperation.

Or that it was because she was fifteen minutes late.

It wasn't as if she was the tardiest date that he had ever had the all-consuming pleasure of waiting for. There had been the coquettish Constable Hartnup, who had actually had to run after him as he stalked away from the restaurant towards his car, thirty-five minutes beyond the appointed hour (in retrospect, this had been a fortuitous happenstance because she had been so remorseful he had established an emotional dominance that had served him well later on).

And there had been plenty of women who had never turned up at all.

It didn't help that it was a pub that was strange to him and that he suspected the bitter was off.

She wasn't that attractive, anyway.

He had all but decided to get up and walk out – an idea that came to him quite suddenly, as if he were being manipulated, thoughts put into his head for someone else's amusement – and was finishing his slightly unpleasant beer when she walked in and he saw the dress she was wearing. If there had only been ten true things in the universe, one of them would have been that Maeve Gillespie was eye-poppingly attractive.

She looked around, unable to see him through the crowds and the smoke, and he was torn between unwillingness to stand up and fear that someone else would claim her. He compromised by half-heartedly waving his arm while trying to look as if it was all nothing to do with him. She saw him, smiled and as she walked towards him he saw the make-up and decided fiercely that she *was* attractive.

He stood up. The old bloke beside him roused himself from his torpor to stare at him as if he had started transmogrifying into half man-half cucumber.

'I didn't think you were coming,' he admitted, not because he wanted to but because the rest of his mind was temporarily out of business.

'I know, I'm late,' she said. 'I'm sorry.'

He failed to appreciate the irony that she displayed no outward sign of this sorrow at all. 'Not at all, not at all.'

While the old bloke stared at them, he enquired, 'Drink?'

As if she had come into the pub for a pair of socks and top-up card for the mobile phone.

'Vodka and orange, please.'

He bought himself a pint of lager as well, hoping that he would have more luck with that.

She smiled gratitude as she took a sip. He knew the perfume she was wearing but couldn't name it; it reminded him of Marcia, a girl who had possessed a tongue that could have graced an anteater.

'I thought we'd eat at Olave's.'

She nodded but not enthusiastically. 'I've heard that's good.'

It was certainly expensive, so he bloody well hoped it was.

Silence settled like a bad odour between them; the old bloke next to them ignored them fiercely. Sauerwine, his mind still paralysed, was only saved from inanity by Maeve saying suddenly, 'Is this allowed?'

'Is what allowed?'

She shrugged. 'This. You, me, going out.'

Manfully ignoring his own vague qualms he said confidently, 'Why shouldn't it be?'

She said diffidently, 'Well . . . I found the body . . . '

'You *spotted* it,' he interrupted.

Her smile was brief. 'Doesn't that make me a suspect?'

'Only if you did it.'

She didn't seem to appreciate his flippancy and into her silence he was forced to add, 'You didn't, did you?'

At last she smiled, a pleasant and warming thing.

'No,' she answered. 'I didn't.'

'There we are then. No problem.'

Her smile broadened and she took a sip of her drink. 'Good.'

He also had a drink, trying to suppress yet again the feeling that he was doing something that was, if not totally forbidden, at least unwise. It was to take his mind off this qualm that he asked, 'How's business?'

It wasn't the most auspicious of questions but he at least thought it safe. Usually he took out policewomen and so asking about their job led to a conversation about how dirty were the locker-rooms, or about how appalling Superintendent Sod had been that day; surely asking a farmer such a question was unlikely to prove controversial.

Yet the atmosphere became suddenly difficult. She frowned, looked intensely at him, said, 'Why do you ask?'

Surprised, he protested his innocence. 'Just making conversation.'

She continued to stare for a few seconds more before relaxing, nodding. 'I'm sorry.'

She said nothing more, preferring another sip of her drink. He enquired tentatively, 'Touchy subject?'

With a small smile she murmured, 'If you must know, business is bloody awful.'

This wasn't going the way that Sauerwine had intended; he felt as if he was moving through a freshly sown field of barbed wire as he said, 'I'm terribly sorry, Maeve. I didn't know . . . just small talk, nothing more.'

Another nod but she remained silent. The old bloke snorted, quite possibly in derision at Sauerwine's ineptitude. Desperation increased rapidly in his breast as he tried frantically to think of another conversational gambit.

It was Maeve who saved the day. 'So why did a good-looking man like you became a policeman?'

It wasn't a brilliant question – it wasn't even an interesting question – but it signalled something to him.

Someone looking for friendship.

Eisenmenger arranged to examine the five bodies taken from Gerard's well and the one removed from the river on the same morning that Sauerwine made his first significant stride towards identifying the river corpse. It was Gerard's computer that led them in the right direction. Beckwith was struggling with the list of missing persons, working through the computer files to see if he could further refine his crude ranking system, presently based purely on age, by using height and weight, and so it was Meckel, now out of uniform, who brought Sauerwine the detailed forensic analysis of the hard disk.

Sauerwine asked, 'Have you read this?'

'No, sir.'

'Has Beckwith?'

'No.'

He handed it back. 'Don't give it to me, give it to Beckwith. First thing to do is to cross-check any names on the disk with any on his missing persons list.'

Thus chastised and having received his first lesson in detection Meckel retreated but it was only thirty-three minutes later that Sauerwine's peace was once more disturbed, this time by Beckwith who, followed by Meckel, burst into his office.

'I think I may have identified the body in the river, sir.'

Sauerwine didn't need to say anything as Beckwith continued, 'One of the names on the list is Clive Ewart. He was fourteen years old and he disappeared on the twelfth of December from his home in Cheshire.'

'Why do you think it's him?'

Beckwith looked – indeed, felt – as if he were going to burst. 'Because Gerard was in contact with him.'

Sauerwine stared at him for a second before saying simply, 'Shit!'

'Oh, yes. The transcripts off the disk are clear and very, very graphic. Gerard was clearly enticing him into some sort of sexual relationship.'

Sauerwine had grabbed the computer report and was eagerly perusing the text; he quickly spotted a potential flaw however. 'These are dated the twentieth and later.'

'Sir?'

'So it's after the date Ewart disappeared.'

Beckwith couldn't see the problem. 'It connects Gerard to one of our missing persons. Maybe Gerard wasn't the reason Ewart went missing, but that's not essential, is it?'

Meckel said, 'If we can prove that the body in the river is Ewart, I can't see that it matters at all.'

Sauerwine had to admit that he couldn't see that it did, but he could not ignore the fact that something was worrying him. 'OK,' he decided. 'Contact Cheshire and get hold of any dental records and see if they've got anything suitable for DNA.' This was addressed to Meckel; of Beckwith he asked, 'You wanted to attend a post-mortem, I believe?'

Beckwith nodded warily.

Sauerwine smiled warmly. 'It's your lucky day. You can attend six at once.'

Meckel was wandering from room to room in Kenneth Gerard's house and was looking at the titles in the study when he heard a key go into the lock of the front door. He stopped immediately, listening intently and wondering who this newcomer might be. He was there unofficially, having yet to be allowed to get a close look at the place where Gerard had lived and, quite possibly, killed. It had occurred to him that while Sauerwine and Beckwith attended the autopsies, he might make use of the time to rectify this omission. Meckel had been peripherally involved with murder enquiries on rare occasions, but never before had he been at the nucleus and he wanted to immerse himself completely in the experience and take advantage of his temporary privileges.

It was possible that this visitor was, like him, a person with authority to be there, but Meckel was a cautious man – his wife had always said that he would be the last into heaven on the day of the Second Coming – and he did not call out. The house was secured and warning tapes hung around the perimeter threatening any would-be trespassers, but nonetheless . . .

This person had a key.

He heard rustling and breathing that was stertorous; he knew of no colleague who breathed quite like that.

Then he heard humming. Beethoven's Ode to Joy.

He was confident that it wasn't an official presence but neither did it sound like someone with nefarious intent.

He moved quietly to the door, opened it and crept along the landing.

The humming had mutated into breathless and tuneless singing in which Meckel heard a woman's voice.

He walked to the top of the stairs from where he could hear that the voice was coming from the kitchen. He descended the stairs slowly and softly; twice there was a creak but not loud enough to disturb the diva; he then moved along the hall to the kitchen door and pushed it open.

An old woman. Short and stout, grey-haired but dressed quite smartly in what Meckel guessed would be called 'floral print', she was wearing blue rubber gloves and was scrubbing at the top of the cooker.

He coughed.

She looked up, mid-bar, and ejected a short scream, alarm causing both her eyes and mouth to open. He came into the kitchen holding up his warrant card.

'Police.'

She didn't look particularly reassured until she had actually taken the card from his hand, examined it minutely and religiously compared his physiognomy with his photograph. Then, as she handed it back, an immediate wave of relief spread over her face and then over her body which had been continuously rigid but which now relaxed.

'Oh, Lord, you frightened me!'

Meckel said, 'Would you mind telling me who you are and what you're doing?'

Still breathing heavily she said, 'I'm Mrs Christmas.'

Meckel knew the name vaguely but it hardly qualified as an explanation of her unwarranted presence on a crime scene. 'And why are you here?'

'It's my day.' She said this as if he were being rather stupid.

'I'm sorry?'

'I do two days a week for Mr Girdlestone.'

Meckel saw through the gloom. 'You clean for him.'

'That's right.' Having thus seen to his enlightenment she turned back to the cooker.

He stepped forward. 'I'm sorry, Mrs Christmas, but you can't stay here.'

Stopping once more she asked, 'Why not?'

Because the last thing you want in a crime scene is someone coming along and hoovering up the evidence.

'Didn't you see the tapes? The ones telling people to keep out?'

She frowned. 'Oh, yes.'

Finding himself becoming exasperated he enquired, 'Then why didn't you?'

Her explanation was simple. 'That doesn't apply to me, does it? I mean, I'm the cleaner.'

He shook his head. 'Not today, Mrs Christmas. Not for some time to come.'

She looked crestfallen. 'Oh.'

He picked up the scrubbing brush in one hand, took her arm in the other and led her to the sink. 'Now, you take those gloves off, then I'll take you back home.'

As they were walking along the path in the front garden he said, 'You've got a key.'

'Yes. It's for when Mr Girdlestone's away.'

He nodded then suggested softly, 'Perhaps you'd better give it to me.'

When she looked doubtful he said, 'We'll keep it safe.'

She still looked uncertain but she opened her purse,

rummaged through it and produced a key on a ring; tied to it was a tag on which was Girdlestone's name.

'Clean for a lot of people, do you?'

'I clean four houses. Mr Girdlestone, the Verner-Morrisons, Dr Potts and Mr Sneddon.'

He couldn't resist playing the policeman.

'And what is Mr Girdlestone like?'

'Oh, he's a gentleman. An absolute gentleman. And such a scholar, too. He's very clever. Why, do you know, I was once doing a crossword in *The Lady* and I asked him if he knew the capital of Papua New Guinea . . . and he knew, just like that! He didn't have to look it up, he just knew.' She frowned. 'Do you know the capital of Papua New Guinea?'

'No, I don't think so.' This was actually a slight fabrication; he knew for certain that he didn't know.

'No,' she said and sighed. 'Neither do I any more.'

Fighting his growing awareness that he was in the presence of madness he asked, 'Did he ever have any house guests? People to stay?'

She considered. 'No, I don't think so.'

'No one? No one at all? Not even relatives?'

More intense consideration. 'No,' she decided at last. 'I don't think he has any relatives.'

They had walked down the lane and were now crossing over the River Ross towards the actual village. Her house, on the outskirts, was visible on the left about three hundred metres distant. It was as much to fight the silence between them that he asked, 'So what are Mr and Mrs Verner-Morrison like?'

'Oh, very nice.' But she said it in a way that suggested she thought they weren't very nice at all.

'Really?' he asked gravely and she looked up at him and saw the expression on his face and smiled. She giggled.

'No, not really,' she admitted.

'Why not?'

'Oh, she's all right – a bit precious and too much make-up – but not horrible, like he is.'

His experience of Alec Verner-Morrison meant that he couldn't really argue. In any case Mrs Christmas was mining her theme with gusto. 'Do you know, he once accused me of not cleaning properly! Me! I mean, I've never been so insulted. I used to clean for Sir Gideon Kelly – *he* was a gentleman. *He* never accused me of not cleaning properly. Why, once he commended me on how clean I kept the family silver, and he used to say that he could have used the grand piano in the music room as a shaving mirror . . . Anyway, it's not as if they're particularly clean and tidy . . . '

'Make a lot of mess, do they?' Now he was partly making small talk, partly playing the policeman.

'She leaves the bedroom looking as if there's been an explosion in a cosmetics factory . . . I don't think either of them has ever learned to wash up . . . that son of theirs lives like an animal . . . '

He got the picture but Mrs Christmas had only finished a preliminary sketch and she had plenty of paint that she now wanted to ladle on. 'And when they've had one of their house parties, well, the things I could tell you . . . '

He was about to change the subject when she dropped into her diatribe, 'All sorts of *devices* . . . '

Intrigued, Meckel asked, 'Devices?'

She stopped abruptly and turned to face him. It was cold and there was a wind blowing from the river that found its way into his bones. She came very close to him so that he could see that a small blood vessel had burst in the corner of her eye. Nodding eagerly she said, 'You know . . . *toys*. And some of the stains!'

He raised his eyebrows, reflecting how there was such a thing as too much information, but his informant had not finished.

'I don't know what they get up to, but they won't let me come in for days on end when they're there, and then they make so much mess . . . '

He suddenly realized what she was describing. 'Are you saying, Mrs Christmas, that Mr and Mrs Verner-Morrison indulge in orgies?'

Her eyes widened, allowing him to see that the area of haemorrhage in the white of her eye was stellate in outline. As she did this, she nodded her head slowly, holding his eyes with her gaze in a vicious grip. 'Yes, *orgies!*' she hissed.

And with that she began walking again, leaving him to catch her up. Before he could indulge in further curiosity regarding the social habits of the Verner-Morrisons she enquired, 'You don't really think Mr Girdlestone had anything to do with those horrible things in his well, do you?'

She seemed unable to think of them as human.

'Well . . .'

'I don't believe it . . . I won't believe it. He's such a nice man. He always gives me a small gift on my birthday . . . He never forgets – I don't have to remind him . . .'

They had reached her cottage. Meckel saw curtains twitch in the next-door window as Mrs Christmas, stopping before her garden gate, almost under the cover of the overhanging thatch of the cottage, made one last plea. 'I'd have known, you know. I'd have known if there was anything unpleasant going on in that house . . . Take Mr Verner-Morrison, now – he's such a nasty man that I could imagine him doing horrible things, but not Mr Girdlestone. He's a gentleman . . .'

She had opened the gate and was actually addressing the dark wood of her front door as she made this last remark. She no longer seemed to be aware of Meckel's existence as she unlocked and opened the door, then closed it behind her.

As Meckel walked away (causing another twitch of the Wiedemanns' curtains) he was left to ruminate that Gerard would know where to go for a testimonial.

Helena sighed. She even went so far, as she looked at herself in the bathroom mirror just after cleaning her teeth, as to murmur, 'Oh, dear.' She was not a habitual swearer (she sometimes winced at John's exuberant use of profanity although he was not particularly prone to such vulgarity unless under circumstances of extreme aggravation) but her feelings at that point came close to provoking her to break her custom. Even alone she did not yield, though.

What to do?

Possibly she was being stupid; she was a cautious woman, someone who believed passionately that 90 per cent of human action was detrimental, 90 per cent of its inaction either advantageous or neutral. Perhaps, then, she should wait.

Except she had a feeling that she was dealing with the 10 per cent where action was required.

She only hoped that she was right.

Even Eisenmenger found it hard. There were moments during the first ten minutes of his examination when he thought that there was no oxygen in the room, that every breath he took consisted of pure miasma, of molecules arising from the six bodies that rotted in front of him. Sydenham, as was his way, managed to appear insulated from this, maintaining a degree of superiority that would have made Zeus himself ashamed. His first words to Eisenmenger – 'Johnny! We meet again!' – were a clear message that he at least had erased all memories of their last encounter when Eisenmenger had highlighted the inadequacies of his post-mortem technique.

Eisenmenger had smiled and said as cheerfully as he could, 'Hello, Charles. We do, as you say, meet again.'

'Indeed, indeed.' He had indicated the body bags, each one of purest white, each exuding vapours that were liquid and faecal. 'Your audience awaits.'

Sauerwine was there, holding everything in lest it should erupt in an unpleasantly messy manner; his presence was purely official but he was aware that he had unfinished business with Tricia. As soon as she had let him in he had been aware of a simmering anger within her and directed squarely at him; Beckwith, who had followed him in, had in contrast proffered more friendly body language. Not that he could blame her; when he had left her on the night of the first autopsy he had promised to ring her and . . .

. . . And he'd had a murderer to find . . .

He now stood near the doorway, regularly leaning backwards and turning his head to the right to take in a further draught of reasonably fresh air from outside. He occasionally eyed his sergeant and was once again more than a little perturbed by his behaviour, not least because Beckwith seemed unconcerned by the degree of rottenness, the maggots, the blow-flies and the green sliminess. He looked almost happy to be there.

All six of the corpses were out, occupying every table as well as a portable trolley, their only clothing soiled white plastic body bags that had been fully unzipped and turned down. Gloom and decrepitude combined with this surfeit of cadavers to impart a gothic air, one that was strengthened by the cold and damp so that plumes of water vapour rolled forth every time someone spoke or breathed heavily. The subjects were arrayed in order of putrefaction, so that Ewart, the body from the river and apparently the last to die, was closest while the dissection table farthest from Eisenmenger displayed something whose approximation to humanity was solely in terms of overall size and shape; all other parameters were more vegetable than animal.

He walked up the line, a general making an inspection like no general had ever made before, stopping at the most decayed body. He had been given Sydenham's reports and had read them several times, making copious notes, but deliberately not trying to hypothesize or conclude from this source of data alone. He did not want to think the way that Sydenham had thought, did not want to allow himself to become infected with another's rationalizations and, more importantly, another's irrationalizations. He wanted to start from point zero.

Examining all of his patients took three hours.

He found that Sydenham had done a good job in terms of observation, given the material with which he was working. Even on the most decayed of the corpses the marks of a ligature around the neck could still be made out; the signs of anal intercourse were undoubtedly present in the least putrefied and could be vaguely discerned in all. There were no other obvious signs of violence, nor was there obvious natural disease. The corpses all appeared to be adolescent, although this was less obvious in some than in others; there were no broken bones and he could see no major lacerations. Sydenham had made an attempt at subcutaneous dissection and, Eisenmenger was happy to admit, this would not have been easy given the state of the subjects but he gained the distinct impression that the attempt had not been enthusiastic. He knew that the chance of a further, more complete dissection yielding anything useful was small but he knew also that he could not afford to miss anything, no matter how tiny. Accordingly, having picked up a scalpel and then approached the corpse of Ewart, he began to complete what Sydenham had started by peeling back the slimy green skin from around the neck and lower jawbone.

'Ha!' This from Sydenham.

Eisenmenger ignored him.

'I've always been of the opinion that flaying the corpse is mostly showmanship, and nothing to do with science. Especially when dealing with something so nearly reduced to primordial ooze.'

Without looking up Eisenmenger said, 'You never know, Charles.'

Sydenham sniggered. 'Really? Are you going to make a prat of yourself on all these poor sods? What do you hope to find when you flay that particular specimen?' He indicated the body at the far end where, despite all of Tricia's precautions and deterrents, maggots continued to wriggle and drop from the corrupting flesh. 'A bar code with Mr Gerard's name on it?'

Which was precisely what Eisenmenger did not want to find. He continued in silence.

After about ten minutes, Sauerwine disappeared; after forty-five Sydenham disappeared, keeping company with a loud sigh and a theatrical shake of the head. Tricia remained attentive but after ninety minutes (he was still on only the third body) Eisenmenger looked up to see her suppressing a yawn. He straightened up, caught a painful twinge of stiffness in his lower back and said, 'Take a tea break. I won't need any more help for at least an hour.'

She opened her mouth to argue but he said, 'I won't offer again,' and she closed it again and left with a grateful nod. As he bent back down he groaned to himself, trying to cope with the worrying idea he might have adopted a vertical posture for the last time.

He worked on.

A further thirty minutes and then Tricia reappeared, refuelled on tea and chocolate bourbon biscuits; Eisenmenger hardly noticed, partly because of his concentration on the task at hand, partly because his back was agony. He was now on the fourth body.

He had reached the fifth before Sydenham reappeared, Sauerwine following. 'For God's sake, Johnny! Haven't you got a home to go to?'

He remained bent down but looked sideways at Sydenham. 'No point in doing something half-heartedly, Charles.'

'It all depends on what you're doing.'

Eisenmenger resumed his task which, at that moment, was dissecting the skin around a penis.

Somehow Sydenham made his sigh echo around the room.

More silence for another twenty minutes.

Eventually Eisenmenger had finished, which meant that he had to straighten up. At his groan there came forth an answering guffaw from Sydenham as if wild beasts were sending forth mating calls across the Veldt.

'Getting old, Johnny?'

'Aren't we all?'

'Ha! Indeed, indeed.' He turned to Sauerwine, who was actually talking in an undertone to Tricia, and said in a slightly overloud voice, 'That's why I avoid doing things that are entirely unnecessary.'

Eisenmenger said nothing, merely smiled; it was a tired smile but then he was very tired. At the back of his head there was the idea that he would never ever escape the smell. He stood, arms folded, surveying the corpses as Sydenham asked in a voice supersaturated with sarcasm, 'And did you find anything?'

All of the corpses were now on their fronts and he was looking thoughtfully at each in turn. He turned to Sydenham and admitted in a distracted tone, 'Not much. Superficial contusions on the anterior of the left thigh of the third one and a subcutaneous haematoma in the scalp of the youngest.'

'Really? Really? And what does that tell you? Have you worked out the killer's inside leg measurement? Does he have a liking for Camembert cheese and dress on the right-hand side? How about telling me who's going to win the Grand National?'

Eisenmenger hadn't been listening. He was standing alongside the buttocks of Ewart as he bent down, ignoring the seriously angry twinges emanating from the region of his lumbar spine, and spread them once more.

'What are you going to do now? Give us an estimate of the size of the killer's todger?'

It was like being barracked by a drunk in the audience. He glanced up at Tricia. 'Could you help me?'

She came across, standing on the opposite side of the dissection table. He asked, 'Could you spread the legs?'

This unusual request proved harder to execute than might have been expected because the hip joints seemed to have been welded into place. In the end it was only accomplished by Tricia grasping one slippery green foot and Eisenmenger grasping the other, after which they pulled in opposite directions. As the legs came apart Sauerwine moaned a low, 'Oh, my God,' and Sydenham said with a certain degree of inevitability, 'Make a wish.'

When the angle between the thighs was great enough Eisenmenger dropped his leg and moved to make a minute inspection of the area thus exposed with both his eyes and his fingers. Straightening slowly he ignored Sydenham's mocking grin and said to a slightly breathless Tricia, 'I'm afraid I want to do the same with all of them.'

'What on earth are you doing, Johnny? Is this some sort of parlour game?'

Eisenmenger said tiredly, 'Just a whim, an idea, Charles. Nothing more.'

Sydenham harrumphed but Sauerwine had swapped his look of nauseated horror for one of concern. He had seen Eisenmenger like this before and it had resulted in a complete upset of a very nicely constructed theory.

One by one Tricia and Eisenmenger separated the legs of the cadavers, after which Eisenmenger leaned down gingerly and made a minute inspection of the anus, the base of the scrotum and the perineum, the area in between.

This complete, he stood up, said with a smile to the mortuary technician, 'Thank you.'

Then he began to divest himself of his protective garments. 'All done?'

'Yes, thank you, Charles.'

Sydenham nodded, looked at his watch and then announced, 'Well, I'm due to have a drink with the Chief Constable, so I'll be off.'

Sauerwine was about to say something to him but what it

was will never be known for Sydenham was gone, as if whisked by supernatural powers from the sight of mortal man. Eisenmenger washed his hands and then sat down on a stool in front of a bench where there was a dictation machine that he was ignoring. He wrote copious notes in pencil on sheets of A4 paper.

Sauerwine, unable to suppress his anxiety, said, 'May I ask what you've found? Do you agree with Dr Sydenham that all six had been sexually abused and asphyxiated?'

'As far as I can tell. Given the state of decomposition, there's always going to be room for doubt, but in none can I find convincing evidence to suggest any other violent or otherwise unnatural cause of death.' He paused, then added, 'Of course, one can never be absolutely certain about toxicological causes in these cases.'

'And you'd agree that the final act in Ewart's death was drowning?'

'It's a very reasonable assumption. There's certainly water in the lungs.'

Having given Sauerwine some reassurance Eisenmenger turned to Tricia who was zipping up the body bags and hosing them down. 'Do you want a hand?'

'That's all right. At least no one's going to view these poor sods, so I don't have to spend hours making them look good.'

Eisenmenger returned to his thoughts.

When the last body bag had been zipped and washed down, Tricia said, 'How about a cup of tea or coffee, Dr Eisenmenger? You must be thirsty.'

'Coffee would be good.'

She was just about to leave the dissection room followed by Sauerwine when she suddenly paused. 'Would you mind telling me what you were looking for between their legs?'

He looked up and smiled. 'Testicles.'

Of course.

She nodded as if he had been searching for a five-pound

note that had slipped down the side of the armchair. It was Sauerwine who asked curiously and (it had to be said) nervously, 'Why?'

Without a trace of irony Eisenmenger replied simply, 'They haven't got any. They've been cut out of all six bodies.'

If Eisenmenger had dropped his trousers and presented the assembled company with his white-skinned buttocks he could not have produced a greater shock.

'What?'

Eisenmenger looked up from writing whither he had returned after imparting this grenade. 'They've all been castrated.'

Sauerwine found his head doing a slow waltz around the room. What did that mean? Did it undermine his case against Gerard?

Tricia said, 'I wonder why.'

At which Eisenmenger smiled. 'Good question.'

Sauerwine at last found his voice, and it was an anguished one. 'Why is everything so complicated when you get involved?'

Eisenmenger thought this unfair. 'Mathematics teaches us that from chaos comes forth complexity, Inspector. Simplicity is a man-made construct, an artefact we manufacture to try to cope with a very big and very difficult universe.'

But such philosophical considerations proved to be meagre compensation for Sauerwine.

Duct Street Billiards and Snooker Club was as far from the kind of place that Helena would have spent the evening in as was Titan or any of the other moons of Saturn. Duct Street itself was a grimy place, never a somewhere that people had lived, more a passage between more salubrious locations, a thoroughfare, a route. It consisted mostly of the backs or the sides of factories and the majority of those had lost out in the economic miracle that she had been told had happened at the turn of the twenty-first century; there was a kind of spectral, romantic beauty about this post-industrial landscape but only during the day or in the protection of a locked car.

In the darkness of the evening, with damp around her and more rain threatened, with a bitterness to the air that she inhaled and a feeling of being watched, the post-industrial landscape seemed a hostile and unwelcoming location. It was certainly not a place for a middle-class female lawyer to find herself.

Maybe I should have let John do this. How hard can his job be? What's six post-mortems, after all?

But such thoughts only annoyed her. She was behaving in this way because society had conditioned her to do so; it was all in her head. The club was here because the rents were low, not for any nefarious purpose.

Easy.

She pushed open the door.

'Yes?'

He was big, she realized at once, but then a brief moment's consideration and the forward movement of the speaker into the half-light and she saw that she had been totally mistaken.

He was *huge*.

'Oh.'

'Can I help you?'

He was wearing a dinner suit and black tie and nothing fitted.

Nothing *could have* fitted. Helena was doubtful if anyone anywhere made formal evening wear of such dimensions.

And then there was his smile. It sat upon his face much as a clown's smile is only artifice, painted on and just as easily removed.

'I . . . I want to go in.'

If he felt this to be unlikely he failed to show it. He was the perfect straight-man as he said, 'Members only. You a member?'

She had the idea that he would have said exactly the same if she had been the Queen in full ceremonial regalia and accompanied by Prince Philip, a state coach and three dozen footmen. She shook her head. 'Can I become a member?'

Without a moment's pause, without any consideration, without a single nerve impulse reaching higher than the most basic of cerebral operations, he held out his hand. 'Twenty quid.'

She was slightly surprised that it was so easy. She brought her handbag round and felt inside for her purse. The twenty pounds that she found and presented were taken before her hand had stopped moving.

She had expected a receipt, maybe even a membership card.

All she got was a nod.

Prudence – not always her friend – whispered that she should say nothing.

The entrance hall had been small and dark; the room in which she found herself was darker but because it was so much larger it was far less claustrophobic. The overall darkness, arching away into nothingness above her head, was dispersed by regular tetrahedra of light over snooker tables and into these silhouettes of men would periodically bend and from them the echoing crack of ball hitting ball could be intermittently discerned. A more rectangular lumination ahead told her where there was a bar. She estimated that there were over twenty tables of which at least half were occupied; maybe it was the darkness but she could see no other woman there.

When she entered, no one looked up, there were no stares, nothing changed. Her entrance made no alteration in the clockwork.

She walked towards the bar in front of her; as she did so she moved between two occupied tables and accidentally brushed against one of the players as he crouched to play a shot.

'Sorry.'

He had already whirled around, his attitude one of belligerence. He was young and shaven-headed and she could see a tattoo on his neck that, to her, was as good as an invitation to the fight. His face, a mask of anger, barely relaxed when he discovered that it was a woman. 'Be fucking careful.'

She saw only that if she argued, there might be a price to pay.

'Sorry,' she repeated.

He held her gaze for a while and she came through the fear to appreciate the context; this was a dance, as ritualistic as the Sir Roger de Coverley. She was expected now to reinforce her contrition; any deviation from this would be taken as provocative. Accordingly she looked briefly down at the cigarette butts on the floor and, magically, he relented and slowly turned back to the snooker table.

Feeling strung even more highly she at last arrived at the bar.

The barman was serving a small, late middle-aged man who had a weasel face and an unnatural obsession with denim. She waited patiently, trying decide what to drink; she felt that she would be unlikely to get a decent Chianti Classico or Sancerre and the idea of quaffing a pint of Tetley's or Hofmeister was somewhere a long way beyond the limit of her imagination. She ignored the peanuts in the bowl by her elbow because she couldn't ignore all the grubby fingers and fingernails that had previously been dipped into them.

The barman came across to her.

'Can I help you?'

My God, you're sexy.

This came to her as if she had overheard it on an open line, a radio signal bounced off the ionosphere and directly and unintentionally straight into her head.

She said, 'Vodka. Vodka and tonic, please.'

He smiled. He had long brown hair and precipitous cheekbones; his smile revealed so many teeth that he seemed to have been blessed by God with double the normal number. He was a good ten years younger than her, but that not only didn't matter, it seemed a positive advantage. She could see that he was appraising her, could see also that he liked what he saw. She had dressed casually in tight blue jeans and black blouse and more than once she caught his eyes flicking up and down her.

'Ice and lemon?'

'Yes, please.'

She watched his back, partly because she wanted to but mainly because it obscured most of the available horizon and she had nowhere else to look. He turned around, put a tumbler with some clear fluid in it down on the bar in front of her and reached under the bar for the tonic bottle; all the while his grin remained and his eye didn't leave her. They were nice eyes, too; dark grey and amazingly clear, even in the relative gloom of the snooker hall.

He picked a slice of lemon from the saucer with a cocktail stick, then shook it into the glass; as he spooned some ice into her drink he asked, 'Like snooker, do you?'

This threw her off guard and she found herself saying without proper thought, 'I find most ball games boring.'

The grin remained as he suggested, 'Perhaps I should teach you about ball games.'

She hadn't drunk a drop but somehow she felt intoxicated. She smiled sweetly and, indicating the glass, 'How much?'

'Five pounds.'

It seemed a lot but she paid up without protest. 'I'm only here to look for someone.'

'You found someone.'

Despite herself she smiled.

He said at once and in mock wonder, 'You *do* smile!'

This was so cheesy she wanted to reach for some crackers. 'Someone called Kernohan. Barry Kernohan.'

He said nothing to this. Another man came to the bar, this one bearing two empty beer glasses; after he had refilled them with lager he returned to Helena. 'Kernohan? Never heard of him.'

The vodka was nice. 'I was told that he worked here. As barman.'

'Maybe he does. They've got at least six of us on a rota. We hardly meet.'

'Oh.' After another sip of vodka she asked, 'Is there a manager I can talk to?'

'There's certainly a manager, although whether you can talk to him . . . '

'I wouldn't take up much of his time.'

He was shaking his head and leaning towards her conspiratorially. For the first time she was aware of the definition of his musculature beneath his shirt. *He works out.*

He said in a low voice for her ears only, 'I really wouldn't. He doesn't take kindly to people asking questions. Gets angry, gets the help in.' He gestured with his eyes and head towards the way in and towards where the bouncer lived. She nodded in comprehension.

'Ah.'

He straightened up. Another thirsty snooker player appeared and required service. Helena was almost at the end of her vodka and when he came back to her he asked, 'Another one?'

Before she had a chance to refuse he was already pouring the spirit and putting in the ice and the lemon, and she parted company with another fiver.

There was no change to give her, of course; having closed the till he turned back to her and said, 'So, what do I call you?'

She had said, 'Helena,' before considering the wisdom of giving her real name.

'I'm Justin.'

'Just Justin? No second name?'

'I'll swap you. Mine for yours.'

She was about to refuse, then thought, *What the hell?*

'Flemming.'

'And mine's Wegener. Justin Wegener.'

He held out his hand and she saw how long his fingers were, how delicate and fine; it occurred to her that they were artist's fingers. When she shook his hand she felt smoothness and warmth and was unaccountably aroused. He said thoughtfully, 'You know, now I come to think of it, there was a chap called Barry who worked here.'

'Barry Kernohan?'

He shrugged. 'But he did work the bar. I never got to meet him – we were always on different shifts – but maybe he's the one you're looking for.'

'How long ago did he leave?'

He thought about it. 'Three months, I guess.'

'Do you know why he left?'

'He got hurt, I think. Some sort of accident.'

She asked hopefully, 'Could it have been a fight?'

He was uncertain, however. 'Could have been.'

From behind her came a sudden burst of shouting. He looked up, over her head, his face immediately interested. She turned around and saw in the darkness two figures silhouetted by a table light, squaring up to each other.

'Excuse me.'

Justin was walking to the end of the bar, then lifting the flap to escape its confines. She turned back to the source of the commotion. She was about twenty metres distant and it was difficult to make out precisely what was happening until one of the pair lunged forward. The other one staggered back, then came forward and a punch was thrown. The tables around were forgotten as an audience began to form, for the most part silent but with occasional calls of encouragement. Justin reached the ruckus just as the two protagonists began to circle around one another; one of them had picked up his snooker cue and was waving it around under the nose of his friend and making sure that he couldn't reach his own cue. She watched as Justin, without pause, stepped up behind the

148

one with the snooker cue, snatched it from him then pushed him over. It was at this moment that the entrance door opened and Helena's friend, the bouncer, emerged looking neither mean nor menacing, just businesslike. The altercation had broken out quite close to the door and so before either of the two amateur boxers could involve Justin in their display of the pugilistic arts the bouncer had grabbed the one on the floor, hauled him up, twisted his arm into a lock and whisked him away; meanwhile Justin had moved in on the other one. Clearly drunk, the remaining boxer took a feeble swing at him which he dodged with careless ease; a single jab to the point of the chin ended the matter. The bouncer came back in and dragged the now unconscious troublemaker out by the legs.

The crowd dissipated with astonishing speed, a silent diaspora gone back to their previous labours even before the bouncer and his cargo had gone through the door. Helena found herself watching Justin in some admiration as he walked back to her. It was clear that not only was he not fazed by this incident, he had enjoyed it.

'I'm impressed,' she said.

A modest smile. 'It was nothing. It happens quite regularly.'

'And are you paid to break up fights? Isn't that what the bouncer's for?'

'I don't mind. I know most of the bar staff would stay well out of it, but it's not usually nasty stuff. Occasionally they try it on with knives but even then they're so pissed they can hardly hold them at the right end.'

She was not normally impressed by brawn but in Justin she saw an elegance and a refinement that suggested here was no mere animal.

'Where were we?' In this question she found an intimacy that was quite exciting.

'Barry Kernohan.'

'Ah, yes.'

'Do you know where I can find him?'

'As I said, I hardly really knew him.'

Her disappointment was short-lived, though. He left her to serve someone else and when he returned said, 'I reckon I could find out for you, though.'

'Could you?'

'Sure.' Then he seemed to experience a sudden doubt. 'Why do you want him?'

She had been wondering how she would answer that question when it came. In the midst of this uncertainty the truth crept in. 'I'm a lawyer.'

He interrupted. 'Are you really? Sexy *and* brainy . . . '

'And I think that Mr Kernohan might be an important witness in a case I'm working on.'

'What kind of case?'

'Murder.'

He was intrigued. 'Really?'

She nodded.

'That wouldn't be the Bell case, would it?'

Surprised, she said, 'Yes. Do you know anything about it?'

'Sorry. Only what I've heard. Bell and his wife used to come in here from time to time.'

'Then I'm sure you see how important it is that I talk to Mr Kernohan.'

His smile was broad and sincere. 'Absolutely.' Then, 'What I suggest is, that you give me your phone number. I'll ask around, see what I can dig up.'

Which placed her squarely into a dilemma. Part of her didn't want to give anything of herself away, but another wanted very much to talk to Justin again. In the end, though, she had no choice and she gave him her mobile number.

He noted it down and then smiled. 'I'll see what I can come up with. Hopefully I'll be able to satisfy you.'

She found herself smiling just as slyly as he did. 'I'm sure you will.'

***

150

Eisenmenger had booked himself into one of the two inns in Rendcomb, The Lamb, finding himself in a room where all the straight lines had long ago decayed into irregular curves and all the flat surfaces such as ceiling, walls and floor were now warped into gentle undulations that deceived the eye and suggested to him that the entire universe had been put through some sort of cosmic Hall of Mirrors.

And then there were the noises. The floor creaked sporadically as he walked around but, intriguingly (and annoyingly), an identical footfall on an identical spot on a different perambulation would elicit a different sound. Although he had yet to sleep in it, he had already discovered that the mattress not only afforded the interesting experience of being hard in some places, soft in others and apparently non-existent in a few, it also squeaked quite alarmingly at the slightest movement. The plumbing supplied not only water that was lukewarm no matter which tap he used but also a quite astonishing repertoire of grunts, gurgles and moans.

These phenomena when combined with the faded wallpaper, the seriously distressed and rickety furniture, and the antique (or was that antiquated?) light fittings, produced a sense of period English charm that Eisenmenger guessed was better observed than experienced.

Tonight, though, he was too tired to care.

Having dragged himself into his room he stripped, showered, dressed himself in jeans and a rugby shirt and then sat on the bed. After the symphony of squeaks had settled he found his mobile phone and called Helena to tell her of his findings.

Not surprisingly, she found what he had to say both fascinating and baffling.

'Their testicles?'

'That's right. All twelve of them.'

'Couldn't they have just . . . *decayed?*'

'There'd have been *something* left. Anyway, in each case

there was an incision in the perineum where'd they'd been removed.'

'The what?'

'The perineum. It's the bit that keeps your legs together and that, in my case, keeps my scrotum from getting scrunched between my legs and, in your case, stops your backside from meeting your frontside.'

'But why remove them?'

He leaned back on to the pillow accompanied by an atonal symphony of reverberating sounds. 'Therein lies a question.'

'And do you have an answer?'

He sighed and thought long and hard. 'Possibly, but I also have another question.'

'What?'

'Is it the kind of thing that Kenneth Gerard might feel like doing?'

Which Helena managed to handle without any hesitation at all. 'No. Absolutely not.'

'You can be certain of that?'

'Yes.'

There were times – and they arose not infrequently – when Eisenmenger felt that he and Helena occupied two universes that existed in parallel but that never quite met; in his there were few highly probables and a vanishingly small number of certainties, whereas in hers, most things were definite and there were only two shades of colour.

'Can you be so sure? I mean, it's been a good few years since . . . '

'This was not done by Kenneth Gerard, John. I told you, whatever else he is, Kenneth Gerard is not a murderer and even if he did end up killing someone he is not the kind of man to remove, for whatever reason, the testicles of his victim.'

He had hit his head too many times on this particular wall. Eisenmenger was a pragmatist when it came to immovable objects, especially when he could see the dried stains of his own blood on them.

And anyway he had a feeling that she was probably right.

'OK, so we move ahead on the theory that Kenneth Gerard is innocent.'

'Which brings us back to my question. Why do it?'

He was staring at the ceiling; more accurately he was staring at the nicotine stains that had presumably been there for twenty, thirty, maybe even fifty years. 'I suppose it's just conceivable that we're dealing with a mad scientist who has isolated a rare chemical from the testes of asphyxiated young men – perhaps one that rejuvenates elderly female virgins.'

'Let's put that one on the back burner for now.'

'Fair enough. Which leaves my other ideas. The first of which is that they're removed as trophies. Some sort of emasculation . . . '

'Does that suggest a woman?'

'Or an inadequate man.'

'And the second idea?'

One of the stains on the ceiling resembled an old woman; when he looked at old stains or patterned wallpaper he always saw old women; what did that say about him?

'That the killer removed them to eat them.'

After that Helena took a while to find her voice again. 'Eat them? Cannibalism?'

'Why not? It's actually far more common than many people think.'

She didn't thank him for this nugget of information. 'Maybe in your world, John, but not in mine.'

'Well, I don't think we need to debate the prevalence of human cannibalism at this precise moment. The point is that it provides an explanation of the castration of the bodies.'

'But why? Why on earth would anyone want to eat the testicles?'

'Because these are homo-erotic murders. The death is a part

of the experience; it's even conceivable the victims are willing participants, playing their parts with as much sexual pleasure as the killer. There are precedents for people offering themselves for sacrifice not only willingly but even insistently. The earliest recorded instance occurs in ancient Central American and South American civilizations where there's a lot of evidence to suggest that the human sacrificial victims not only didn't protest at their fate but actually wanted it. One could, without too much of a stretch, bring in the current vogue for suicide bombers, where the psychology is one of willingly dying in a particular manner in order to go to paradise.'

Helena felt as if she had called up Dial-A-Professor as she listened to him prattle on. She at last managed to intercede with, 'But suicide bombers have an overwhelming religious belief and they aren't cannibals.'

'No, but if you take a strictly pragmatic view you can define religion merely as a set of beliefs bringing with them advantages for the believer. Using that definition, men or women who gain extreme sexual gratification from sado-masochistic acts can be lumped into the same generic type. The ingestion of the testes is merely a distortion and extension of the concept of penetration; it might also be seen as assimilating the victim, ingesting his sexual being.'

He left her without any idea of where to go except to accept that he might be right. 'You've convinced me even more that Kenneth Gerard is innocent,' she told him.

'Maybe I have, but I doubt that anything I've uncovered is going to convince Inspector Sauerwine that he's got the wrong man. If I know the constabulary, once they've decided they know who did it, they tend to become slightly blind to other possibilities.'

'I'll get a psychological profile. Prove that Kenneth couldn't have done it.'

'Of course, but will that be enough?'

'What do you mean?'

'You're asking your expert to prove a negative. I bet the Crown will get another expert to say that there may well be circumstances where such behaviour is not out of the question – and then we're back to square one.'

'All the same, if I don't get a profile that's favourable to our case, we're doubly screwed.'

'Sure.'

'And if that isn't enough, we'll just have to find the real killer.'

He sighed. 'We?'

'Well. you're down there, aren't you? You may as well hang around for a few days, see if anything turns up.'

Already the mattress was fighting back.

'But if they charge Gerard with five more murders, then you'll have to come back here.'

'He's already charged with one. That means they'll be in no hurry about these other five since he's not going anywhere now. I doubt whether I'll be needed in the near future. There doesn't seem much point in swapping places.'

When she wanted to Helena could have given lessons on stubbornness to a rock.

He asked resignedly, 'How's it going with the Bell case?'

'I've found a possible lead on Kernohan.'

'A strong one?'

'I'm hopeful. I went to the snooker club where he worked. He's left but the man behind the bar is going to see if he can find out where he might have gone.'

'Well, take care. It doesn't sound as if Kernohan and Bell move in very nice circles.'

'Don't worry, I will.'

Helena put the phone down, lay back in the easy chair and closed her eyes. She thought about what she had just been told; actually she felt slightly sick at what she had just been told. It was typical of Eisenmenger that he should regard the discovery as fascinating and intriguing, be seemingly untouched by its awfulness.

Still, it strengthened her conviction that she was right to defend Kenneth Gerard.

God, she felt awful.

This was an abrupt realization but once made it carried with it the armour plating of certainty. She felt bloated and tired; the slight feeling of nausea, she now appreciated, could not be laid in its entirety at the feet of Dr John Eisenmenger.

Perhaps she'd eaten something, or perhaps she had a bug.

She then remembered.

Her period was due.

She drifted off into a doze.

'It doesn't change anything.'

Beckwith found himself enjoying the spectacle of a Meckel who wasn't getting it all effortlessly right. To hear the strains of desperation only added to the pleasure. Silence was allowed to join them in the room for a few, desperate moments.

'What I want to know,' put in Superintendent Burr in a portentous and menacing voice and completely ignoring Meckel's opinion, 'is why it was left to the defence pathologist to uncover it.'

Sauerwine found all eyes turning towards him, as if he were in some way responsible for Sydenham's inadequacies. He said, 'Dr Sydenham tells me that he overlooked the objects in question through pressure of work.'

Burr leaned forward, the only exercise he was ever seen to take. '"Objects in question"? They're balls, man, so call them that. They're nuts, knackers, plums, testicles.'

'Yes, sir.'

Burr hadn't finished. 'And what does he mean, "pressure of work"? He's paid a lot of money to perform these autopsies and I don't expect to get a crap service and a lot of pathetic excuses.'

Sauerwine felt that it was unfair that he should be the one catching all the blame. 'I didn't choose him, sir. I believe it was the Chief Constable who . . . '

But Burr, whether for reasons of diplomacy or unadulterated viciousness, had no interest in his subordinates attempting escape by means of invoking the name of the Chief Constable. 'It doesn't matter who it was. He did a poor job and at the very least we've been made to look a load of total prats in the eyes of the defence. The question is – does this materially alter matters? Does it put a hole in the case?'

Meckel was desperate to reassure the superintendent. He almost left the seat and fell on his knees before the desk as he said quickly, 'I'm sure it doesn't, sir.'

Beckwith thought it but Burr said it. 'You may think it doesn't, Constable, but if I was paid a pound every time a constable got it wrong, I'd be a billionaire by now.'

Meckel thus dismissed (very much to the pleasure of Beckwith), Burr turned his gaze back to Sauerwine. 'What do you think, Inspector?'

Sauerwine cleared his throat, straightened up slightly in the strangely uncomfortable seat that his buttocks were now caressing and took this opportunity at rehabilitation. 'It boils down to whether or not Gerard is capable of such behaviour, sir.'

'And is he?'

Sauerwine liked to believe that he was more than just a bog-standard copper. 'I think a psychiatrist would say that this kind of behaviour indicates a desire to — '

'Forget the Freudian bullshit. Do you think he cut their knackers off?'

Spotting that the tide in his affairs was rapidly reaching flood proportions and knowing that he had to take it, Sauerwine said promptly, 'I've got no doubts at all that he did.'

Beckwith closed mental eyes, Meckel relaxed and Burr merely stared for a long time. 'Just get me a psychiatrist who's going to say that.'

'No problem.' And from the way he said this few would have guessed that he felt some alarm at the road he was now treading. Burr, however, had decided to move his attention on to a new victim. Accordingly it was of Beckwith that he enquired, 'So, tell me, Sergeant. What do you think?'

No spotlight ever shone brighter or with greater radiant energy than the one now beating down on Beckwith; not only was Burr gracing him with a gaze that spoke of no great liking, but also Sauerwine was treating him to the sort of scrutiny that would have melted lead. Meckel, he noticed in his peripheral vision, stared at the patch of carpet between his heavily shod feet.

He said carefully, 'If I can sort of work backwards, I think we've got excellent evidence that links Ewart to the other five victims – mode of death and mutilation of the bodies both indicate one murderer – but I'm slightly worried about the evidence that links Gerard to Ewart . . . '

'What are you talking about?' Sauerwine's vocal cords had tightened due to incredulity and therefore his voice had risen to an interesting pitch. 'We've got DNA confirmation that it was Ewart in the river, and Gerard was in contact with him via computer, the body was dumped in the river right by his house. What more do you want?'

Beckwith had tried to be constructive but, as had happened so often before in his life, his well-meant criticism had been received awry. Feeling both flustered and defensive he pointed out, 'We've got no forensic evidence actually linking him to any of these murders. Also, this business about castration, it doesn't seem to fit in with his profile at the time of the last offence.'

Sauerwine opened his mouth to speak and might, from the look on his face, have produced a vocal pitch that would have threatened the windows and upset a few dogs in the neighbourhood had Burr not said, 'He's dropped out of sight for years, Sergeant. It's plenty of time in which to change, become even more depraved.'

'Yes, sir . . . '

'And anyway,' Sauerwine joined in, having become just calm enough to adopt a tone that was appreciable by human auditory apparatus, 'this is early days. I'm certain that when we've identified the other victims, they'll all be linked to Gerard.'

Burr nodded, then asked, 'How's that going?'

Sauerwine was back in total control. He oozed confidence and relaxation. 'Gerard's computer disk is proving very interesting, sir. He was in contact with a great many people, almost all of whom were young men. We're correlating these names with names from the missing persons' lists and hopefully the other five victims will match one of those. We only need one more positive and I think we can safely say that he's going down for a long, long time.'

Burr had achieved the object of the meeting which was chiefly to reassure himself that when he spoke to the Chief Constable later in the day he would be able to look really rather competent. As they filed out, Sauerwine gave Beckwith one hard and frankly malevolent stare before stalking away. In contrast Meckel, who was following him, gave him a sympathetic smile and Beckwith was left to wonder which of these he found harder to take.

Beckwith returned home in time to give Janet a hand with the bath routine. Freddie was boisterous and Beckwith got thoroughly soaked and left a considerable quantity of water on the bathroom carpet; by the time he had read him a story – then read him another because Freddie begged him to – it was half an hour after Freddie's normal bedtime. Freddy's eczema wasn't too bad; his asthma hadn't bothered him too much either. Exhausted but somehow happy with life, Beckwith came down to the kitchen where Janet was cooking a mixed grill.

'Thanks for that. It's a great help.'

'I'm sorry I can't do it more often.'

'I don't expect you to. You've got your job to do. That must come first.'

He found her reasonableness suddenly irritating. She was so bloody nice, forever understanding; he sometimes thought that she would have forgiven him a dalliance with Cindy, a possibility that brought him such deep shame he nearly drowned in it. Why did she have to see his point of view all the time? She played the martyr, didn't complain, just suffered, and he felt himself to be the monster, the uncaring one. He didn't want to feel an ogre, yet every look, every gesture, every understanding word added another detail to his coat of monstrousness.

'No, it shouldn't,' he said. 'It shouldn't at all. You and Freddie should.'

'Don't be silly . . . '

'For Christ's sake, don't argue, Janet.'

He was as shocked as she was by his angry tone; she stared at him, then began to cry. Blindly she found a chair at the kitchen table, flopped down at it, head in hands. He looked on as she sobbed, his feelings of shame an excuse for inaction. 'God, I'm so tired,' she said between tears and he noticed that even at this point she wasn't angry with him.

She dropped her head down on her forearms, continuing to cry.

At last, feeling that it was too late, he walked over to her, put his hands around her shoulders. 'I'm sorry, Jan. I shouldn't have snapped at you.'

She shook her head. 'I'm being silly.'

Did motor neurone disease make you emotional? He didn't know. He hadn't wanted to join his wife in surfing the net, garnering details of the means of her death. She said, 'You must be tired. Isn't the case going well?'

There she went again; reasonable enough to drive a man insane. She didn't even have the humanity to use her illness as a weapon against him; why couldn't she be more like him? Why couldn't she be nasty, insecure, vicious?

This time he bit down on the irritation. 'It's going very well. We've got the murderer.'

'That's good!'

That's it – always look on the bright side. You'll be doing that the day you die . . .

He actually felt himself blush with embarrassment as this thought slithered into his head.

He smiled weakly. 'Yeah. Isn't it?'

The meal had been good but the film had been mediocre yet Sauerwine didn't mind; nor, he thought, did Maeve. He fancied himself an amateur student of body language and from the way she had leaned towards him, and the way that she had pushed her upper arm against his, he reckoned that the signs were good. He had driven her back to the farm and they sat there now, in her living room, drinking coffee and liqueur, eating the rather expensive chocolates he had given her.

Their chat had been intimate and she had not stopped smiling all evening; her laugh was frequent and delightful. Her eyes were doe-brown, the laughter lines exquisite. She had on an emerald-green dress that accentuated her figure, a ruby brooch, a bracelet that matched.

He found himself falling in love for the first time since Sally had left and he had discovered too late that she was more than a regular date, that she was someone whom he did not wish to lose. He was sufficiently versed in the ways of love that he did not let this conviction show, that he still affected a degree of laconic distance.

Never show them you're too interested.

He didn't have a book of rules, at least not one that he could articulate, but he had been playing the mating game long enough to know what to do when.

Inevitably the conversation came around to her relationship with her husband.

'You're still legally married?'

'Yes, 'she admitted. Then, 'Does that bother you?'

'Not at all.' It did, actually, but not enough to stop him wanting to see her again. He sipped the liqueur. 'Do you mind talking about it?'

He suspected that she was not entirely telling the truth when she said, 'No. It's probably best for you to know the background.'

'Which is?'

'When we married, I genuinely loved Richard. It didn't last long.'

'What changed your opinion?'

But it was apparently not best for him to know that particular bit of the background. She said unconvincingly, 'We drifted apart.'

Sauerwine's living was made, though, by winkling out the flesh of a story. 'Why?'

'It doesn't matter.'

She looked distressed, though; it made him want to help her.

'Please, tell me.'

He was good at body language but only in fits and starts. His interest in why the Gillespies might have become so estranged obliterated his part-time academic pursuits and he failed to notice that this was not a line of enquiry that brought her pleasure.

'We just didn't get on.'

'He didn't hurt you, did he?'

'Oh, no.' She was sure on that point.

'Was it another woman?'

'No.'

Sauerwine's subconscious noted that she had withdrawn in upon herself, that her legs were together, her head down, her shoulders forward; it noted it but failed to ring up his conscious which was all a-busy on finding out facts. 'Then why?'

He had backed her into a corner. She could say only the truth. 'He's gay.'

Which surprised him.

'Gay?'

A nod.

'Then why . . . ?'

She was torn between reticence and desire to please, to enter into intimacy with him. Eventually desire won out. 'He was desperate for money for his farm. I brought money with me.'

'Which was good for him, but what about you? What did you get out of it?'

'I thought he loved me; that's what I wanted. '

'But you stayed.'

She smiled weakly. 'I did, didn't I?'

He couldn't understand. Someone other than a policeman might have left it at that, at least until later, but Sauerwine was in full investigatory mode. 'What's kept you here?'

She finished her liqueur but found that he was still looking at her. Having put her glass down on the table she looked at it for a while. 'I was naive. I'd been left a lot of money by the death of my mother – my father had died when I was young – and there was no one to advise me. I failed to spot that the marriage put everything I own into this farm. Irrevocably.' She looked up at him. 'The marriage goes, I lose it all.'

At last he understood. 'Oh.'

She continued to scrutinize him. 'Is that a problem?' she asked.

'No . . . '

'I mean, you weren't pinning your hopes, were you?'

It took him a moment to comprehend what she meant. 'God, no!'

She was eyeing him. 'You're sure?'

'This isn't important!' He waved his arm around. 'It's you I like, Maeve. Honestly.'

He reached out to her, took her hand, leaned across, took her arms. 'You must believe me.'

And she did. He came to sit beside her. 'I'm sorry. I shouldn't have pried.'

He kissed her. It wasn't their first but the others had been on the cheek. They both enjoyed it.

Enjoyed it very much.

She led him upstairs to the bedroom and then they made love. He felt as if he had been set free from a prison.

Only afterwards did he resume the conversation. 'What happens if you divorce him?'

As lovers do, they were lying side by side, his arm behind her head, hands upon each other. The light was still on. 'He'll lose the farm,' she said after a long pause; she spoke not to him but into her dilemma.

'Why?'

'We've taken out extra mortgages – a lot of them. They're all in our name. If I go, the bank will call them in – he'll be ruined.'

She said this with infinite sadness.

'Would that bother you?'

It took her a long time to answer and when it came her response was slow and laden with tears.

'Oh, yes.'

Melanie Munro's voice was deep and husky so that, when Eisenmenger had booked his room at The Lamb by phone, it had given him the immovable impression that she was some sort of diva, a woman who moved in a slinky manner and whose eyes would be expressive of unquenchable sexual desire. In the event, the landlady turned out to be a rather pleasant, rather plump and rather businesslike woman who, for Eisenmenger at least, had as much sex appeal as a beanbag. She didn't smoke but presumably decades spent licensed to dispense beers, wines and spirits in premises where the great majority of people did had resulted in enough passive ingestion of cigarette smoke to have inflated a one-to-one scale model of the Albert Hall. He also observed a liking for Irish whiskey that probably did a good job of stripping away the surface lining of her throat and vocal apparatus on a daily basis, and that would also have done interesting things to her voice.

When Eisenmenger came down the next morning he felt as if he would have had more rest if he'd dispensed with the bed and slept half in and half out of the bath and this despite the fact that the cold tap had an incurable drip. He tripped on the uneven stairs and nearly fell head first down them, saving himself only by clinging to the newel post. Had he died at that moment it would have been no compensation to know that he had done so in one of the oldest coaching inns in England.

Breakfast, however, proved to be excellent and Melanie Munro an attentive hostess.

'Eggs all right, Doctor?'

'Delicious. And gorgeous black pudding.'

'It's not a full English without black pudding.'

He looked out of the window. 'It's given up raining,' he observed.

She dampened his enthusiasm at once. 'Later this morning, they say.'

His seat afforded him a view of the main thoroughfare in Rendcomb; it was the kind of view seen on a hundred thousand jigsaw puzzles, a million boxes of all-butter short-bread, a billion postcards. She emptied the coffee pot into his cup, then held it up. 'More?'

'Please.'

She took it out along with his empty plate, leaving him with toast and a variety of jams.

He was the sole breakfaster and liked it that way. The dining room contained about twelve tables, all covered with white linen clothes. A grandmother clock clicked away in the corner, a curiously contemplative sound as if an elderly person were thinking deeply, making regular involuntary noises. Landscapes and prints of horses hung about the walls; a clatter of dishes and roar of running water came faintly from the kitchen. It ought to have been wonderfully relaxing and heart-warming, it ought to have been a perfect picture of a perfect England, but it wasn't. In fact, if he hadn't been looking into the murders of six men he wouldn't have spent more than ten seconds there. Everywhere he looked he saw cold calculation, a scene painted as artfully to deceive as theatre scenery.

He ate toast that he had spread with apricot jam and looked occasionally out of the window, seeing a small number of passers-by, a larger number of cars. Mrs Munro reappeared with his coffee.

'Are you here on holiday?' she asked, having put the coffee pot down in front of him.

'Business,' he said.

She nodded. 'At least you're not a reporter.'

'Reporter?'

'Oh, yes. Haven't you seen them?'

Of course he had. Few who hadn't shuffled off their mortal coil could have been unaware of them. The news that five bodies had been discovered in a well was unlikely to have failed to wake the fourth estate from its restless slumbers, and they had prowled relentlessly around the streets of Rendcomb for the last few days.

'I hadn't really noticed.' Eisenmenger found that he was good at disingenuous.

'Oh, goodness, yes. When the news broke about Mr Girdlestone they were everywhere, asking everyone about him. One or two of them stayed overnight while they were digging up the bodies. Uncouth, most of them.'

'Girdlestone. Is he the one that's been accused?'

'That's right! They've found five bodies in his well!'

There was something about mass murder that induced exclamation marks to grow like grass.

'Golly.'

'Yes. All young boys.' Before he could reply she emphasized her meaning. 'They were all young boys!'

She was looking at him with a knowing expression.

He played his part. 'Are you saying — ?'

She was desperate to tell him and was happy not to let him finish.

'Yes! He's a paedophile!'

'Are you sure?'

She couldn't believe he should ask such a question. It was as if once the tag had been attached there could be no removal, that the application of the name defined that to which it was attached. *Ceci n'est pas une pipe,* only in reverse.

'Do you know what he did?' It wouldn't have mattered whether he did or no, for before he had finished the inhalatory part of the respiratory cycle she was telling him. 'He enticed six young boys into his house, then butchered them.' She looked towards the kitchen where, presumably, tender ears were straining to hear what she had to say; Eisenmenger had the impression of a roomful of fresh-faced seven-year-olds all wondering what the adults were gossiping about. Then she turned back to him. 'They say he cut off their willies.' This was uttered in a whisper with a strange accentuation of the lips as she sounded the final word and Eisenmenger found himself astonished at how closely, yet how inaccurately, this unfounded rumour mirrored actuality.

She little knows . . .

Yet this was not the worst. Another glance towards the kitchen for reassurance that no innocent faces were peeping through the gap, then, 'Some people say that he ate them!'

These were presumably the same 'they' and the same 'some

'people' who told people about the woman down the street who was no better than she ought to be.

'Did you know him?' He asked this in a hushed tone in order to stay in camouflage.

'Slightly.' He was about to ask her opinion of Kenneth Girdlestone né Gerard but was saved the task. 'I always thought he was a bit weird . . . '

It was a phenomenon he had encountered before. History was rewritten; when mud was thrown it not only stuck, it covered; it not only covered, it stank.

'Did he keep himself to himself?'

'He never came in here.' Which was presumably something of a sin. 'I used to see him walking in the village quite frequently, though.'

'He's a teacher or something, isn't he?'

This caused an exacerbation of her symptoms. Another glance kitchenwards before, 'I know!' This was followed by, 'He taught mathematics. Perfect for a child-abuser, don't you think?'

Quite why mathematics should be the subject of choice for paedophiles was lost on Eisenmenger. Nevertheless he nodded enthusiastic agreement, then rather soiled his credentials by asking, 'But I understand that there's no evidence that anyone in the neighbourhood has gone missing. I mean, it doesn't look as though any of his pupils have gone missing . . . '

She sniffed at this rather meek plea of mitigation. 'That's as maybe, Doctor, but would you send *your* child to him to learn about square roots and suchlike?'

Finding this rather difficult to answer he said merely, 'Since I don't have any, I really couldn't say, Mrs Munro.'

She sensed some sort of victory but was gracious enough to content herself with a small smile and eyebrows that were barely raised enough to be noticeable. She said, 'Well, I'm sure Mr Verner-Morrison is regretting employing him.'

'Verner-Morrison?'

'He owns Bridge Farm. He's very rich. Mr Girdlestone was teaching Ben, his son.'

'Was he? Oh, dear . . .'

'I know! What a shock it must have been.'

Feeling that he had heard enough propaganda directed against Kenneth Gerard he stood up. 'That was a delicious breakfast.'

'We aim to please. Will you want dinner?'

'Yes, please.'

She smiled. 'Good.'

Ben knew at once who was responsible for the imperious knocking on his bedroom door. For fifteen years such a knocking had punctuated his life; if it had not been a fusillade of knocks, it had been his name shouted imperiously or even just the second person pronoun yelled angrily.

His father was not an easy man to live with.

He didn't answer, though, because he was too deep in misery.

His room was typical of his age and sex. Posters adorned the walls – a mix of attractive and scantily clad females, and unattractive and thankfully overclad rock bands – and the emulsion on the walls was deeply and darkly depressing. It was untidy and the windows were forever shut, producing an atmosphere to which Ben was wholly inured but which the occasional visitor found surreptitiously disconcerting. It didn't help that he appeared to keep forgetting where the washing basket was.

The knocking returned.

'Ben? Ben?'

He didn't answer.

He heard muffled muttering; unbelievably and despite not being able to discern a word he could hear in these primordial sounds how irritated his father was.

'Ben?' This time the voice was softer and without the bass tones.

He sighed. 'Yes, Mum?'

'Can we have a word?'

He looked around the room although he didn't know why. 'Yeah.'

There was a brief pause before the door opened slowly.

His mother came in first. She peered around the door, saw him lying on his bed, smiled and then said with a smile, 'Hello, Ben. Can I come in?'

'Sure.'

His father followed her, of course, looking not only angry and flustered (as usual) but also (as unusual) trying to smile reassuringly. 'Ben,' he said, to which Ben failed to reply. He didn't even get off the bed, contenting himself with leaning back on his elbows. Eyeing them warily he asked, 'What do you want?'

His parents exchanged glances.

Oh, great. It's 'serious'.

'We wanted to ask you about . . . Mr Girdlestone.'

Ben's face remained unchanged. 'What about him?'

'You've heard the news, haven't you?'

He nodded, not taking his eyes from his parents. His father appeared nervous, certainly an unusual happenstance; his mother's voice was gentle and enquiring which was also something he had heard only rarely.

'Well,' continued his mother, 'we were just wondering . . .'

But she lost her way and ended the sentence with an embarrassed shrug. His father suddenly exploded. 'For Christ's sake, Cherie!' To his son he said, 'Did Girdlestone ever do anything? You know . . . inappropriate?'

Ben frowned. '"Inappropriate"?' He asked, 'What do you mean, Dad?'

'Did he ever touch you, or maybe suggest things to you?'

His face didn't alter. '"Touch me"?'

Alec Verner-Morrison lost what remained of his temper. 'The bastard's a fucking paedophile! Did he molest you?'

And abruptly Ben was as angry as his father. 'Oh, don't be stupid! Of course he didn't molest me! What do you think I am, a little boy of six?'

'No, but — '

'Anyway, he's not a paedophile! And he's not a murderer, either!'

His mother broke in. 'That's not what the police are saying, Ben. They say — '

Almost shouting now, Ben said, 'I don't care what they say! They're wrong. He's not a killer!'

His father's face was becoming suffused and he took a step forward. 'Now look here, Ben, we're only concerned for your welfare . . . '

'Yes, yes,' was his wife's contribution.

'Well, you don't have to be. Nothing happened. Nothing at all.'

He glared at them for a moment, then turned away to face the wall. His father opened his mouth as if to continue the debate but his wife frowned and shook her head fiercely. Then she gestured that they should leave their son alone.

As they descended the staircase Verner-Morrison moaned, 'I just don't understand him. What the hell's wrong with him?'

'He's at a difficult age.'

'He was born at a difficult age and he'll probably die at one, too.' He shook his head. 'I don't know, I just don't seem to see the world the same as he does.'

'He's obviously very loyal to Mr Girdlestone. They must have got on really well.'

'Just as long as that cunt didn't fiddle with him, that's all.'

Upstairs in his room, Ben Verner-Morrison was crying.

The whole of the house and garden was surrounded with fluttering yellow plastic tape which in black capitals advised him that it was a crime scene, and that he (and indeed any other passer-by) was to keep out. Maybe they had obeyed this

171

injunction but that didn't mean the house had been ignored; someone – perhaps more than one – had daubed on the front garden gate the words, FUCK OFF, YOU POUF, in striking pink paint, and a stone had been thrown through a ground-floor window. Eisenmenger walked past the front of the house looking at it, wondering if these proto-vigilantes had stopped to think that Gerard was only a tenant and that it was not his property they were vandalizing. He turned the corner into the lane that ran from the bridge up into the forest on the hillside.

This brought him alongside the back garden; the tape continued on his left-hand side and Eisenmenger walked beside it. There was a low privet hedge over which he could see much of Gerard's garden, see how neat it was, see the garden shed and the greenhouse and the well. About a hundred metres further up the slope was a large Victorian house set well back from the road; he doubted that he could be seen by anyone in that house and there was no one in the road. Unless someone had stationed themselves sniper-like in the trees, this meant he was unobserved.

He ducked under the tape at a point where a gate was set into the hedge. He unbolted it, slipped through and closed it again. Looking around he saw that he would now be visible only to someone passing in the lane.

The garden had suffered the effects of a heavy police presence which, combined with the incessant rain, had turned large areas of the lawn and flowerbeds into mud pools. Small shrubs had been trampled, a Russian vine and a handsome honeysuckle which had once climbed a trellis with easy aplomb now hung backwards, half torn from their assured grip. Someone had trodden their heavy-footed way through the newborn clusters of velvet blue, white and yellow crocuses.

The well was before him.

There was more tape around and over the well and no way that Eisenmenger was going to inspect it without leaving traces of his interference. He pulled the tape away carelessly because there was no point in doing it any other way.

The heavy metal plate that covered the well had once been secured with metal bolts but he knew that this was no longer the case. It was very heavy to lift (in fact he had to find a spanner from the shed to lever it up enough to get his fingers underneath) and the grating noise that was made as he slid it to one side was hideously loud. He was thankful that the house and garden were relatively remote; the chances that the noise would be heard were minimal.

'I don't think you're allowed to do that.'

The lid dropped back down with a deafening clang. If he'd actually been in the process of lifting the lid by his fingertips he'd probably have lost a couple of digits so great was the shock of this slightly querulous observation that came from behind him. He swung around to see, atop the hedge, the head and shoulders of a little old lady with grey hair and large, almost terrified eyes.

Recovering himself as best he could he smiled and said, 'Hello.'

'The police told me off for going in to clean.'

A light flicked on in his head. 'You clean for Mr Girdlestone?'

'I used to. They won't let me any more.'

He walked towards her, held out his hand over the hedge. 'How nice to meet you. My name's John Eisenmenger.'

She seemed surprised by his amicability. 'Oh.' As she shook his hand he felt how dry and warm was her flesh. She said, 'Jennifer Christmas.'

'A pleasure,' he assured her. He could hear how oleaginous he was being and hoped that he wasn't overdoing it.

'What were you doing?'

Before responding he looked up and down the lane and she did likewise, following his actions but delayed by a moment. Then he leaned towards her. 'I think Mr Girdlestone might be innocent.' This confidence produced an immediate reaction.

'Oh, so do I!' Her face became transformed by relieved pleasure; what followed suggested huge relief that she had found an ally at last. 'Everyone else is being horrible about him. Have you seen what they've done to the front of the house? It's shocking. It's uncivilized, that's what it is. And they're saying the nastiest things in the village about him, but I know better. I work for him and I know what a gentleman he is.'

Eisenmenger was nodding as he was thinking that here was a plea of mitigation that most accused murderers would have killed for. He said carefully, 'I'm glad to hear you say that, Mrs Christmas.' He paused, then asked, 'There's no possibility that you could be mistaken, is there? I mean, some people can be very deceiving.'

'Oh, no.' This was produced with such certainty that Thomas the Doubter himself might have had second thoughts about his second thoughts. 'I can tell, you know. Just because I'm an old woman doesn't mean that I'm stupid, Mr Eisenmenger. I remember that once this man came to the door pretending to be from the gas company and I knew at once that he was a fraud, even though he showed me his card and it was embossed and it had this emblem on it . . . '

'And was he? A fraud, I mean.'

'Oh, yes.' She looked at him and nodded, and irony might not have been invented as she said without a hint of a smile, 'Of course, it helped that I don't have gas . . . '

Eisenmenger found himself liking Mrs Christmas.

He decided then to take a chance; he needed to make friends in the village. 'Look, I don't suppose you'd be able to help me, would you?'

A doubtful look, one that was faintly theatrical yet totally bewitching. 'I don't know. Is it illegal?'

Well, it was, actually, but at that moment Eisenmenger failed to find the three-letter affirmative in his lexicon. Instead he moved another centimetre closer after another three hundred and sixty degree survey of the horizon; still they were alone unless the CIA had a covert listening post in the post-box opposite. 'I'm looking for evidence to prove that Kenneth Girdlestone might be innocent. Whatever else he might be, I don't believe that he's a murderer. Would you like to help me?'

She also checked out their surroundings, just in case he had missed a bloke in a raincoat with a wooden leg and a pair of binoculars. 'Yes!' she hissed at him, presumably hoping that the sibilance would disrupt any advanced electronic listening devices pointing in their direction.

He lifted the fluttering yellow tape and opened the gate. 'Come in,' he offered.

She scurried inside and Eisenmenger reflected how only old ladies and butlers scurried.

'What do we do?'

Already it was 'we'.

'The bodies were found in the well.'

'The first one wasn't.'

'No, but the other five were.'

She appeared to be less than enamoured with his detective skills. 'Why?' she asked.

'Why what?'

'Why were there five in the well, yet one in the river?'

He opened his mouth, then shut it again, finding he had no answer to that. Why, indeed? Maybe Mrs Christmas was going to prove more than just a convenient source of local information. 'Do you know, Mrs Christmas, I think that's a very good question.'

He turned his attention back to the well, its cover still off-centre where it had dropped and exposing part of the stonework. He pushed it further to one side with some difficulty and peered down into the darkness.

'What are you doing?'

His voice echoed dankly as he said, 'Just getting some idea

of how deep the well is, how difficult it would be to throw in a body.'

She tried to join him in his inspection but was too short to see deeply into its darkness. 'Is it deep?'

'About twenty, maybe thirty metres.'

'How horrible!'

He pulled back and began to look at the stonework on top of the well wall, finding nothing that would magically give him the identity of the murderer. He turned his attention to the metal plate while his elderly companion had her attention on him.

The bolts he found particularly interesting.

'What have you found?' he was asked after a short while.

'Someone has cut through the bolts, see?' He showed her where he had brushed off the superficial rust revealing a relatively smooth-cut surface flush with the metal plate.

'Oh, yes.' She paused. 'But couldn't Mr Girdlestone have done that?'

Eisenmenger was discovering that Mrs Christmas had a disturbing habit of asking awkward questions; he found it a rather intriguing habit. Looking at her gravely, he said, 'Before we hypothesize, let's look around a little more.'

Checking only to ensure that they were still unobserved he began to look around the rest of the garden, including especially the greenhouse, the shed and the area behind it. The anvil's previous resting-place had been covered with a plastic dustbin lid. He examined the impression in the earth with great care. Inevitably Mrs Christmas enquired, 'Is there something important there?'

He straightened up, was caught by a sudden twinge of lumbar pain, and winced as he said, 'The edges are clean.'

'And?'

'And so it was lifted straight out. One go. Could you have done that?'

'Goodness me, no.'

Thinking of his back he said, 'I doubt whether I could, either. Which means that we are dealing with someone strong. Also it explains how whoever it was managed to manoeuvre a corpse and an anvil over the side of a boat on the river. Not easy.'

'No,' she nodded.

'Still,' he said cheerfully. 'Let's look on the bright side, Mrs Christmas. It lets you out.'

She giggled.

Having found nothing else but evidence of a large police contingent that had milled about the garden and trampled everything of horticultural interest, Eisenmenger stopped in front of the back door to the house, looking inside. From behind him Mrs Christmas asked, 'You're not going to break in, are you?'

The tone was breathlessly excited, as if she were desperate to hear him confirm her fears. He duly obliged and was unable to resist a sly grin as he did so. 'Why not?'

Another giggle. 'How? Will you break a window? Jemmy the lock?'

For the first time he had to disappoint. 'I'm sorry,' he said as he held up the keys that Helena had given him. She in turn had obtained them from the owner, Kenneth Gerard's landlord, after parting with fifty pounds.

'Oh.'

The kitchen was cold and there was already an un-mistakable air of a house abandoned, as if it too had given up on its owner. By the sink Eisenmenger saw a scrubbing brush which Mrs Christmas picked up at once with a 'tut' and then proceeded to put in a cupboard. A fly – where would a fly come from in the winter? – droned in lazy, jagged laps of the kitchen; some hyacinths in a pot on the kitchen table were wilting and Mrs Christmas, this time with a sigh, took it at once to the sink for resuscitation.

This done she asked, 'What are you looking for?'

He shrugged. 'I may know when I find it, but then again I may not.'

From her understanding nod and the way her eyes widened slightly she found this gnomic utterance way beyond normal human comprehension.

For the next forty minutes they went from room to room. Mrs Christmas was most upset by the glass of the broken window that littered the living room. She repeatedly muttered, 'Oh, dear,' for some minutes afterwards. Occasionally Eisenmenger would ask her questions about Gerard and his habits; he showed most interest in the study. 'Did he spend a lot of time in here?' he asked as he looked around in unconscious imitation of Meckel.

'Very much so.'

'Working at the computer?' There was a space on the desk where it had once sat, and wires trailed from the printer and the monitor, no longer connected to anything.

She frowned as she tried to recall. 'Sometimes. Not always.'

'I don't suppose you ever saw what he was doing on it?'

'It's all gobbledegook to me, I'm afraid.'

He had expected as much.

At last they returned to the kitchen and the fly, its lonely patrolling guardian. They sat at the table. 'Would you like a cup of tea?'

'We'd better not,' he said. 'Thanks, anyway.'

She couldn't wait long before asking, 'Have you discovered anything?'

He smiled sadly. 'It doesn't usually work like that.'

'Oh.'

She seemed so downcast by this that he felt compassion enough to rescue her from silence. 'You remember that you asked why the last body was put in the river?'

'Yes.'

'I think, Mrs Christmas, that that was a very good question.'

'Was it?'

He smiled. 'Yes, I do.'

She considered this, looking down at the grain in the wood of the table. Then, looking up at him, she enquired, 'Why?'

He leaned back, arms stretched out, hands clutching each other by fingers entwined. 'The well is quite deep enough to have hidden ten, twenty more bodies, so why hide the sixth in the river? The river is a poor place to hide anything, even if you tie it to an anvil and dump it in a deep pool. If the level drops there's a danger that it might be exposed, if the river floods then the line may break and free the body, as seems to have happened. Whereas the well is a far more secure place.'

She said nothing but was watching and listening intently.

'The well had been covered with a heavy metal plate secured with four sturdy bolts. The murderer knew that it was the perfect place to hide the bodies and so cut through the bolts to access it. Now, the police will say that the well was at the bottom of Kenneth Gerard's garden and so he had easy access but, as we've shown today, anyone could have got into the garden from the road, unobserved and unknown to Kenneth Gerard.'

'Yes!' She exclaimed this as if he had just produced an eleventh commandment, one that was so obvious it was a wonder no one else had spotted it.

'Also, the police will say it was Kenneth Gerard who sawed through the bolts but that doesn't explain your point, Mrs Christmas.'

'You mean why was the sixth body in the river?'

'Exactly. You see, it occurs to me that by his own story, he noticed that the cover on the well was movable. If we suppose that he didn't examine the bolts carefully and merely assumed that they had rusted through – there was superficial rust on the cut surfaces – and he didn't bother to move it to one side to look inside it, then his story is logical. He sought to secure the cover as completely as possible by piling heavy breeze blocks on top of it, just in case some children decided to investigate it.'

She signalled that she was following him by a frown and a slow nod.

'So things were suddenly changed . . . maybe our murderer decided suddenly that the well wasn't such a good place to hide the bodies. Maybe he decided there was a bit too much attention being paid to it.'

She said nothing but looked deeply involved with the pattern of his thoughts.

'And that leads us on to his substitute hiding place . . . '

'The Deeps?'

He nodded. 'Exactly. He knew enough to know that they existed and that they were near . . . very near, indeed.'

She looked at him, mouth open ever so slightly. She had caught from his tone that this was significant but did not appear to grasp any details. After a brief pause he explained, 'I don't think a stranger to the area would have known about them.'

She emerged from her spell. 'You mean he's local?'

'Almost certainly. How else would he know about the well and about the existence of the Deeps at Rendcomb?' He smiled. 'I think also that we are safe in our unconscious assumption that we are dealing with a man.'

'Are we?'

He smiled. 'The anvil,' he explained.

She looked momentarily chastised. 'Oh. Yes, I see.'

'I would say that it's time we left, wouldn't you?'

They stood up and he ushered her out of the back door. There was a sense of inevitability about the drops of cold rain that were just starting to fall. They walked back down the garden; before they left Eisenmenger returned the well to approximately its former state, then held the garden gate open and lifted the tape so that Mrs Christmas could walk out.

In the lane she asked, 'What will you do now?'

'Have a cup of coffee. Would you like one?'

She giggled. 'Yes, I think I would.'

***

'Ben! Ben!'

Verner-Morrison prowled around the large living room having already prowled through the dining room, the kitchen and the entrance hall. He had repeatedly called his son's name throughout his patrol, infusing an increasing amount of vexation into every iteration. He was fed up with prowling.

'Where the hell is he?' he muttered.

He stalked back into the entrance hall, then out into the damp, grey air. 'Ben! Ben!'

Nothing.

'Jesus H! Where is the little git?'

He fought a feeling of helplessness, one that was his constant tormentor these days. He could not help but feel that it had been the biggest mistake of his life when he had given up the business for 'retirement' to the country. Now everything seemed so much harder – harder to cope, harder to stay on top, harder to keep his mistress . . .

Did Cherie know? He sometimes wondered.

What he did not dare wonder was whether she cared . . .

A large jeep turned into the long drive, its engine's roar pounding out, echoing into the dankness, disturbing the world through which it moved. It took several minutes to reach the farmyard, with Verner-Morrison waiting impatiently in the cold while it did so. His wife got out. She glanced briefly at him, forgot to give him a welcoming smile, and went around the back of it, reappearing with four carrier bags in her hands. She strode towards him and, as she passed, asked, 'Are you just going to stand there?'

'I can't find Ben.'

Over her shoulder, 'Have you looked in his room?'

'Of course I bloody have!'

She had disappeared inside the house, leaving him with nothing to do but feel impotent; he didn't want to feel impotent, he wanted to feel important, but since he had made his money and pulled out of active participation in the car trade this feeling had become as rare as tits on a bull. She re-emerged from the house, conferring on him a glance that she might have given a dog with a lamp-post and a weak bladder. 'Are you rooted to the spot?'

He began to follow her to the car, stood there while she loaded him down with plastic shopping bags. 'He's been as miserable as sin for the last few days. What the bloody hell's the matter with him?'

'He's got exams this year. I expect he's worried about them.'

'Some bloody girl, I expect.'

'I don't think he knows many girls.'

She slammed the back door of the car and picked up the rest of the bags from the ground. He began to trudge away with Cherie following, both of them laden with shopping. Over his shoulder he said, 'He bloody well should, then. Maybe that's what his problem is.'

They tramped through the hallway and into the kitchen where the bags were deposited in a growing pile by the breakfast bar. 'Why do you want him?' she asked.

'I want to make sure that he's going to be around at the weekend. We've got a party coming and you're going to need help.'

'You're not going ahead, are you? Not with all that's happened?'

'Why not? That's what we agreed.' He asked this with a frown on his face and a tone that suggested she was being dim. This was not quite Cherie's recollection of the way the conversation had gone but she was used to the poverty of her memory, the way that it never seemed to get things quite right, especially those memories of conversations with her extremely better half.

'That was before. We didn't know then that there was a mass murderer in the village.' She had her hands on her hips now and when she uttered the words, 'mass murderer', she did so with a wave of them.

'What's that got to do with us?'

She couldn't believe how stupid he was being. 'There are police everywhere!' This was pointed out incredulously.

'So?'

For one instant a disinterested observer might have supposed that Mrs Verner-Morrison was on the point of fainting, given the fact that her eyes closed for a long time and she swayed slightly. 'What if they come calling during the . . . *party*?'

The said disinterested observer might also have noted the emphasis applied thickly to the last word of this sentence.

'They won't.' This was a simple answer consisting as it did of two words; they were delivered with a degree of confidence that suggested omniscience few in the mortal realm can muster.

'Oh, yes? How can you be so sure?'

'Why should they? What's all this palaver got to do with us? That sicko, Girdlestone or Gerard or whatever his name was, did what he did in the village. I never met the man and you barely talked to him, only to drop Ben off and pick him up . . . ' His voice faded as his face folded into a thoughtful frown. 'He is telling the truth, isn't he?'

She didn't understand.

'Ben. He is telling the truth? About Girdlestone, I mean.'

She heard in the question a fearful vulnerability that had been absent for many years. It brought back memories of a different life, one in which they had danced together to the same tune in a romantic light, rather than to different tunes in different rooms under different moons.

She smiled with the pleasure of long-lost remembrances and put her hand out to his arm. 'Of course he is,' she said softly. 'Ben wouldn't lie to us. You know that.'

She was scrutinized intensely for a second and then Alec was back and the past was where it should be, long and gone and without any import at all. 'Yeah,' he said. Then with complete certainty, 'Yeah, I know.'

He coughed but she knew that it was no more than a cover to have her remove her hand. 'Anyway, that's not relevant. The point is, what Girdlestone was up to had nothing whatsoever to do with us. I don't see why I should lose out on a very, very lucrative source of income just because of something that's happened in the village.'

'But it's not as if you need the money.'

'What's that got to do with anything? I might not need it, but I still want it. There's nothing wrong with that, is there?'

'No,' she agreed but it was a doubtful assent, riddled with hesitancy.

Nevertheless it was enough for her loving and oh-so-better half. 'Right. So the party goes ahead.'

And that was that.

The file on Clive Ewart was emaciated, comprising merely skin, few bones and no flesh. It told Sauerwine only that Clive Ewart had been experiencing an unhappy home-life because six months before he had announced his homosexuality to his parents; neither had liked it but his mother had at least made an effort at accepting it. According to the report, his father had taken it as some sort of affront, a deliberate insult. Sauerwine could not find surprise at such a reaction; it was all too familiar. Puritanically heterosexual fathers unable to accept the sexual orientation of their offspring cropped up with alarming frequency in his work.

There were no details about the row that had finally decided young Clive to fly the nest but Sauerwine could guess that it would have held few innovations in the endlessly repeated pattern of human behaviour. Anyway, it didn't matter; Clive had left with nowhere to go and no one to go with. Thereafter his life had, as far as the official record was concerned, entered oblivion; the discovery of his body had been merely the death announcement, the period mark to his life.

He had had no friends that they could identify, no obvious

places that he could have gone, nowhere that he might reasonably have run to. His computer – they all had computers these days – had failed to turn up the names of either Gerard or Girdlestone or, indeed, any name that might have served as an alias to the murder, but Sauerwine wasn't unduly concerned. It was inconvenient but not catastrophic; he knew that he already had enough to snare Gerard.

In fact, young Clive Ewart had done little more than most adolescents when it came to using his computer. In addition to writing and researching his homework essays, he had indulged in violent computer games, numerous Internet chat rooms and downloading pornography. Interestingly, he had sampled both heterosexual and homosexual varieties, although the latter had become more prevalent in latter months. The list of sites was tediously titillating – Throb and Gristle, Fuckanory, Sodom and Gomorrah, Cuntry Life . . .

Sauerwine dropped the file to his desk and sighed.

There was nothing of use here.

Eisenmenger took Mrs Christmas back to The Lamb for coffee and chocolate cake, a commodity for which his new assistant had an apparently insatiable appetite. As he sat opposite her in front of the elegant but faded curtains of the bow windows it seemed to him that she consumed it with frightening rapacity.

He could not quite believe her. She was clearly genuine and he could see that she would prove an invaluable source of local information, but she was already becoming curiously . . . *adhesive*.

'Nice?' he enquired.

'Ooh, yes. I do like The Lamb's chocolate cake.'

He nodded and smiled. Somehow he had already guessed that.

'Did Gerard – Girdlestone – have many visitors?'

She considered this whilst a smear of chocolate in the

corner of her mouth was distorted into a variety of topologies by the small chewing movements of jaws. 'Hardly any, I think.'

'A loner, then?'

'Yes. I would say so.'

'He didn't teach at home?'

'Only Ben.'

'Ben?'

'Ben Verner-Morrison. His parents own Ashbrook Farm.'

Eisenmenger considered this. 'How many pupils did he have?'

'I don't know really.' She had wiped the corners of her mouth with a napkin but succeeded only in diluting and spreading the chocolate. He noticed how much powder she had on her face. 'At least ten, possibly fifteen.'

'So why did he teach all the others at their homes, yet not Ben?'

She seemed to regard his question as a direct challenge to her, as though she were being called to account for this aberration. After much concentration she offered hesitantly, 'Well, I do know that Mr and Mrs Verner-Morrison are very private people.'

'Don't like visitors?'

She shook her head. 'Mr Verner-Morrison especially. He can be most abrupt. I remember once I turned up and one of his parties had gone on a bit longer than expected . . . he was most put out, I think. He sent his wife to shoo me away. Said I should go home . . . Of course, I can't complain because they still paid me . . . '

'You clean for them as well, do you?'

'That's right. Tuesdays and Thursdays.'

'Do you clean for anyone else?'

'Dr Potts and Mr Sneddon.'

He had finished his coffee long ago but Mrs Christmas didn't seem to mind it cold. He asked, 'Would you like some more cake?'

She looked at him over the cup, her eyes wide and spark-ling with joyous naughtiness. 'No!' she exclaimed quietly. 'You devil, you! Are you trying to get me into bad ways?'

'Isn't it too late for that?'

She put the cup down, smiling and chuckling. 'You know, I do believe it is . . . but, no, I mustn't. One slice is more than enough.'

He sighed in mock disappointment at his failure, then returned to the subject in hand. 'You must know a lot about Rendcomb. Have you lived here long?'

'All my life.'

'I expect you know a few secrets.'

She giggled. 'A few.'

He leaned back, his head brushing the curtain behind him. 'You could be very useful to me, Mrs Christmas.'

'Could I?'

'I think so.'

'How?'

'Because you know the place, know its people. I don't.'

'Is that important?'

He became conspiratorial. 'Essential. You see, if Kenneth Gerard didn't kill these boys, then someone else did, and that someone lives around here.'

Her mouth and eyes opened in perfect synchronization. 'No!'

He nodded gravely. 'Yes.'

She became incapable of speech, forced to stare at him. He went on, 'Which means it is very likely that you know the person responsible for the murders.'

He was laying it on with a trowel, he knew, but felt that it was a wise investment of his time and attention; he needed Mrs Christmas, needed her local expertise, her ears and eyes (two commodities that he suspected were exceedingly acute when it came to the foibles and attitudes of the inhabitants of Rendcomb) and he judged that a liberal dosing of schlock horror would entice her into co-operation.

'You want me to help you find out who is?'

'Would you?'

She was so excited she seemed to be swelling before his eyes; he feared for the no doubt robust elastic of her nether garments. 'Golly, yes!'

'Good.' He offered his hand across the table and she shook it formally.

'What shall I call you?' she asked.

'My name is John, Dr John Eisenmenger.'

'You're a doctor?'

'A pathologist.'

She made a face. 'You mean you . . . ' Her voice dropped. ' . . . *dissect* people?'

'Sometimes.'

She was looking on him with new eyes, ones that were at once fascinated and slightly appalled. She decided, 'Well, I can't call you John, then. It will have to be Dr Eisenmenger.'

He was about to argue but she cut him short. 'I mean it. I have never called a doctor by his first name and I never shall.'

He shrugged and smiled, then said, 'And I shall call you Mrs Christmas.'

Of this she approved.

To celebrate their new partnership they had more coffee over which Eisenmenger asked her if she knew of anyone in the village who had had reason to dislike the maths tutor. 'No,' she decided after a period of consideration that was as deep and long as it was painful to behold. She seemed to think that this was a failure on her part for she followed this up with, 'I'm sorry.'

Eisenmenger was in consideration of his own and didn't hear her for a few seconds. 'Uh?' Then he realized what she had said. 'It's all right, in fact, it's a very significant negative.'

'It is? Why?'

'Because it suggests that revenge is not a motive.'

She nodded enthusiastically. 'I see.' This, though, was followed by a frown. 'No, I don't.'

He explained patiently. 'We need to discover the reason why the bodies were all placed in or around Kenneth Gerard's property. Most serial murderers distribute their victims' cadavers in different locations in an effort to confuse the investigation. There must, therefore, have been a very good reason in the killer's mind for putting them all in the one place. I think if we discover what that reason was, we'll have made significant progress.'

He was beginning to find the pained expression that she adopted when working through his cerebrations quite beguiling. His mother had died before she had grown truly old and he had never really known his grandmothers; Mrs Christmas almost matched the idealized concept of elderly widowhood. She said at last, 'So you wondered if the murderer might have had a grudge against Mr Girdlestone?'

He shrugged. 'It was the least likely possibility. These people weren't killed solely to get Kenneth Gerard sent to prison; if revenge had been the reason for choosing his property as a cemetery, it could only have been a subsidiary one.'

'So why then?'

'Well, the most obvious one is the well. A perfect place to hide bodies, and that brings us back to the last body which was not in the well but the river.'

'Yes! Why was that?'

He realized abruptly that he was being subtly pumped and he laughed to himself at the arts of inquisitive old women.

'The well, as I said, was the perfect place to deposit the bodies. My assumption is that our murderer knew that because he lived around here . . . '

'But he could have put them anywhere,' she objected. 'It's so rural around here, they could have been dumped in the woods somewhere. Nobody would have found them for ages.'

'Maybe, and maybe some rambler would have stumbled across the first one within a week. It would have been a risk and that risk would have grown with every corpse. It's actually very hard to get rid of a body completely, to make them vanish. They don't burn easily and they take years to rot down. Much better to hide them.'

More pondering and while she did this he added, 'So let's assume that he knew about the well, knew that it was covered over and to all intents and purposes a place that no one was going to look in for a long, long time. His first visit under cover of the night is to scout it out, then to saw through the bolts that hold the cover in place. Once he's done that he has his hiding place and after every murder all he has to do is to tip the next body into the well and carefully reposition the metal plate.'

'How does he get the bodies to the garden?'

Once again she had asked a pertinent question.

'In the boot of a car. He parks at a safe distance up the road, probably off the road in the woods just in case some late-night reveller spots it; remember, this is probably three o'clock in the morning. Thereafter he has to trust to luck and carry the body the rest of the way. If someone does come along, though, that would be a problem, I guess . . . '

'No, it wouldn't. There's a drainage ditch that runs the whole length of the road down to the river. He could just drop the body into that and jump in after it if someone came along.'

He smiled. 'You see? That's why I need you.'

She actually blushed.

'Five times he goes to the well and five times he makes his carnal deposit. The sixth time, though, he discovers a problem.'

'Mr Girdlestone had covered the well over.'

'Which presents our murderer with a problem.' He paused, thinking hard, trying to place himself in the murderer's mind. 'A dozen breeze blocks on the well. Hard work to move but not insurmountable; our murderer's strong – strong enough to heave bodies around the countryside, strong enough to lift up anvils with relative ease.'

'Perhaps he was disturbed.'

'Maybe.' Yet he knew it wasn't that. The occasional car, or possibly a wandering party straggler, would have soon passed leaving the killer to his work. More likely something had decided this person that the well was no longer such a good place to hide his victims.

'I think,' he said at length, 'that he was spooked. Perhaps he saw not only the breeze blocks on the well but also that the cover had been moved – Gerard says he noticed the cover was loose so it's quite feasible that he dislodged it. I think he made the decision then and there to look elsewhere.

'But where? He had the body with him, the night was passing and he wanted rid of it.'

His new assistant was transfixed, staring at him as if he were speaking divine truths in tongues. He asked, 'Is that the only well around here?'

She took a moment to come back from wherever he had taken her. 'Yes,' she decided. 'There are several on my side of the river – I've got one myself – but I think Mr Girdlestone's is the only one around here.'

'And to have taken the body over the river would have been dangerous because by doing so he was going further into the village and therefore more likely to be discovered.'

She nodded and he continued his flight of fancy. 'And then he remembered the river, more specifically, the Deeps. Holes up to ten metres deep in a river which was for the most part only two metres deep. And they were convenient, too. Right by the bridge, not fifty metres away. He would know where to find a boat; all he needed was something of sufficient weight and something with which to attach it to the body. A scout around the garden soon solved those problems.'

Mrs Christmas appeared to believe that she was in the presence of supernatural forces as she first stared at him, then shook her head, then said, 'That's amazing!'

He couldn't stop himself smiling, even though he knew deep within himself that he was fundamentally wrong.

Not that that bothered him half as much as the even smaller voice that told him perhaps he was *fatally* wrong.

But how?

Mrs Christmas, ignorant of small, or even very small, voices said, 'It makes so much sense.'

'But it doesn't actually tell us who did it.'

Her enthusiastic wonder was temporarily dented. 'No,' she agreed. 'I suppose it doesn't.'

There was silence for a moment. He had long ago finished his second cup of coffee and she now did likewise. He said, 'We'd better go.'

He got up to pay the bill and she followed him out into the entrance lobby of the inn where she put on her heavy black woollen overcoat. He looked in the mirror while she buttoned this up to her neck, his thoughts lazily tumbling over themselves, a slowly roiling liquid of half-considered ideation.

And then he remembered a phrase she had used.

'What did you mean when you mentioned parties at the Verner-Morrisons'?'

She paused at the top button, always the most difficult. 'He has parties. Well, he calls them parties . . . '

He looked at her. 'And what would you call them?'

Having successfully negotiated the final button she patted her pockets for her gloves; only when she had found them did she say, 'I think he has orgies.'

Eisenmenger raised his eyebrows. 'Do you?'

'Oh, yes. Do you know, he's got this enormous statue of his wife in his hallway? And it's nude!'

The Verner-Morrisons were starting to interest Eisenmenger. 'Does he, indeed?'

'She's a prostitute, of course. You can see it at once.'

Which, since he hadn't met her, he felt unable to judge.

'But I got the impression that these "parties" last quite a long time.'

'They do. People arrive on Friday and don't usually leave until Monday, sometimes Tuesday.'

It sounded to Eisenmenger to be a jolly long time to indulge in orgying. 'Always the same people?'

'I don't know. He doesn't like anyone else being around. He positively chases them off. Says that his guests want privacy.'

It was conceivable that Verner-Morrison held house parties of the type common at the start of the twentieth century when the rich and feckless would gather for formal dinners and games of croquet on the lawn, but somehow Eisenmenger doubted it. Mrs Christmas completely refuted this hypothesis with her next remark.

'Their minibus nearly ran me over last year.'

This was said in a tone that clearly demanded more sympathy than it received.

'Minibus? The guests arrive by minibus?'

Mrs Christmas rode the disappointment womanfully. 'Usually; and quite often there's more than one, too.'

He gazed at her thoughtfully. 'Do you know, Mrs Christmas, I think I'd quite like to see where the Verner-Morrisons live.'

'He won't want you there. He's having one of his parties this weekend.'

Eisenmenger smiled. 'Even better.'

Gerard's computer sang.

It sang with increasing clarity to Sauerwine, Beckwith and Meckel; it serenaded them, to their ears, in the sweetest of tones; its melodies beguiled them, told them in siren song all that they had previously only suspected, all that they wanted to know. It confessed in these chordant notes the sordidness of what it had been asked to do, of websites visited, rooms chatted in, e-mails sent. It gave to them all that they needed to know about the habits and tastes of Kenneth Girdlestone, né Gerard. It whispered in urgent tones the names of five of the youngest of men with whom he had talked and shared intimacies, all of whom had since disappeared; in each case the dates of these messages coincided with their disappearance. Their files were sought and carefully perused. The dental records were sought and then compared with the residents of the mortuary.

All five matched and thus the victims were christened.

Andrew Abbott, Jacob Blackfan, Charles Diamond, William Josephs, Thomas Miller.

Their files were sought and carefully dissected by Sauerwine, Beckwith and Meckel but nothing connecting them sprang out, proclaiming the reasons why they should have ended up scattered around Kenneth Gerard like discarded sex toys. No common themes ran through their histories, other than the normal ones of runaways – dissatisfaction, disenfranchisement and naivety.

When Helena returned to the flat after a fruitless hour spent with a gentleman who was on remand for indecently assaulting his daughter's pet rabbit, she assumed that the message on the answerphone would be from John. She was tired and depressed and feeling in need of ablution as she always did on returning from visits to clients in prison; it was as if the sins of others were concentrated there, seeping out of the walls, polluting the air, tainting the water, and her mere presence within the confines of a place of detention seemed always to make her dirty and violated. She could do nothing more until she had showered. Only then, clad in clean clothes and a glass of chilled Sancerre in her hand, did she listen to the message from Eisenmenger.

Except it wasn't.

'Hi, it's your favourite bartender. How's things? Are you screening your calls? I bet you do. Someone like you would get a lot unwanted attention. If you're in, pick up because I've got something for you . . . '

He paused, waiting perhaps five seconds before continuing,

'Playing hard to get, eh? Give me ring when you're free. I think you'll be interested.'

He gave out a number, which Helena didn't get down the first time and had therefore to replay the message.

Eagerly she dialled the number.

'Hello?' The voice was as she remembered it, silky and smooth and strangely alluring.

'Justin? It's Helena.'

'Well, so you do care.'

'I've only just got in and heard your message.'

'And discovered I might have something you want.'

She smiled at his teasing; found herself wondering why it was so easy to like him. 'And do you?'

And discovered at that point that she really rather enjoyed liking him.

A deep sigh came down the phone line. For some unaccountable reason she wondered what he was wearing. 'Do you know? I think I do.'

Which was more or less the time that she was shocked to notice that she had started to wonder what he wasn't wearing. With something of a jolt she brought herself back to reality and whilst severely reprimanding herself for silly schoolgirl fantasies enquired, 'What?'

'I've made contact with your friend, Kernohan.'

'Where is he?'

'It's not as simple as that. He's a very cautious man. Seems he's had a bad experience at the hands of your client.'

Which attitude Helena could well understand. 'What do we do?'

There was a thoughtful hesitation before, 'Why don't I try to arrange a meeting – the three of us. He might come if he knows I'm going to be there.'

Helena didn't particularly want a third party – even one as juicy as Justin – present whilst she talked to Kernohan, but she could think of nothing better. Planning that she would be able to get rid of Justin after the introductions had been made, or perhaps arrange further meetings in private, she agreed.

'OK. Where and when?'

'Unfortunately I'm not around for a few days. I'll let you know when I get back.'

Sneddon's curriculum vitae stated that he came from a farming family and had attended agricultural college. At his peremptory interview (held at one of Verner-Morrison's car showrooms) he had impressed with his confidence and knowledge and he had been offered the post at once; as far as he was concerned, he had succeeded, too, producing a small profit each year. It had been the Verner-Morrisons who had proved the problem. Alec Verner-Morrison was rude and scathing, treating him like a servant rather than as a manager. His successes were overlooked, his occasional failures the cause of rage. He had thus grown to hate Alec Verner-Morrison and his Barbie-doll wife.

But then things had changed.

William Sneddon now watched the anonymous white minibuses pass by his small cottage while on his face was a look of controlled excitement. For over three years he had watched the same unmarked vehicles arriving at the farm once a month, watched them depart three or four days later; Alec and Cherie's guests for their 'parties'. At first he had been merely intrigued, but his job as farm manager had in those days been hard and he had yet to prove himself to his employers.

Then, though, he had come to learn the truth of those parties.

That he should was inevitable; he was about the farm at all hours of the day and night, needed often to consult Verner-Morrison on some aspect of the business. It would have required a state of catatonia not to see what he had seen, hear what he had heard, and not then draw conclusions therefrom.

He had not been particularly shocked.

Far from it, indeed; he had rather boldly put to the Verner-Morrisons a proposition for partnership, for expansion and a rather more professional approach to their activities. His terms had been generous to them; he could bring a certain degree of experience and certain foreign contacts; they would merely have to increase their investment; he would in turn guarantee to increase their returns.

They had liked his plan.

Alec Verner-Morrison could not, however, accept his farm manager – his employee – as a partner, no matter how junior. He continued to treat Sneddon as an underling but Sneddon didn't mind. Cherie was pleasant to him, which was nice; he was making more money than he had ever thought possible; he was picking up titbits from the table of the parties.

He was also extracting a sort of revenge on Verner-Morrison, with his victim completely unaware of it. In every way he had the upper hand; that he knew their secrets and they did not know his, was a source of much pleasure to William Sneddon.

His revenge was not just cold, it was chilled to zero, frosted and delicious.

Oh, so delicious.

The telephone rang and he turned away to answer it.

Sauerwine was feeling good about life for the first time in a long time because for the first time in that same long time he felt unoppressed by work. With Gerard in custody and charged with all six murders, his only concern was to prevent Burr taking all the credit. He thought it unlikely that the corpulent and static superintendent would fool anybody into believing that he had been solely or even mainly responsible for the successful completion of the case but he didn't want to risk it. Yet how to proceed? He was not good at office politics whereas Burr was, had achieved his lofty vantage point by this facility. He did not think it would be productive – might even be disastrous – if he called the Assistant Chief Constable and pointed out directly that his had been the main contribution to the apprehension of the county's first serial killer. So indirect means would have to suffice; where and when better than an informal soirée at the Chief Constable's house? It had been rumoured that even Burr was going to attend, although few really believed that this miracle of perambulation was going to occur; even if it did, Sauerwine could only imagine him sitting in a corner in a groaning armchair, the horsehair stuffing and springs protruding at a variety of angles acute and obtuse whilst conveying a sense of complete hopelessness encased in extreme corpulence.

It was with irony that was so unconscious as to be deeply comatose that he was perusing this problem and completely forgetting Meckel's contribution when the telephone rang.

'Sauerwine.'

'Someone on the line for you, Inspector. Mrs Gillespie.'

Of course Sauerwine accepted the call.

'Maeve? It's Andrew. Something wrong?' He was aware of the informality and found it oddly dissonant, yet peculiarly reassuring.

'Not at all. I hope you're not busy.'

'Nothing that can't wait.'

He was completely unconscious of any sense that this exchange was in any sense gushing.

'I wanted to thank you for last night.'

He wanted to thank her; wanted to go down on his knees and worship her. Before he had met her he had been starting to think that he had been cursed, destined to wander the seven seas of love and never once making port.

'I certainly enjoyed it; I hope you did.'

'It was wonderful.'

'Any come-backs?'

She knew that he meant her husband. 'Richard's not around.'

'Good.'

She paused. 'He'll have to find out sometime . . . I mean, if it lasts.'

'Of course, of course . . . '

'I have to admit, I'm not looking forward to telling him, if that day comes.'

'You think he'll be violent?'

She hesitated. 'I don't know . . . it'll be a shock. I just don't know how he'll react.'

'Don't worry,' he reassured her. 'I'll be there for you. I won't let you do it alone.'

'I know you will.'

The conversation lapsed into a sort of self-conscious self-contemplation, before she asked, 'When can I see you next?'

'How about tonight?'

She sounded beautifully, wonderfully, genuinely distressed as she said, 'I'd really love to, but I've got a meeting with the accountant this evening, and that's likely to go on for hours. She's very thorough – not that that's going to help. She can be as thorough as she likes with our accounts, they're still a disaster area.'

'You can't put her off?'

She wanted to but she knew that she couldn't. 'I'm sorry.' Then, 'I'm free tomorrow night, though . . . '

Now, had the devil appeared one night to Andrew Sauerwine (perhaps when he was undressed and about to step into the shower) and then offered him the choice between another night with Maeve Gillespie (with eternal damnation thrown in) and an evening with Chief Superintendent Burr, the Chief Constable and (doubtless) their wives, there is little doubt that he would have chosen the pitchforks and the unpleasantness with burning oil, except for the fact he just had to be there . . .

'I'm sorry, Maeve, but I can't.'

'Oh.'

He felt as if he were being tortured. 'I really would love to . . . '

'When then?'

At least she sounded genuinely sorry. He suggested as the next best thing he could offer, 'The night after, then?'

She didn't speak for just a second but then said, 'You'll come early?'

'I'll come straight from work.'

'We can eat in. Taste my cooking – maybe you'll have second thoughts.'

'I sincerely doubt it.'

Maeve Gillespie put the phone down, felt torn by feelings of excitement and feelings of doom. Her excitement lingered on from her night with Sauerwine, at the prospect of seeing him again, this new and therefore wondrous thing, but the doom was an old companion, its lingering having lasted for years, its stale breath never now departing.

Was Andrew Sauerwine the thing that she had been seeking now for many years? Was he the key to the door to a passage out of her torment?

If so, what would Richard say or do? He was not a violent man, but he was passionate, if not about her, then doubly so about the farm; if her departure brought his world down, how would he react?

She was tired. Not only tired of how she had been forced to live for so long, but truly, profoundly exhausted. It was not just the exertions of last night, either. She had not slept well for a long time, her slumber punctuated, punctured even, by dreams of a surreal and disturbing aspect. She had never been a heavy sleeper but of late her bed had become a place of comfortless endurance, a part of a meaningless ritual. The dreams were not exactly nightmares but they were somehow disquieting and always barely remembered, leaving her waking state one of depression and vague dread. If it carried on too much longer she would, she resolved, visit the doctor, but not yet. She doubted whether the doctor could do anything anyway, except offer her cursory counselling and possibly pills; the former would be useless, the latter would be anathematical.

Was this what she had been dreading? The arrival of someone who would force her to a decision, bring down the house?

She took a breath of deep, cold air, ran her fingers through her hair. *Pull yourself together, Maeve. There are things to be done.*

She found it difficult to come to terms with the odd fact that the deeper into financial mire they sank the more people seemed to want forms from her and the longer those forms became. The bank wrote to them, it seemed, every week, the feed merchant at least twice a month and the second and third mortgage-holders on the farm had increased their frequency of written communication from yearly to monthly since they had missed payments ten weeks ago.

What did it matter if she pressed the nuclear button and divorced Richard? It would only precipitate something that was heading towards them with the relentlessness of a winged avenger. Bankruptcy would in many ways be a blessed relief, a release from her lightless prison. Freedom from Richard.

She regretted many things in her life but early marriage to Richard was way up there, top of the list, a crowning achievement, completely lacking in radiance, completely overwhelmed by vainglory. His land and her money had seemed in the early days to be the perfect marriage but the early days had been few in number and a long time ago. When she had first met him, Richard had appeared to be a charming, handsome man; a young farmer who had inherited his father's failing farm and who was determined to resurrect it. The romance had been rapid; 'whirlwind' was the word so beloved of romantic novelists but in Maeve's case the second part of their relationship had been when the whirlwind had started, when she had discovered, too late, that he wasn't interested in having a sexual partner, only a source of cash. The act of her discovery of the truth – she had caught him in flagrante with a gentleman he had picked up at the West of England Show – still caused her to burn with embarrassment and intense fury, a volatile mix; it had been a hard way to discover that love did not come into the reckoning of their relationship.

She lived in the farmhouse and took care of the business side, only helping out with the manual tasks at busy times such as harvest; he lived in a house on the edge of their land, two cottages knocked into one, and of his social life she knew nothing. Over this time they had learned to work together but in a cold and purely formal manner; a loveless marriage had become a loveless business partnership. They talked as colleagues, nothing more; when they argued it was over the accounting or the cost of something; they never found occasion to laugh when in each other's company.

She had found herself trapped, though. The foolishness of her youth had meant that she had signed everything over to the company that was the farm and in which they had equal shares. Divorce would mean she would lose everything. In the early days there had been a chance that she could at least recoup something, that she could take profit from her invest-ment, but the precipitous downturn in farming had ended that. In the space of one year meagre profit had turned into major deficit; since then they had been buried deeper and deeper in loss and debt.

It was only an added, though extremely bitter irony, that she had had to work so hard and in such isolation that until now there had been no chance of meeting someone to take her away from the hell in which she lived.

That was about to change, she was sure.

In unconscious imitation of his wife, Richard Gillespie also put the phone down, a smile of greedy satisfaction lingering long after it had any right to. He wouldn't make a lot out of this, but it would help. He reckoned he could count on a few hundred a month in cash and then there was the subcontracting work that was going to come his way. No longer would the Verner-Morrison estate bring in outsiders to work the land; it would be undertaken by Richard Gillespie. All the ploughing, drilling, spraying and harvesting, all the forestry, all the land maintenance.

All done by him – or through him – and all done at premium rates.

Premium rates plus.

He sighed, got up and went from the living room to the kitchen. He found a bottle of champagne, looked at it. It was old – he had bought it when Maeve had agreed to marry him but circumstances had prevented him from opening it. Circumstances had in fact prevented him for ten long years. It wasn't much of a life that had no cause for celebration in even a decade, he reflected bitterly.

Until now.

He had no champagne flutes, contented himself with a highball glass which he raised in a mock toast. He took the bottle and the glass back to the living room and sat down at the old photograph album.

This he gave another toast.

'Who were you talking to?'

Verner-Morrison had put the phone down hurriedly as soon as Cherie had come in, discovering yet again that there was no innocent way to do it.

'A business associate.'

She looked at him hard for just a moment longer than he found entirely comfortable. Then, 'They're here.'

'Good.' He left the room to greet his guests. Cherie lingered, went to the phone and retrieved the number of the last incoming call.

It had been withheld.

Mrs Christmas gave directions while Eisenmenger drove. He had not planned matters in quite this way and felt slightly baffled about it. He had intended that Mrs Christmas should give him directions to the Verner-Morrisons' house but her ability to describe how to reach it had proved non-existent; she had been completely without the ability to see in her head whether to turn left or right, whether he needed the second or the third turning off the roundabout, whether it would take him two minutes or two hours to get there.

'I'm terribly sorry. I get so confused. I usually walk, you see; take shortcuts.'

His fortitude had surprised him; somehow the aggravation she engendered was nullified by the dotty charm.

'I'm sure if you took me with you I could tell where it is . . . '

And reluctantly he had agreed.

It wasn't far to the turning off the road that led to the Verner-Morrisons' farm and within ten minutes they were parked in a lay-by. 'Whose house is that?' he asked, indicating the small cottage on the corner of the turning into the lane.

'Mr Sneddon's.'

'You mentioned him, didn't you? You clean for him?'

'That's right.'

'What does Mr Sneddon do?'

'He's the farm manager for the Verner-Morrisons.'

'He lives alone, does he?'

'That's right.'

It occurred to Eisenmenger that Mr Sneddon might well have a shrewd idea of what was happening on his employer's property. He got out of the car.

'What are you going to do?'

'First, talk to Mr Sneddon. Then I'm going to wander along the lane to the farmhouse.'

Mrs Christmas seemed to be perturbed by this plan of

204

campaign. 'Is that a good idea? I mean, Mr Verner-Morrison gets very cross with people who call during his parties.'

Eisenmenger smiled. 'I'm a stranger in the area. How am I supposed to know that?'

'Well, I won't come, if you don't mind.'

'Of course. You stay here.'

He was not surprised to discover that the small house was empty, assuming that Mr Sneddon was out, presumably hard at work farm managing. He looked through the windows and saw a relatively spartan interior; presumably easy money for Mrs Christmas.

The sound of his footsteps coming up the long lane that led towards the farm was loud in his ears and had the crisp ringing sound of cold winter's air. The gate to the farmyard was closed and it was decorated with a large sign on which were the words (in red) PRIVATE PROPERTY – NO ENTRY, but there was a small stile to its right which he climbed over. Once on the other side he looked around the farmyard.

Like Meckel he was immediately struck by its tidiness; it was a model farmyard, an idealized representation of one, a toy that had been built on a one-to-one scale. He saw the restored tractor in the centre and thought that he could so easily be looking upon a museum, a relic of a past that had never been.

He saw also the security lighting that so liberally adorned the buildings, the alarm boxes on the main farmhouse and three of the barns. Parked discreetly in one of those barns were two white minibuses. He began to stroll towards the yard, trying to look both casual and unobtrusive, a trick he had always found difficult. He got into the yard and stopped in front of the open barn. Behind the minibuses, largely hidden by darkness, he saw lighting equipment and big black boxes, similar to ones he had seen at rock concerts.

As he stood there the front door to the farmhouse opened and a tall man came out dressed in jeans and black polo-neck shirt; a baseball cap adorned his head and he held a clipboard. He stopped abruptly when he saw that there was a visitor, spun round and called something into the house. It wasn't long before a third actor entered the scene, this one a small, more rotund man; while the first stood where he was, this newcomer headed for Eisenmenger. He had a shotgun broken over his arm.

'Oi!'

Eisenmenger adopted an instant smile around which he moulded his features into an expression of befuddlement. The man approached him, striding across the washed bricks of the yard, gesticulating: that this was Mr Alec Verner-Morrison could not have been clearer to Eisenmenger.

'This is private property! Clear off!'

'Is it? I am sorry.'

'Didn't you see the sign?'

Eisenmenger looked behind him back towards the gate, the direction that Verner-Morrison was indicating. 'No.'

'Well, there's a bloody great sign there that tells people like you not to come in.'

People like me? Eisenmenger fought the urge to enquire what kind of person he was.

'My name's John Eisenmenger, Mr Verner-Morrison.'

'So?'

'I'm looking into the murders in the village.'

For the first time Eisenmenger saw a small break in the carapace of confident hostility.

'What's that got to do with me?'

'Your son was taught by Kenneth Gerard, I believe.'

'Who are you?'

It was an inevitable but unwelcome question. 'I'm working for Mr Gerard's defence.'

'Are you? Well, in that case you can piss off double quick-time. I'm not doing anything to help that bastard.'

'Even if he didn't do it?'

'He's an animal. I'd kill everyone like him if I had my way.'

'Nevertheless, he deserves to be punished only for what he's done, Mr Verner-Morrison.'

'Fuck him.' As punctuation he locked the gun into place, an act of deliberate menace. 'Go away.'

'I'd like to talk to Ben, if I may.'

'The police have talked to him already.'

'It would be most useful if I could . . . '

'Like I said, fuck him. And fuck you, if it comes to that. If you're not off my property in ten seconds, I'm going to aim this at you and fire it. The closer you are, the more damage I'll do.'

He brought the gun up; it was a double-barrelled shotgun and Eisenmenger had seen on many occasions how much damage could be done by one at close range. He kept the smile, though, as he said, 'And bring the police here? Would you really want that?'

'I don't care. Let them come.'

Eisenmenger nodded whilst wondering if ten seconds really meant ten seconds; he decided to get to the point. 'I think you're making hardcore pornography here, Mr Verner-Morrison. I think the last thing you'd like is a police investigation of a "shooting accident".'

'Bollocks.'

Rather worryingly, Eisenmenger didn't hear the slight falter in tone that he had been expecting; what distressed him even more was that the gun came up to his head. He thought seriously about turning and running as visions of some of the shredded faces and exploded heads he had autopsied came over the mental horizon.

Surely he wouldn't really do it?

'I have a companion in a parked car at the end of the lane; if she hears a shot or if I don't return in thirty minutes, she will phone the police.'

The gun remained where it was.

Oh, shit.

One last go.

'I want ten minutes with your son, Mr Verner-Morrison. I don't care about the filming equipment or the minibus for the actors and film crew; I don't care what you do in the slightest. I just want a brief chat with your son and then I'll be gone.'

He couldn't look at the gun any longer; if he were going to have his face turned into pizza he'd rather have his eyes closed, he decided.

'Alec!'

Eisenmenger opened his eyes to see the gun being lowered, a look of angry resignation on Verner-Morrison's face while behind him a small, blonde woman stood in the doorway of the farmhouse.

'Ten minutes,' he said sullenly. 'And no longer.'

In Burr's office – now the centre of the investigation when the enormity of the crime had come to be appreciated, when the press interest had exploded and the political connotations had spread like a virulent contagion throughout every move the police might make – Sauerwine, Beckwith and Meckel looked through the evidence that mounted against Kenneth Gerard and unanimously concluded that they had a case that was beyond refute. Sauerwine felt in his bones that he had the murderer in custody, that whatever his protestations Gerard was guilty.

Only the details bothered. The forensic psychologist was quite happy that Gerard might well have indulged in such sex games as had been participated in by (inflicted on?) the victims, yet the removal of the testes remained a problem.

Burr had read the report and, in a tiresome repetition of past behaviours, appeared to hold Sauerwine directly responsible for its contents.

'What the hell's he talking about?'

Sauerwine wasn't actually sure. 'Well . . . ' As luck would have it, his uncertainty was irrelevant because Burr didn't let him finish.

'I'd have thought it was bloody obvious why he took the knackers.' Burr seemed to have a problem with using the anatomically correct descriptor. 'Trophies.'

He glared at Sauerwine, mute challenge to enter combat. Sauerwine stepped gingerly into the ring. 'As far as I understand it, sir . . . ' He paused, perhaps in hope that he would again be saved the trouble of ending his sentence; the disappointment of an embarrassing silence forced him to continue, feeling that he was wandering aimlessly and only just in the general direction of the sentence's end. ' . . . the psychologist is saying that he doesn't believe that such behaviour fits Gerard's psychological profile.'

'Bollocks!'

No one laughed at this witticism.

'Of course he is,' continued Burr. 'Remember the Hospital Killings?' This last was addressed to Meckel who nodded. To Sauerwine he said, 'One of the porters was going about strangling nurses with urinary catheters and surgical clamps. Some wanker of a psychologist gave us a report thick enough to use as a diving board; said that the murderer was probably black, probably abused as a child and almost certainly had a history of minor sex crimes.'

Clearly expected to take in interest in this trawl through the archive Sauerwine enquired, 'And was he?'

Burr leaned forward. 'Sandra Swann was white, a virgin and as ugly as sin; she just had a problem with anyone prettier than her.'

Sauerwine took the point.

'All the same . . . ' Burr looked pensive. They all paused, wondering – fearing – what was coming. 'A confession would be nice . . . '

He looked at his inspector with something that the kind might have described as a smile, the cruel as a smirk.

Eisenmenger could not help but notice that he was being

shepherded by Mrs Verner-Morrison through the large house, presumably to keep him away from the more intriguing activities of the household; despite this, he saw enough to appreciate that his guess had been right and that Verner-Morrison's 'parties' were not, as Mrs Christmas had suggested, orgies, but carefully organized filming sessions. As they passed one room the door opened and out came a stunningly attractive young woman dressed in a short black robe that was only loosely tied; her head was completely shaved. She looked at Eisenmenger as he passed, her face betraying no interest at all. Behind her was a tall man who was stark naked. He was well muscled and had long hair. He also had an impressive erection upon which an expensive-looking camera was focused.

'Come on. This way.'

Feeling inadequate Eisenmenger hurried after her.

'You will be gentle with him, won't you? He's been terribly affected by this business.'

He assumed that she was talking about the murders although he couldn't help wondering what effect hardcore pornography was having on their son. They arrived at a large room at the rear of the house, which contained a huge plasma screen television. An adolescent boy sat cross-legged on the floor in front of this, his attention rapt on images of dark corridors and flashing lights; as they watched there was an ear-splitting howl and a mechanoid monster jumped out of the shadows, dripping blood from its mouth. The loud explosion that destroyed it (completing it with gobbets of crimson flesh flying in all directions) made Eisenmenger jump, although no one else reacted.

'Ben?'

No reaction. On the screen the walls of the corridor moved past them as if they were walking down it.

'Ben? Ben?'

With a sigh the screen froze just as a giant arachnoid thing began to be discernible scuttling towards them. Without looking round, 'What is it?'

'There's someone here who'd like a word with you.'

At last he faced them and Eisenmenger saw a good-looking young man behind an expression of boredom and rebellion. 'I don't want to see anyone.'

'But, Ben . . . '

He had turned away without even glancing at Eisenmenger. His mother looked at her guest and shrugged. 'I'm sorry, but what can I do?'

Ben was slumped forward, a portrait of abjection.

Eisenmenger said softly, 'Ben? I'm sorry to bother you. My name's John Eisenmenger; I'm here because I'm trying to prove Kenneth Gerard innocent.'

To his mother's eyes the effect of these words on her son was nothing less than miraculous. He straightened up, looked around at Eisenmenger and asked, 'Really?' He now carried a look of hope.

Eisenmenger nodded and Ben looked at his mother. 'It's OK, Mum. I'll talk to him. You can go.'

Thus dismissed, Cherie Verner-Morrison returned to the film-set and her supporting role (which involved performing oral sex with two men at once). Despite the concentration required for the scene she couldn't stop wondering why her son had been so eager to talk to this newcomer.

Helena hated reunions because she believed that the dead past should not influence the present, that that which had gone before was a troublemaker best left to lie asleep and alone. She tore up letters that invited her back to school, back to university, back to that which had left her life; she tried to move ever forwards, preferring to stride always onwards rather than paddle in the pools of remembrance.

As she sat there in that poky room of the remand prison of the city, she could think only that she was now being forced to re-enter a dance that she no longer wished to dance. She, Sauerwine and Gerard were back in this gavotte, only Beckwith was missing, Meckel being a late replacement on the dance-card.

'Why did you do it, Gerard?'

Her client had taken another step on the journey from innocence to guilt, his progress marked by the omission of a title; the surname now was the order of the day.

'Do what?'

'Cut out their testicles.'

'I told you. I didn't.'

'Somebody else cut them out, then? You only abused them and murdered them? You had an accomplice?'

Helena interjected tiredly, exhausted by repetition, 'Can we forget these pathetic tricks, Inspector? My client has already told you that he didn't abuse or murder or castrate anyone.'

'I don't think it's a game, Miss Flemming. I'm sorry if you take what has happened lightly . . . '

'I don't. I consider the treatment of my client to be a matter of the very gravest importance, which is why your pathetic attempts at verbal trickery are beginning to annoy me.'

Sauerwine found himself stung by this; he wasn't used to having his interrogation technique criticized, in fact, he'd always been rather proud of it. He opted in the face of this negative critical reaction to select for a different strategy.

'What did you do with them, Gerard?'

'Do with what?'

'Their testicles. Mount them, burn them, keep them in a pickle jar?'

Gerard looked nauseated. 'I didn't do anything with them because I didn't do anything to those unfortunate young men.'

'The names are all over your computer, Gerard. Your conversations with them, your invitations to visit, your promises of a good time.'

'I don't know how that got there.'

'So it wasn't you?'

Gerard's skin might never recover, seemed to have been lost in grease and pallor, a dying thing covering an ailing man. He shook his head and his thin and lank hair barely moved. 'No.'

'So who was it? Who else has access to your computer?'

It was Sauerwine's trump, the card that beat all others and, as he had known, Gerard could only lay down his hand and capitulate. 'No one.'

Sauerwine nodded, grim but satisfied. 'No one,' he repeated. He looked at Meckel. 'You're a bright chap, Constable. Perhaps you can help.'

Meckel made a play of deep consideration. 'Mrs Christmas has a key,' he pointed out.

Sauerwine turned to his victim. 'Your housekeeper has a key. Perhaps it was her.'

Gerard watched him from eyes that were not so much bloodshot as a peculiarly luminous yet dark magenta. He managed a smile that was sadder than tears. 'I shouldn't think so.'

'No?' Sauerwine was astonished. 'Does anyone else have a key?'

Gerard's hesitation in shaking his head was heartbreaking. 'No,' he whispered.

'Oh.' Sauerwine turned once more to Meckel. 'No one else has a key.'

'Perhaps someone broke in,' was the next inspired suggestion of said constable.

Sauerwine, by now established as the go-between, enquired, 'Had any burglaries recently?'

Gerard's eyes were wide and unblinking, seemingly held in an unbreakable grip by Sauerwine's not unhandsome features. 'No.'

'Oh. Oh, dear.'

He let the significance of this admission lie in front of them on the table, not visible to anyone but huge in all their minds.

After a long while he asked softly, 'So why did you castrate them, Gerard?'

And so the song cycle continued through the long and cold and dreary day.

Left alone, Eisenmenger sat on the floor next to Ben Verner-Morrison and tried to ignore the pain in his back and the protestations of his tendons. The young man eyed him warily. 'Are you telling the truth?'

'About helping Kenneth Gerard? Yes.'

'They all hate him.' He didn't specify whom he meant by this.

'He's a convicted paedophile, Ben.'

He shook his head vehemently. 'No.'

Eisenmenger didn't argue. Instead, 'I don't think he's a murderer, though.'

'He's not that, either.'

Eisenmenger could smell something in the breeze but ignored it for the moment. 'You never for one second got the impression that he might be in some way . . . violent, or sinister?'

'Never once. He was always kind and gentle; he was always ready to help. Nothing was too much trouble.'

Eisenmenger nodded in complete understanding. He said nothing for a moment while Ben looked down at the console in his hand.

'Your parents,' he said eventually. 'Does what they do bother you?'

Ben shook his head mutely.

'It's a big secret, though.'

This time a shrug. It had obviously been made clear to Ben that he was not to discuss it, unless he didn't really know what it was that they were doing . . . ?

'It's pathetic.' This quite unexpectedly.

Eisenmenger held his silence.

214

'They think they're so clever, fooling everyone. He's so proud because of all the money he makes under everyone's noses, but I think they're stupid. They're a joke. Them and their silly porno films.' He dropped the console into his lap and Eisenmenger saw how miserable and lonely this only son was. '*Cuntry Life*! Pathetic! God, they make me sick. I've got a tart for a mother and a pimp for a father.'

Eisenmenger felt as if he were paddling in someone else's grief; he found it unpleasant, almost slimy. 'How long have they been making them?'

'Two, three years. Saddoes.'

Eisenmenger left it a few seconds before his next question. 'Do you love Kenneth Gerard?'

The boy's head jerked up and round to him at that one. Suspecting a trick question he opened his mouth and, Eisenmenger could see, was about to issue a strong denial. Eisenmenger held up his hands. 'I won't tell your parents, Ben.'

It stopped him speaking but it wasn't enough to elicit admission. Eisenmenger said wistfully, 'Kenneth Gerard needs all the friends he can get, Ben. I'm sure it would mean a lot to him if I could tell him that you're thinking of him.'

At which Ben Verner-Morrison began to sob and Eisenmenger had to hold him and comfort him . . .

When he got back to the car Mrs Christmas asked him breathlessly, 'Well?'

Eisenmenger sat back and thought. 'Nothing that helps us much, I'm afraid.'

Mrs Christmas made a face. 'Shame,' she said.

'How's it going at your end?'

'Martin Bell's trial has been set for a fortnight Tuesday.'

'Any progress finding Kernohan?'

'My contact's away at the moment. I'm hoping to meet up with him the day after tomorrow. How about you?'

Eisenmenger was sitting by the window in his hotel room. The chair was considerably more comfortable than the mattress which, as the night approached, he found himself eyeing with some trepidation. 'Nothing concrete. Not much more than local colour, I'm afraid.' He thought it unwise to discuss Gerard's relationship with Ben Verner-Morrison – technically an offence – on the phone.

'I'm worried about Gerard. He's showing the strain.'

'Is he in solitary?'

'Oh, yes. But that doesn't stop all the intimidation.'

Eisenmenger could imagine.

'It's going to take time to crack this, Helena, and that's assuming I can do it at all.'

'I have faith in you.'

'That may not be enough.'

'Don't be so pessimistic. Haven't you got one of your famous feelings yet?'

Well, actually, he did. Or rather he had a feeling that he had a feeling. An intimation that there was something to be discovered here, perhaps something that he had already seen or heard or been told but that he had yet to recognize. He had no idea what it was or even if his impression was accurate, only that it might be there.

'Nothing I'd want to die in a ditch for.'

The conversation meandered on for ten minutes. When they parted he put down the phone and went down to dinner. Helena stayed where she was in her lounge and looked at the phone for a long time.

Eisenmenger spent the next day alone but only because Mrs Christmas was fully booked, first cleaning for William Sneddon, then attending the hairdresser for her weekly appointment; he had the feeling that had she been able to escape her commitments she would have applied herself to the role of Watson with singular tenacity. The bed had proved no less a thing of vindictiveness and spite and for much of the day he felt as if he were in a fugue state, semi-divorced from reality. He talked to Kenneth Gerard's neighbours in the morning and found many that refused to discuss the matter; those that did had, with startling perspicuity, suspected him all along of malevolence and nefariousness. In the village few people claimed to know him and those that did were of a similar mind. Just before lunch he wandered down to the river by Gerard's house and looked from the bank out to where the body had been hidden. No great revelation was bestowed upon him, no astounding ideas struck him and he considered that he had achieved little.

At something of a loose end in the afternoon, he decided to drive out to where the body of Clive Ewart had been found. He did this not because his expectations were great but because he was rapidly running out of places to go or people to talk to.

He parked the car in front of the slightly run-down farmhouse, got out and looked around. Through a gap between the house and a grain hopper he spotted a figure prone under some sort of agricultural machine and walked over to it. The machine was old and rusty and had a lot of metal spikes and sharp-looking circular blades at one end; to Eisenmenger it resembled an industrial-sized mincing machine.

'Mr Gillespie?'

The figure remained under the machine and the voice appeared to come out of its metallic heart. 'Who's asking?'

'My name's John Eisenmenger. I was wondering if I could talk to you about the body in the river. The one that washed ashore here.'

A short sharp clang followed. 'You a reporter?'

'No.'

Another clang. 'Police?'

'No.'

This time two more. 'Then why should I talk to you?'

Eisenmenger knew what was coming now. He said, 'I'm looking into the matter because Kenneth Gerard is my client.'

No more clangs. Just a moment's silence before the body wriggled out and Eisenmenger found himself staring down at the face of Richard Gillespie. 'You don't want me. I never found the body, my wife did. Ask her.'

'Did you know Kenneth Gerard?'

'Never met the man.'

Whether this was true or not Eisenmenger could not judge and he had to take Gillespie's word as truth. 'Where is she?'

Gillespie was already wriggling back under the mincing machine, presumably to resume the delicate repairs he was undertaking on it. 'In the house, I expect.'

The clanging recommenced, this time unbroken, and Eisenmenger walked away taking some comfort – not much – from the lack of overt hostility to his cause. He went to the front door of the farmhouse and rang the bell.

No answer.

He rang again, but again, no answer.

'Oh, well,' he said to himself and walked back to the car.

Richard Gillespie continued to knock seven bells out of whatever it was as he drove away.

In fact Eisenmenger missed Maeve Gillespie by only fifteen minutes; she had been shopping at the supermarket. Richard saw her arrive but failed to tell her that she had had a visitor. She didn't even acknowledge her husband, going straight inside with her bags of shopping.

Twenty minutes later, the shopping stowed, she sat in her office, strong black coffee in a mug before her, thoughts sluggish. She finished this, then made another but found that coffee, no matter how strong or in what volume, failed to inject energy into her thinking that morning. A particularly bad night, an especially deep despond, afflicted her. She couldn't think properly and was edgy and bad-tempered; she found it impossible to concentrate on her paperwork and even a walk with Bessie in the bracing, rain-laden morning wind failed to revivify her.

Where was the vet's bill? It was due today, she was sure, and he had been paid late the month before. Nor was he a forgiving gentleman, likely to cock a sympathetic ear to her tale of a disastrous potato price last year. With seven other accounts or bills due to be paid that week and funds for fewer than half that number she had to prioritize; she elected to appease the vet this month, perhaps to disappoint the next.

Except she could not find his invoice.

She had once been methodical (*you're just an obsessive bitch* had been her loving husband's pithy observation) with most paperwork correctly and neatly filed, and the little that showed tidily placed. Not now, though. Now she had not the heart to bother herself over such trivia; there were too many other problems besetting her to worry over misfilings and missed appointments.

Except when invoices that had to be paid went missing.

She could have rung the vet up and asked him how much he was owed but she didn't feel able to face his sour sarcasm and heavy-footed innuendo about her inability to pay. She tried to recall where and when she had last seen it.

It had been a week ago, she suddenly remembered. Richard had been incensed by it, unable to believe that it was accurate. 'He's trying to rook us. He knows we're having trouble and he's just trying it on. Using us to make up for his losses when someone's gone bust and not paid him.'

'That's rubbish. He might be hard but he's also fair; he's not a crook.'

'Isn't he? He tried to overcharge for penicillin last year.'

'That was an honest error.'

'Well, why don't I just take this and make absolutely sure that he hasn't made another "honest error"?'

And he had snatched the paper from her and walked out.

Relieved that she knew now where it was she went outside but her husband had vanished. Fifteen fruitless minutes of searching around the yard and then she went back inside and picked up the phone receiver. She received no answer when she dialled the number of his house. She proceeded to dial his mobile, but it was switched off.

'Great.'

She had an appointment in Rendcomb at the hairdresser's and she also desperately needed to get some more dog food for Bessie, special stuff that the vet had recommended; it would be an ideal opportunity to drop the cheque into the vet's practice, but only if she could find it.

This was typical of Richard. He disappeared for hours on end sometimes and she had never discovered where he went or why. She suspected but could not prove that he had a boyfriend somewhere, which was fine as far as she was concerned; what annoyed her was the fact that he didn't even tell her that he was going to disappear or for how long. She was fed up with having to apologize for his absences.

She often wondered whom it was that he was seeing. Some married man, perhaps, a respectable husband, indulging a secret fantasy with her husband. Lucky Richard.

It was with more than a tint of sourness that she regarded the irony that he had time and opportunity for pleasure while she, the woman he had duped, had none.

Until now.

Her smile was as sour as citrus.

Until now, perhaps.

Whatever the cause of his absence she wanted that invoice. It was most likely that he had just left it in the cab of the tractor or one of the cars, she decided.

She was wrong, she discovered, having spent twenty minutes searching through the sweet papers, diesel receipts, dried leaves and mud on the floor of first the tractor and then the Jeep, nominally hers; the other car – the Volvo – was gone, presumably because Richard had it. Bessie sat on the damp ground outside and looked at her expectantly, obviously thinking that it was time for a walk.

Unless he'd lost it completely – and that wouldn't have surprised her – it was either in the Volvo or at his house. She tried the phone again, once more without success.

Damn!

She thought about leaving it, but she couldn't. She wasn't going to give the vet the chance to lord it over her again. As she sat in the Jeep she tried to recall the amount, at least approximately. Was it three hundred and fifty pounds? Or two hundred and fifty?

Double damn!

Impulsively she opened the door of the Jeep, called Bessie to sit beside her, then turned the key in the ignition, put it into gear and drove away from the farmhouse down the narrow lane through muddy puddles. He'd be mad, she knew, if – when – he found out, but she couldn't help that. She needed that invoice and she needed it today and if he didn't like it, then he shouldn't be such a moron . . .

He lived a good three kilometres away, the river's ribbon snaking lazily on her right as she drove; only at the last did the road swerve away to the left and leave it behind her. Now she was driving gently with the boundary of her own land on her left while on her right was broken woodland that formed the outskirts of the Verner-Morrisons' land; this continued for five minutes or so before she arrived at her husband's house.

She had to admit that he had done a good job on it, but then he should have done, given the amount of money he had spent. When she had complained he had pointed out that it was an investment, that as a farm asset, the enlarged and renovated house would be very valuable.

She wondered how long it would be before they had to realize that asset.

The Volvo wasn't there.

The house fronted directly on the lane while behind it was a small paddock cordoned off from the rest of their land; direct access on to the farm could be obtained by a five-bar gate. There was no attempt at cultivation of any kind. One of the two original front doors had been bricked up, the other made taller and wider. Her knock produced no reply, as she had expected.

She looked around, decided to try phoning him one last time and for one last time was left defeated. She looked around again, feeling foolish. She had no key and no idea how she could get in; why had she bothered coming?

The chances that he had left a door or window unlocked were small but not zero, and this now seemed to be the only course of action left available. With Bessie at her heel she began to move around the house trying the lower storey windows without success; she moved around to the side and as she did so her attention was diverted by a car moving swiftly along the lane. Feeling inexplicably guilt-ridden she stopped and stared, even moved slightly in against the wall until it had passed. She couldn't see who had been driving. Before she turned back her eye was caught by smoke rising above the woods on the opposite side of the road. She knew that there was a cottage there but she had thought it derelict; the smoke rising in a thin plume suggested that it came from the chimney. Presumably it had been renovated, no doubt another money-making exercise by Alec Verner-Morrison; she reflected how unfair it was that he had so much money, she so little.

She resumed her patrol, arriving at the back door, finding to her surprise and delight that it was unlocked.

Idiot, she thought unkindly. *Anyone could walk in.*

She looked around, didn't see anyone.

Didn't see that she was observed from the shadow of the trees.

Justin's next message was concise. 'I'll be at Dizzie's Jazz Club in Montpelier at eight tonight. Meet you there.'

Helena fought the pleasure that this prospect brought.

The kitchen was a tip and was exactly as she had imagined it would be; it was a cliché of a room with unwashed plates, piles of opened and unopened mail, heaps of unironed clothing. There was dust on most of the surfaces and there was a fine layering of grease almost everywhere, one that became thicker as the cooker was approached.

She allowed the scene to feed her disdain for him.

Bessie was fascinated by this pot-pourri of odour and began to move excitedly around the room from nook to cranny to alcove to crevice. She decided that it was too dangerous to let the dog wander around the house, fearful that Bessie would knock something over or chew something; a reluctant Bessie was ordered back out. She wouldn't wander far.

The remainder of the ground floor was equally chaotic; her husband had clearly no love of the arts of the housewife. She looked from room to room on seas of disorder, lifting piles of magazines, DVDs, CDs, newspapers, gently moving scattered snack packets, wincing at crumb-covered furniture, acutely aware that the vacuum cleaner had enjoyed a long, quiet and peaceful life away from strenuous activity.

She couldn't see the invoice anywhere, not even on the dining-room table which had probably never been used as its manufacturer had once intended; now it was a resting place for circulars and offers of credit cards and, their inevitable consequence, unpaid credit card bills.

Where would he put it? Upstairs?

She was loath to trespass further into his sanctum but having come so far she would not be deterred at the last. She walked up the stairs quietly, listening for creaks as if she might awaken ghosts. Three bedrooms and a bathroom, one of the bedrooms no more than a box-room, used for storage; she saw there a rowing machine and a bike and boxes. The back bedroom was clearly unused and smelled faintly musty; the main room at the front was a surprise.

It was huge, for a start, and here she could see that he had given his imagination a degree of freedom it had been denied elsewhere within the house. The mirror behind the bed for one thing, fully two metres by two; the bed itself was king-sized and the linen on it of royal blue and silk. Opposite the bed was a large plasma screen underneath which were a DVD player, surround sound stereo system and video recorder. DVDs and videos were everywhere and all of them she discovered quickly (and not particularly to her surprise) were pornographic.

Hardcore.

The covers were enough to make her eyes water.

She looked at only the first few, dropped them hurriedly as if they were singeing her fingers and would have moved on had she not glanced down at the next one on the pile.

This one she grabbed as if it were precious metal. *An Everyday Story of Cuntry Fucks.*

In the foreground, arrayed on a blanket on a lawn, was a couple. The young lady was long-haired and full-bosomed; she lay on her back and had her mouth full and her eyes closed. Her friend (clearly a close friend) was tall and muscular and, she had to admit, handsome; hair tied back in a pony tail, he was on his knees and there was a smile on his rugged features as he searched for something in a place normally only a gynaecologist ventured. As arresting as this pose was, her attention was caught by the context. It was an open-air view, a walled garden, and the house to which it belonged was very familiar.

She stared for a long time at that photograph then began to search through the rest of the DVDs. It didn't take long to find another one that she found fascinating. This time it was an indoor scene depicted on the front, this one involving three 'actors'; they were all men, all naked and all apparently the best of friends. On his knees in the middle was someone she couldn't see very well, mainly because his face was buried in someone's groin, his lips and tongue clearly wrapped around a large and erect penis; the man with the pony tail was back, this time at the back, his hands on his companion's hips. She could see enough to make her clench her buttocks together involuntarily.

But she looked again because her memory told her faintly that she knew one of these actors . . .

The one in the middle . . . she was sure of it.

But from where?

She could not recall.

And anyway, she found their stage quite distracting. She knew that room; not well, but as well as anyone would know their neighbour's house. She looked through every DVD that was there, found another half-dozen with scenes on the front that she thought she recognized. She desperately wanted to view one of these films but didn't dare try to do so in Richard's house using equipment she didn't understand. Had it all been filmed there, or was it just the cover shot?

She decided to risk taking one from its box and secreting it in her pocket; she selected one that was apparently hetero-sexual and without obvious deviancy then decided that she had spent long enough in her husband's inner sanctum. She left hurriedly, came down the stairs and was on the point of walking out when her eye was caught by a piece of paper in the living room, tucked in beside the clock on the mantel-shelf. She plucked it out and found that she had succeeded in her mission for it was the vet's bill.

It was with a small smile on her face that she turned and walked out into the kitchen. She looked around one last time, her face expressing her disapproval at what she saw. Her back was to the door when it opened.

She spun round, expecting Richard and afraid of his reaction.

It was then that she felt her heart first freeze, then thud into action as the newcomer strode into the room, came right up to her. The face before her was smiling. The hand scythe was raised, but not for long.

Helena enjoyed the delicious tingling of guilt as she walked down the stairs of the basement jazz club. She was doing something that was forbidden, that she would not admit to anyone, that was a secret; everyone needed secrets, places to go that were unknown to others, that were especially unknown to those who were close. The closer the better.

She told herself afterwards that she intended nothing; it was merely a fantasy. Everyone had fantasies – they were a part of normal human existence – men especially. John, she was sure, had fantasies. In fact, come to think of it, she could describe the subject of those fantasies with perfect precision.

Beverley Wharton.

Tart.

Her image lived with Helena, etched there in perfect clarity, every damned curve and every come hither look.

He denied it, of course, but then he would, wouldn't he? She could tell that, whatever he said, he had always fancied the underwear off her and he still did. And there was the question of had he or hadn't he ever slept with her. It was not, she told herself fiercely, the fact that he might have slept with someone else, merely that he might have slept with *her*.

And she certainly wasn't intending to sleep with Justin.

All she wanted to do was enjoy a break from the norm, a chance to be with a rather gorgeous-looking man who clearly thought that she was worth a second, maybe a third, look.

The club was well soundproofed because she hadn't heard anything until she pushed the heavy black-painted door open and heard a saxophone solo suddenly loud and sexy around her. It was dark and full of yellows and deep oranges and shadows. Tables were arrayed before her, black and white photographs of people who she assumed were jazz greats peppered the deep ochre walls. It was smoky and warm and took her at once back to her student days when visits to clubs, bars or pubs had been everyday occurrences and when life had been something to enjoy.

She saw him quickly, standing in the corner, near the stage with his back to the small bar. She walked across the room, weaving a curving course between the tables. The club was about two thirds full, most of the faces turned to the small stage ahead of her. It was, she noted, a curiously motley crowd, all ages and all fashions, as many female as were male; not at all as she had imagined the audience at such a venue would be.

The saxophone ended and amidst the respectful applause Justin glanced round, saw her and smiled as he stood. 'Hello, Helena.'

She looked around to emphasize the point that there should have been a third party present. 'Where's Kernohan?'

'Coming presently. Drink? Vodka and orange?'

She nodded. The saxophone had left the stage and there was a lull filled by incomprehensible conversational babble; behind her she heard a couple arguing about bathroom fittings. When Justin returned they had settled on gold taps but little else.

'You're a jazz buff, are you?'

He shrugged. 'I guess you could say that.'

'Do you play?'

His reply was gilded by slyness. 'Yes . . . but not music.'

She ought to have ignored this pathetic pun but somehow the leer on his face was appealing and the twinkle in his eye was deliciously tempting. 'You're very, very naughty. Do you know that, Justin?'

The leer broadened. 'Oh, yes. I know that very well.'

She couldn't stop herself smiling and had to drop her head to hide a slight blush. She felt his eyes on her and sort of liked it that way.

His mobile rang; the ring tone was a cockerel. 'Sorry,' he said, although he neither looked nor sounded it. 'Yes?'

She watched him listen, saw the frown and the glance in her direction.

'Look, she's here with me now,' he said.

More listening.

'Barry, there's nothing to be frightened of.' He glanced at her again. She had caught the name, was listening with reinvigorated interest. 'I'm sure there'll be no harm in talking to her . . . '

He raised his eyebrows at her and she nodded.

' . . . She's saying, "Yes," Barry. You won't come to any harm. Just pop down to the club for an hour. No one will know.'

Yet more listening before, abruptly, he pulled the phone away from his ear and looked first at it, then at her. Waggling it in his fingers he said to Helena. 'Sorry. He's got cold feet.' He deposited it in his pocket.

She had guessed as much. His tone, she judged, was less than unhappy. 'Why?'

'Marty Bell has a reputation. In fact, in Barry Kernohan's case, the word around here is that it's more than just reputation.'

'Oh? And what is "the word around here"?'

He put folded arms down on the table behind his bottle of lager. 'That Martin Bell beat up Barry Kernohan for mouthing off.'

'So, does "the word around here" say what he was mouthing off about?'

'That Suzy Bell had an affair.'

'And did she?'

He shrugged. 'How the hell should I know?'

Which was reasonable. She sipped her vodka and he upended his bottle of lager. Contemplatively she asked, 'What shall we do now?'

'We could just have a good evening . . . ?'

'We could,' she said, 'except that we have to get to speak to Barry Kernohan.'

228

If he noted the use of that particular personal pronoun he kept it to himself. 'It's that important?'

'Very.'

He took another drink. 'You're a lawyer, right?'

'Yes.'

'So would I be right in saying that you're working for Martin Bell?'

'I'm his defence lawyer, yes.'

He said nothing but there was a look on his face that suggested he could have spoken at great length.

'Something wrong?'

'As I said, Bell had a reputation.'

'I think we've established that.'

'Bell was mean. He beat up on Suzy and he beat up on anyone who was in the wrong place at the wrong time. He made a lot of people very uncomfortable, made a lot of them very pissed off.'

She raised her eyebrows. 'What's that got to do with me?'

'I think you'll find there are a lot of local citizens who think that Martin Bell's right where he should be. You might have trouble finding people who have a good word to say for him.'

'Kernohan?'

'For one, yes.'

He stood up and without asking went to the bar. Whilst she considered what he had said she absent-mindedly watched him. The club was filling up and the atmosphere was becoming hotter and smokier. He had on tight white jeans allowing Helena to see that the well-defined musculature was not confined to his chest.

God, I bet he's fantastic with his clothes off.

As though a freak telepathic line had opened up between them he turned at that moment as he waited to be served and smiled at her.

Where, she wondered, was this going?

It was quite obvious what he wanted out of it, but what

about her? Should she even be here? Was she solely searching for a witness who might throw light on the murder of Suzanne Bell? Or was she also seeking something else?

Was she really so dissatisfied with John? Life with him could hardly be described as boring, but then again he was no Apollonian figure of bronzed manhood either. It wasn't that she felt sick when he took off his clothes – far from it – and she had yet to insist that they make love in the dark, but he did not *exude* sex.

That was it. He exuded many things – charm, intellect, kindness, honesty – but not sex. He was good at lovemaking but she did not look at him and think that the next bang would be the big one.

Whereas Justin.

She felt aroused every time he touched her . . .

But she didn't want to sleep with him. She was quite firm on that. Definitely not . . .

'My, you look serious.' As the whispered words came into her right ear she smelt for the first time that he was wearing a strong yet sweet scent, something that was casually expensive. She looked around at him as he leaned across to put her drink on the table in front of her; she could see the right side of his chest under his shirt, could see that the skin was smooth and bronzed.

'Not really. Just trying to figure out how to entice Mr Kernohan to help.'

He sat down, drying his hands on his trousers. 'Money might help.'

'Might it?'

He nodded, took a sip of lager. 'When I was putting out feelers for him, I caught a whisper that he owes for a car. Owes quite a lot, and we're not talking about a main dealer. The guys who sold him the car won't be going through the courts to get their cash.'

'How much?'

'I don't know. I could find out, though.'

She couldn't see that it would do any harm. 'OK.'

'Fine.' He leaned forward. 'That's business done with for the moment; now let's enjoy ourselves.'

She raised her eyebrows. 'What *can* you mean?'

Four musicians were making their way on the stage. He flicked his hand towards them with a lazy grin. 'Listen to the music.'

Richard Gillespie drove back to his house long after night had fallen, slightly drunk, probably over the limit. He no longer cared. He had been celebrating his first piece of good fortune for a long time; why shouldn't he get pissed? Tomorrow he would begin to cash in, make up for lost time and lost money.

The presence of his Jeep outside the front door surprised him, even alarmed him. His wife had rarely visited him in the all the years of their separation and he had grown accustomed to this solitude; his space had become private, he had become a single man in all but name. She had no business to visit him uninvited.

He got out of his car and went up to the car, finding it open but this did not surprise him. He smelled dog. He pulled his head out of the car and then looked around.

He suspected that he'd left the back door open. *She'd better not have gone in the house.*

A rising feeling of ire propelled him around the side of the house. He was right, the back door *was* open.

'Maeve! Maeve!'

He stood in the doorway but there was no answer.

His right hand reached out for the light switch, found it, then found that it didn't work.

'Bugger,' he murmured. He wanted to go to bed, not fart around replacing light bulbs. He stepped inside, closed the door behind him, found himself leaning suddenly against it.

'Oops,' he said to himself.

He pushed off, feeling fairly confident that he knew his way around even when slightly drunk and in the dark.

Unexpectedly he collided with something on the floor. It was heavy and metallic and it made him stumble and then fall heavily to his hands and knees, a loud noise of clanking his only companion.

'Bugger,' he said again, this time wincing. How had that got there? He reached out and discovered that it was the coal scuttle. He didn't understand. He certainly hadn't put it there . . .

Then the person who *had* put it there hit him very hard and he collapsed into unconsciousness.

Sauerwine returned from his date with the hierarchy of the constabulary profoundly melancholic. It was worse than he had feared – not only had Burr somehow managed to acquire the praise and reward for Gerard's arrest for himself, he had also completely overlooked that he had had any help. To hear him talk – and Sauerwine had heard him talking a great deal in the past three hours – he had guided 'his team' with consummate skill, had foreseen every discovery, advised the chaps every time they seemed to be going wrong, supervised with textbook leadership, strategic skill, diplomacy and strength; he had even had the infernal cheek to suggest that Sauerwine had not thought Girdlestone was the guilty man, had only seen the true and righteous path when Burr had talked him through the gigantic stock of evidence against him.

Sauerwine had had to stand there, glass of cheap and near-undrinkable red plonk in his hand, and allow this travesty of truth to be related before him, the Assistant Chief Constable apparently lapping it up, slapping Burr on the arm in a comradely, probably Masonly, manner, laughing uproariously at all the pathetic jokes.

No, it had not been a good night.

232

It was nearly midnight, but he desperately wanted to be cheered up.

He was destined for disappointment.

He rang Maeve's number which was not answered. Rang her mobile, which was switched off. Rang the house again, still without provoking reply.

Where the hell was she?

She hadn't said that she was going out, had she? He had imagined that she was going to be at home, but perhaps he had been mistaken.

Yes, that was it. He had been mistaken; she was out.

He wondered where and with whom, though.

And this peculiarly irrational paranoia – that perhaps she was two-timing him – began to grow within him as he lay that night in bed. He knew how illogical it was but that didn't matter.

Eisenmenger returned to talk to Maeve Gillespie early the following morning, finding neither Richard nor Maeve there; he did, however, come across Inspector Andrew Sauerwine who arrived shortly after he did. The two men greeted each other warily outside the front door to the farmhouse.

'Good morning, Inspector.'

'Doctor.'

'If you're looking for either of the Gillespies, I'm afraid you're out of luck.'

Sauerwine frowned. 'Oh?'

'Richard Gillespie was here yesterday afternoon but now neither of them seems to be around.'

'You came round yesterday?'

'That's right.'

'And Mrs Gillespie wasn't around then either?'

'No.' Eisenmenger caught concern in Sauerwine's reaction. 'Problem?'

But he received no reply. Sauerwine asked, 'Is there another way in?'

Eisenmenger didn't know and so they walked around the outside of the house. At the rear was a small enclosed yard with high brick walls in which was set a tall wooden gate. Inside the yard were dustbins, two rusting bicycles, piles of flowerpots and empty fertilizer sacks in an untidy pile weighed down with a brick. There was a door into the farmhouse that Sauerwine discovered was unlocked. He didn't hesitate, walking straight in and calling out, 'Mrs Gillespie? Maeve?'

Behind him Eisenmenger watched Sauerwine's demeanour and heard his use of the first name; being ignorant of the dysfunctional nature of the Gillespies' marriage, this surprised him but he said nothing. Clearly, though, this was more than a policeman looking to speak to a witness.

The kitchen sported unwashed dishes and mugs in the sink, a dishwasher that was empty, a range cooker. The top of the cooker was devoid of pots or pans. Sauerwine looked around briefly and was immediately gone into the room beyond; it was idle curiosity that made Eisenmenger look into the top oven.

'Inspector?'

Sauerwine returned to find Eisenmenger looking surprisingly domesticated, for his hands were clad in oven gloves and he was carrying a glass casserole dish. He put this down on the surface by the cooker, took the lid off. What was inside was akin to dark brown slurry.

'A trifle overcooked, I think,' commented Eisenmenger.

Sauerwine closed his eyes.

Justin had left a message on the answerphone.

Barry Kernohan apparently owed nine hundred and fifty pounds; he would agree to meet and talk to Helena for half of this sum.

Aware that it was highly likely that this would prove to be money wasted, that even if Kernohan's information proved

234

useful she would never be repaid, Helena decided to accept the offer.

'I want this treated as a crime scene.'

'But, sir . . . '

'What?'

The interrogative was as good as a sign on the map written in blood – *Here Be Dragons* – but Beckwith felt that he had procedure on his side. 'She hasn't been missing for very long.'

'Your point, Sergeant?'

'It would be unusual . . . '

'I don't care. I have reason to believe that her disappearance might be suspicious. I want the farm treated as a crime scene and I want her husband found. He's not around and I don't know where he is. You get over here while I go to his place and see if he's there.'

Beckwith was an awkward and argumentative individual, made all the more annoying by his implacable cheerfulness and apparent lack of insight into the effect he had on others, but he could see the smoke signals drifting up on the proverbial horizon, and he needed no Horn, Big, Little or both, to translate.

'Rightio.'

Meckel was sitting next to Beckwith as he put down the phone.

'What's happening?'

'Maeve Gillespie's disappeared, possibly her husband as well. Sauerwine thinks the worst. Wants it treated as a crime until proven otherwise.'

Meckel, ever the loyal servant, accepted this at once. 'What do you want me to do? Arrange forensics?'

'Don't you think it's a bit odd?'

'What?'

Beckwith sighed inwardly at Meckel's innocence; outwardly

he adopted a patronizing and tired attitude. 'Within days of discovering that Rendcomb is home to a man who grooms, assaults and then kills underage boys, we also have this.'

'So?'

'So maybe they're connected.'

Meckel considered this. 'I don't see how.'

'You think it's likely that two sets of major crimes should occur in a small English hamlet at the same time?'

Meckel shrugged. 'They could do.'

Beckwith snorted disgust. 'Just ring forensics, eh?'

Meckel did so, but he didn't let Beckwith see his troubled countenance.

'Why are you so convinced that this is significant?'

Eisenmenger had watched Sauerwine as he phoned, seen the agitation, brewing for so long, come to a head. Sauerwine was tapping his mobile phone against his lip, staring at the blank computer screen. He didn't change his posture as he said, 'She hasn't been answering her phone since last night.'

Is that it? 'Was she in danger?'

Sauerwine still didn't react anatomically. 'I think she may have been.'

'Her husband?'

At last he looked at Eisenmenger. 'If he's gone missing as well, then yes, quite possibly.'

Eisenmenger considered this for a while. His eyes fell upon the empty dog basket. 'The dog's gone,' he commented.

Sauerwine barely heard him.

A car crunched to a halt outside. Sauerwine perked up hopefully and looked through the window; it was a large but battered four-by-four. Eisenmenger saw both interest and disappointment in Sauerwine; it wasn't Maeve Gillespie but perhaps it was news. Frowning, the inspector stood up and went out to meet this newcomer with Eisenmenger following.

A large man with a distressingly overgrown moustache had

clambered out and was looking around. Sauerwine's appearance before him made him stare curiously, a state of affairs that was ended by the production of a warrant card.

In lieu of the presence of the owner, Sauerwine enquired who he was and what he wanted.

It turned out that he was a vet and he wanted paying. Maeve Gillespie had said that she would give him a cheque for the amount owed the day before but no money had materialized and so he had come in person to seek it out.

Sauerwine heard these words and in his head the certainty crystallized into diamond-hard conviction that something was terribly wrong. For the first time, Eisenmenger, too, began to wonder.

Indicating the Jeep and the Volvo, Eisenmenger asked, 'Whose are those?'

Sauerwine's voice came from a face that was set. 'The Gillespies'.'

They got out of the car and looked around. A crow could be heard echoing in the distance, a maudlin sound, somehow full of foreboding. Sauerwine went to the cars, examining them both in turn; Eisenmenger could see his shoulders droop when he discovered that they were both unlocked. His brief perusal was unproductive of anything useful. They went to the front door, receiving no reply when they knocked; Sauerwine's anxiety increased.

'Round the back?' asked Eisenmenger.

They found the back door locked.

'What now?'

Sauerwine, his face grim, said, 'We break in.'

Eyebrows raised, Eisenmenger murmured, 'If you say so.'

Sauerwine wasn't interested in anyone else's opinion; he was clearly a driven man now. He said, 'You go round the house that way, I'll go this; look for an open window, even if it's on the upper floors.'

They met at the front door, without success. Sauerwine sighed, thought briefly, then bent down to pick up a stone from the path. Without warning he broke the glass in the panel beside the front door; having knocked out the shards that clung to the frame he reached inside to turn the lock.

'Just as well it wasn't double-locked,' said Eisenmenger as the door swung open. Stepping inside after Sauerwine he added, 'If Richard Gillespie's been having a kip we should be getting a visit from him in fairly short order.'

The silence, though, was proof that no one slept in that house.

It was both empty and ransacked. The living room had been turned upside down, bookshelves emptied, drawers pulled out and tipped over, the cushions ripped from the seats; the carpets had even been pulled up. The dining room had been similarly treated; when they went upstairs, the bedrooms had not been ignored. Indeed, particular attention had been paid to the main bedroom where the degree of disorder seemed to be especially frenetic. Completely baffled, Sauerwine stood in the middle of this mayhem while Eisenmenger poked around.

'What the hell's gone on here?'

'I'd suggest that you have another crime scene.'

'But what crime? Kidnapping? Burglary?'

'Both, perhaps.'

'If Richard Gillespie abducted his wife, who's turned over his house?'

'What makes you so certain that Gillespie's the guilty party?' Eisenmenger was looking curiously at Sauerwine from his position on the floor by the bed.

Sauerwine, clearly uncomfortable under this scrutiny, shrugged. 'I think it's more likely.'

'Well, I think we can assume that he wasn't guilty of all this.'

'Maybe Maeve came here looking for something . . . he interrupted her.'

'Such as what?'

Sauerwine didn't know. He said only, 'I don't know, but it must have been Maeve who did this . . . '

'Her or a third party.'

Sauerwine considered this in silence. Eisenmenger was looking through the DVD titles. 'There's a lot of porn going on around here.'

'What do you mean?'

Eisenmenger explained about Verner-Morrison's sideline.

'I must pay him a visit.'

'The point is,' said Eisenmenger, 'is it all relevant?'

'What to?'

'To the deaths of six teenage boys.'

Sauerwine couldn't believe what he heard. 'Are you joking? Of course it's not.'

Eisenmenger said nothing, a lack of protest that was apparently remarkably aggravating.

'This is a domestic . . . nothing more.'

Eisenmenger said only, 'Maybe . . . I just don't think it would be a good idea to exclude anything at the moment . . . '

'I can't see how this connects with anything. You're sadly deluded if you think that this is going to help your client.'

But Eisenmenger wasn't so sure. He had picked up a *Cuntry Life* DVD. The name rang a bell, as did the scene on the front; like Maeve Gillespie before him, he began to wonder.

Blackmail?

Had one, or both, of the Gillespies been blackmailing Verner-Morrison over his activities? If that were the case, though, why leave the DVD here? And was it a strong enough reason for blackmail?

Eisenmenger couldn't convince himself.

Something else, he thought.

They went downstairs, only the kitchen left to look in.

They were unprepared for what they found.

Blood everywhere, apparently centred on a spot near the

cooker. No body, just blood. They stood side by side and looked around the room, then at each other.

'Jesus.' Eisenmenger wasn't sure whether it was he or Sauerwine who said this.

After a long, long time, Sauerwine got out his mobile phone and contacted Beckwith, telling him that they now had another job for forensics.

'Have you heard the news?'

Mrs Christmas had sought him out. She was wearing the same heavy black woollen coat but today she sported a small round hat, also black. It wobbled slightly whenever she became animated. Mrs Munro came into the dining room.

'Good afternoon, Mrs Christmas. How are you today?' She produced this solicitous statement as she began to clear the remnants of Eisenmenger's luncheon from the table.

'Fine, thank you.'

They were polite but formal; even Eisenmenger – never the most insightful of social commentators – found his antennae being twitched. When they were again alone, Mrs Christmas leaned across to him. 'That woman's no better than she ought to be.'

Which statement left Eisenmenger's intellect reeling; he nodded to demonstrate a degree of comprehension but it was an understanding of the spirit rather than the letter of the utterance.

Said woman returned. 'More coffee?' she asked Eisenmenger whilst managing to ignore the Mrs Christmas-shaped hole in the vicinity. He declined. Left alone with the table cleared Eisenmenger was able to enquire which news in particular she had heard.

'About Mrs Gillespie! She's disappeared!'

How did it spread? Gossip in Rendcomb seemed to disseminate at faster than light velocities.

He said cautiously, 'I had heard a rumour.'

'And they say that her husband's missing, too. Do you think it's him? Is he the murderer?'

'I don't know.' Which was simple and true; he *didn't* know. Serial killers were supposed to be slaves to a pattern, unable to avoid repeating the mistakes of history, which meant that future actions could be predicted; thus was the art of the forensic psychologist born. With that as mantra, there was no way that the disappearance of Mrs Gillespie could be seen to be the work of the person who had previously despatched six under-age men. The police would surely see it as an unfortunate coincidence; after all they had the guilty party in remand prison, so unless he had tunnelled out from beneath the latrine bucket, it *had* to be completely unconnected.

He, however, had a different perspective. Starting from the premise that Kenneth Gerard was *not* the killer, it followed that there was still a serial killer at large. Anything like the disappearance of Maeve Gillespie was therefore potentially of great significance, even if it failed to fit the pattern of what had gone before; either that or there was not only a serial killer in the neighbourhood but also a wife-killer. Since few cities harboured more than one such killer at any one time, he found it difficult to swallow the possibility that Rendcomb did.

How, then, to explain the apparent change in modus operandi, perhaps modus vivendi?

Eisenmenger didn't know yet and was loath to spend too much time in possibly pointless speculation. Mrs Gillespie might yet turn up – perhaps she had been called away to a sick relative – and no one would have a problem any more. True, Sauerwine (clearly with knowledge that was hidden to Eisenmenger) feared the worst, but he had behind him huge resources; for the time being Eisenmenger would let others worry about Mrs Gillespie.

Mrs Christmas – exhibiting signs of disappointment that he was less than animated about Mrs Gillespie's disappearance –

abandoned this weapon and selected another from her armoury. 'Have you made any progress?'

Which presented him with a dilemma. Much as he found her delightful, he also found her strangely cloying. When he was with her he was forever possessed of the idea at the back of his head that he was again in the presence of his mother. Not that that was necessarily an awful thing, merely that he could not bring himself to react to her in a normal way.

Yet he knew that he needed her knowledge, if not her discourse.

He took a deepish breath and suggested that they go for a walk as he did not want to be overheard. Having put on his coat, they wandered down the small high street, out past Mrs Christmas's cottage and then on to the bridge. They leaned on the stone parapet and looked down into the unwelcoming grey waters moving turgidly beneath them (or at least Eisenmenger did, Mrs Christmas could really only see the wooded horizon ahead). It wasn't actually raining but there was drizzle in the air.

'I'm lost, Mrs Christmas. Something's going on, but I have no idea what. I know what the Verner-Morrisons are doing but I don't know if it's relevant to the six deaths; if Mr and Mrs Gillespie really have gone missing, then what are we to make of it? Is that in any way connected with the deaths?'

Mrs Christmas looked into his face, sympathy for his plight radiating out of the black wool of her coat. 'They always were a funny couple, the Gillespies.'

'In what way funny?'

'They weren't really married, not what I call married. My Ron would have said it was a "marriage of convenience".'

He assumed that Ron was Mr Christmas but didn't dare ask lest he be dragged down a meandering, one-way cul-de-sac. In any case what she was telling him was far too interesting. 'Let's walk along the towpath and you can tell me more.'

And so as they strolled slowly by the languidly flowing grey waters of the Ross, Eisenmenger learned of the old Gillespie farm that had been handed down to Richard in a state of near collapse, of the long and proud history of Gillespie farming in the area that had come close to its end.

It was at this point that Eisenmenger commented on the vast store of knowledge that Mrs Christmas possessed. 'How long did you say you've lived here, Mrs Christmas?'

'All my life.'

'Which is how long?'

'Longer than my teeth but not as long as my smile.' Mrs Christmas sounded like an excited schoolgirl and Eisenmenger could not help but grin.

'So Mr Christmas came from around here too?'

She nodded. 'Ron was an apprentice butcher. Very handsome, very "eligible", as they used to say. He was quite a catch.'

'And you caught him.'

'I did, didn't I?'

He would have left the subject then, had he been allowed.

'The first few years were wonderful,' she continued wistfully. 'I've never been so happy.'

As she faded slightly towards the end of this utterance, social etiquette condemned him to ask, 'It didn't last?'

'Oh, it lasted a fair time. Six years Ron was with me. Then he got blood poisoning.'

'I'm sorry.'

'It was an occupational hazard. He died quite quickly, really, despite the antibiotics.'

Eisenmenger felt awkward, as if he had blundered into a private meeting, perhaps a lovers' tryst. He kept a respectful silence until she added more brightly, 'Still, he left me with a baby boy.'

He seized this line of optimism. 'Really . . . ?'

She nodded. 'Until I lost him, too.'

He now felt doubly crushed, even more unable to comment. He was rescued by Mrs Christmas. 'Where were we?'

Admiring her resilience he replied, 'You were telling me about the Gillespies.'

'Oh, yes. Well, most of us thought that Richard's choice of wife was most inappropriate. Maeve was a girl who he'd met in London – no one knew where or how. She was very personable – knew which knife to use and how to write a letter – but it was obvious to everyone that she and Richard had very little in common. He was a pleasant young man but a *farmer*. He didn't have many of the social graces, whereas she seemed to have too many, if anything. Also she was far brighter than Richard; if there's one thing my parents taught me, it was not to marry a man who's more stupid than you are.'

These sepia-tinged observations seemed to come from far back in the past, an alien world unexplored by Eisenmenger. He was lulled into soft nostalgia.

'Anyway, he's gay.'

Had any other person in the entire universe produced these three words he would have assumed that they were just repeating gossip.

This, though, was Mrs Christmas.

He stared at her, and she stared back.

'Gay?'

Her nod was solemn, which left him to digest this concept.

'But he married her, anyway,' he pointed out

'He did. Everyone smiled and made the best of it, of course. It was quite a happy day, as I remember it, but it wasn't long before it became obvious that things weren't going too well.'

Which he could well understand.

'Such as?'

'Little things, I recall. She lost her sparkle. He made comments in the pub. That kind of thing.'

He prompted her. 'Yet they're still married.'

She smiled slyly. 'And living in separate houses.'

He joined her in the smile. 'There is that.'

She commented mysteriously, 'There's more to marriage than love.'

He raised his eyebrows and she enjoyed her advantage for a moment before explaining, 'Young Maeve brought money with her. Lots of it.'

She said this in a knowing way, not quite winking at him but very nearly. He nodded slowly, then commented, 'As you say, "a marriage of convenience".'

She was pleased that he understood.

They walked on, now quite deep into the woodland. The path had levelled out and turned to the right, then again to the left. 'It's been like that for a long time. Of course, the irony is that the farm's still not doing well, despite all Maeve's money.'

'But they remain together.'

She shrugged. 'Until now, perhaps.'

Before he could say anything she added, 'Maybe she had a life assurance policy.'

Eisenmenger lay in bed unable to sleep, not because it was possibly the least comfortable resting-place since Prometheus had been chained to his rock, but because he was making no progress in the case. He was discovering all sorts of interesting titbits – pieces of history, fragments of gossip, fascinating facts – about all sorts of local inhabitants, but he was most definitely not discovering who had really murdered six, possibly seven or even eight, people.

Did it matter if Alec and Cherie Verner-Morrison made hardcore pornographic films in their farmhouse? Who cared if the Gillespies had a sham marriage and lived apart? Was it significant if Richard Gillespie had had a taste for pornography, for sexual fantasies? It certainly didn't matter if they were heterosexual but the DVDs in his room had been of a varied and exotic character, and they had included sadistic homosexual ones.

Something mattered.

'You again?

Eisenmenger smiled. 'Me again.'

'What now?'

The rain that had held off for a while was starting to fall once more and Eisenmenger suggested, 'How about letting me in?'

Verner-Morrison didn't look as if he wanted to but Cherie popped up behind him and said, 'Come on, Alec. Let the poor man in. He's freezing.'

She practically shoved her husband out of the way. 'Come in, dear.'

Eisenmenger entered, murmuring, 'Thank you.'

Cherie Verner-Morrison was dressed a little more demurely than the last time Eisenmenger had seen her. She took his coat while her loving hubby looked on sourly. 'I don't know what you said to Ben, Mr Eisenmenger, but he certainly cheered up after your chat.'

'That's good, Mrs Verner-Morrison. He's a very pleasant young man.'

'Cherie, please.' Her husband snorted, which they both failed to hear. 'Come through.'

She ushered him into the lounge, bade him sit. 'Drink?'

He was about to refuse but she went on, 'I'm having champagne. Would you like some?'

It seemed churlish to refuse and so she poured him a glass while Alec Verner-Morrison glowered at them. As she gave it to Eisenmenger she whispered not unloudly, 'He can't have any. Doctor's forbidden him.'

She seemed to find this inordinately amusing.

Eisenmenger sipped his champagne.

'What's this about?' Verner-Morrison had leaned forward.

'A lot of people have died around here.'

'I've already talked to the police about that.'

'Did they show you their photographs?'

'Yes.' Verner-Morrison was ostentatiously bored.

'And you didn't recognize any of them?'

'Nope.'

'It's not possible that they were . . . actors?'

Verner-Morrison seemed to take exception to the emphasis Eisenmenger placed on the word. 'No.'

Eisenmenger turned to Cherie. 'Are you certain, too?'

She nodded. 'I tend to get to know the actors we use quite well.' She giggled and Verner-Morrison scowled.

It was good champagne.

'Is that all?'

'Do you have a lot to do with Richard Gillespie?'

'Not really. Why?'

'He's disappeared. So's his wife.'

Verner-Morrison laughed. 'Ha! Surely not together?'

He was scolded at once. 'Alec!'

'What?' Verner-Morrison was all innocence. 'Everyone knows what's been going on. The farm's nearly bankrupt, they can't stand each other . . . '

'It might be serious.'

If Verner-Morrison was concerned, he hid it with a shrug. 'Well, he hasn't turned up here, if that's what you mean.'

Cherie cast a glance at Eisenmenger as if to apologize for her husband. He suggested to her, 'Tell me about the porn business.'

He had tried to make it sound conversational, an idle enquiry much as he might have asked about the bathroom fittings, but clearly his attempt at subterfuge and subtlety fooled no one. Verner-Morrison had had enough. He stood up. 'No more. You've interfered enough.'

'I think – '

'What Girdlestone – whatever his name is – got up to had nothing whatsoever to do with us. I mind my business, I expect you to mind yours. Got it?'

'But – '

'No "buts". The last time you came, I took a shotgun to you. You were lucky then, don't risk it.'

Eisenmenger was about to indulge in a bit more arguing but Cherie shook her head silently at him and he decided to let discretion overrule valour. He drained the champagne from the glass, stood up and with a smile at his hostess said, 'Thank you for your hospitality.'

He ignored his host.

She showed him out and in the hall she said, 'I'm sorry about Alec. He's a bit touchy these days. Pressure of work . . .'

From which Eisenmenger presumed that the porn business was a fairly competitive arena. She opened the door and said in a low tone, 'If you think it's important, I'll talk to you later. Alec's taking last week's rushes to be edited in London. Why don't you come at three? We can chat then.'

The call from Burr came much as death might come – wholly expected in the course of things, yet wholly unwelcome. Sauerwine had enough to worry about without the added pressure of Burr's demands. It was now well over twenty-four hours since Maeve Gillespie had last been heard from and the knowledge that he had at least been justified in initiating a missing person enquiry sooner rather than later was scant comfort. He had a feeling of dread deep within him and not all of it was due to his fear of Burr's anger.

'What the bloody hell's going on in Rendcomb now?'

He had not been bade to sit, a bad sign. Burr was leaning forward – had rolled forward might have been a more apposite description – and his face was red and glowering.

'The Gillespies have disappeared, sir.'

'Disappeared? What do you mean, "disappeared"? "Disappeared" as in "been disappeared", like they do in Latin American and Middle Eastern countries?'

'I don't know, sir, but Maeve Gillespie did not turn up for

an appointment yesterday evening and she has not been seen at the farm for over twenty-four hours. Her husband, Richard, is also missing.'

'Perhaps they've gone away together. A spur of the moment decision . . . '

'They were estranged, sir. Relations were not good.'

'Even so . . . '

'And we found spilled blood in Richard Gillespie's house. A lot of it.'

'Whose blood?'

'We don't know yet.'

Burr considered this. 'Theories?' he asked.

'I have reason to believe that Richard Gillespie may have killed his wife, sir.'

Burr stared at him and Sauerwine found this scrutiny uncomfortable; Burr didn't exactly have gimlet eyes, but he did have the facial apparatus to make his scrutiny uncomfortable to bear. He also, as it turned out, had a worryingly perceptive take on the matter in hand.

'"Reason to believe"?' he asked. 'Tell me more.'

There was a certain arachnoid quality to this invitation.

'Well, sir, she led me to believe . . . '

Burr nodded. 'She made a statement . . . ?' This was half a question, half a conclusion, all of a tricky one to respond to.

'Not formally, sir.'

'I see. Carry on.'

'It's possible that her husband might have had reason to harm her.' He went on to explain the domestic arrangements that existed in the Gillespie household.

'And is this likely? That she would want to leave her husband?'

Sauerwine was finding that the more he explained, the harder Burr's questions became. He said as neutrally as he could, 'Yes, sir.'

Burr returned to staring. He licked his lips as if contemplating lunch. 'Would you mind telling me,' he invited slowly, 'why you initiated a missing person enquiry before the usual twenty-four-hour period? Before, indeed, you had evidence that a crime had been committed?'

Burr was no longer the corpulent and torpid demigod who lived above them; now he was a man who had not risen through the ranks merely by chance and the hydrodynamics of constabulary politics. The question was a good one and, as with most good questions, it was tricky to answer.

'I had a hunch, sir . . . '

Burr nodded slowly, not in agreement but in understanding. 'A hunch,' he repeated. He was good at repeating what people said to him, as if savouring it, trying it out for size, testing it. All the while he was still staring.

All in all, he stared for a goodly while.

Then, 'OK, you had a hunch, and maybe you were right. What have you done about it?'

'A search of the farmhouse has turned up nothing, sir. There's no indication of a struggle but there's no suggestion that she packed or anything like that; she doesn't appear to have planned to leave, at least not for any length of time. Richard Gillespie's own house appears to have been ransacked. Apart from the bloodstains, forensics have drawn a blank.'

'So what conclusions have you come to?'

'I think that Maeve Gillespie may have come to harm and that Richard Gillespie may be implicated.'

'And the fact that his house was ransacked?'

'Possibly a diversionary tactic, sir.'

'Or possibly evidence of a third party.'

'Yes, sir, but . . . ' He was forestalled by a wave of the hand. More contemplation.

'You seem very keen to implicate Richard Gillespie.'

Sauerwine didn't blush, didn't even smile; he managed an expression that suggested outrage (without being too theatrical) at any unspoken implications inherent in this suggestion. Nicely understated, it was, too. 'If not him, then who else?'

Burr nodded slowly at this quantum of wisdom. He said in a contemplative manner, 'And we all know the statistics about murderers being known to their victims.'

'Exactly.'

'And it's nothing to do with the Gerard business?'

Sauerwine's smile was born from absolute confidence. 'Nothing at all, sir.'

Despite Cherie Verner-Morrison's reassurances Eisenmenger was still nervous as he opened the gate to the farmyard and walked towards the front door. He was not, however, shot at or threatened and reached the porch unmolested, albeit experiencing a not inconsiderable degree of twitchiness.

He rang the doorbell and waited.

And waited.

He rang again but this time there was an answer at once . . .

. . . By Mrs Christmas.

'Oh!' she exclaimed. She was dressed in a housecoat and had a can of spray polish in her hand. From behind her Cherie came out to see who it was; in contrast, she was dressed in a bright red towelling robe. She was wet.

Eisenmenger, looking somewhere between Mrs Christmas and the somewhat distracting Cherie Verner-Morrison, said with a smile, 'Hello. Can I come in?'

Mrs Christmas, having overcome her surprise at finding him calling on the Verner-Morrisons, said hesitantly, 'Well . . . yes . . . I suppose so . . . '

Cherie came forward. 'Of course he can, Mrs C. Let the poor man in from the cold.'

She stood aside. On her face was an expression that flitted uncertainly between curiosity, understanding and speculation. There was a pause before Cherie said, 'Thank you, Mrs C. Please carry on . . . '

Taking the hint, Mrs Christmas nodded and walked away; he could see that she was desperate to know the reason for his visit.

Only when the door had closed behind the old lady did Cherie say to him, 'Sorry I didn't get the door. I was swimming and didn't hear the bell.'

'Is it convenient?'

She smiled. 'Oh, yes.'

She stood aside and he stepped into the hall.

'I'll take your coat.' She hung it on a hat stand behind the door, then stood and looked at him, hands on hips. She was standing beside her statue; Eisenmenger had the distinct impression that it was quite deliberate. 'What can I do for you?'

He smiled. 'You can tell me about the logistics of running a porn movie business.'

She raised her eyebrows and smiled. She wasn't unattractive; not young, but not unattractive. 'I can do that. There's no aspect of this business I can't give you the low-down on.'

He returned the smile. 'No. I don't suppose there is.' A sigh. 'However, much as I'd love a guided tour, Mrs Verner-Morrison, I'm trying to catch a murderer . . . '

A moment's hesitation, a sign and then she dropped her hands from her hips. 'Oh, well. You can't blame me for trying, can you?'

He shook his head. 'No, I can't, Mrs Verner-Morrison.' By way of compensation he added, 'Not that you have to try too hard.'

She laughed delightedly. 'Tease! But please, call me Cherie.'

'If you'll call me John.'

'Deal.' Then she turned and threw over her shoulder, 'Come on. The champagne calls!'

She led him through the lounge, through French doors to the indoor swimming pool. It was uncomfortably hot and humid, an unpleasant contrast with the rawness in the countryside around them. The view was of the edge of the farmyard, a row of low buildings that had presumably once been pigsties and, behind them, a low range of hills. They sat in wicker chairs around a low marble-topped table on which was an ice bucket replete with champagne.

'So what do you want to know?'

He had taken off his jumper but was still too hot. 'First I just want to make absolutely certain that you've never seen the victims before.'

He had with him a file from which he now took six photographs. She took them, scrutinized them carefully, then shook her head. 'No. Never. '

He believed her.

'There's no possibility that they could have been actors, perhaps minor ones, in the films you make here?'

She took a dainty swallow of champagne and crossed her legs. 'Absolutely not, sweetie. We rarely use more than five or six actors at any one time and a lot of those are regulars. You get to know them quite well.'

She didn't exactly wink but there was undoubtedly a tiny twitch of her left eyelid, one that Eisenmenger decided it would be prudent to ignore.

'Does your husband make the arrangements? The financing, the equipment, that kind of thing.'

'The equipment's all ours, dear. Alec keeps it in one of the barns. Makes more economic sense than hiring it every time.'

'What about signing up the actors?'

'Will does that. He engages the actors, arranges payment, arranges editing and generally acts as Alec's right-hand man on the set. Alec's in charge of distribution, that kind of thing. He's got a lot of contacts in Europe and the US.'

'And where does Sneddon hire from? Where does he get the actors?'

She shrugged. 'As I said, the main stars are regulars – we use them time and again – but as for the smaller parts, I really couldn't say. Drink up.'

She seemed to have a prodigious appetite for the stuff. Eisenmenger complied and was unable to prevent a refill appearing with astonishing rapidity.

'So Will Sneddon does more than manage the farm?'

Her smile was wide and knowing. 'Oh, yes. When we hired him, we quickly realized that he had other, more useful abilities.'

'So you originally took him on just as a farm manager?'

'That's right. We were fairly amateur in those days; nothing more than home movies, really.'

Eisenmenger was fascinated by these revelations. 'He was responsible for setting up this operation?'

'Well, I wouldn't put it quite like that. He discovered what we were up to . . . '

'How? How did he discover it?'

She was surprised by his interest. 'Well . . . I don't know. He must have seen one of the films, I suppose. We only had a limited distribution then. The films were just me and a bloke . . . or another girl . . . nothing more than Health and Efficiency stuff, really . . . and we just used to flog them on the Internet, no questions asked.'

Eisenmenger wondered about this; wondered why he was so interested in this even as he wondered what it all meant. That was the way with his brain; it did things and told him about them afterwards.

Cherie went on, 'Anyway, he came to Alec with a business proposal. Suggested that we should expand; bigger budget, more stars, regular filming schedule. Said he would supply the actors and take care of the local arrangements; even put us in touch with a few distribution contacts he had in Europe.'

'An unusual range of interests for a farm manager.'

She grinned slyly. 'I think he saw that there might be a few perks.'

'And are there?'

She sighed, sipped more champagne. 'I don't think he goes

254

without.' Then, 'Of course, he's actually quite a good farm manager as well.'

'Which presumably helps.'

She put down her glass. 'This is all Alec's dream. He wanted to have a farm but, of course, he knows absolutely nothing about farming, so he hired a farm manager. The first chap we had was rubbish so Alec sacked him, then we hired Will Sneddon. When Will came up with this wheeze Alec jumped at it. I think he was missing business, missing being able to order people around, be in control. This gives him something to do in life.'

'And presumably it gives you a little entertainment as well.'

'Now, now,' she said in a mock scolding tone as she waved her forefinger to and fro. Then she giggled. 'I've always been in this business. Alec first met me when I was doing a glamour shoot at the Berlin Motor Show. When we moved out here I was afraid that maybe I'd died and no one had told me. I used to check my pulse every morning, just to make certain I was still breathing.

'That was why we started making the movies in the first place. Alec had found that life as Farmer Giles wasn't quite what he had imagined and I wanted a little bit more excitement than waiting for the postman to leave a couple of bills.'

'Do you make a lot of money?'

She had her glass again and over the rim she looked at him and winked slowly. 'A little bit.'

A little bit as in shedloads.

He asked, 'So in between shoots, the equipment is put into store?'

'Under lock and key, yes.'

'So who has a key?'

'Alec does, I do and, of course, Will.'

'Can I see it?'

She was unsure. 'Is it important?'

'Probably not, but then who knows?' He paused. 'Please?'

He made this plea deliberately theatrical and she giggled. 'How can I refuse? But I'll have to get dressed first.'

She left him with more champagne and departed to dress, her own glass in hand. Eisenmenger was starting to feel distinctly light-headed; how did she manage to consume such prodigious quantities of the stuff? She must, he ruminated, have a liver like pâté de foie gras.

She returned in tight jeans and black cashmere jumper; they walked back through the lounge, then into the hallway where she put on a thick, white skiing jacket before they went outside.

The barn was set back from the others, its entrance turned away from the rest of the farmyard. She produced a key, which she put into the huge padlock that adorned the door, then pulled the door open. The widening shaft of light revealed a moderately sized huddle of cinematic equipment hiding against the far wall. There was a large camera, a sound boom, six arc lights and numerous black boxes. Eisenmenger walked forward and began to poke around amongst it all. Cherie stood just inside the barn to one side and looked bored as only a woman can.

'What's in the boxes?'

'Sound equipment mostly. Some other bits and bobs.'

As he poked around the paraphernalia he asked, 'Who does the filming?'

'Chap from London. Used to work in commercials.'

'Only one camera?'

'Usually, although we do have two.'

He looked around at her. 'There's only one here.'

'No, there isn't.' She came forward, peering around him. He watched her face form a frown. 'Where is it?' she said as much to herself as to him.

'What's going on here?' The voice was loud and challenging and it startled them both. They turned to see a silhouette in the doorway, one with a shotgun. After a moment's consternation Cherie breathed out and said, 'Will!'

The figure came forward. The gun wasn't pointing at them but there was something distinctly menacing in its orientation nonetheless. He only had eyes for Eisenmenger. Cherie said, 'John and I were just wondering where the second camera is.'

'Were you?' What was the matter with the man? He couldn't stop staring at Eisenmenger, even as he continued, 'It's being serviced.'

'Of course!' She turned to Eisenmenger and, presumably under the impression that he was hard of hearing, repeated, 'It's being serviced.'

'I should have guessed.'

Eisenmenger stepped forward, as much to stake out a bit of territory as for any other reason; he felt as if he were participating in some sort of anthropological exercise as he did so. Cherie didn't seem to notice that there was a distinct atmosphere of challenge and counter-challenge in the air as she said, 'I was explaining the intricacies of our little cottage industry.'

'Is that wise?'

'John's very discreet.' She swung round. 'Aren't you?'

This was slightly tricky as he had already shopped them to Sauerwine so he mustered as much insouciance as he could as he lied, 'Very.'

Sneddon didn't look convinced; looked rather as if he would quite like to use Eisenmenger as a large, soft and pink clay pigeon. 'Your husband wouldn't like you showing this stuff to a stranger.'

Cherie shrugged.

Sneddon was back with the staring at Eisenmenger who had the near-irresistible impulse to smile at him. In lieu of this he asked, 'Do you think I could have a word with you, Mr Sneddon?'

'Why?'

'About the six murders that occurred in Rendcomb.'

'What's that to do with me?'

257

'Nothing, I'm sure . . . '

'That was Girdlestone, the paedophile.'

'Well, I'm not so certain . . . '

'Are you saying it was me?'

Cherie stepped in. 'Don't be silly, Will.'

Eisenmenger explained, 'Not at all, Mr Sneddon.' He was watching the shotgun nervously. 'I don't know if you're aware, but Mr and Mrs Gillespie have disappeared.'

Sneddon eyed him suspiciously. 'Disappeared?'

'Apparently.'

He saw Sneddon working through this, trying to make sense of it. 'What's that to do with me?'

'Did he know about what went on here? The films, I mean?'

Sneddon was looking at Cherie; he seemed reluctant to answer. 'Not that I know of.'

'Are you sure?'

The gun twitched. 'I said so, didn't I?'

With which remark, as it was true, Eisenmenger could find no grounds for dispute.

Sneddon said, 'I think it's time you left.'

Cherie looked about to take issue with this but Eisenmenger forestalled her. 'Absolutely.' To Cherie he said, 'Mrs Verner-Morrison, I would like to thank you for your generous hospitality, but Mr Sneddon is entirely correct. I have out-stayed my welcome.'

'You don't have to leave. We could have more champagne . . . '

'I really must be going.'

He was already moving away. Sneddon stood to one side as he passed.

'All right, then.' Cherie sounded genuinely disappointed, almost sad, and Eisenmenger had a sudden sense of how lonely she was.

Mrs Christmas, in the middle of cleaning one of the spare bedrooms, looked on as he walked across the farmyard.

***

'Help me, Mrs Christmas.'

'Of course, dear.'

Mrs Christmas had just served tea and cake as they sat in her crowded sitting room, a fire burning in the grate. It was some hours after his visit to the Verner-Morrisons and he had met her in Rendcomb High Street; he might have been wrong but he had the distinct impression that she had sought him out, hunted him as prey with the single-mindedness of an assassin. The invitation to tea had been beyond his ability to resist.

'If we assume that Kenneth Gerard is innocent then there are certain fundamental questions that we have to answer.'

'If you say so.'

'All of the bodies were left on or around Kenneth Gerard's property.'

'Yes.' She had her mouth full of coffee and walnut, which meant that her concordance was signalled as much by vigorous nodding of her head as by the muffled vocalization.

'So, is that a coincidence?'

She swallowed the last of her mouthful. 'Is what a coincidence?'

'That the murderer chose to hide the bodies on the property of a man with a criminal record for paedophilia.'

Now she was sipping her tea from a bone china cup that sported overmuch gold gilt and floral patterning. 'It must have been, mustn't it? I mean, no one knew about poor Mr Girdlestone.'

On the face of it, Eisenmenger had to agree but, all the same, he wondered how easy it would be to find out such information. 'But suppose someone did, Mrs Christmas. How might they have found out?'

She seemed to be lost by this question, looking almost distressed by it. 'Well . . . I suppose someone might have stumbled across an old newspaper cutting, or perhaps someone's guest from London recognized him.'

Eisenmenger crunched a walnut. 'Possible,' he conceded.

Mrs Christmas seemed to think the matter settled. 'What next?' she asked.

'We have to explain the extremely incriminating data on Kenneth Gerard's computer.'

'Ah,' said Mrs Christmas perkily. 'I've been thinking about that.'

'And?'

'Mr Girdlestone . . . Gerard . . . was a great man for the Internet. He was always sitting at his computer, I recall.'

Eisenmenger reflected that this habit was rather more likely to incriminate than exonerate the maths tutor, but Mrs Christmas was unconscious of this rumination as she continued, 'Now, I understand that you can *download* from the Internet and that by doing so things are put into your computer.'

'Yes, they are, but . . . '

'So couldn't all those horrible things have been put there by someone else? Someone who wanted to make it seem as if Mr Gerard had been in contact with those poor boys?'

But Eisenmenger was shaking his head and smiling, hoping not to sound too patronizing as he explained, 'I'm afraid it doesn't quite work like that, Mrs Christmas.'

'Oh, dear. Really?'

'Even with all today's technology it would still require physical access to the computer to put that kind of data on the hard disk.'

'Oh.'

She seemed crushed, deflated, and Eisenmenger felt cruel. He tried to emoliate this by pointing out, 'It's quite good, actually.'

'Is it? Why?'

'Because if you'd been right, we'd have had several hundred million potential suspects; as it is, we've only got a few – anyone who could have gained physical access to that computer. As soon as we've discovered who that is, then we've got our guilty party.'

A second's consideration, then, 'Yes, I suppose we have,' she decided. She brightened noticeably.

'Now, the relevant time would be after the discovery of the first body but before Kenneth Girdlestone was arrested. Is it possible that anyone could have tampered with the computer during that time?'

'But why then? Why not before?'

'Because the e-mails were sent and received over a long period of time. The forensic scientists would be able to tell the difference if all of the incriminating data was put on at a single sitting.'

She didn't understand.

'The hard disk in Gerard's computer suggests that over a period of months he was in regular contact with all six of the dead adolescents. There are only two ways that that could be faked; the first is for someone to have broken in there to send and receive the e-mails, and that is impossible to believe. I just cannot conceive that Kenneth Gerard didn't notice that someone else was using his computer.

'The second is that someone swapped hard disks as soon as they realized that the game was up; they put their – incriminating – disk into Kenneth Gerard's computer and took his away. They could only have done that in the short window before he was taken away and his computer impounded.'

'Gosh!'

Eisenmenger said as much to himself as to her, 'The risk would have been that Gerard would have noticed – but the brilliant thing was that the incriminating files were deliberately wiped before the disks were swapped. Gerard wouldn't see them and to the police the act of removal would be guilt-ridden.'

She said tentatively, 'So somebody did something to Mr Gerard's computer just before he was arrested?'

'I think so. Did anyone call at the house that you know of?'

'I can't think of anyone. Of course, I wasn't there all the time.'

'But you can't think of anyone calling when you were?'

'No, I don't think so.'

'Are you positive? What about Mr or Mrs Verner-Morrison? One or both of them could have come to the house, surely? To discuss Ben's tuition.'

'I suppose they might, but I never saw them.'

'What about William Sneddon?'

'Never.'

'Richard Gillespie?'

She shook her head but stopped almost immediately. Eisenmenger watched her intently. 'Have you remembered something?'

'Now you come to mention it, yes.'

'What?'

'It was just before Mr Gerard was taken to the station . . . '

'And?'

'He'd gone out. I was cleaning and . . . Mr Gillespie came to the door. He said that he had some lamb for the freezer.'

'You let him in?'

'Oh, yes.'

'And left him alone?'

'Yes, but not for long.'

'How long?'

'I don't really know. I was cleaning the oven. I hate cleaning ovens. I do it just before Christmas and then on the Spring Bank Holiday. I don't want to do it, but I say to myself, "Jean Christmas, it's about time that the cooker had a good wash and brush-up, and if you don't do it, then nobody else will." So I put on my rubber gloves . . . '

'Let's try to work out how long it might have been.'

She was brought back to his reality. 'Yes, all right.'

'It can't take long to put a few cuts of meat in the freezer.'

She opened her mouth, then, 'He came out to the kitchen, asked me for a cup of tea.'

'Did he? Where exactly is the freezer?'

'It's in the utility room.'

'So were you aware of him in the utility room?'

'Not really. I had my head in the oven. Then he came into the kitchen and asked about a cup of tea. Said he was having a problem with his van. He left me for about five minutes, then came back in. He took the tea out and was gone for another five or six minutes.'

'So in total, he had maybe a quarter of an hour?'

'I suppose so. Would that be enough?'

Eisenmenger nodded. 'The beauty of the modern PC is the relative simplicity of its internal architecture and its modular construction. You don't need much computer know-how to replace a hard drive; four screws that hold the casing, four screws that hold the drive in place, three cables connected at the back. Someone sufficiently practised could do it in five, probably.'

She was amazed.

'You mean it was Richard Gillespie?'

He smiled. 'Could have been, Mrs Christmas, could have been. Don't forget you weren't here all the time, were you?'

'No . . .'

'So possibly someone else visited when you weren't here.'

'Wouldn't Mr Gerard know?'

'He might.' Another thought occurred to him. 'Was Kenneth Gerard in the habit of leaving the door unlocked? It seems to be a fairly common habit around here.'

She said cheerfully, 'Oh, yes. He was very absent-minded.'

Which wasn't what he wanted to hear.

He finished his tea.

Helena's mobile was switched off and there was no answer from the phone in the flat. He left a message and then sat at the table in the window of his room, a pile of documents in front of him; six folders, one for each of the victims, forensic reports on Gerard's computer, forensic reports on Gerard's house and garden, a psychological profile of Gerard, reports of Gerard's paedophile history. All this had arrived in one large parcel by courier from Helena; it had greatly excited Mrs Munro's curiosity but Eisenmenger, as was his way, had been non-committal which (human nature being human nature) had had the effect of arousing her interest even more.

Now, having eaten a dinner of roast pork, apple sauce, cauliflower cheese, roast potatoes, peas, carrots and crackling (the crackling had been good but a mistake, he now felt), he had retired to his room to consider what these documents had to offer. He had a bottle of Pouilly-Fumé by his side as he started on the file on Clive Ewart; he made notes in pencil on a pad of lined paper, enjoying the feel of the sharpness of the pencil's point as he wrote. As the evening wore on he would periodically sharpen the pencil, a ritualistic act of renewal.

For five hours he read and he wrote and all the time he worked things through in his head. At the end of this time he had been through every document twice, had written thirty pages of notes, had finished the wine and had begun drinking water. He looked at his watch and was not in the slightest bit surprised to see that it was two thirty in the morning.

And he still had no definite idea of what had really happened in Rendcomb.

He rather fancied some whisky and, since the bar was long since shut, he broke the rule of a lifetime and raided the minibar, trying not to think how much it was going to cost him. There was no ice but chilled water sufficed.

First principles.

Medical diagnosis rested on building up from first principles; if you didn't have the foggiest notion what the disease was, the only way to get anywhere near the truth was to return to the foundations, those things that you could observe or that you knew must be, then extrapolate from there.

The first assumption he had to make was that Kenneth Gerard was innocent. Making this assumption gave him a different perspective on the geography and chronology of all that had happened. It released him from the blinkers that the police wore.

If so, then he had to account for two pieces of evidence that incriminated Gerard – the computer files and the bodies in the well and in the river. Which meant that someone had deliberately tried to frame Kenneth Gerard. The purpose of the frame was not primarily to put Kenneth Gerard in prison, merely to make sure that no one looked for the right suspect. As soon as the body of Clive Ewart had been washed ashore the real killer had known that his safety depended on ensuring that Kenneth Gerard was convicted of the murder.

No.

He realized that he was guilty of sloppy thinking.

The killer had been far cleverer than that, far more foresighted. The bodies had been dumped around Kenneth Gerard's property for months before anyone knew that a crime had been committed. He had known all along who Kenneth Girdlestone really was and had thought to begin the deception perhaps from day one. It had been tampering with the computer that had been done between the discovery of the body and Gerard's arrest.

Yet even that suggested planning of the most meticulous and impressive kind. He had impersonated Gerard even as he groomed the victims; when the crimes had come to light he had swapped computer disks, and the frame had been complete.

Opportunity.

That then became the determinant. Anyone could have repeatedly dumped the bodies in the well or in the river, but the replacement of the drive required access to the house. That meant that either the house was broken into or it was someone who visited the house in the days between the discovery of Clive Ewart and Gerard's arrest. Someone who had a good knowledge of computers and how they worked.

He somehow doubted that Mrs Christmas was the guilty party.

It was imperative that Helena question Gerard about any visitors to the house in the days before his arrest. He made a note to that effect.

Where is she?

He thought to try ringing her again, decided that it would wait until morning.

There was someone that he knew from Mrs Christmas had visited the house.

Richard Gillespie, who had now disappeared, as had his wife.

Gillespie, who had an interest in pornography, who might well have known what was going on at the Verner-Morrsions' farm, who had threatened his wife. Something had happened at Gillespie's house, something involving the shedding of blood; if it was Maeve Gillespie's then the assumption would be that it was Richard Gillespie who had shed it.

Was it possible that here was yet another trick of misdirection? If Richard Gillespie never reappeared then perhaps those who believed that Gerard was innocent would be tempted to believe that the real perpetrator was Gillespie, that his wife had been silenced because she had discovered something incriminating.

So why didn't he believe that Gillespie was the real killer?

He tried to analyse his doubts. Firstly, did Gillespie have the computer know-how to pull off the trick with the hard disk? Somehow he doubted it; it wasn't that it was a technically difficult thing to do, just that few people knew just how easy it was. Richard Gillespie had not struck him as a man who spent hours hacking into secure sites or finding the cheats in computer games. Secondly, every instinct he had told him that in some way the deaths were linked to the Verner-Morrisons and Gillespie's involvement with them had been peripheral at best. A few odd jobs about the farm did not constitute anything more than a tenuous connection . . .

But it was possible that Gillespie had seen something. The DVDs in his house perhaps suggested that Gillespie had known exactly what was going on . . . what else did he know?

But this was not satisfactory either. The activities of the Verner-Morrisons were not a strong enough reason for blackmail. True, what they were doing was potentially illegal but not apparently linked directly to the six homosexual murders.

A new thought occurred to him.

Gillespie's house had been searched. Maybe the DVDs that had been left behind were irrelevant. Maybe Gillespie had died because of a DVD that was no longer there . . .

Shit!

Suddenly he knew he was right.

And his mind raced through possibilities, but one name kept coming up.

Will Sneddon.

Sneddon might well have the computer knowledge to pull off the switch of the hard disks. He was also intimately involved in the porn operation at the Verner-Morrisons.

. . . And there was the matter of the missing camera.

Was it possible that he was indulging in a little porn business of his own? Perhaps one involving underage boys?

Eisenmenger was desperately tired and knew that he had to sleep, even if it was on a mattress apparently filled with shrapnel and boulders. He had a quick shower, then crawled into bed, his head still full of questions. If anything there were now more.

What about the castrations?

How had Sneddon found out about Gerard's history?

If Sneddon were making his own films, where was he doing it?

He fell into a sleep shot through with images, the most memorable of which was one in which he was looking on in horror as Sneddon cut off his scrotum with a scalpel, his agony only adding to the pain of his asphyxiation as he struggled at the end of rope.

Eisenmenger sought out Mrs Christmas early the next morning but without success. He wanted to ask her about William Sneddon, about his house and about her knowledge of his computer skills. He had called Helena early and had had a long discussion about his theories, asking her to check with Gerard about visitors to his house just before he was arrested, in particular whether Sneddon had called on some pretext.

'I'm seeing him this afternoon. I'll get a list from him then.'

'Could you also ask him if Richard Gillespie was supplying him with lamb?'

'If you think that we need to know that.'

'It would help.'

'I will then.'

Eisenmenger sighed. 'Is everything all right?'

'Fine. Why?'

'You seem a bit . . . edgy.'

'No.'

'Fine.'

'What makes you say that?'

'Nothing . . . '

A pause ensued.

'How's Kenneth Gerard faring?'

'Not good, Not good at all.' She was still in bed, feeling somehow decadent.

'Well, tell him to keep his chin up. I think I can see light at the end of this.'

'Can you? I can't. As far as I can see you've got no idea how or why, just a vague idea of who.'

'If I'm right, the "why" follows fairly logically, and if you tell me that Gerard was visited by Sneddon just before he was arrested, then we not only have the "how", it confirms the whole hypothesis.'

That was typical of John Eisenmenger; he didn't 'theorize', he 'hypothesized'.

'It won't be enough to get my client off the hook.'

'No,' he agreed. 'But at least I'll know where to look for something a little more damning.'

'Be careful. If Sneddon assaulted, murdered and then castrated six young men, he's both very clever and very ruthless.'

'I don't intend to let him know that I'm especially interested in him.'

'So how will you find out more about him?'

He smiled confidently as he told her, 'I have a mole.'

She didn't understand but before she could ask he was off the subject. 'How are things going with the Bell case?'

Which question she found strangely worrying, not least because of the unwanted feeling of guilt that seeped into the world around her. 'Slowly.' She looked around the bedroom, feeling unwarrantably tired.

'Time's running out. Have you managed to find this Kernohan character?'

'I spent an entire night waiting in a jazz club for him to turn up. Apparently he's got cold feet because of Bell's reputation.'

'Why don't you – ?'

'It's all right. I'm on top of it.' She found his immediate assumption that she couldn't cope to be patronizing. She lay back in the bed and looked at the ceiling as she said, 'He's got debts. Ones with people who don't believe in going to law.'

'Bribery?'

'Enticement.'

'Is your information correct? I mean, he's not leading you on, is he?'

Her hand had gone to her breast or, more specifically, the scar; it kept going there, a scab to be picked at. The flesh beneath it was firmer than it ought to have been; her consultant had told her that it was just scarring but it felt so like the cancer she couldn't stop worrying. Her nipple was hard . . .

. . . She thought of last night.

'No. He's in trouble financially and I can offer him a lifeline. I've arranged another meeting tonight.'

She began stroking the skin of her abdomen. She suddenly realized what she was doing and panicked.

What the hell am I doing?

Eisenmenger had picked up the vibes and so it was with some trepidation that he asked, 'You're not meeting him alone, are you?'

'And if I am?'

He sighed. 'Helena, I'm only concerned for your welfare. I'm not trying to be oppressive.'

'So have a bit of confidence. Why do you always assume that I'm some sort of wilting wallflower, unable to look after myself?'

'I don't –'

'Yes, you do. There are times when I think you look on me as a child, someone to boss around and fret about.'

Since he did have a tendency to fret about her, he was momentarily constrained by veracity. 'Helena, please . . . '

'If you must know, I'll be there with Justin.'

Justin? It took him a moment to place the name.

'The bartender?'

'That's right. He's been acting as intermediary.'

He wasn't sure if this was all that reassuring but he was completely sure that to say anything would be . . . well, painful.

'Just take care, OK?'

She caught the tenderness. 'Of course I will.'

He tried to feel reassured.

And failed.

Eisenmenger called Ben Verner-Morrison using the number he had been given and arranged to meet him in his car in the road by William Sneddon's house in the late afternoon. Ben was prompt and got into Eisenmenger's car straight away.

'What's this about?'

'Tell me more about your parents' business.'

'What's to tell? They film people poking each other in various ways.'

'Is that all?'

Ben frowned. 'Isn't it enough?'

'All kinds of sex?'

'Anything and everything.'

'Children?'

'Except that.'

'You're positive?'

'Absolutely.'

'So how does it all work? Who writes the stories?'

Mockingly Ben replied, 'Dad does. Reckons himself at that sort of thing.'

'What about the equipment?'

'Sneddon does all that.'

'He procures the actors, doesn't he?'

Ben smirked. 'Procure?'

'Employ, then.'

'I guess so.'

'Do you know where he gets them from?'

But Ben didn't.

'Did Kenneth Girdlestone know what was going on?'

'No!' This was vehement.

'You didn't tell him?'

Ben looked at him sourly. 'Would you?'

Eisenmenger took the point. 'Did Richard Gillespie know?'

He picked up at once on Eisenmenger's use of the past tense. 'What do you mean, "did"?'

'Does, then.'

Rather coyly he admitted, 'I've seen him about the place. I don't know why.'

Eisenmenger considered what Ben had told him. Here was a hint of the answer, he was convinced. Not all of it, not even the core of it, but the grain around which the answer had grown, had solidified, had become a pearl.

'Are you any closer to proving that Kenneth didn't do it?'

Which was a question that was extremely tricky to answer; Eisenmenger didn't like lying and didn't like prevaricating; trouble was, he didn't like disappointing people either. 'I'm sure, Ben. I haven't found anything to make me think he's guilty.'

It was scant comfort.

Helena found herself feeling dizzy as she emerged from the bathroom.

What did it mean?

She took a deep breath. Stupid question. She knew exactly what it meant.

Trouble.

She had refused to allow it into her consciousness but now it was knocking too insistently, creating a cacophony that was unignorable.

Her periods had stopped.

They had warned her that this might happen, and yet their words had refused to ally themselves with her; they had remained outside her existence, these concepts of sterility. Even when she had been asked directly by the oncologist if she were planning a family, she had thought only of the present, of the *now*; her brain had failed to consider the hypothetical. Of course she had replied that she wasn't planning to have children – she wasn't. She was planning to get rid of her breast cancer, nothing more.

And she had thought that she had beaten it anyway.

Her periods had returned; not brilliantly, it had to be said, but certainly getting better, more regular, more reassuring.

And now this . . .

She could not escape feeling doubly cheated; to have given her the illusion of safety and then snatch it away was cruel.

The oncologist had told her to phone no matter what the problem. She decided to accept his offer.

As she punched in his number she wondered what she would tell John.

She wondered, too, if he would care.

He finally caught up with Mrs Christmas soon after lunch. She was walking over the bridge towards her house just after he had unsuccessfully called there.

'Mrs Christmas!'

She smiled. 'Hello, Doctor.'

He stood and waited for her to join him at the garden gate.

'I've been looking for you.'

She was delighted. 'Have you?'

'I have.'

'Is there news?'

He didn't exactly look around in a conspiratorial manner, but he did drop his voice. 'Not news, but I would like to talk to you about something.'

She looked delighted. 'Really? What?'

'Can we go inside? Perhaps a cup of tea?'

Of course they could have a cup of tea; within fifteen minutes his wish had been granted, and he was partaking, to boot, of Hobnob biscuits.

'What do you want to know?'

'Tell me about Mr Sneddon.'

She was momentarily nonplussed. 'Mr Sneddon?'

'Will Sneddon. Tell me about his house.'

She was hesitant. 'Well . . . what's there to say? It's usually very neat; I almost feel guilty taking his money but there's always the dust, isn't there? I wonder where the dust comes from? I read once in a magazine that it comes from outer space, but then I read somewhere else – or did I hear it on the radio? – that it all came from dead people, that every time I breathe in I'm actually breathing a few molecules of Aristotle . . . or was it Socrates? I don't mean I'm the only one breathing them in, everyone's – '

He had no choice but to interrupt.

'Does he have a computer?'

'Why, yes. It's in the back bedroom.'

'Does he use it a lot?'

She considered for a moment, sipping her tea and staring at the ashes of a fire in the grate. 'I really couldn't say. He's not usually there when I'm cleaning, you see.'

He nodded. Of course. In any case, the question was really irrelevant; he had to get to look at that computer, whether he spent twenty-three hours every day or only one hour every year on the thing.

'I need to get to see that computer, Mrs Christmas.'

'Why?'

'Because maybe it's the one that really talked those young men into coming to Rendcomb.'

Her eyes widened. 'Mr Sneddon?'

He nodded soberly.

'Not Mr Sneddon!'

He shrugged. 'I think he's the most likely.'

She stared at him silently. He felt as if he'd just told her that Santa Claus had been arrested for sexually assaulting one of his little helpers. Her head was shaking slowly and very slightly and not even another sip of tea was able to effect much of a recovery.

He asked, 'When are you next due to clean for him?'

She came to. 'Why, today!'

'Today?' He was surprised and pleased by this stroke of good fortune. Then, 'I thought you said you cleaned for him yesterday. Why so soon again?'

She seemed momentarily lost. 'He asked me specially . . . asked me to wash his curtains. Said they were filthy.'

Eisenmenger wondered what this might imply: bloodstains, perhaps? Whatever the reason for this somewhat unexpected occurrence he decided to take advantage of it. 'Mrs Christmas, I want to ask you a favour.'

Her eyes sparkled. 'You want me to let you look around Mr Sneddon's house!'

'I realize – '

'That would be a betrayal of trust,' she pointed out.

'I know it would, but – '

'It's probably illegal.'

'Probably – '

'How could I live with myself?'

'I don't know – '

'Of course I will!'

This sudden tack in the course of their conversation left him floundering as he was knocked out by the boom swinging around. She went on, 'If he's the murderer, then we have no choice, do we? Who else is going to try to prove Mr Girdlestone's innocence?'

'Exactly.'

Now she was off, freed from the fetters of convention by a higher morality, one that called her to do great but dangerous deeds.

'I'd better make sure the coast is clear, first,' she decided. 'Just in case he's at home for some reason. I could give you a call on your mobile phone when I've checked it out.'

'What time are you going there?'

'Three o'clock. I've got to do some shopping for the Wiedemanns first.'

'Wiedemanns?'

'My neighbours.'

It was a little later than he would have liked. 'What time does Sneddon usually get home?'

'Not until six.'

Three hours. It ought to be plenty of time . . .

'I could keep watch for you,' suggested his eager sidekick, clearly seeing herself in some sort of Blyton-style adventure.

He smiled indulgently. Ever since he had begun looking into this case, Mrs Christmas had bumbled around him, seemingly frantic to become involved. He had been instinctively reluctant to allow her this wish . . . until now.

'You could, couldn't you?'

She nodded enthusiastically, seeming to be positively desperate to participate.

'OK. I'll be in my room at The Lamb. You've got my number?'

She wrote it down in a small, neat hand in a notebook she produced from her handbag. He finished his tea, thanked her and then left.

Mrs Christmas called him at three twenty.

'Dr Eisenmenger? It's Mrs Christmas.'

She was whispering, as if there were a danger of being overheard; it lent an excited air to her voice, which Eisenmenger strongly suspected was an accurate reflection of what she really felt.

'Is everything OK? Are you at the house?'

'Yes!'

'No sign of Sneddon?'

'None at all.'

'I'll be with you in about fifteen minutes.'

Eisenmenger was well aware that Sneddon's house was only three hundred metres from the Verner-Morrisons' farm; he didn't think that the house was visible from the farmhouse itself but Verner-Morrison's land was all around and therefore Sneddon might be anywhere around him. That the sun had fallen almost to the horizon and the air was now growing darker and even colder was, he felt, a help as he parked the car under overhanging trees some hundred metres from the house. He hurried along the side of the road, crouched against the cold, head down. He walked straight through the garden gateway, along the short path and then up to the front door.

The bell was very loud.

Mrs Christmas opened the door almost at once and he thought briefly, *She must have been waiting in the hallway for me.*

'Come in!' she hissed.

She stood back and he stepped inside quickly.

The door closed behind him and he turned, pulling off his coat.

And then someone hit his head with something very, very hard.

After a brief but intense burst of pain he knew nothing more.

He heard the voice first, a drifting and echoing noise that gradually metamorphosed into words that in turn slowly took on character.

Mrs Christmas was talking.

She sounds quite chirpy.

He opened his eyes, found focus. The light hurt his eyes, in fact hurt the whole of his head, and he realized that the whole of his head was immersed in a vat of superheated pain.

She was talking to Sneddon, sitting in a comfortable-looking armchair and sipping tea. Sneddon was nodding and clearly listening but his eyes were on their guest. Eisenmenger looked around the room; just a sitting room, no more frightening than a million others. It might have been Sunday tea with the vicar and with Great Aunt Lucy who had an unfortunate stomach problem.

Except he was handcuffed and manacled to the chair.

Mrs Christmas caught the movement of his head and stopped talking.

'Hello, Doctor,' she said politely. She even had a smile on her face, which was more than could be said for Sneddon whose expression was petrous.

'What's going on?' It was a dreadful cliché and it made him sound like an idiot but he had an awful feeling he *had been* an idiot.

Sneddon spoke for the first time. 'Isn't it obvious?'

And, in a way, it was; Eisenmenger's problem was that he didn't know in which way it was obvious. He looked at his erstwhile assistant. 'Why?'

Mrs Christmas put down her teacup, resting it on the saucer with great care. She said to Sneddon, 'I'd better be going.'

He nodded. 'Probably best if you're not around.' It was a sentiment that didn't do much for Eisenmenger's cheeriness.

She stood up. 'Thank you for the tea.'

She picked up her handbag and moved to the door of the room, both Sneddon and Eisenmenger watching her.

She left the room, closing the door behind her. There was a short pause while presumably she donned her customary black woollen overcoat, then they heard the front door open and shut with a bang.

Sneddon turned back to Eisenmenger who asked again, 'Why?'

For the first time Sneddon smiled. It wasn't a nice smile. 'She's my mother.'

Sauerwine received the news of the DNA analysis with mounting dread. The blood in Richard Gillespie's house was unequivocally Maeve Gillespie's. Not only that, but there was evidence of neural tissue, hair and bone. He felt profoundly depressed as he said to Beckwith, 'It's a murder investigation.'

Richard Gillespie had vanished and there was as yet no sign of him. House-to-house enquires were proceeding and all of Gillespie's friends and acquaintances were being contacted, but now the effort would be stepped up. His photograph would be circulated and more officers would be brought into the investigation; the area around the house would be meticulously searched.

Huge resources would be employed to find both Richard Gillespie and his wife, but Sauerwine now knew that at best they would find only her body.

'What now?'

Sneddon pursed his lips as though he was unsure, as though there were all sorts of things they might do – perhaps a game of Monopoly, or cribbage, or perhaps they would share a toasted cheese sandwich and a bottle of stout.

Or perhaps Eisenmenger would be killed.

Sneddon looked at his watch; it was dark outside but Eisenmenger had no idea how late it was. There were no clocks in his line of view. 'Time to go.'

'Where?'

But Sneddon wasn't interested in idle questions. He left, the room, returning a moment later with a heavy metal pipe about half a metre long, as well as a roll of parcel tape. He said, 'We can make this easy or we can make this hard.'

'Make what easy?'

'I'm going to take you out to the car. I want you to co-operate; if you decide not to, I'll have to teach you some discipline.'

He was smiling again and Eisenmenger had the strong impression that Sneddon would have liked a bit of unco-oper-ativeness.

'Well?'

Eisenmenger had one set of handcuffs on his wrists and two more that attached his ankles to the legs of his chair. He was brave but not reckless. 'I'll co-operate,' he promised.

Sneddon stepped forward and began to wind parcel tape around his head, covering his eyes and mouth, leaving only his nose exposed. He wound the tape round and round and round, the harsh static noise of unwinding tape loud in Eisenmenger's ears.

Her heart was *hammering*, and not just because she had had to rush from her appointment with the oncologist.

For God's sake, woman! Pull yourself together. What are you? A schoolgirl?

The ring wasn't answered for a long, long time. She stood outside the door and looked around the hallway; it wasn't a bad hallway, but it was a hallway. It was a place to pass through, not to live in. The door next along was opened, the chain still on, and Helena saw half of a small, elderly face peering out at her. She couldn't see enough to determine whether there was disapproval upon the features of the old lady, although she just *knew* that there was. The eyes remained to regard her even as the door before her opened. Justin was wearing a Ralph Lauren T-shirt and she briefly wondered how he could afford such designer clothing.

'Come.' He stood to one side.

She had thought that the address was surprisingly good and it transpired that the decoration in the flat was no less impressive. She told herself sternly that it was her own prejudicial attitudes whispering to her that suggested this was far too good for a barman. Before she could follow up on these politically incorrect thoughts the door was shut and he had taken her jacket and she could smell his eau de Cologne.

'You've got a nosy neighbour,' she commented.

He laughed. 'She's just jealous. Doesn't like to see or hear anyone else enjoying themselves.'

Hear?

'Drink? Vodka?'

'Please.'

She sat where he indicated, on a two-seater sofa in dark blue material.

'When is Mr Kernohan getting here?'

He was mixing the drinks and appeared not to hear. He gave her a drink, sat beside her and asked, 'What do you think?' Meaning the flat.

'It's lovely.'

She sipped her vodka. It was strong.

He nodded. 'Not bad for a barman, eh?'

He took a sip of his, she another of hers.

'No. Nor's the drink.'

They laughed together at this witticism. 'So, about Mr Kernohan.'

'Have you got the money?'

'As promised.'

'Good.'

And that was that. She sensed something wrong, was glad that she had made precautions.

He leaned back with his arm behind her, perfectly at ease. 'Of course, I don't just keep bar.'

She smiled. 'Somehow I guessed.'

He leaned towards her. 'Would you like to know what else I do?'

Already her drink was half gone. It was a very nice drink. 'Amaze me,' she suggested.

He smiled at the ceiling. His legs were apart, his shirt unbuttoned enough to show smooth chest. 'What would you say if I told you that I star in porn films?'

She had expected him to say something about modelling or acting; on reflection, she wasn't entirely wrong.

'Really?' It wasn't so much that this was not what she had expected him to say, more that she had trouble saying it. Her tongue didn't seem to be connecting properly with her teeth or mouth.

Why was the light so bright, the background music so intrusive?

'Absolutely.' He came even closer. 'Do you know, I've got a cock the size of a cucumber?'

Had her head not been starting to rotate in an anti-clockwise direction she might have reprimanded him on his lack of social etiquette, but she had other things to think about. She tried to concentrate on her right hand, sliding it down to the pocket in her slacks. 'You don't say,' she remarked, except that it came out as, '"thay".'

'I do. And the stamina of a stallion.'

She took a deep breath. 'Barry Kernohan's not coming, is he?'

A smile. 'No.'

'He never was, was he?'

'No.'

His fingers had moved to her blouse. One button, two button, three button, four . . .

'Were you ever in contact with him?'

She wanted to move but her head was full of rushing sounds and her limbs were curiously unwilling to do what her head told them to. His fingers found the top of her bra, tunnelled under the bright red lace, found her nipple. The bloody thing was hard, as if it had a life of its own.

'Actually, no,' he admitted. He didn't sound too upset.

Her fingers moved further into her pocket. Why had she worn slacks that were so tight? Why couldn't she think properly? What was she feeling for?

My God, he's turning me on . . . I don't want to be turned on . . .

He put his mouth down on her breast, allowed his tongue to flick her nipple gently. Her fingers found what she was looking for but she couldn't get a grip on it. The room was beginning to spin faster, his breathing was loud in her ears.

He said dreamily, his voice barely a breath in her head, 'I can show you things you've never even dreamed of. That would be good, wouldn't it, Helena?'

'What have you given me?' she asked, to gain time. 'Rohypnol?' Her voice was smothered by cotton wool. Her fingers were growing numb too, while the muscles in her arms were starting to grow weak, lazy.

'Something like that. Nice and compliant.'

And then she realized. Despite the swirling room, the discordant noises, the muscles and nerves that were no longer hers, she realized.

'You were the lover. You were Suzy Bell's lover.'

Thuzy Bell, she heard. Her fingers now seemed to be little more than fat pork sausages, as sensitive as stuffed cannelloni, but she at last managed to get a grip.

Her blouse was completely undone now. He dragged her down from a sitting position to one prone, then stood over her and began to unbutton his trousers. 'That's right.'

One thing was certain, he hadn't lied about the cucumber. She could hardly take her eyes off it as it emerged and he said proudly, 'Now, I know you want to do this, Helena. I know that you're really turned on by me, so why not make it easy?'

'What turned on Suzy?'

Thuthy.

He had pulled off his shirt so that he was completely naked, now leaning down over her to begin to undo her slacks. He paused. 'Suzy? She liked it rough. Learned that from her old man, I guess.'

She had to fight to keep conscious, fight to remember what she was holding in her hand. 'And you gave it to her rough?'

He held up his hands in a submissive gesture. 'I'm just here to please, Helena.' His hand went to the cucumber. 'Just here to please.'

By now he had exposed her knickers . . .

Which was when, with an effort that she was only ever

going to achieve once, she brought her hand out from her pocket, flicked the switch and thrust the stun gun deep into his scrotum, right at the base of the cucumber.

She'd never heard such a delicious scream.

Eisenmenger came to in complete darkness and in deep coldness. He was bound and gagged and had been folded into a foetal position; his head was crammed against something hard, his knees were resting on a hard ridge and when he tried to straighten his legs he found that they were only a couple of centimetres from something solid. His head was sore and his left side was numb because he had been lying on it. He had pins and needles in both his calves and his fingers. There was a smell of dust and damp and oil.

He was in the boot of a car.

He knew that it wasn't moving because apart from the sound of the wind and the soft patter of rain on the boot lid above him there was absolute stillness and silence. He wondered how long he'd been there, how long he would remain there.

He wondered, too, what would happen to him at the end of his time there.

When the police arrived they found a most intriguing tableau, something that might have been a vignette from a Feydeau farce. Helena, still half-undressed, was asleep on the floor by the sofa; Justin was unconscious, his head having banged against the wall. This, in turn, had brought down an expensive print of London in the eighteenth century; it hadn't hit him but the glass had shattered and fallen on him. It all looked almost like the fall-out from a drunken party except for the fact that Justin's next-door neighbour had heard a piercing scream that sounded as if someone were being murdered . . .

. . . And Justin was almost completely naked and bearing burn marks across his genitalia.

They shook Helena gently and she came to quite easily, although she was groggy and almost drunk. They sat her up and draped a blanket around her that was supplied by the neighbour; she clung to it as if it were keeping her afloat.

'Can you tell us what happened?'

Eyes closed, breathing asthmatically with her mouth open, Helena heard the question, took a while to work out what it meant, took a while longer to work out something to say in response.

'He tried to rape me.'

She said the words but as she heard them she was thinking that they were strange, alien things indicating an alien concept. What had happened had happened to someone else in another place, in another time.

They looked at each other and while thus doing she said, 'Would you fetch Inspector Starry? I'd quite like to talk to him.'

Amazingly he'd actually fallen asleep when the car began to move. He felt it move sharply backward, stop, then even more rapidly forward and to the right, the engine revving hard. The boot compartment filled with the smell of exhaust.

Wherever they were going the road was smooth. After what he judged to be ten or fifteen minutes the car slowed slightly, then swung round to the right, then accelerated again. Another period of about the same time, then they slowed again; the exhaust fumes were becoming almost intolerable.

He must have a hole in the exhaust. Perhaps he's planning to asphyxiate me.

The car almost stopped this time, then once more turned to the right, stopping almost immediately. He heard a door open, the engine still running; the rain had eased and he heard what might have been footsteps on gravel, a faint clanking, then a squeak.

He's opening a gate.

The footsteps returned and the door was closed, then the car moved forward a few metres and once more halted.

A good countryman; he closes the gate behind him.

After another pause terminated by the sound and vibration of the car door closing they moved off again but the journey this time was far less congenial and Eisenmenger was thrown around as the car bumped and jerked its way forward.

We're in a field.

This part of the journey seemed to be endless, presumably stretched into eternity by the discomfort. They stopped at last and this time the engine was switched off. He heard the car door open, then nothing for a few minutes.

It was during this time that he became aware of just how full his bladder was.

The boot was opened; the grey morning sky was behind Sneddon as looked down on him. He said nothing as he held up another syringe – how many of the bloody things did he have? – took the plastic cover off it and plunged it into the side of Eisenmenger's buttock. As he pushed the plunger down the initial pain of the needle penetrating flesh gave way to a rapidly crescendoing, almost immediately unbearable agony that fired down his leg and forced him to try to straighten it despite the confined conditions. He groaned, clenching his eyes tightly, but none of these was helpful in relieving the torture.

He knew what had happened even if it made no difference at all; Sneddon had injected the tranquilliser into his sciatic nerve, an elementary mistake. In hospital it would have been a cause of much paperwork – Adverse Clinical Incident reports, memos, complaints, perhaps a call for compensation – but Sneddon neither knew nor cared. His expression didn't even change as he watched Eisenmenger slide downwards into unconsciousness.

The police surgeon took her blood which hurt as he did it and continued to hurt for an hour or so afterwards. She gradually became clearer in the head, enough to refuse to be moved to hospital for a 'thorough' examination; she had enough knowledge to know that that would mean an 'intimate' examination.

'He didn't rape me. There's no need.'

'Are you certain?'

She shook her head, noticed that the world moved groggily around long after she had come to rest. 'No. He wanted to, but he never got around to it.'

The surgeon raised his eyebrows at Starry and shrugged. Starry made a face and the surgeon moved away. Helena opened her eyes. She was cold and shivered slightly, pulling the blanket closer about her. The woman police officer sitting beside her put her arm around her shoulders.

'Could we go over again what happened here?' Starry was wandering around the room, hands behind his back, his attitude suggesting a degree of cynicism.

Her mouth was absurdly dry, no matter how much water she drank. She said, 'I came here because I understood that we would be meeting Barry Kernohan.'

'And who was your friend?'

'He knew about Suzanne Bell's affair. Knew who might have been her lover.'

Starry asked, 'Who is he? What's his name?'

'Justin something . . . ' Her brain wouldn't do her bidding, the surname remained elusive. 'He's a bartender at the snooker hall in Duct Street.'

'And you thought this Justin bloke would lead you to Barry Kernohan who would tell you about this mythical lover who . . . what?'

'Who really killed Suzanne Bell.'

Starry might have been trying to suppress a smile but an independent judge would have been equivocal on the subject. 'So you came here to his flat . . . he jumped on you and you fought back.'

'That's right.'

'With a Tasor.'

She stared back at him. 'Yes.'

'And are you aware of the law regarding such devices?'

'And are you aware of the law regarding date rape?'

'That doesn't excuse – '

'Inspector, if I'd had a pair of gardening shears I'd have used those and then he might have had a proper reason to complain.'

He said nothing for a while then nodded. 'Fair enough.'

She tried to banish the thirst with more water, emptied the glass, handed it to the policewoman beside her who got up and went into the kitchenette. Starry remarked, 'This is a very nice flat for a barman.'

Helena felt nausea wash around her head, billowing in her stomach. It took a moment's concentration to defeat it.

'He has a sideline. Pornographic movies.'

Starry raised his eyebrows. 'Does he, indeed?'

'I can vouch for the fact that he's an outstanding actor.'

Another glance around the room. 'Perhaps I should try that. The pension might need supplementing.'

She tried a smile, found the flesh of her cheeks cold and waxen. 'Why not?'

The policewoman returned with more water, which Helena took thankfully. Starry knelt down by the television, under which there was a wooden cabinet; in it there were perhaps a hundred DVDs. He began pulling them out, looking at them, then tossing them down on the carpet. There were a few that were mainstream; most, though were pornographic; a lot of them pictured Justin on their cover.

'Fond of himself, wasn't he?' he murmured.

He had a lot to be proud of.

He came across something that made him stare, then an expression of disgust formed on his face. He dropped this one as if it were hot, then looked at his fingers as if they were covered in something less than pleasant.

He stood up. 'We'll talk to him about this in due course. What he did – tried to do to you – is the main thing.'

Helena wanted to retire to her bed and not see the light of day for at least a week but she hadn't finished. 'No, it's not.'

Surprised, 'What does that mean?'

'Compare his DNA with the semen samples from Suzy Bell.'

'What will I find if I do?'

'You'll find that he's the man who made love to Suzy Bell just before she died; just *as* she died.'

'You're saying that he did it? That he murdered Suzanne Bell?'

She nodded.

He was polite and his condescension was all the more marked for that. 'Even if you're right, it doesn't mean that he killed her. Even if he was her lover, it doesn't change anything. It just confirms that Martin Bell had a superb motive for killing his wife.'

'He's just tried to rape me, for Christ's sake!'

'I'll admit that perhaps Mrs Bell had a pretty poor judgement about her lovers, but that doesn't mean Justin was responsible for her murder.'

'Ask him for an alibi for the time of the murder then.'

For the first time he looked less than certain. 'I will,' he promised after a pause.

'And talk to his other lovers. You may find a pattern of behaviour involving systematic beating.'

He looked at her thoughtfully, perhaps having a problem with the commanding tone she had adopted. 'OK,' he agreed finally.

She finished the glass of water. Was that her fourth or her fifth? 'And now I'm going to go home, if someone will give me a lift.'

Starry wasn't quite at the head-scratching phase but he was certainly looking perplexed. He felt that he had lost control of the situation; victims weren't supposed to tell him what questions to ask, where to look for answers. He nodded at the policewoman, feeling suddenly unsure of himself.

Helena stood, stepped forward. For some reason, although she was perfectly anchored, although she was at complete and perfect rest with respect to her position in the universe, all that was around her suddenly lost its grip. The room, the world, the solar system, the Milky Way, the local cluster and all of its friends close and far began to spin. She'd never enjoyed funfairs and, anyway, this was no fun.

Another step, just to make sure that it wasn't a meeting of ley lines or maybe the spot where Merlin had shuffled off the proverbial, but this, if anything, only worsened the effect.

She fell to her knees and hands, the thick carpet proving surprisingly ineffective in providing any sort of cushioning. This brought her face to face with the DVDs that Starry had tossed on to the floor.

Starry had stepped forward and ostensibly tried to stop her, one of those gestures that people make but that never quite seem to do anything useful at all. The policewoman had been rising from the sofa and also moved forward emitting a gasp but she was too far from her to stop the fall.

'Are you all right?' Starry crouched down beside her, putting his hand out to rest on her shoulder.

The cosmos was slowing down now, but that didn't mean she felt any less peculiar; somehow the act of deceleration was if anything worse. In any case she had to concentrate greatly on controlling her gastric sphincter.

Gastric sphincter! You have a lot to answer for, John Eisenmenger.

Deep breathing.

'Sure,' she said at last.

With Starry on one side and the policewoman on the other they began to help her to her feet. Her vision, previously blurred, cleared . . .

'Wait.'

She reached for the DVD that had caught her eye.

Justin, completely naked, stood while a young gentleman knelt before him; the latter clearly had a liking for long green salad vegetables.

She knew the face, knew it from photographs she had seen in the case prepared against Kenneth Gerard.

The young gentleman was Clive Ewart.

He came to and was again cold but this time it was worse; he was indoors but the place was unheated and draughty. There was no carpet, just bare, dusty, floorboards.

And he was naked.

Bound – his hands were handcuffed behind his back, his ankles manacled – but no longer gagged, he lay on his side. The pain in his right leg had been replaced during his unconsciousness by an intense bony ache, one that made his teeth want to clamp together; he had severe pins and needles the entire length of that leg, as well as in his fingers. His head ached and there was a taste of oil and metal in his arid mouth.

He had something around his neck . . .

He couldn't see what it was but he could somehow guess.

It was a noose.

The room was high-ceilinged and clearly in a derelict house of some sort. In the corner he could see a crude kitchen complete with butler sink, portable gas burner and small fridge. Opposite it was a mattress on the floor, the bedclothes neatly made. A large plasma screen television and DVD player were arranged on a low table in front of the bed; their presence was strangely incongruous.

Sneddon was a tidy man.

In contrast to these signs of domesticity there were other items, things less likely to be found in the average suburban residence.

Three portable floodlights, for instance.

And a large camera, complete with microphone and small playback monitor.

These were pointed at Eisenmenger who, he now discovered, was on a small and low wooden stage to which the manacles were attached by a centrally placed heavy metal bracket; he might be able to stand but he wasn't going to shuffle off anywhere.

'Oh, shit.'

Starry was starting to find Helena really rather tedious. It was bad enough that she had practically written the script for his interrogation regarding her own rape and then tried to overturn his very nice case against Martin Bell, but now she wanted to conduct her own interview regarding a case that wasn't his and that, as far as he understood, had been solved very satisfactorily, thank you.

'This is very irregular,' he said, aware that he was speaking in police clichés but unable to phrase it in any other way.

'Well, you, do it, then.'

'Do what, precisely?'

A headache had arrived to replace the nausea and giddiness; it was a headache that was psychotically angry and out for blood.

'He was making films with Clive Ewart, one of the dead men found at Rendcomb.'

'And . . . ?'

'Maybe he knew the others.'

They were sitting in the rear of a police car. She had her head back on the seat, eyes closed while she felt the inside of her skull pulsate.

Starry enquired sarcastically, 'Having tried to scupper my case against Martin Bell, you've decided to start on the one against Kenneth Gerard, have you?'

'Yes. I have.'

He emitted a noise like a small geyser discharging into the environment and there followed silence between them while they drove through heavy rain. The car was cold.

'Even if he did know them, what does that prove? Do you think he's the killer of them as well?'

'No.' If he was pleased to hear this, he was less delighted by her follow-up. 'But nor do I think Kenneth Gerard was.'

He eyed her balefully. 'Is there anyone you're not defending?'

'I've turned down Hitler and Satan. Didn't like their aftershave.'

'I can't let you talk to him, it would be most irregular.'

'You're surely not going to ignore what I've told you, are you? He might be a material witness in a case of serial killing.'

He looked as if that were precisely what he wanted to do but after a moment's uncertainty he said finally, 'He's in hospital at the moment; unaccountably he's got some nasty burns to the scrotum. We could pay an unofficial visit to him while he's there.'

They had put Justin into a side room and given him a nice policeman to talk to, just so that he didn't feel lonely. In fact he had been detained overnight in hospital because of the loss of consciousness rather than anything that might have been done to his nether regions. Starry came into the room, nodded at the police constable who left without saying a word, then stood at the end of the bed. Justin was wearing pyjama bottoms and a little cotton gown; he lay on top of the bed, his legs apart. He had to do this because there was clearly a lot of dressing around his scrotum. He didn't look happy.

'What the fuck's going on here?'

Helena came into the room.

'What's that bitch doing here?' To Starry he said, 'She assaulted me. Have you seen what she did to my tackle?'

'She tells a different story.'

'She's a liar. She came on to me at the snooker hall, pestered me, then when I finally gave in, she gets out that stun gun – '

'Shall we talk about this when we get you down to the police station? We should have the lab results back on the blood samples we took from Miss Flemming by then . . . you can explain the date rape drug. You've got all night to cook something up.'

Justin opened his mouth but nothing came out; the expression around his eyes was far more eloquent.

Starry continued, 'Tonight I want to talk to you about another matter.'

'What's that?'

'Miss Flemming tells me that you're something of a film star.'

'What of it?'

Helena sat herself in a chair in the far corner, saying nothing. Starry moved to stand with his back to the blinds at the window.

'Are you?'

Warily Justin shrugged. 'I do some bit part acting.'

'Some bit, judging by the covers of the films in your flat.'

Helena noted that Justin couldn't stop the smile appearing, although he refrained from comment.

'I'd like to talk to you about one of your fellow actors. Gentleman by the name of Ewart. Clive Ewart.'

'Don't know him.'

'You're sure?'

'Positive.'

Starry looked at Helena. She said, 'Show him.'

Starry took the DVD from his pocket, tossed it on the bed. Justin stared down at it. 'Oh. You mean him.'

He didn't try to make it sound convincing.

'Yes, we mean him.'

'I just knew him as Clive. Never got to know him well enough to learn his surname.' Which, judging by the photograph, was a little difficult to believe.

'But you knew him.'

'Yeah, sure.'

'This film. Where was it made?'

But Justin's memory was proving strangely unreliable. He shrugged. 'Can't recall.'

294

Starry took in enough breath to inflate him quite visibly.
'Try harder.'

Justin stared at the DVD box for a few seconds more, his face a picture of concentration that was blatantly false. Eventually, 'No. Nothing comes to mind.'

The look of cockiness on his face failed to persuade his interrogators of his veracity.

There were times when Starry felt as if he were in a recurring nightmare where suspects lied in a variety of unconvincing ways until doomsday. Why was there no creativity in fabrication? Surely confabulation should have been the most liberating occupation known to mankind?

He said, 'Clive Ewart – the man who is in that picture with his mouth around your genitalia – was found two weeks ago, having been in the river for some time. He was murdered, the victim of homosexual rape and castration.'

There was a silence but that did not signify tranquillity. This piece of information had a curiously animating effect on the previously confident Justin. His glance kept transferring from Starry to Helena and back again, as if they were each too hot or too bright to be gazed upon for long. His whole attitude became tense, his face rigid with worry. After the shock had subsided he began, 'Now, just a minute . . . '

'You'll have heard about it, of course. You can't have missed it, what with the papers and the television coverage.'

'Yeah, I didn't realize . . . '

'I don't know about you, but I'd say that DVD suggests you had a homosexual affair with poor Clive. That would make you a suspect.'

'I didn't! For fuck's sake, that was business, that was acting.'

Starry sneered. 'Acting? It's hardcore, Justin. Whatever you did, you really did it. There was no CGI involved.'

'I'm not a queer. What I do I do for money.'

'And that's better, is it?'

'I didn't kill him.'

'So tell me about this great work of art,' suggested Starry, gesturing at the DVD. 'Tell me where it was made.'

But Justin was not keen. 'I don't remember. I do a lot of this stuff, you know.'

'Can you remember when it was made?'

He looked again at the DVD but that was not a key to open his memory. 'I dunno. Last year, maybe.'

Starry turned again to Helena, his face a grimace. He implied he thought that this was a waste of time. She suddenly stood up, came to the end of the bed.

'Was it made in Rendcomb?'

He smiled at her. 'Never heard of the place.'

'You don't make films for Cherie and Alec Verner-Morrison?'

He shook his head. 'Can't say I do.'

'So who do you make them for? Or do you make them yourself?'

He shrugged. 'It varies. I do a lot of stuff abroad.'

I bet you do.

She saw the lie come into his head, creeping in behind the eyes, the light of deception. 'That's where it was. That's where I met him. Abroad. Denmark.'

'Denmark.'

He nodded, a sly grin dancing about his mouth and eyes. 'That's it. Near Legoland.'

Starry was getting restive. She knew that she had little time left. Nodding in apparent acceptance of his falsehoods she said, 'OK. Now we're going to talk about Blackfan, and Diamond, and Josephs, and Miller, and Abbott.'

His confidence didn't so much slip as disintegrate. 'Who?'

She repeated the names.

He was cautious. 'Never heard of them.'

'Haven't you? Are you sure of that?'

'Positive.'

'They've been in the news, too. They're the other five

296

victims. They all suffered the same fate as poor Clive Ewart –
homosexual murder.'

'So?'

She smiled. Afterwards she liked to think that it was this
smile that did it. She said through it, 'You've appeared in films
with all of them.' This might have been true, she just didn't
know.

He was genuinely horrified. 'What?' He looked at Starry,
found succour there. 'You've got to be joking! This is nothing
to do with me! I might have been in the same films as them,
but . . . '

'If you don't want to be involved, tell us where you filmed
them.'

'This is complete bollocks . . . '

He seemed to be looking around the bedspread for
something, perhaps a place to hide. His mouth was working,
he was almost talking to himself. Then he jerked his head up,
looking straight at Starry. 'I'll admit that I came on a bit strong
tonight, OK? Maybe I got a bit naughty . . . but I don't know
anything about this.'

Starry said mildly, 'Then tell the lady what she wants to
know.'

He didn't want to but the thought of being implicated in six
murders was a strong incentive. He said eventually in a low
voice, 'Rendcomb. They were filmed in Rendcomb.'

She relaxed. She thought that she could guess what he was
going to say. 'At the Verner-Morrisons'?'

He was back examining the bedspread, his mouth working
again. Perhaps he didn't hear the question because his next
remark was not a direct answer. 'Look, I make a living filming
these things. I go where the money is, do what the script calls for,
OK? If it says shag a woman, I shag a woman; if it says shag a
man, then that's what I do; shit, I've even shagged animals.'

'You worked for the Verner-Morrisons in Rendcomb,
though, didn't you?'

297

'They became a regular gig. Nothing too *extreme*, if you know what I mean. One on one, two on two, two on one; old man Verner-Morrison likes stuff using the back door, but nothing heavy. Nothing violent, and he wasn't interested in man on man. He wanted his wife in most of it – gave him a kick, I guess. It certainly gave her one.'

Helena didn't understand. 'So this wasn't filmed at the Verner-Morrisons'? Then where?'

'Yes, it was.'

Now he'd lost her completely.

'At the Verner-Morrisons', but not *by* them.'

'Then who?'

'William Sneddon.'

John had mentioned Sneddon, she recalled. 'The farm manager?'

He smiled sourly. 'Amongst other things.'

'He made these films . . . what? Without telling them?'

'Sneddon's a creep – not exactly unusual in the business – but he's a smart man. He saw that there was unused capacity in the Verner-Morrisons' operation and there was a market waiting to be tapped. The cameras and lights weren't being used most of the time; they were just being left in storage. Why not borrow them for his own productions?'

'What market was he trying to tap?'

'How shall I put it? The heavier end.'

From what hardcore Helena had seen in the course of her career, it was all fairly heavy but Starry said immediately, 'Children?'

'No.' Justin was quick, desperate, to deny. 'Not that.'

Starry was suddenly interested. 'Except that he was only fifteen,' he pointed out in a tone that flowed with cynicism, waving his hand at the DVD on the bed.

'I didn't know! He said they were legit.'

'And you didn't ask too many questions.'

'They sure looked old enough.'

Starry smiled sourly. 'Ignorance is no excuse. The charges are mounting up, Justin.'

'I didn't fucking kill them, though.'

Helena said, 'So what do you mean by "heavier"?'

He shrugged. 'At first Sneddon just wanted the standard homosexual stuff; nothing anyone had too much problem with. If they did, they shouldn't have been there. But then he started to get interested in other things. Got keen on fisting for a while; went into great close-up on that, he did. Got a right hard on.'

Helena asked, 'This was when?'

'About six months ago.'

'And how many actors were involved?'

'For every film it was just me and one other.' He gestured at the DVD. 'He was one of the last. Nice kid. Scared, though.'

Didn't that bother you?

She tried not to imagine what emotions had been going through their minds as they were filmed by Sneddon. She asked, 'And after the "fisting"?'

'For the next few films he went in for an S and M thing. Whips, leather, chains, that sort of thing.'

'Did Sneddon ever participate in any of this?'

'You must be joking! Stayed firmly behind the camera, shouting instructions. But you could tell that he was getting his rocks off on what he was filming. Creamed his jeans on more than one occasion.'

She noticed that Starry was taking more interest now.

'He never approached you?'

Justin snorted a laugh. 'He did once, actually.'

'What did he say?'

'It was quite early on. He sidled up to me after a day's filming. Suggested a cosy tête-à-tête.'

'What did you say?'

He looked disdainful. 'I put him in the picture about the way it works. I'm not a fucking poof. Gave him a flea in his ear and suggested that he should keep his prick to himself.'

'Where did you stay?'

'I used to check into a hotel in Bishops Shrieve. It's nice and anonymous, the kind of place where nobody cares and nobody notices. Sneddon used to ferry me to and fro.'

'And the other "actors"?'

Justin shrugged. 'I think they stayed with him.'

She flicked a glance at Starry; on his face was a deep frown and he was listening intently to every word. Back to Justin she said, 'How long did this go on?'

He shrugged. 'About once every six weeks."

'And the last one was when?'

'Just before Christmas.'

Which was when Clive Ewart had died.

Starry suddenly asked, 'That last film you made . . . was that the one that Clive Ewart made with you?'

Justin had to think, as if the young men he had acted with had just been receptacles for his sperm, grist for his mill. 'I'm not sure I remember,' he decided at last. 'Possibly.'

Probably, I think.

'How many films did you make?'

'About ten. We're due to start another one next week.'

Helena and Starry looked at each other; she didn't say anything. She didn't need to.

Starry came to the bed, put his fists on the duvet and said in a low voice to Justin, 'Do you have any idea how much shit you're in?' Maybe Justin was going to answer, maybe he had measured the shit levels to the nearest millimetre, but he wasn't given the chance. 'I thought I had you for attempted rape – I still do – but, wonder of wonders, I find that you're an accomplice in at least six homicides . . . '

'This is crap! I didn't know what was going on.'

'Didn't you really? So what did you think was happening?'

Justin got fed up with the view in Starry's direction, turned to Helena. "It can be like that in this business. You don't ask questions, you just take the money.'

She found herself so disgusted it was difficult to speak. 'How much were you paid?'

'For the films? Only a thousand a time.'

She couldn't keep the sneer from her face. 'Well, that's more than Clive and the others were given. All they got was murdered.'

Starry picked up the DVD and, ushering Helena before him, went to the door. Before he left, he turned to Justin one last time. 'I'll be back tomorrow. We've got a lot to talk about.'

He was almost gone before something else occurred to him. 'And while you're lying there, you might like to think up an alibi for the murder of Suzy Bell.'

Beckwith took the call because Sauerwine was with Burr. There had been no news regarding the disappearance of the Gillespies. No one had seen anything of them, no one had heard anything, no one had any ideas where Richard Gillespie might have gone. They all knew of their marital difficulties but no one knew details; no one *wanted* to know details. They had just gone public with a plea to one or both of the Gillespies to get in contact with them; this plea had not made mention of Sauerwine's certainty that Richard Gillespie was the murderer of his wife.

Beckwith's attitude changed from boredom to intense interest as he listened. Meckel was watching him and, as he put the phone down, asked, 'Something turned up?'

Beckwith was genuinely bewildered. 'I don't know.'

Sauerwine entered the room. Over the past few days he had changed, becoming morose to the point of catatonia; when asked a question, he was prone first not to answer, then to grow angry when the questioner persisted. Beckwith had taken to minimizing communication with his superior but what he had to say now prompted him to revise this stratagem.

'Sir?'

Sauerwine walked on.

301

'Sir?'

Sauerwine turned, a deep frown on his face. 'What?' He didn't sound particularly interested.

'There may be a development in the Gerard case.'

Sauerwine's frown became so deep as to become positively subterranean. 'Development?' he demanded. 'What do you mean?'

Beckwith found his courage beginning to wither on the vine. 'That was Inspector Starry. Do you know him?'

'Vaguely.'

'He said . . . ' He found his voice petering out in direct correlation with his audacity.

'Well? What did he say?'

Meckel, too, had been intrigued by this news; he was looking on with great avidity.

Beckwith, feeling that with every word he was writing another sentence of his indictment, recounted the gist of Starry's conversation. He thought that he had been perfectly erudite but Sauerwine had a problem.

'Hardcore pornography?'

'Yes, sir. He's on his way here now to discuss it.'

'William Sneddon?'

'That's the name he gave me.'

Of Meckel he asked, 'Have we talked to this William Sneddon?'

'He's the farm manager of the Verner-Morrisons.'

Verner-Morrisons? Sauerwine suddenly recalled Eisenmenger's remark about the Verner-Morrisons making pornographic films.

He walked slowly into his office; incredibly, he appeared now to be even more downcast than before.

Helena had already tried Eisenmenger's mobile three times and each time had only been connected to the answering service; she didn't think yet another urgent plea to call her as soon as possible would help much. She rang The Lamb and heard Mrs Munro's deep, throaty tones; like Eisenmenger before her she thought irresistibly of bronzed Amazons and come-hither curves.

'Could I speak to Dr Eisenmenger, please?'

'I don't think you can.'

Which was not the answer Helena had expected; in fact it sounded positively obstructive.

'Why not?'

'Because I don't think he came in last night, which was rather annoying, because he'd said he would be in for dinner.'

'And he hasn't been down for breakfast?'

'Not yet.'

'Could you go and check his room, please?'

'Well, I suppose I could.'

'It's very important.'

'Hold on.'

She heard the receiver clunked down on to a wooden surface, heard background noises of a kitchen and one or two voices talking in a distracted, conversational manner while she ran through thoughts. *Perhaps he stayed somewhere else last night, somewhere innocent . . . perhaps he's got a lover . . .*

A picture of Justin, naked and ready for action, intruded . . .

Surely not a lover . . .

Justin was replaced by Beverley Wharton . . .

But she's nowhere around this case . . .

'Hello?'

'Yes?'

'There's no answer from his room. I don't like to use the pass-key . . . '

'It doesn't matter.'

She put the phone down. It was of no consequence whether Mrs Munro used her pass-key or not; the room was empty.

John Eisenmenger was missing.

Sauerwine felt as if some stupid child had picked a single,

small thread in his grubby blue jumper, pulled and then kept pulling; he felt as if the thread had lain in a growing pile of spiralled wool as more and more of it had came away; as if once the jumper had gone, the space once occupied by it had started to go but, this time, as thread fell to the floor the hole in the universe had actually grown in size, and now the whole of the universe was unravelling while he was forced into inaction, while he could do nothing but wonder where it had all gone wrong.

He sat in his office and listened to what Starry had to say, looked on as Helena nodded, adding occasional comments, layering on emphases. Meckel and Beckwith were there too, but he did not feel particularly supported; Meckel, yes, but Beckwith . . . ?

'All right,' he said, trying to salvage some sort of connection between this new information and his once watertight case, 'so you've got some testimony to suggest that Sneddon was using these young men in pornographic films. I don't see that that in any way exonerates Gerard. It proves that they were in the area so, if anything, it could be seen to strengthen the case against him. If he had somehow found out about the films . . . '

'But they were staying with Sneddon.' Helena tried to keep calm in the face of this intransigence.

'That's hearsay. As far as I understand it, this Justin bloke didn't know that for certain.'

Starry shook his head in agreement and Helena said, 'Well, you at least need to talk to him.'

'We will, don't worry.'

'And what about John? He's missing.'

Sauerwine was finding Helena just a little bit tiresome; he had noticed this feeling before. 'He appears to be,' he agreed cautiously.

Dumbfoundedness did not come easily to Helena – she was more a get-bloody-incandescent-and-put-your-spoke-in kind of a person – but this refusal to acknowledge what to her was obvious left her bereft of both breath and speech for several seconds.

She turned to Starry for help, yet he merely failed to spot that she was looking in his direction. By the time she turned back to Sauerwine she was capable of locution again.

'What?' she demanded.

'Well, he's only been missing twelve hours or so. There might be a hundred innocent explanations for his absence.'

Beckwith, also in the room but outside of the conversational circle, shook his head and reflected that Sauerwine's attitude to missing persons seemed to have mutated in the past three days.

'But he's the third disappearance in less than a week. You're convinced the first two are suspicious, why not this one?'

Put like that it was slightly awkward to explain this sudden epidemic of vanishings and Sauerwine was backed into a vague, 'It could all be coincidence . . . '

Helena narrowed her eyes; having got over her dumbfoundedness, she found loquacity to come easily. 'Coincidence?' she said scornfully. 'In the space of a year at least six young men have been murdered in Rendcomb and now three more people have disappeared in the course of a few days. That's one hell of a coincidence.'

Somewhat defensively Sauerwine spread his hands wide, his elbows on the desk. 'Look, I got bollocked for jumping the gun with the Gillespies. I don't want the same fate again, OK?'

'But you've got to start looking now . . . '

'I'm sorry.'

Helena looked ready to explode, might well have done, had Beckwith not then spoken without actually realizing he was going to. 'Why don't I poke around, ask a few questions? Sort of unofficially.'

Sauerwine was uncertain for a moment, then saw the benefits. Burr would be extremely unlikely to discover

Beckwith's perambulations and it would keep Helena quiet.

'Why not?' he decided.

Eisenmenger's hotel room gave them no clues, gave Helena only a profound sense of melancholic dread. The book by the bed (*Our Mutual Friend*, halfway through), the glass of water beside it, his clothes, the half-completed crossword – all these were reminders on both a visceral and an intellectual level of his recent presence. His notes on the table by the window were the sole sign that he had been investigating anything at all. She and Beckwith sat and read them for over an hour; at the end of it they looked at each other.

'He suspected Sneddon,' she said quietly.

'It looks like it.'

'And now he's gone.'

'It looks like it.'

She looked at Beckwith, at his painfully fair hair and slightly juvenile facial expression, and wondered if he was any use at all. 'Is that all you've got to say? "It looks like it"?'

She feared for a moment that he would repeat this four-word mantra, and perhaps he was about to, but if so he realized it in time to save his soul and said instead, 'The question is, what did he do about it?'

'He'd try to find evidence. He'd know that your inspector wouldn't budge without a confession signed in blood and witnessed by the Pope and the Archbishop of Canterbury.'

Beckwith wasn't sure that Sauerwine was 'his inspector' any more but let it pass. 'So he'd presumably talk to Sneddon. Inspector Sauerwine's going to do that; there's no point in us doing it as well.'

Helena wondered if Sauerwine would ask the right questions. She looked again at the notes; they were messy and yet somehow erudite, perhaps because of the small, regular handwriting. She saw the name, 'Christmas'.

'We could speak to her. She seems to have been helping him. Maybe she'll have some idea of what he did.'

It had turned warm in a damp, uncomfortable, winter's kind of a way. It was so moist they might have been walking under water, an impression heightened by the gloom of the day, the heavy dark grey clouds overhead. Helena felt as if she were a long way underground, a place where light and happiness were banished. The curtains of the cottage next door twitched as they walked up the garden path to the cottage that Mrs Munro (who, to Helena's surprise, had turned out to be more droopy than curvy in the flesh department) had indicated was the domicile of Mrs Jean Christmas.

The lady who answered the door was somehow perfect for her abode. Short and slightly dumpy, grey and lined, kindly-looking eyes, a slightly bewildered expression on her face as Helena explained their mission.

'Oh, dear. Disappeared, you say?' She thought about this, a worried frown on her face.

'You wouldn't know what he was planning to do yesterday, would you? Where he was going?'

'No, I'm afraid I don't.'

'You didn't see him? Contact him at all?'

'Not yesterday. I was busy all day, you see? I do some part-time work cleaning. It doesn't pay that much and, to be honest, some of the people who employ me are no better than they ought to be, but at least it gives me a little bit of pocket money . . . the pension doesn't go far these days, you know . . . '

'Did he mention William Sneddon at all?'

Thus arrested in her monologue, Helena saw the old lady appear to reset her nervous system and attempt to concentrate on this new enquiry. 'Not especially,' she decided eventually.

My God, she's vague. Has she got all her marbles?

'He didn't say that he was going to talk to him, perhaps look around his house?'

307

A definitive shake of the head. 'Oh, no. Definitely not.'

Helena sighed and Beckwith felt quite sorry for her. In some ways she reminded him of Cindy. He said to Mrs Christmas, 'He gave you no indication of what he was planning to do?'

'No, nothing at all.' She became slightly agitated. 'I do hope Dr Eisenmenger's all right. He was such a nice man.'

'If he should get in contact with you, would you let me know as soon as possible?' He gave her a card.

'Of course I will.'

As they were walking back to the car he asked, 'What do you want to do now?'

'Sneddon's house. Maybe he went there, snooping around.'

They got in the car and as Beckwith was accelerating away from the cottage she said, 'It's funny. She used the past tense. Almost as if she knows he's already dead.'

'Slip of the tongue. People are always doing it when someone goes missing.'

She had no alternative but to agree with him. After all, what could a sweet innocent old lady have to do with any of this?

On their way to the Verner-Morrisons, Sauerwine and Meckel had in fact already called at Sneddon's house but, receiving no reply, they proceeded up the farm track to the Verner-Morrisons. The door was opened by a dyspeptic Verner-Morrison whose mood failed to be improved by the appearance of warrant cards.

'Can't a man get any peace around here?' he demanded.

Sauerwine thought savagely that since *he* wasn't getting any, he couldn't see why a jumped-up little dick like Verner-Morrison should. 'I wouldn't be here if it wasn't important, sir.'

'What is it?'

'May we come in?' Although syntactically this was a question, in every manner it was an order. Looking as if he had swallowed a hornet Verner-Morrison complied. Cherie came out to see who was calling.

'There are a couple of matters I'd like to clear up with you, Mr Verner-Morrison.'

'This is bloody police harassment. What do you want now?'

'How about forming a discussion group on pornography?'

'What?'

'I'd like to talk about pornography. Is it a necessary evil? Or perhaps it's a necessary good, a safety valve for society?'

Verner-Morrison looked uncomfortable, uncertain. 'What's that got to do with me?'

'Because you're a pornographer.'

Verner-Morrison had been built for bluster; it was his thing, how he coped with life, how he got through the day, overcame the many obstacles of modern life.

'You what?' These monosyllables were a curious musical phrase, first descending, then rising. They were almost a caricature.

'You're a pornographer, Mr Verner-Morrison. You make pornographic films.'

He watched Verner-Morrison making calculations, what to sacrifice, where to retrench. 'I wouldn't call them – '

'I would. They're hardcore pornography.'

Verner-Morrison was in a pedantic mood. 'They're adult entertainment,' he protested.

'Really?' Sauerwine glanced at Cherie Verner-Morrison: her cleavage was deep enough to ski down. 'They're very adult, I understand.'

Verner-Morrison wound himself up for a bit of indignation. 'I don't do anything illegal – '

'Your farm manager helps you out.'

Verner-Morrison was slightly disconcerted by this change of direction. 'Of course he does. I employ him to help out on the farm.'

Sauerwine shook his head. 'He manages your film enterprises as well.'

'What of it?'

Cherie decided to add her twopennorth. 'There's nothing wrong with what we do.'

'We can discuss that later. As it is, I'd first like to speak to William Sneddon.'

Verner-Morrison detected an inch of grace and grasped it eagerly. 'If you want to speak to him, you'll have to check with his secretary.'

'Where would I find her?'

This was a stupid question. 'In the farm office.'

With an aura of supreme calm that he didn't in any way feel, Sauerwine asked, 'Perhaps you could tell me where to find it, sir.'

Verner-Morrison was only too keen to draw them away from the scent. 'Of course. I'll take you over there.'

They were hustled out of the house, Cherie looking on with an unreadable expression on her face as Verner-Morrison marched across the farmyard, fully confident that he would be followed. She closed the door as slowly and as quietly as possible, then returned to the lounge with a very troubled look on her face.

Ben, who had heard everything, sat at the top of the stairs and did not move. Everyone was interested in Will Sneddon . . . Why?

Will Sneddon was all right, wasn't he? He'd always got on well with him . . .

He thought back through the last few years. He hadn't had a great deal to do with Sneddon, really. Weeks would go by without seeing him; except recently – he'd been around a lot recently.

Was that significant?

John Eisenmenger had been interested in Will . . .

The memory of a summer's night last year in the wood came back to him. Surely not . . . ?

He would have to tell Eisenmenger.

He heard Sneddon come in, felt the transmitted vibration of

his heavy footsteps through the stage. He lifted his head but his view was severely restricted; he tried to ignore his bladder which, to judge by the pressure, was now approximately the size of a prize-winning pumpkin. He was shivering almost constantly now, a low-level trembling against which occasional shudders would fall.

He watched the lower half of Sneddon walk around to stand in front of him, then crouch down. It was some, but only some, comfort to him that Sneddon was dressed not in plastic or rubber but in normal clothes.

'Good. You're awake.'

He was conversational; matey, almost. Eisenmenger said nothing.

'You haven't tried to stand up? Why not?'

He had in fact, but his right leg was almost completely dead and he had soon fallen again.

Sneddon waited a few moments for an answer then, when none was forthcoming, straightened up again and said merely, 'Oh, well. You will soon.'

He disappeared again and Eisenmenger let his head fall.

He heard the sound of a rope being pulled through a pulley, a high and shrill sound that lasted maybe a second, was then repeated. Again and again Sneddon pulled on the rope and then he felt the first tug at the noose; with each screech of the pulley, the tension increased and he felt his head being pulled off the stage. He had to lift himself off the stage, assume a sitting position, but still the screeches came, still the upwards pull on his neck. Because of his dead leg there was no way he was going to stand up with his hands bound behind his back but he had help. Now that he was in a sitting position the knot of the noose was at the back of his neck and the rope rose vertically to the ceiling above him; the screeches continued relentlessly and he felt the pressure on his trachea and larynx increase and quickly become intolerable. He struggled to get to his feet, but couldn't manage it, falling back only as far as the noose, ever rising to the ceiling, would allow. He made gurgling noises, for a moment unable to regain his balance and swinging on the rope; more screeches, the noose rose higher, his right buttock rose off the stage, the pain in his throat worsened. He could barely breathe now but still the screeches came and still the noose rose. He scrambled to get to his knees but his right leg wasn't his any more, hadn't been his for a long time now. His head was swelling with blood, beginning to feel as if it might explode; he could no longer get breath into his lungs, he felt sick, felt as if his eyes might pop out of their sockets.

And still the screeches came.

At last he found first his left knee, then his right; relief at last. Even the shooting agony in his right leg was somehow pleasant.

But the relief ended as yet more screeches sounded. In his effort to get up his body had twisted around and now he could see Sneddon, see him pulling time and time again on the rope, see the look of delicious concentration and expectation.

Then the noose bit into his throat again and Sneddon was for the moment forgotten as he attempted to get to his feet. He had to use the noose, hang there to the right, so that he could straighten his left leg enough to put the foot down; then, because the right leg just would *not* obey his instructions, he could do nothing other than wait for the screeches to take the noose higher and higher. He had, in effect, to raise himself by a combination of resting his weight in the noose and pushing up with his left leg.

This time he nearly passed out so great was the pressure in his head, so tightly was his throat crushed, so little air passed through it, but he managed it at last. He had to put most of his weight on his left leg, found it difficult to balance. He was breathing as if he'd just run half a marathon, might have just swallowed kettle descaler, felt light-headed even as his brain pulsated so forcefully he thought his eyes were being pushed forward.

But the screeches hadn't stopped.

The knot of the noose rose up and for the first time he thought, *I'm going to die.*

He spoke – gasped – at last. 'Are you going to kill me?'

Sneddon didn't react; he just kept on pulling.

The pressure on his throat was back. If Eisenmenger had thought to repeat his question it quickly became impossible. His chin went up and though it brought some relief there was another pull on the rope and it was gone.

He stretched his head up as far as it would go . . .

Another screech . . .

The pressure increased . . .

He lifted his heels off the stage . . .

Another screech . . .

The pressure worsened . . .

He went on to tiptoe, shut his eyes, knew that there was nowhere else to go, knew that he was going to die . . .

Nothing.

He couldn't see Sneddon, couldn't turn very easily; he heard a slapping noise and guessed – hoped – that he was tying off the rope.

A sigh, one of satisfaction. Footsteps came around; even when Sneddon was in front of him he could barely see him because his chin was so high.

'You're not much, are you?'

Eisenmenger guessed that crucifixion was probably a thousand times worse than this, a philosophical concept he found hard to appreciate. Speech was severely curtailed but he made a special effort for Sneddon.

'Fuck off.'

Sneddon ignored him. 'Some of the young men I've invited here have been quite the donkey.'

Eisenmenger said nothing.

Sneddon reached out, grasped his testes. 'Still, not bad sweetmeats.'

'So you are a cannibal?'

'Words, Dr Eisenmenger, mere words.'

'Do you cook them or eat them raw?'

'Does it matter? You won't be partaking.'

'Everyone thinks they're Hannibal Lector these days. It's very tedious.'

Sneddon's face betrayed sudden irritation. He walked away beyond Eisenmenger's field of vision, then came back and held up for Eisenmenger's appreciation a hand scythe. 'This is sharp.'

He put the curved blade against Eisenmenger's abdomen, pressed and drew it slowly along for a full second. It wasn't deep but it hurt almost intolerably and it bled freely, a deeply crimson curtain. Eisenmenger's face was screwed into agony and he uttered a stifled cry of pain, unwilling to give Sneddon too much satisfaction.

'Don't annoy me too much, Dr Eisenmenger. Whilst you're still alive, you're capable of feeling a distressingly large amount of pain.'

'If you're going to kill me, just get it over with.'

Sneddon laughed. 'Where's the fun in that?' He sighed. 'Still, even if you're not the biggest banana in the bunch, it doesn't really matter.'

Eisenmenger didn't want to know why, had a strong premonition that this was not good news. 'Why the testes, Sneddon? Why not the liver as you're supposed to do?'

Sneddon paused, thinking hard. Then in an almost contemplative voice he said, 'It started out of curiosity. I'd eaten sheep's testicles in North Africa and found them delicious . . . '

'I thought you only liked young meat. I'm a bit too old and tough for you, surely.'

Sneddon nodded in agreement. 'I fear so . . . ' He suddenly brightened. 'Mustn't complain. Better than nothing, eh?' He reached out and began to stroke Eisenmenger's thigh. 'What with all this fuss, I don't know when I'm going to get another chance . . . '

'I don't think you'll find me as willing as your previous partners.'

Sneddon was in earnest agreement. 'I'd already guessed that perhaps you didn't partake of the more exotic kinds of coupling . . . '

There was something about his tone that gave Eisenmenger no cause for optimism. He quickly discovered that his foreboding was based upon secure foundation.

'You've heard of amyl nitrate, haven't you? Of course you have. You're a doctor. You know what it does.'

Oh, yes. Eisenmenger knew what it did.

Sneddon told him anyway.

'It relaxes the sphincters. Makes penetration easier.'

Thank you for that.

As Eisenmenger feared but had expected, Sneddon had a vial of the stuff in his pocket.

'I'll piss on the floor.'

Sneddon was momentarily nonplussed. 'Pardon?'

'It'll make me piss on the floor.'

He looked at the vial, then at Eisenmenger, made a decision.

'Piss away. I'll be at the back.'

He uncorked the vial.

Then his mobile rang. He looked at the number that came up, frowned, hesitated.

'Someone important?' Eisenmenger tried to sound as laconic as possible and wondered why. He was scared shitless – what did it matter if he showed it? Brave defiance was hardly likely to make Sneddon think better of his evil ways and repent of the Lord.

Sneddon didn't reply, clearly thinking hard.

The blood from the abdominal wound was slowing but the whole of Eisenmenger's front below it was now covered in sticky red, heading down his thighs and beginning to drip from his knees. The pain was just as severe as ever.

Eisenmenger tried again. 'You're wanted by someone; your

caring boss, I'd guess,' he said. Then, 'You had to change your plans when you were told that I was getting close to you. What have you told the office, Sneddon? Your mother's died?'

'Shut up.'

Sneddon made a decision, switched the phone off.

'It might be important.'

'It can wait.' He smiled. 'Now. Are you going to co-operate?'

'Are you going to drop dead?'

Sneddon actually laughed. 'No,' he replied simply. 'You are.'

'Don't bet on it.'

Sneddon considered him, then came to stand very close to Eisenmenger, reached out and stroked with the knuckle of his left hand Eisenmenger's penis. He said thoughtfully, 'I've got twenty-four hours before I have to get back to civilization. That's a long time. How are you feeling now, John? You've got a problem with that leg, I see; do you think the other's going to cope well? And your neck's a bit stretched, I think; bit of a strain on the back, I should imagine.

'Twenty-four long hours, John. One thousand four hundred and forty minutes; God knows how many seconds. It won't be long before each second seems like its own minute; quite quickly after that, they'll start to feel like hours.'

And all the while he stroked Eisenmenger.

'But don't think,' he continued, 'that I'm relying on your lack of stamina. I have other means of persuasion, should they prove necessary.'

'Really? And what would they be?' He was trying to ignore what Sneddon was doing, yet to his shame it wasn't working. Try as he might he couldn't stop the stimulation from affecting him.

Sneddon said lazily, 'I don't think you want to know, John. I really don't think you want to know.'

In desperation Eisenmenger took his bottom lip between his teeth and bit down hard. The pain made his head reverberate, ringing with a high-pitched tone, and he felt warm blood in his mouth and running down his chin, but it had the desired effect; whatever Sneddon was doing was no longer of interest.

Sneddon stopped, looked up at him. He said softly, nastily, 'Go on, then. Play your games. Maybe I'll stop being nice sooner rather than later.'

'I'm sorry, there's no answer.'

'And he said that he had to go to London unexpectedly?'

'That's right.'

'But he didn't say why?'

'No. I didn't ask . . . I didn't like to.'

Verner-Morrison decided that it was time to play the employer. 'What the hell does he think he's doing? Buggering off like that without telling me.'

Sneddon's secretary, Yvonne, clearly felt that she had to apologize for her superior. 'He did say that it was very important.'

'I don't care if it was a death in the bloody family – he should have told me.'

'Does he have any family?'

'As I recall his CV mentioned a grandfather. Parents are dead, I think.'

Sauerwine felt frustrated and didn't like it; he had the feeling that he was being stalled, that he was being kept away from something. 'When did he say he'd be back?'

'He said probably tomorrow. We've got contractors coming in the day after, so I'm sure he'll be back for that.'

Verner-Morrison muttered, 'He'd better be.'

Deeply dissatisfied, Sauerwine left, trailed by Meckel.

Outside, Sauerwine asked, 'What do you think?'

Meckel didn't know. He was confused; the case against Gerard had been perfect, yet here was information that seemed to suggest they'd been wrong.

'He can't be on the run, sir. He doesn't know about this new evidence.'

'No.' From the way that he said the word, it was clear that it was shot through with caveats.

What if Eisenmenger were really missing? If Sneddon was the killer, then his absence might have quite sinister implications.

Yet if Eisenmenger was just momentarily out of contact for some entirely innocent reason, then Sneddon might really be in London on an urgent but presently unexplained errand that had nothing to do with anything. This might all be a complete waste of his time; he should be actively looking for Maeve, not wasting his time running after victims who didn't exist, criminals who were innocent.

He thought of Burr and what the fat man might say if he called it wrong.

Beckwith was looking for Eisenmenger. Until he had been missing for twenty-four hours – only a few hours to go – Sauerwine would do nothing officially.

And there was no reason to think that Sneddon had been alerted to their suspicions . . .

'No,' he said again, this time with more certainty. He strode to the car. 'I think we can wait to speak to Mr Sneddon.'

Beckwith returned with Helena to the hotel. There had been no calls from Eisenmenger, nothing had changed. She sat in gloom in front of the handwritten notes and tried to not let fear cloud her judgement. On their way back Beckwith had taken a call from Meckel – Sneddon was apparently in London although all attempts to contact him had failed.

She said after half an hour of empty waiting, 'You may as well go. There's nothing more that I can think to do at the moment.'

But Beckwith begged to differ. He could hang around for a little while longer.

To what end, though? She would have to sit and wait for Eisenmenger to make contact or, if her worst fears were confirmed, enough time passed for Sauerwine to initiate a full police enquiry into his disappearance.

Beckwith, though, was insistent.

'If you need to go anywhere, you'll be stuck; you haven't got a car and you've got more chance of getting a gondola than a taxi in Rendcomb.'

She was about to continue the argument, then realization dawned. *He's smitten.*

She rather liked that idea. Second in just a few weeks; she couldn't be *that* unattractive . . .

Then sanity shouted loud enough to be heard. She'd nearly been seriously hurt playing silly games and flirting; it wasn't a good idea to go there again.

'Really . . .'

'Look, let's brainstorm.' It was a sign of Beckwith's keenness to remain that he had slipped into management speak. 'Maybe we've missed something.'

She was doubtful. Brainstorming in her experience was little better than intellectual masturbation, achieving nothing of practical value, only a false sense of satisfaction in what was effectively onanism. Beckwith rolled relentlessly on, hoping enthusiasm would triumph.

'Look, if you're right, we need to work through the consequences . . . try to mimic what Dr Eisenmenger would have done.'

It was a nice idea but she knew John Eisenmenger and Beckwith didn't; replicating his thought processes would not prove an easy task. She asked, 'Such as?'

Beckwith was momentarily stalled. Just because he had had the idea didn't mean that he knew where to take it. Then, 'The one thing that always bothered me about the case against Gerard was the location. Where he did it.'

'It doesn't seem to have bothered the good inspector.'

'We didn't find a speck of forensic evidence in the house, or the garden; we even looked in the shed, but there was nothing.'

'And what do you deduce from that?'

'That he murdered them somewhere else.'

'Then why bring them back to the house to dispose of them?'

Beckwith looked at her, nodding slowly and slightly. 'Exactly.'

They stared at each other, he on the bed, she by the window, then she said suddenly, 'So if we assume that Sneddon is actually the murderer, where did he kill them? He can't have done it in his house, can he? I mean Mrs Christmas cleans the house – she might notice something. It would be too dangerous.'

'I don't know,' said Beckwith doubtfully. 'I shouldn't think she's the most observant of people.'

'No, no. Justin said that the victims stayed with Sneddon. He can't have had them in his house, it would have been noticed by somebody, even if Mrs Christmas missed it.'

Beckwith leaned forward, elbows on knees. He found himself wanting to be on side with Helena. 'Where then?'

Even as he asked the question they both realized the answer. 'The farm,' they said simultaneously. Helena carried on, 'How many acres is it?'

Beckwith didn't know precisely. 'It's big, though. Maybe five hundred.'

The momentary happiness that Helena experienced was crushed as she appreciated the scale of their task. Beckwith, though, was more positive. 'It may sound a lot but if you think what we're looking for, most of it we can discount; it must be some sort of building, maybe a caravan, and my guess would be that it would be in woodland. There can't be much woodland on Verner-Morrison's farm.'

She turned to the papers on the table. 'There's an Ordnance Survey map here.'

She spread it out and Beckwith came across to look at it. He surreptitiously looked at her, saw how smooth her skin was, how full and deeply coloured were her lips; he recognized her perfume but couldn't place it.

Helena was concentrating on the map, leaning over it; Beckwith caught a glimpse of light blue lacy bra.

'There's actually quite a lot,' she decided eventually. Beckwith wrenched his eyes from the distraction and his mind back to the task. Most of the eastern half of Verner-Morrison's land was wooded. He sighed and Helena said, 'Shit.'

The profanity made him smile secretly, made her seem human, approachable.

She sat heavily back down in her chair while he continued to look over the map. Staring out of the window at the High Street she saw a teenage boy hurrying towards the inn, thought nothing of it. She felt deep despair, fearful that it might already be too late for John.

Beckwith said, 'Why don't we ask Verner-Morrison? He should know what's on his own land.'

She couldn't raise much enthusiasm; from what John had said of the man he'd probably never even visited most of the land that he owned. 'I suppose so. I can't think of anything else to do.'

He wanted to reach out to her, put his hand on her shoulder in an encouraging and friendly way, knew that he wouldn't.

There was a knock on the door. Helena called, 'Come in.'

The door opened and the teenager she had seen in the street entered hesitantly.

'Yes?'

He looked puzzled. 'I was looking for Dr Eisenmenger. I was told . . . '

Helena smiled, came towards him. 'My name's Helena Flemming, this is Detective Sergeant Beckwith.'

He still didn't understand.

'Dr Eisenmenger's gone missing.'

'Oh . . . '

'Who are you?'

'Ben Verner-Morrison.'

Beckwith became interested. 'Alec and Cherie's son?'

A nod.

Helena said, 'Come in. What did you want with John?'

She bade him sit in her chair by the window. He was very nervous, especially of Beckwith. 'I wanted to talk to him . . . about the murders.'

'What about them?'

But he looked across at Beckwith, didn't answer.

She reassured him. 'It's all right. Sergeant Beckwith is here to help.'

He concentrated on talking to Helena, not taking his eyes from her, as if to banish Beckwith. 'He didn't believe that Mr Girdlestone was the murderer.'

She nodded. 'I know.'

'He was asking about Will, Will Sneddon. He asked if I'd noticed anything out of the ordinary.'

'And have you?'

'I didn't think about it at the time . . . '

'What?'

But he lost concentration, glancing across at Beckwith, a strange hesitancy taking hold. Helena put out her hand to him. 'Ben? You can speak openly. Whatever you say won't leave this room.'

She gave Beckwith a hard stare, as if to challenge him to argue. He essayed a twitch of a smile and she returned to Ben. 'What did you want to tell Dr Eisenmenger?'

'About six months ago, in the summer, I was in the woods and I saw Will – Will Sneddon.'

'And?'

He frowned. 'He was with someone.'

'Who?'

'We didn't see. It was dark.'

'We?' This from Beckwith and Helena shot him a glance that had it been a blow-dart would have left him dead in five seconds.

Ben started to look scared again. She said quickly, 'It doesn't matter, Ben.' She went on, 'What time of day was this?'

'Late.'

'How late?'

'About ten, eleven at night.'

'It was dark?'

'Yes. They were walking through the wood.'

All very interesting but she couldn't see why this was significant. 'Why are you telling us this, Ben?'

'Because of something he said. I didn't think anything of it then; but now . . . '

'And what was that?'

'He said, "I've got a surprise for you tonight, Jacob."'

Jacob. Jacob Blackfan? Her glance at Beckwith was this time friendlier; he, too, had suddenly become extremely interested. 'Where was this?'

'In Battledown Wood.'

'Show me.'

She showed him the map on the table; Beckwith came over and looked on from the back of the crowd. He pointed at the south-eastern border of his father's land; Richard Gillespie's house was quite close. 'There.'

Beckwith asked, 'Are there any buildings around there?'

'Only some old mining cottages. Nobody's lived there for years.'

'Could you take us there?'

He nodded uncertainly.

'Aren't you going to speak to Inspector Sauerwine?'

Beckwith, who was driving, didn't reply. This was a problem he had been wrestling with for a while now. He suspected that he should let his superior know what was going on, but he thought also that he was fed up with being sidelined, with having to take what warmth he could from the reflected limelight hogged by Meckel. He was, though, conscientious.

323

He was not a maverick, acting instinctively, constitutionally incapable of acting by the rules; he was a rules-man, conventional, keen to remain within the boundaries.

'Turn right here,' said Ben from the back.

It didn't look like any kind of a road to Beckwith. It wasn't just unpaved, it was erupted, mud and stone thrown down haphazardly so that there were deep ruts, potholes that were ravines and elevations that were mountainous. They weren't in a four-wheel drive and it showed immediately as they were flung around violently and erratically. The trees were set relatively far back but the day was dull and the overhead sky was little cause for an uplifted heart. It felt to Helena as if they were travelling across Arctic tundra, the roof of the world only a cold winter's breath away.

Beckwith drove on and thought about Helena's question, debated the possibilities. This was probably going to prove a futile excursion, so no point in saying anything; yet what if it weren't, what if they were driving towards the murderer of six? Was he really planning to take him on helped only by an attractive but untrained and hardly muscular solicitor and a fifteen-year-old boy?

'How far is it?' he asked Ben.

'Not much further.'

They were travelling downhill, still bouncing around, still moving up and down, occasionally sliding.

'Are you?' asked Helena again.

Feeling obliged to say something, he admitted, 'I don't know.'

She stared at him. 'You must.'

'This is probably a waste of time . . . '

They hit something the size of an oil tanker and Beckwith felt the steering squeal and grind with the shock. Helena was jerked forward, putting her hand out to the dashboard. Despite this she still kept her eyes on Beckwith, still managed very clearly to convey disagreement with what he'd just said.

'You must,' she repeated.

The road up ahead came to an end and Ben said, 'You have to walk from here.'

They hadn't reached anywhere and there was no obvious reason why the road should have given up at that moment; it was as though it had come to its sense, realized the futility of its mission, seen the future and decided that somewhere it had gone wrong.

Beckwith started to get out but Helena hadn't finished. 'You must,' she repeated.

He paused, then broke. He knew that he must, had known it all along. He nodded and got out his mobile. His call to the station found Sauerwine and Meckel absent; he could have called Sauerwine direct but opted not to. He left a message telling them where he was and why he was there. He declined immediate assistance. 'I'll let you know.'

Helena had been waiting outside. Through habit he locked the car.

'What's happening?'

'I've told them where we are.'

'Are they sending help?'

'Not immediately. I'll let them know if it's required.'

She didn't look happy but Beckwith was already saying to Ben, 'Which way now?'

'This way.' He set off through the woods, apparently just blundering through ferns and bramble that were above waist height, but it soon became apparent that there was a path of sorts; it was intersected by fat tree roots and ivy trails, and it rose and dropped precipitously, but it was just about a path. Beckwith followed, then Helena.

A machete would be nice.

She had guessed from what Ben had said – from what he had not said, as much – that he had been with a lover; that the lover was Gerard followed from what Eisenmenger had learned. A place such as this would be ideal in the summer for those who did not wish to be observed, those who had privacy to cherish and a world to avoid. They were effectively walking along a lovers' lane.

An hour had passed. Eisenmenger was still unable to bear weight on the right leg and he ached – no, he was in agony – all through his body. The strain of stretching and resting on just the ball of his left foot was starting to overwhelm him. His weight was bearing more and more heavily on the rope around his neck, a tactic that had initially brought some small relief; it was long gone now and whenever he tried to rest more on the rope it brought only a choking sensation.

Sneddon was lying down on the mattress. He had been watching homosexual pornography for all this time, his eyes intent on the screen, casting only very occasional glances over at his prey. Now he rose from the mattress and came over to Eisenmenger.

'Tired?' he asked.

Eisenmenger wasn't able to speak.

'Will you co-operate?' He held the amyl nitrate. 'Make life easy?'

Eisenmenger's suggestion that he should go forth and multiply was made from a larynx that was slowly being crushed. His head was starting to pound, his vision was going red and moist.

'No? Oh, dear. I'm growing impatient, I'm afraid.'

He walked behind Eisenmenger, his footsteps loud. There was a brief pause and then he walked back to stand in front again. He held up a hammer.

'Last chance, my friend.'

Eisenmenger didn't know what to say. Surely not . . . ?

Sauerwine took the message from the station when they were the other side of Rendcomb.

'What the bloody hell's he up to now?' he asked, although

it was extremely doubtful if Meckel was going to provide any answers. Accordingly the constable remained taciturn on the subject, asking instead, 'What would you like me to do, sir?'

'Drive on. He said he'd call if he needed assistance.'

It seemed to Meckel to be a reasonable decision and, accordingly, they drove on, away from Rendcomb.

'It's through there.' They were deep in the woods now, the light almost aquatic; they might have been in some giant terrarium. Ben had stopped and was pointing up the track at a vague shape in the distance.

Beckwith was suddenly feeling as if he'd made a bit of a boo-boo in not requesting back-up. 'Right,' he said as confidently as he could manage, 'you two stay here. I'll nip on ahead and see what's what.'

Before Helena could argue – he guessed that she would – he strode off.

Helena looked at Ben who looked at the ground. She said gently, 'Thanks.'

He looked up. 'What for?'

'For doing this. You may have saved John's life.'

He shrugged, looked embarrassed. 'It's probably nothing.'

Which was when they heard the cry.

Beckwith was only a hundred metres from the house when it came and it was all the louder in his ears, all the more anguished. He began to run, stopped almost at once. The woods suddenly seemed a very perilous place, threatening, full of shadow and hiding place. Police training kicked in and he crouched down as he found his mobile phone, autodialling Sauerwine's number.

'What now?'

Sauerwine addressed this to the phone before taking the call but he responded to Beckwith with little grace. 'Yes?' he demanded.

He heard Beckwith breathing heavily and whispering, for a moment wondering if the idiot were playing some sort of silly game with him. 'Sir, I'm at an abandoned cottage deep in the woods on the southern side of Verner-Morrison's estate. There's just been some sort of cry of agony from the cottage . . . I need back-up.'

Sauerwine sat up, his mind's pictures and beliefs dancing around, changing, becoming locked into new configurations. Suddenly Beckwith wasn't a bit of a useless irritation, he was a colleague in danger, perhaps serious danger.

'Don't do anything. Stay where you are until we get there. Leave the mobile on so we can get a trace on you. Is there anyone with you?'

'Miss Flemming and Ben Verner-Morrison are further back, sir.'

What was this? A family picnic?

'Well, make sure they don't do anything stupid.'

'Yes, sir.'

Meckel was already turning the car; they were several kilometres from Rendcomb. Sauerwine contacted the station, ordered a trace on Beckwith's phone and some assistance to meet him at Beckwith's last recorded position.

Sauerwine's only comment to Meckel was, 'Get there quickly.'

Sneddon brought the hammer down with no more emotion than he might have shown when driving home a nail, and with no less force, his target the fourth and fifth toes of Eisenmenger's right foot. The pain wiped out for a moment everything that had gone before; the aching of his muscles, the bone-deep hurting of his sciatic nerve. The cramps were gone to be replaced by something so extreme he felt it claw at his brain, throw a cloak of darkness over his eyes for a second. Amidst all this he felt the crack of the bones, a bursting of blood vessels.

He opened his mouth and it was half a scream, half a cry.

Instinctively he tried to jerk his foot up, felt himself lose balance then swing to the right, held up by the noose; the grip around his neck tightened and he began to choke, his head to explode. He hopped, cramp rearing up the back of his left leg, the manacle restricting his movement; the only way he could regain his balance and relieve the pressure on his throat was to put his right foot down again.

More near-unendurable agony. He tried to balance on the ball of the big toe, and this helped, but it did not extinguish the pain.

Sneddon had watched this with great but detached interest.

'Going to co-operate now?'

Eisenmenger could hardly talk, for a moment felt that he had perhaps already uttered his last words. Sneddon hefted the hammer thoughtfully but was patient. At last Eisenmenger said as distinctively as he could, 'You'll have to kill me.'

Sneddon smiled. He didn't argue, didn't even look sorry, merely crouched down in front of Eisenmenger and raised the hammer again.

Beckwith had started to run back to Helena and Ben when the second cry came again. This time it was more of a scream, more a thing of despair, one made the more shocking by being suddenly terminated with a horribly suggestive finality. He turned, said into the open phone line, 'I can't wait any longer.'

He plunged headlong forward.

When Sauerwine was told about the second cry and about Beckwith's decision he and Meckel were still over a kilometre away from Verner-Morrison's estate.

'Get an armed unit there as well,' he said.

Helena had largely obeyed Beckwith's injunction not to move, edging forward only slightly. The second cry, though, was a different matter. She recognized in it something of Eisenmenger's voice. Turning to Ben she said, 'I'm going to see what I can do. Don't go any nearer.'

She was gone before he could reply.

Sneddon had this time hit the right foot at the base of the second and third toes. Eisenmenger was beginning to black out, as he lost his balance and his weight fell on the noose, pulling it even tighter. It was an automatic thing that allowed him to hop, trying to get his weight on the sole of his left foot; more than once he put down his right foot because he had to, but only for the merest instant.

He barely noticed his erection.

'Well, well,' murmured Sneddon.

Eisenmenger eventually found some stability. He was close to unconsciousness and part of his mind recognized that he was therefore close to his death. He was barely putting any weight at all on his right foot but could feel that it was swollen and burning with red heat. His legs were trembling violently. It would not be long before he could no longer support his weight.

Beckwith charged through the undergrowth as quickly as it would allow, unaware that Helena was behind him.

Sneddon, a large smile on his face, said, 'Shall I put you out of your misery?'

Eisenmenger could no longer reply, could barely hear him.

Taking silence as assent, Sneddon crouched down, raised the hammer.

This time he aimed for the left foot.

Beckwith could see the cottage clearly now. It was in a small area that was relatively clear of vegetation, that had presumably once been a garden; there was a dilapidated hut on the far side, even a broken-down swing. He broke into the clearing, running heedlessly . . .

330

His left foot landed on a carefully placed gin trap.

The cry from outside came just as the hammer had reached the top of its travel, halted it, made Sneddon look suddenly around, his games forgotten. He stood up, a worried frown on his face, then walked to the door behind Eisenmenger.

He picked up his shotgun as he left the room, snapped it into position.

Sauerwine and Meckel arrived at Beckwith's last position.

'Have you got a fix on Beckwith's phone yet?'

'He's about three kilometres to your north, sir. There should be a track on your right that you can take into the estate.'

Meckel began to move forward while they both scanned the line of the woods.

'There,' said Sauerwine, pointing diagonally ahead.

Meckel turned off.

'Get a bloody move on,' suggested Sauerwine.

Meckel accelerated, the car bounced, jumped and crashed through the mud.

'Sir?' The voice on the radio sounded worried.

'What is it?'

'I don't know what's happened, but it sounds as if Sergeant Beckwith's been hurt. He's just cried out.'

'Shit.'

To Meckel, 'Faster.'

Sneddon came to the door of the cottage, saw Beckwith at once. He had fallen forward and to his left. He was now sitting upright, his back to Sneddon, clawing frantically at the metal jaws of the trap. Sneddon grinned, advanced, the gun held low but pointed at Beckwith.

Helena mistook Beckwith's cry for Eisenmenger's voice. She ran even faster, tripped on a tree root and fell heavily, almost colliding with an oak tree head first, only being saved as her hands reached out and broke the impact. Winded she just paused for the briefest possible moment then began running again, no slower.

Ben didn't know what was going on but knew that he couldn't stay put. Was Will Sneddon really a killer? As incredible as it seemed, he wasn't too young to recognize that those cries had been the cries of someone in pain. He started to walk slowly after Helena. When Beckwith's cry rang out through the wet woodland, he too started to run.

Sneddon came to within ten metres of Beckwith, then raised the gun to his shoulder. He said nothing. Beckwith was gasping for breath, grabbing frantically at the trap whose metal teeth had embedded themselves deep in his left calf, cracked the tibia; his blood-soaked leg was blazing with pain, his ears pounded with the sound of his heart.

He didn't hear Sneddon.

It wouldn't have mattered if he had.

Helena ran forward, her hands still ringing with the impact of the oak tree. She saw Sneddon before she saw Beckwith, saw the posture and the gun. She opened her mouth to cry out but was too late.

The gun fired, first one barrel, then the other.

Ben was sprinting now.

Sauerwine and Meckel had just reached Beckwith's car. They were out of theirs and so heard the shotgun's fire.

Sauerwine looked at Meckel, his face registering the shock of what the sound implied. Meckel looked no less appalled but was even quicker off the mark than his superior.

Helena stopped as the shots went on, perhaps five metres from

Beckwith. She saw a look of surprise, not pain, on his face as he sat there, as if someone had just tapped him unexpectedly on the shoulder while he worked away at something, deep in concentration, perhaps tying a daisy chain. The look, though, was frozen there, the last expression he would ever have, the one he would carry with him into the cold earth. The whole of his left shoulder was gone, the bone, flesh and blood ripped and ragged; shreds of pink lung peeped out, his neck excavated above it. Blood pumped up, not spouting but bubbling out. There were spatters of blood on his chin and around his eyes. His hands were still reached out to his leg where Helena saw the trap and, irrationally, she winced, as if all his other problems were minor, only from this could she produce sympathy.

David Beckwith fell slowly to his left as Helena's gaze found Sneddon's. He betrayed no surprise as he reached in his pocket for two more cartridges, his eyes never leaving Helena.

She knew that she had to tackle him, no matter how futile it might prove; to stand still would be her death, even if to run would only delay matters.

She charged forward.

Eisenmenger began to weaken for the last time. His calf muscles would no longer support him. His body began to droop.

Sneddon had the first cartridge in and was slotting the second home, when he saw Helena charging at him. He snapped the gun straight and brought it up as Helena ducked down.

Ben came into sight, saw Helena collide with Will, low and hard, as the first barrel went off. It missed Helena and Will staggered backwards, fell heavily on his backside. Ben came on, noticed but didn't register Beckwith's body, ran by it, not stopping, towards Helena and Sneddon who were grappling on the ground.

The gun was pointing towards him.

The gun went off.

Sauerwine and Meckel heard the third gunshot, then the fourth. They carried on running as fast as they could, the ground impeding them, laying traps for them.

Eisenmenger slipped into unconsciousness, felt his body drop and the noose once more begin to crush his throat. As the pressure in his head increased he found academic thoughts drifting into his mind.

. . . Death by hanging may occur by any of several mechanisms . . .

. . . Direct crushing of the larynx or pharynx will result in a reduction or cessation of air entry into the lungs, probably exacerbated by the tongue being forced against the oropharynx . . . there will be an immediate cessation of venous return from the head and, if the force is sufficient, an eventual impedance of arterial blood to the brain with subsequent hypoxic injury . . .

The sound of the shot echoed around the wood but Helena couldn't hear it; her head had been next to the gun as it had gone off and she had been totally deafened, even as she continued to fight Sneddon. She didn't see Ben crumpling around the tattered red wound that had been his abdomen. Sneddon, though, was too strong. He managed to grab her shoulders, twisted her round, fell on top of her. Pinning her to the ground he straightened his arms then looked down on her.

'And who might you be?'

He wore a smile as a cat would.

She wriggled to try to break free but with no effect.

'Answer me,' he suggested. It was not an idle suggestion.

She tried again, failed, then relaxed. 'Where's John?'

'Oh! A friend of John's!' He sighed. 'Dear me. What a shame.'

He rose from his knees, put his left foot on her chest heavily. The gun came up but this time he held the warm barrel. The stock rose in a high arc, paused and began its rapid descent towards Helena's head.

. . . In judicial hanging, of course, death is designed to occur by severance of the vertebral column and spinal cord at a level which is incompatible with life . . .

Sauerwine ran into the clearing, Meckel close behind. They saw the heavy gun descending fast.

Helena thrust the Tasor into the inside of his left thigh, flicked the switch. Sneddon jerked, convulsed, and the pressure on her chest was relieved. She had just enough leeway to twist to her right. The stock of the gun was no longer being driven by Sneddon who was all but unconscious, in the act of falling, but it still had downwards momentum. It caught her on her ear, making her head ring, her ear scream in hot protest.

Sneddon hit the ground just as Sauerwine and Meckel arrived; while Meckel rolled Sneddon over and cuffed him, Sauerwine knelt by Helena. 'Are you all right?'

Her head was making sweet if slightly atonal music but she fought to clear her mind. 'John's in there,' she gasped. 'Go and get him.'

Sauerwine ran inside, Helena following as quickly as she could. Meckel had briefly checked Sneddon's pulse and breathing, was even now tending to Ben who was alive but badly injured.

. . . Of course, the commonest cause of death in hanging is extreme vagal stimulation, nerves which run through the neck and which have a role in regulating heart rate . . .

Sauerwine ran into the room, saw Eisenmenger, naked and

335

manacled, barely struggling at the end of the noose. The rope ran up to a roof gable where there was a pulley, then down to the floor to his left where it was secured, having been tied off in a slipknot. He pulled the rope and freed the knot; Eisenmenger slid slowly to the floor, slowly enough for Sauerwine and Helena to break his fall.

. . . Extreme stimulation will actually stop the heart completely . . . this is, incidentally, thought to be the mode of death in so-called 'dry-drowning' in extremely cold water . . .

Part Three

Helena had been expecting a call from her oncologist. During her visit he had performed a lot of tests, had promised that he would let her know the results.

He was merely keeping his promise.

She might have been there for a visit – come and look around your local station. Certainly her attitude did not suggest the gravity of the charges against her. Even her solicitor was having trouble coping with the absurdity of the position. It was a joke, wasn't it? This harmless old lady charged with aiding and abetting the murders of six people, the kidnapping and torture of another?

She didn't deny it, though.

Sauerwine had thought that he would have a problem; he was well used to interrogation but all his techniques were aimed at questioning the young, the strong, the guilty, the unashamed, the strong, the hard; how was he going to deal with this vulnerable old woman?

He needn't have bothered.

Mrs Christmas had a strong streak of practicality in her make-up. As she explained to Sauerwine, 'I've never liked lying . . . I only did it because Will asked me to.'

'Will Sneddon is your son?'

She nodded; a proud smile came upon her face. 'That's right.'

'Sneddon is a pseudonym?'

'Yes. He didn't want people to know who he really was.'

'Why not?'

She opened her mouth but her solicitor – a gloomy, cadaverous individual who looked as if he would have been quite satisfied if laughter were to be made a capital offence – intervened. 'You don't have to answer that. It's not for you to explain the motives of someone else.'

She looked at him; it was difficult to tell whether she pitied him, laughed at him or merely didn't understand him. 'I want to.'

To Sauerwine she said, 'He had done some silly things as a child. He thought that people would take against him.'

Take against him? Sauerwine looked at Meckel. Had he just heard right?

He asked her then, 'Mrs Christmas, are you aware of what your son is accused of?'

'Yes.'

She said this as if she thought the question stupid; of course she was.

Sauerwine could feel the moorings that kept him attached to terra firma being severed one by one. He tried not to show distress as he asked, 'Aren't you at all . . . . disturbed by that?'

She frowned. 'No.'

He experienced brief panic, then realization erupted. *Of course* . . .

He paused, trying to phrase his question as gently as he could. 'Look, Mrs Christmas, the evidence is overwhelming . . . '

'Oh, I know that, dear.'

'You do?'

She nodded.

'Your son did it?'

She opened her mouth but was not allowed to speak. Her friend, the corpse, said, 'My client does not wish to answer that question.'

338

'Why not?' This question came not from Sauerwine but the corpse's client. It successfully perturbed the undead no end. 'Well . . . '

She ignored him. To Sauerwine she said, 'I'm afraid he did.'

The last anchor to the earth was severed and Sauerwine was floating free; he was drifting through the atmosphere, the winds of surrealism buffeting his craft, normality shrinking rapidly into a misty distance.

He got out his sextant and made a final attempt at navigation. 'You're saying that you know your son committed six murders?'

He glanced at the tape recorder just to make sure that it was still going round, that life hadn't completely gone tits-up.

It might have been his imagination but there was a playful pause before she said gravely, 'Yes.'

His voice has changed. I wonder if it'll ever be the same again.

But it wasn't just his voice that had changed. The Eisenmenger Helena sat with in the hospital side room was withdrawn, almost depressed; he said that he wasn't – if pressed he would deny it and he would smile and occasionally laugh and even make his characteristic dry remarks – but she could see beyond that, see that the kernel was keeping itself separate, apart.

It reminded her of the man she had come to know – nearly lost – following the suicide of Marie, his previous girlfriend. She wondered if Tamsin had returned to talk to him this time.

'Mrs Christmas has been charged with six counts of accessory before and after the fact.'

He shook his head. The television was on and his eyes kept moving towards it, then away again; that was new, too. The old Eisenmenger would have been able to keep his mind on the matter in hand.

'John, she nearly got you killed. She was complicit in the deaths of six innocent people. She was also complicit in the attempt to frame Kenneth Gerard with the murders.'

'He wasn't entirely innocent himself, don't forget.'

'We're all guilty of something.'

He didn't rise to the bait. Instead, 'So how's Ben?'

'Better now. It was touch and go for a long time. They had to operate seven times and at one time there was a fear that he'd have a permanent bag.'

His right leg still wasn't right. It had been five weeks now and there had been significant improvement but it was decidedly stiff and there was still less than full sensation. His right foot was still encased in a cast, as well.

Nobody was telling him that he wouldn't limp for the rest of his life and he wasn't asking.

'Has there been any trace of the Gillespies?'

She shook her head.

'And there are probably at least four more bodies, some-where,' he reminded her. 'He and Justin made ten films.'

She nodded. 'I know, but Sneddon's not talking.'

He asked mischievously, 'Got himself a clever defence lawyer, has he?'

'Ha, ha.'

He smiled. *Well, that's something.* But even as she thought this she saw distance behind the eyes. *Make him talk about things.* This was what she had been advised to do by the consultant neurologist she had confided in.

'I don't quite understand all of the details,' she said.

'Mmm? Really?' His eyes had wandered again to the television; a quiz show, not entirely dumb-dumbery but hardly anything to bother Wittgenstein or Bertrand Russell. He came back to her. 'Like what?'

'Well . . . ' In fact she had a pretty good idea of what had gone on, but hey-ho . . . 'What exactly was Sneddon doing?'

'Sneddon was fulfilling his sexual fantasies on a grand scale. Those sexual fantasies were homosexual and sadistic and as time went on they became increasingly depraved. When he discovered what the Verner-Morrisons were up to he saw an opportunity to increase his income by becoming not only farm manager but also intimately involved in the porn movie production business.

'I suspect at first that he contented himself with the money and the added bonus of free and easy sex but he was more interested in homosexual sex and the Verner-Morrisons weren't. What to do, therefore? Well, the equipment was lying idle for long periods of time, so why not branch out even further? Why not make his own films? Your friend Justin was recruited – I gather Justin is a complete professional, not minding what he screws as long as he's paid for it – and all that was required then was to find someone for him to screw on camera.

'I don't know much about the porn business but I should imagine the homeless and the runaways are a ready source of acting talent. Sneddon already had contacts because he was casting for Verner-Morrison, but I suspect for these pro-ductions he worked alone. He groomed young men, those that were unhappy at home, that wanted out and wanted to make money. The ones he fancied, he enticed to Rendcomb. They starred in his film with Justin, with Sneddon looking on from behind the camera.

'But even that wasn't enough. Sneddon was a voyeur but he was also a man who had sexual demands of his own. Somewhere along the line, he developed a fixation with auto-asphyxiation; perhaps he even tried it himself, but the thing about this particular sexual experience is that it's rather perilous. One false move and you're no longer aroused, you're pushing up the daisies. Not for Sneddon, I suspect.

'Yet he discovered how pleasurable it was to coerce others to experience it, and experience it to the point of death. He would get his rocks off while the unfortunate in front of him asphyxiated. I wouldn't be surprised if he filmed that as well, but purely for his own, private viewing.'

'Sauerwine said that they've uncovered a large library of porn in the cottage . . . they're looking through it now.'

He nodded, said sourly, 'Lucky them.'

'What about the cannibalism?'

He was back looking at that bloody quiz again; she felt like getting up from her chair and yanking the plug from the socket.

'Part of the descent, I suppose; a descent into depravity. I would guess that he wasn't even thinking of anyone dying when it started off. The first one was probably a mistake, a sexual game gone a bit too far. Then, as he got used to the idea that his partners were expendable, it became normal. The thing with the testes possibly came about as a way of commemorating them, a piece of them – to Sneddon, an important piece of them – living on. Or maybe they were trophies, possibly it was even some sort of fertility thing. I don't know. Anyway by this time Sneddon was, to use a technical psychiatric term, completely and utterly bonkers.'

He was sitting in a chair, dressed, but this was a recent development; like Ben Verner-Morrison he had had a stormy course following the arrest of Sneddon. In addition to the problems with his foot and the sciatic nerve in his right leg, the degree of laryngeal trauma he had suffered had necessitated a tracheostomy and a long stay in ITU. The wound on his abdomen had been relatively superficial but had become infected with MRSA; he had developed cellulitis and subsequently septicaemia. There had been times when Helena had been seriously concerned that he might not survive. Even now, with the worst behind him, he still suffered pain from the wound and would wince with relatively slight movements of his torso.

She commented, 'I suppose it's Mrs Christmas's role that I really don't understand.'

He didn't reply at first, and not because he was lost in the television. With a slow smile he said eventually. 'I liked her; liked her a lot.'

'She betrayed you to him. She helped him cover up what he was doing.'

'She betrayed me to her son,' he pointed out. 'Mother love. Frighteningly powerful stuff. I'm sure she didn't condone what he did – probably would rather it wasn't happening deep down – but she couldn't stand aside and not help him.'

'How could she do it? He was torturing people, raping them, cannibalizing them . . . '

'People have a marvellous capacity for accepting the unacceptable, believing two opposites simultaneously, saying one thing one day, the complete contradiction the next – and each time believing it. They believe what is demonstrably untrue – astrology, spiritualism, homeopathy – and they refuse to believe what is unarguably true. It's part of being human. We all believe what it makes us comfortable to believe; we disbelieve on a similar principle. It keeps us sane.'

'But even so . . . '

For the first time he seemed to find animation from somewhere as he said, 'When I think of what Jean Christmas was willing to do for her son it frightens me, but it's always been that way, and it always will be. The urge to protect her child is strong in every mother and in some it's essentially a psychosis. It's human nature, Helena, the way she's wired. Just as Sneddon and Gerard are wired to act in the ways we've seen.

'If there's one thing you learn quickly when dealing with mental disease, it's that you can't rewire a personality. It's set from the day we're born and until the day we die.'

And ever more shall be so.

The line from the old song came back to her and, with it, came realization of the irony that they should be talking about mother love . . .

An auxiliary nurse came in and asked if he'd like something to drink, Eisenmenger declining on the principle that he was feeling better and wanted to stay that way. When the door closed she was about to speak but before she could he asked, 'Have you found out the history of Mrs Christmas and her son?'

'Sauerwine says that what you were told by Mrs Christmas wasn't exactly true. Christmas senior died early and left her to raise her son, William, alone. Apparently she couldn't cope with him and by the time he was twelve he had already been in trouble with the law on several occasions. Then, he was accused of indecently assaulting his class teacher; the case was dropped but Mrs Christmas and her son thought it wise to disappear for a while. They moved out of the area for a few years, during which time he went to agricultural college.

'He hadn't become a saint, though. Another charge of indecent assault, this time against a fellow student, but again there was insufficient evidence.'

Eisenmenger shook his head slowly. 'Perhaps he began to believe that he was destined not to be caught,' he murmured.

'He did, though, spend five years in prison, shortly after graduating. It was for manslaughter.'

Eisenmenger showed genuine surprise. 'Really?'

'He got into a fight in a pub after a rugby match. He smashed a bottle, did a spot of facial rearrangement and topped it off with a swipe across the poor chap's throat. He bled to death.'

'And one wonders if his interest in homosexuality might have been awakened whilst he was serving time at the Queen's pleasure.'

Helena continued, 'When he got out, he looked up his mother. It was she who told him about the job at Verner-Morrison's.'

'I bet his CV didn't mention indecent assault and man-slaughter.'

'I doubt whether his CV had much connection with reality at all.'

'Not that that's unusual.'

Her heart lifted when she heard the lightening of his tone. She said, 'Sneddon's hair was dyed and, of course, he had the beard; it was over twenty years since he had last been in the village. It was extremely unlikely that anyone would recognize him.'

'But clearly he couldn't go around calling Mrs Christmas, "Mum". Having her clean his house, though, was a nice touch; they could reminisce for a couple of hours a week over a cup of tea without fear of discovery.'

'We're fairly sure – although she hasn't admitted it yet – that she was instrumental in arranging the alibi, the one that framed Kenneth Gerard. At some stage she found out what her son was doing. She's a nosy old bat who had probably spent half her time at Gerard's house nosing through personal possessions. Somehow she discovered that he had a past, possibly it was one of the books with the name "Gerard" instead of "Girdlestone" inside. She did some more prying, found out the full story. When son Will asked her if she knew a good place to hide a body, she presumably said, "It's funny you should say that . . . "'

'Which leads us to ask whether there are a few more bodies yet to be found, the ones he disposed of before he discovered that Kenneth Gerard had a nice, deep well in his garden.'

'And then there are the Gillespies.'

'Yes, the poor Gillespies.'

'Sauerwine thinks that Gillespie found out about his "unofficial" use of the Verner-Morrisons' equipment and tried to cash in on the deal. He was desperate for the money in view of the financial state of his farm.'

'Maybe.'

She smiled. 'Or maybe not?'

'Richard Gillespie had lived in the area all of his life. He knew Rendcomb; he knew everyone who had ever lived here in his lifetime . . . '

She saw at once what he was implying. 'He recognized Sneddon.'

'It's extremely possible, I think. When Sauerwine and I were looking around his house, I noticed that he had been wandering down memory lane; he had got out some old school photographs. I wonder if he approached Sneddon hoping to get a little bit of money for keeping quiet about his true identity. Unfortunately he was completely oblivious of the fact that Sneddon had turned into a serial killer.'

'And Maeve Gillespie?'

'The likeliest explanation is that Sneddon felt that he couldn't risk letting her live in case she knew what Richard was up to. In order to cover up the double murder he deliberately made it look as if Richard might have killed her; he created the impression that Richard Gillespie was some sort of sex addict, too, just to muddy the water.'

She considered this. 'Unless he or his mother confesses, I suspect we'll never know for sure.' Then, 'I wonder where the bodies are.'

He shrugged, had stolen a glance at the television; the quiz had finished, a news bulletin had started. 'Verner-Morrison owns a lot of land,' he remarked. 'Chances are they're somewhere on that.'

She found herself watching the television with him. The silence seemed to entice her to confession, seemed to lead her inexorably to revelation, draw her into intimacy.

The words when they came – only two, neither of them complex or obscure, only one in any way charged with meaning – announced themselves as much to her as to him. They were clothed in an everyday tone – *Pass the salt, I'm completely knackered, Where's the butter?* – almost, in fact, an undertone.

As the newsreader handed over to the weathergirl (an honourable profession almost completely unrelated to meteorology) she said, 'I'm pregnant.'

There was no stunned silence, no pause while Eisenmenger's consciousness assimilated the meaning of this simplest of sentence constructions, one that included the most basic of verbs – *to be*, the concept that expresses the most fundamental

346

of philosophical concepts, that of consciousness. His head jerked around, the television at last banished from his concerns. The look on his face was one of surprise but she could not judge whether it was delighted or appalled surprise. His mouth opened and it was at this point that the pause came. Only a small one, but significant nonetheless.

Then he said, his eyes wide, his voice low, possibly wondrous, possibly dread-filled, possibly both, 'Oh, shit.'

Her heart fell to earth as she thought that he saw only horror at the prospect.

But then he smiled.